About the Author

Two of my most heartfelt beliefs about writing suspense fiction are these: First, it's a craft—a skill that can be learned and refined and improved with practice. Second, we writers of suspense fiction have a duty to entertain and to—as the other moniker for the genre suggests—thrill our readers.

In rereading the first version of this book, which I wrote thirteen years ago, I realized that, while it was a perfectly acceptable dramatic, character-driven study of life on Wall Street, it didn't make my—and presumably my readers'—palms sweat.

It didn't, in other words, thrill.

I considered just letting the book stand as a curiosity among the suspense novels I've written but I felt the nag of the second belief I mentioned above—that overarching duty to readers. I know how much I enjoy the experience of reading a roller coaster of a story and I felt that the premise of this novel and the characters I'd created would lend themselves to more of a carnival ride of a book. Hence, I dismantled the book completely and rewrote nearly all of it.

I had a chance recently to write an introduction to a new edition of Mary Shelley's Frankenstein and during the course of researching her work I learned that she significantly revised the novel thirteen years after it was first published (how's that for a coincidence?). Many of the changes in the later edition of Frankenstein reflected the author's altered worldview. Not so in the case of Mistress of Justice. The current edition stands true to its view of Wall Street in the chaotic era of the 1980s—takeover fever, uncontrolled wealth, too-chic-for-words Manhattan clubs, ruthlessness in boardrooms and bedrooms . . . and the many hardworking lawyers who wished for nothing more than to help their clients and to make a living at their chosen profession.

My special thanks to editor Kate Miciak for giving me this chance and for helping this book realize its potential.

—J.D., Pacific Grove, CA, 2001

Praise for *Mistress of Justice* and Jeffery Deaver

Also by Jeffery Deaver

JEFFERY
DEAVER

MISTRESS OF JUSTICE

HODDER

First published in Great Britain in 1992 by Hodder & Stoughton
An Hachette UK company

This Hodder paperback edition 2016

3

A CIP catalogue record for this title is available from the British Library

Paperback ISBN 978 1 473 63191 5
eBook ISBN 978 1 848 94178 6

Typeset by Palimpsest Book Production Ltd, Falkirk, Stirlingshire

Printed and bound in Great Britain by Clays Ltd, Elcograf S.p.A.

Hodder & Stoughton policy is to use papers that are natural, renewable and
recyclable products and made from wood grown in sustainable forests.
The logging and manufacturing processes are expected to conform to
the environmental regulations of the country of origin.

Hodder & Stoughton Ltd
Carmelite House
50 Victoria Embankment
London EC4Y 0DZ

www.hodder.co.uk

ONE

Conflicts of Interest

"Let the jury consider their verdict," the King said, for about the twentieth time that day.

"No, no," said the Queen. "Sentence first—verdict afterwards."

—Lewis Carroll, *Alice's Adventures in Wonderland*

CHAPTER ONE

The drapery man had been warned that even though it was now well after midnight, Sunday morning of the Thanksgiving holiday, there would very likely be people in the firm here, attorneys and paralegals, still working.

And so he carried the weapon at his side, pointed downward.

It was a curious thing—not a knife exactly, more of an ice pick, but longer and made of a blackened, tempered metal.

He held it with the confidence of someone who was very familiar with the device. And who had used it before.

Dressed in gray coveralls bearing the stencil of a bogus drapery cleaning service and wearing a baseball cap, the big, sandy-haired man now paused and, hearing footsteps, slipped into an empty office. Then there was silence. And he continued on, through shadows, pausing for a long moment, frozen like a fox near a ground nest of skittish birds.

He consulted the diagram of the firm, turned along one corridor and continued, gripping the handle of the weapon tightly in his hand, which was as muscular as the rest of his body.

As he neared the office he sought, he reached up and pulled a paper face mask over his mouth. This was not so that he wouldn't be recognized but because he was concerned that he might lose a fleck of spit that could be retrieved as evidence and used in a DNA match.

The office, which belonged to Mitchell Reece, was at the end of the corridor, not far from the front door of the firm. Like all the offices here, the lights were left on, which meant that the drapery man wasn't sure that it was unoccupied. But he glanced in quickly, saw that the room was empty and stepped inside.

The office was very cluttered. Books, files, charts, thousands of sheets of papers. Still, the man found the filing cabinet easily—there was only one here with two locks on it—and crouched, pulling on tight latex gloves and extracting his tool kit from his coverall pockets.

The drapery man set the weapon nearby and began to work on the locks.

███████

Scarf, Mitchell Reece thought, drying his hands in the law firm's marble-and-oak rest room. He'd forgotten his wool scarf.

Well, he was surprised he'd managed to remember his coat and briefcase. The lanky thirty-three-year-old associate, having had only four hours' sleep, had arrived at the firm around 8 A.M. yesterday, Saturday, and had worked straight through until about an hour ago, when he'd fallen asleep at his desk.

A few moments before, something had startled him out of that sleep. He'd roused himself and decided to head home for a few hours of shut-eye the old-fashioned way— horizontally. He'd grabbed his coat and briefcase and made this brief pit stop.

But he wasn't going outside without his scarf—1010

WINS had just reported the temperature was 22 degrees and falling.

Reece stepped into the silent corridor.

Thinking about a law firm at night.

The place was shadowy but not dark, silent yet filled with a white noise of memory and power. A law firm wasn't like other places: banks or corporations or museums or concert halls; it seemed to remain alert even when its occupants were gone.

Here, down a wide wallpapered corridor, was a portrait of a man in stern sideburns, a man who left his partnership at the firm to become governor of the state of New York.

Here, in a small foyer decorated with fresh flowers, was an exquisite Fragonard oil painting, no alarm protecting it. In the hall beyond, two Keith Harings and a Chagall.

Here, in a conference room, were reams of papers containing the magic words required by the law to begin a corporate breach of contract suit for three hundred million dollars, and in a similar room down the hall sat roughly the same amount of paper, assembled in solemn blue binders, which would create a charitable trust to fund private AIDS research.

Here, in a locked safe-file room, rested the last will and testament of the world's third-richest man—whose name most people had never heard of.

Mitchell Reece put these philosophical meanderings down to sleep deprivation, told himself to mentally shut up and turned down the corridor that would lead to his office.

Footsteps approaching.

In a soldier's instant the drapery man was on his feet, the ice pick in one hand, his burglar tools in the other. He eased behind the door to Reece's office and quieted his breathing as best he could.

He'd been in this line of work for some years. He'd been hurt in fights and had inflicted a great deal of pain. He'd killed seven men and two women. But this history didn't dull his emotions. His heart now beat hard, his palms sweated and he fervently hoped he didn't have to hurt anyone tonight. Even people like him vastly preferred to avoid killing.

Which didn't mean he'd hesitate to if he were found out here.

The steps grew closer.

■■■■■■

Mitchell Reece, walking unsteadily from exhaustion, moved down the corridor, his feet tapping on the marble floor, the sound occasionally muffled when he strode over the Turkish rugs carefully positioned throughout the firm (and carefully mounted on antiskid pads; law firms are extremely cognizant of slip-and-fall lawsuits).

In his mind was a daunting list of tasks to complete before the trial that was scheduled in two days. Reece had graduated from Harvard Law fourth in his class, largely thanks to lists—memorizing for his exams volumes of cases and rules of law and statutes. He was now the firm's most successful senior litigation associate for much the same reason. Every single aspect of the case—the civil trial of *New Amsterdam Bank & Trust, Ltd. v. Hanover & Stiver, Inc.*—was contained in a complicated series of lists, which Reece was constantly reviewing and editing in his mind.

He supposed he'd been reviewing his lists when he'd neglected to pick up his scarf.

He now approached the doorway and stepped inside.

Ah, yes, there it was, the tan cashmere given to him by a former girlfriend. It sat just where he'd left it, next to the refrigerator in the coffee room across from his office. When he'd arrived that morning—well, make that *yesterday* morning at this point—he'd stopped first in this canteen room to make a pot of coffee and had dropped the scarf on the table while getting the machine going.

He now wrapped it around his neck and stepped out

into the corridor. He continued to the front door of the firm. He hit the electric lock button and—hearing the satisfying click that he'd come to know so well, thanks to his thousands of late hours at the firm—Mitchell Reece stepped into the lobby, where he summoned the elevator.

As he waited it seemed to him that he heard a noise somewhere in the firm—nearby. A faint whine of a door hinge maybe. Followed by the *snick-snick* of two metal objects faintly colliding.

But then the elevator arrived. Reece stepped in and began once again reciting his scrolls of lists silently to himself.

"I think we may have a misunderstanding," Taylor Lockwood said.

"Not really," returned the voice, also female though much older, from the phone.

Taylor dropped into her squeaky chair and rolled against the wall of her cubicle. *Not really?* What did *that* mean? She continued, "I'm the lead paralegal on the SCB closing. That's at four today."

It was 8:30 A.M., the Tuesday after the Thanksgiving holiday, and she'd just arrived back here after a few hours' sleep at home, having spent most of the night at the firm, editing, assembling and stapling hundreds of documents for the closing this afternoon.

Ms. Strickland, on the other end of the line, said, "You've been reassigned. Something urgent."

This'd never happened that Taylor knew about. It was general knowledge—as solid as Newton's laws—that a law firm partner was incapable of handling a business closing without the presence of the paralegal who'd worked on the deal. Law is manifest in the details, and a firm's paralegals are the gurus of minutiae.

The only reason for a last-minute reassignment was if a major screwup had occurred.

But Taylor Lockwood did not screw up and a cursory

review of her ball-busting work on the case over the past weeks revealed no glitches the remedy for which would involve her summarily getting kicked off the deal.

"What're my options?" she asked the paralegal supervisor.

"Actually," the word stretching into far more syllables than it had, "there *are* no options."

Taylor spun her chair one way, then the other. A paper cut inflicted by a UCC security agreement last night had started to bleed again and she wrapped her finger in a napkin with a happy turkey printed on it, a remnant from a firm cocktail party the week before. "Why—?"

"Mitchell Reece needs your help."

Reece? Taylor reflected. So I'll be playing with the big boys. . . . Good news, but still odd. "Why me? I've never worked for him."

"Apparently your reputation has preceded you." Ms. Strickland sounded wary, as if she hadn't known that Taylor had a reputation. "He said you and only you."

"Is this long-term? I'm taking a vacation next week. I'm scheduled to go skiing."

"You can negotiate with Mr. Reece. I mentioned your schedule to him."

"What was his reaction?"

"He didn't seem overly concerned."

"Why would he be? *He's* not the one going skiing." Blood seeping through the napkin had stained the turkey's smiling face. She pitched it out.

"Be in his office in an hour."

"What sort of project?"

A pause, while Ms. Strickland perhaps selected from among her quiver of delicate words. "He wasn't specific."

"Should I call Mr. Bradshaw?"

"It's all taken care of."

"I'm sorry?" Taylor asked. "What's been taken care of?"

"Everything. You've been transferred and another paralegal—two actually—are working with Mr. Bradshaw."

"Already?"

"Be in Mr. Reece's office in one hour," Ms. Strickland reminded.

"All right."

"Oh, one more thing."

"What's that?"

"Mr. Reece said you're not supposed to mention this to anyone. He said that was very important. Not to anyone."

"Then I won't."

They hung up.

Taylor walked through the carpeted cubicles of the paralegal pen to the one window in this part of the firm. Outside, the Financial District was bathed in early-morning, overcast light. She didn't care much for the scenery today. Too much old grimy stone, like weathered, eerie mountains. In one window of a building across the way, a maintenance man was struggling to erect a Christmas tree. It seemed out of place in the huge marble lobby.

She focused on the window in front of her and realized she was looking at her own reflection.

Taylor Lockwood was not heavy but neither was she fashionably bony or angular. Earthy. That was how she thought of herself. When asked her height she would answer five-five (she was five-four and a quarter) but she had a dense black tangle of hair that added another two inches. A boyfriend once said that with her hair hanging frizzy and loose she looked like she belonged in a pre-Raphaelite painting.

On days when she was in a good mood she believed she resembled a young Mary Pickford. On not-so-good days she felt like a thirty-year-old little girl, standing pigeon-toed, impatiently waiting for the arrival of maturity, decisiveness, authority. She thought she looked her best in imperfect reflections, like storefronts painted black.

Or Wall Street law firm windows.

She turned away and walked back to her cubicle. It was now close to nine and the firm was coming awake, growing busier—catching up with her; this was usually the case; Taylor Lockwood was often one of the first employees to arrive. Other paralegals were making their way to their desks. Shouts of greetings—and warnings of impending crises—were crisscrossing the paralegal pen, war stories of subway snarls and traffic jams were exchanged. She sat down in her chair and thought about how abruptly the course of life can change, and at someone else's whim.

Mr. Reece said you're not supposed to mention this to anyone. He said that was very important. Not to anyone.

Then I won't.

Taylor glanced at her finger and went to find a Band-Aid for the paper cut.

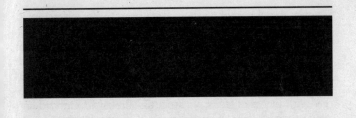

CHAPTER TWO

On a warm morning in April of 1887, a balding, thirty-two-year-old sideburned lawyer named Frederick Phyle Hubbard walked into a small office on lower Broadway, slipped his silk hat and Prince Albert coat onto a hook and said wryly to his partner, "Good morning, Mr. White. Have you secured any clients yet?"

The life of a law firm began.

Both Hubbard and George C. T. White had graduated from Columbia Law School and had promptly come under the acutely probing eye of Walter Carter, Esquire, the senior partner at Carter, Hughes & Cravath. Carter hired them without pay for a year then turned them into professionals at the end of their probation by paying them the going salary of twenty dollars a month.

Six years later, the two men—as ambitious as Carter had pegged them to be—borrowed three thousand dollars from White's father, hired one law clerk and a male secretary and opened their own firm.

Though they dreamed of offices in the state-of-the-art Equitable Building at 120 Broadway they settled for less.

Rent in the old building they chose near Trinity Church was sixty-four dollars a month, which bought the partners two dark rooms. Still, their quarters had central heat (though they kept the office's two fireplaces going throughout most of January and February) and an elevator that one operated by pulling a thick rope running through the middle of the car with pieces of tapestry carpeting Hubbard's wife had cut and stitched; the felt pads provided by the building management were, Hubbard felt, inelegant, and he feared they might "impress clients adversely."

Over lunch at Delmonico's on Fifth Avenue, where Hubbard and White sunk much of their first profits feeding existing and would-be clients, they would brag about the firm's new letterpress, which used a damp cloth to make copies of firm correspondence. The firm had a typewriter but the lawyers wrote most of their correspondence in ink with steel pens. Hubbard and White both insisted that their secretary fill the firm's ink-blotting shakers with Lake Champlain black sand. The men had looked at, though rejected, a telephone—it would have cost ten dollars a month (besides, there was no one to call but court clerks and a few government officials).

In school both men had dreamed of becoming great trial lawyers and during their clerking days at Carter, Hughes they'd spent many hours in courtrooms watching famous litigators cajole, charm and terrorize juries and witnesses alike. But in their own practice economics could not be ignored and the lucrative field of corporate law became the mainstay of their young practice. They billed at fifty-two cents an hour though they added arbitrary and generous bonuses for certain assignments.

Those were the days before income tax, before the Antitrust Division of the Justice Department, before the SEC; corporations rode like Assyrians over the landscape of American free enterprise and Messrs. Hubbard and White were their warlords. As their clients became exceedingly wealthy so did they. A third senior partner, Colonel Benjamin Willis, joined the firm in 1920. He died several years later of pneumonia related to a World War One mustard gassing but he left as a legacy to the firm one railroad, two banks and several major utilities as clients. Hubbard and White also inherited the matter of what to do with his name—appending it to theirs had been the price for both the colonel and his fat clients. Nothing of the bargain was in writing but after his death the remaining partners kept their word; the firm would forever be known as a triumvirate.

By the time the mantles passed, in the late 1920s, Hubbard, White & Willis had grown to thirty-eight attorneys and had moved into its cherished Equitable Building. Banking, corporate law, securities and litigation made up the bulk of the work, which was still performed as it had been in the nineteenth century—by gentlemen, and a certain type of gentleman only. Attorneys seeking work who were in fact or by appearance Jewish, Italian or Irish were interviewed with interest and cordiality and were never offered positions.

Women were always welcome—good stenographers being hard to find.

The firm continued to grow, occasionally spinning off satellite firms or political careers (invariably Republican). Several attorneys general issued from Hubbard, White & Willis, as did an SEC commissioner, a senator, two governors and a vice president of the United States. Yet the firm, unlike many of its size and prestige on Wall Street, wasn't a major political breeding ground. It was common knowledge that politics was power without money and the partners at Hubbard, White saw no reason to forsake one reward of Wall Street practice when they could have both.

The present-day Hubbard, White & Willis had over two hundred fifty attorneys and four hundred support employees, placing it in the medium-sized category of Manhattan firms. Of the eighty-four partners, eleven were women, seven were Jewish (including four of the women), two were Asian-American and three were black (one of whom was, to the great delight of the EEOC-conscious executive committee, Latino as well).

Hubbard, White & Willis was now big business. Overhead ran $3 million a month and the partners had upped the billing rates considerably higher than the small change charged by Frederick Hubbard. An hour of a partner's time could hit $650 and in big transactions a premium (referred to by associates as a no-fuck-up bonus) of perhaps $500,000 would be added to the client's final tab.

Twenty-five-year-old associates fresh out of law school made around $100,000 a year.

The firm had moved from sooty limestone into glass and metal and now occupied four floors in a skyscraper near the World Trade Center. An interior designer had been paid a million dollars to awe clients with dramatic understatement. The theme was lavender and burgundy and sea blue, rich stone, smoky glass, brushed metal and dark oak. Spiral marble staircases connected the floors, and the library was a three-story atrium with fifty-foot windows offering a stunning view of New York Harbor. The firm's art collection was appraised at close to fifty million dollars.

Within this combination MOMA and *Interior Design* centerfold, Conference Room 16–2 was the only one large enough to hold all of the partners of the firm. This Tuesday morning, though, only two men were sitting here, at the end of a U-shaped conference table surfaced with dark red marble and edged in rosewood.

Amid an aroma of baseboard heat and brewing coffee they together read a single sheet of paper, gazing at it like next of kin identifying a body.

"Lord, I can't believe this." Donald Burdick, the man pinning the sheet to the table, had been the head of the firm's executive committee for the past eight years. At sixty-seven he was lean and had sleek gray hair trimmed short by a barber who visited Burdick's office fortnightly, the old Italian brought to the firm in the partner's Rolls Royce— "fetched," as Burdick said.

People often described the partner as dapper but this was offered only by those who didn't know him well. "Dapper" suggested weakness and a lack of grit and Donald

Burdick was a powerful man, more powerful than his remarkable resemblance to Laurence Olivier and his suede-glove manners suggested.

His was a power that could not be wholly quantified—it was an amalgam of old money and old friends in strategic places and old favors owed. One aspect of his power, however, did lend itself to calculation: the enigmatic formula of partnership interest in Hubbard, White & Willis. Which was not in fact so mysterious at all if you remembered that the votes you got to cast and the income you took home varied according to the number of clients you brought to the firm and how much they paid in fees.

Donald Burdick's salary was close to five million dollars a year. (And augmented—often doubled—by a complicated network of other "investments," to use his preferred euphemism.)

"My Lord," he muttered again, pushing the sheet toward William Winston Stanley. Sixty-five years old, Stanley was stout, ruddy, grim. You could easily picture him in Pilgrim garb, cheeks puffing out steam on a frigid New England morning as he read an indictment to a witch.

Burdick was Dartmouth and Harvard Law; Stanley had gone to Fordham Law School at night while working in the Hubbard, White mailroom. By a crafty mix of charm, bluntness and natural brilliance for business he'd fought his way up through a firm of men with addresses (Locust Valley and Westport) as foreign to him as his (Canarsie in Brooklyn) was to them. His saving grace among the society-minded partners was membership in an Episcopalian church.

Burdick asked, "How can this be accurate?"

Stanley gazed at the list. He shrugged.

"How on earth did Clayton do it?" Burdick muttered. "How did he get this many in his camp without our hearing?"

Stanley laughed in a thick rasp. "We just *have* heard."

The names contained on the list had been compiled by one of Burdick's spies—a young partner who was not particularly talented at practicing law but was a whiz kid at getting supposedly secret information out of people at the firm. The list showed how many partners were planning on voting in favor of a proposed merger between Hubbard, White & Willis and a Midtown law firm, a merger that would end the life of Hubbard, White as it then existed, as well as Burdick's control of the firm—and very likely his practice of law on Wall Street altogether.

Until now Burdick and Stanley were convinced that the pro-merger faction, led by a partner named Wendall Clayton, would not have enough votes to ram the deal through. But, if this tally was accurate, it was clear that the rebels probably would succeed.

And the memo contained other information that was just as troubling. At the partnership meeting scheduled for later this morning the pro-merger side was going to try to accelerate the final merger vote to a week from today. Originally it had been planned for next January. Burdick and Stanley had been counting on the month of December to win, or bully, straying partners back into their camp. Moving the vote forward would be disastrous.

Burdick actually felt a sudden urge to break something. His narrow, dry hand snatched up the paper. For a moment it seemed he would crumple it into a tight ball but instead he folded the paper slowly and slipped it into the inside pocket of his trim-fitting suit.

"Well, he's not *going* to do it," Burdick announced.

"What do we do to stop him?" Stanley barked.

Burdick began to speak then shook his head, rose and, stately as ever, buttoned his suit jacket. He nodded toward the complicated telephone sitting near them on the conference table, which unlike the phones in his office was not regularly swept for microphones. "Let's not talk here. Maybe a stroll in Battery Park. I don't think it's that cold out."

CHAPTER THREE

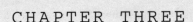His eyes were the first thing about him she noticed.

They were alarmingly red, testifying to a lack of sleep, but they were also troubled.

"Come on into the lion's den." Mitchell Reece nodded Taylor Lockwood into his office then swung the door shut. He sat slowly in his black leather chair, the mechanism giving a soft ring.

Lion's den . . .

"I should tell you right up front," Taylor began, "I've never worked in litigation. I—"

He held up a hand to stop her. "Your experience doesn't really matter. Not for what I have in mind. Your discretion's what's important."

"I've worked on a lot of sensitive deals. I appreciate client confidentiality."

"Good. But this situation requires more than confidentiality. If we were the government I guess we'd call it top secret."

When Taylor was a little girl her favorite books were

about exploration and adventure. The two at the top of her list were the Alice stories—*Wonderland* and *Through the Looking-Glass*. She liked them because the adventures didn't take the heroine to foreign lands or back through history; they were metaphoric journeys through the bizarre side of life around us.

Taylor was now intrigued. *Lion's den. Top secret.*

She said, "Go ahead."

"Coffee?"

"Sure. Just milk, no sugar."

Reece stood up stiffly, as if he'd been sitting in one position for hours. His office was a mess. A hundred files—bulging manila folders and Redwelds stuffed with documents—filled the floor, the credenza, his desk. Stacks of legal magazines, waiting to be read, filled the spaces between the files. She smelled food and saw the remains of a take-out Chinese dinner sitting in a greasy bag beside the door.

He stepped into the canteen across the hall and she glanced out, watched him pour two cups.

Taylor studied him: the expensive but wrinkled slacks and shirt (there was a pile of new Brooks Brothers' shirts on the credenza behind him; maybe he wore one of these to court if he didn't have time to pick up his laundry). The tousled dark hair. The lean physique. She knew that the trial lawyer, with dark straight hair a touch long to go unnoticed by the more conservative partners, was in his mid-thirties. He specialized in litigation and had a reputation of his own. The firm's clients loved him because he won cases; the firm loved him because he ran up huge tabs doing so. (Taylor had heard that he'd once billed twenty-six hours in a single day; working on a flight to L.A., he'd taken advantage of the time zones.)

Young associates idolized Reece though they burned out working for him. Partners were uncomfortable supervising him; the briefs and motion papers he wrote under their names were often way beyond the older lawyers' skills at legal drafting.

Reece also was the driving force behind the firm's pro

bono program, volunteering much of his time to represent indigent clients in criminal cases.

On the personal side, Reece was *the* trophy of the firm, according to many women paralegals. He was single and probably straight (the proof wasn't conclusive—a divorce—but the ladies were willing to accept that circumstantial evidence as entirely credible). He'd had affairs with at least two women at the firm, or so the rumor went. On the other hand, they lamented, he was your standard Type A workaholic and thus a land mine in the relationship department. Which, nonetheless, didn't stop most of them from dreaming, if not flirting.

Reece returned to his office and closed the door with his foot, handed her the coffee. He sat down.

"Okay, here it is—our client's been robbed," he said.

She asked, "As in what they do to you on the subway or what they do at the IRS?"

"Burglary."

"Really?" Taylor again swallowed the yawn that had been trying to escape and rubbed her own stinging eyes.

"What do you know about banking law?" he asked.

"The fee for bounced checks is fifteen dollars."

"That's all?"

"I'm afraid so. But I'm a fast learner."

Reece said seriously, "I hope so. Here's your first lesson. One of the firm's clients is New Amsterdam Bank & Trust. You ever work for them?"

"No." She knew about the place, though; it was the firm's largest banking client and had been with Hubbard, White for nearly a hundred years. Taylor took a steno pad out of her purse and uncapped a pen.

"Don't write."

"I like to get the facts straight," she said.

"No, don't write," he said bluntly.

"Well, okay." The pad vanished.

Reece continued. "Last year the bank loaned two hundred fifty million dollars to a company in Midtown. Hanover & Stiver, Inc."

"What do they do?"

"They make things. I don't know. Widgets, baubles, bangles, bright, shiny beads." Reece shrugged then continued, "Now the first installments of the loan were due six months ago and the company missed the payments. They go back and forth, the bank and Hanover, but it's pretty clear that the company's never going to pay the money back. So, under the loan agreement, the whole amount comes due—a quarter-billion dollars."

"What'd they do with the money?"

"Good question. My feeling is it's still sitting somewhere—hell, they didn't have *time* to spend that much. But anyway, what happens at New Amsterdam—our revered client—is this: The economy melts down and the bank's reserves are shrinking. Now, the government says to all banks, Thou shalt have X amount of dollars on hand at all times. But New Amsterdam doesn't *have* X amount anymore. They need more in their reserves or the feds're going to step in. And the only way to get a big infusion of cash is to get back Hanover's loan. If they don't, the bank could go under. And that results in a couple of problems: First, Amsterdam is Donald Burdick's plum client. If the bank goes under he will not be a happy person, nor will the firm, because they pay us close to six million a year in fees. The other problem is that New Amsterdam happens to be a bank with a soul. They have the largest minority-business lending program in the country. Now, I'm not a flaming liberal, but you may have heard that one of my pet projects here—"

"The criminal pro bono program."

"Right. And I've seen firsthand that the one thing that helps improve shitty neighborhoods is to keep businesses in them. So I have a philosophical stake in the outcome of this . . . situation."

"And what exactly *is* the situation, Mitchell?"

"Earlier in the fall we filed suit against Hanover for the two hundred fifty million plus interest. Now if we can get a judgment fast we can levy against the assets of the company before the other creditors know what hit them. But if there's a delay in enforcing that judgment the company'll go into bankruptcy, the assets'll disappear and New Amsterdam might just go into receivership."

Taylor tapped the pen on her knee. She didn't mean to be projecting the impatience she felt though she knew maybe she was. "And the burglary part?"

He replied, "I'm getting to that. To loan the money the bank made Hanover sign a promissory note—you know, a negotiable instrument that says Hanover promises to pay the money back. It's like your savings bond."

Not like one of *mine,* Taylor reflected, considering what *theirs* was worth.

"Now the trial was set for yesterday. I had the case all prepared. There was no way we'd lose." Reece sighed. "Except... When you're going to sue to recover money on a note you have to produce the note in court. On Saturday the bank couriered the note to me. I put it in the safe there." He nodded at a big filing cabinet bolted to the floor. There were two heavy key locks on the front.

Shocked, Taylor said, "*That's* what was stolen? The note?"

Reece said in a low voice, "Somebody took it right out of my fucking safe. Just walked right in and walked out with it."

"You need the original? Can't you use a copy?"

"We could still win the case but not having the note'll delay the trial for months. I managed to finagle a postponement till next week but the judge won't grant any more extensions."

She nodded at the file cabinet. "But when... how was it stolen?"

"I was here until about three on Sunday morning. I went home to get some sleep and was back here by nine-thirty that morning. I almost thought of camping out." He gestured toward a sleeping bag in the corner. "I should have."

"What'd the police say?"

He laughed. "No, no. No police. Burdick'd find out that the note's missing, the client too. The newspapers..." He held her eyes. "So I guess you know why I asked you here."

"You want me to find out who took it?"

"Actually, I'd like you to find the note itself. I don't really care who did it."

She laughed. The whole idea was ridiculous. "But why me?"

"I can't do it by myself." Reece leaned back in his chair; the singing metal rang again. He looked at ease, as if she had already accepted his offer—a bit of haughtiness that irritated her some. "Whoever took it'll know I can't go to the cops and he'll be anticipating me. I need somebody else to help me. I need you."

"I just—"

"I know about your ski trip. I'm sorry. You'd have to postpone it."

Well, so much for the negotiations, Ms. Strickland....

"Mitchell, I don't know. I'm flattered you called me but I don't have a clue how to go about it."

"Well, let me just say one thing. We work with a lot of, you know, private eyes—"

"Sam Spade, sure."

"Actually, no, *not* Sam Spade at all. This's what I'm saying: The best detectives're women. They listen better than men. They're more empathic. They observe more carefully. You're smart, popular at the firm and—if we can mix our gender metaphor for a minute—the grapevine here says you've got balls."

"Does it now?" Taylor asked, frowning and feeling immensely pleased.

"And if you want another reason: I trust you."

Trust me? she wondered. He doesn't even know me. He— But then she understood. She smiled. "And you know I didn't steal it. I've got an alibi."

Reece nodded unabashedly. "Yep, you were out of town."

She'd gone to Maryland to spend the Thanksgiving holiday with her parents.

Taylor said, "I could've hired somebody."

"I think whoever was behind the theft *did* hire somebody." A nod toward the cabinet. "It's a professional break-in—the burglar picked the lock and, whatever you see in the movies, that ain't easy. But the point is that you don't have a motive, and motive is the number one reason somebody becomes a suspect in a crime. Why would *you* steal it? You have a good relationship with everybody at the firm. You don't need money. You've applied to law school—three of the best in the country. Besides, I just can't imagine Samuel Lockwood's daughter stealing a note."

She felt a troubled jolt that he'd peered so far into her life. "Well, I suspect Ted Bundy had upright parents too. It's just that this is out of my depth, Mitchell. You need a pro—one of those private eyes you've hired before."

"That wouldn't work," he said bluntly, as if it were obvious. "I need somebody with a reason to be here, who won't raise eyebrows. You'll have to poke into a lot of different places at the firm."

Like Alice on the other side of the looking glass.

Still seeing the hesitancy in her face, he added, "It could work out well for you too." He toyed with his coffee cup. She lifted an enquiring eyebrow and he continued, "I'm a trial lawyer and I lost my delicacy the first time I ever stood up in court. The fact is if that note doesn't turn up and I lose the case then I'm not going to make partner this year and that just isn't acceptable. I might even get fired. But if we *can* find it and nobody learns about the theft then it's pretty likely I'll make partner here or, if I don't want to stay at Hubbard, White, at some other firm."

"And?" she asked, still not certain where his comments were headed.

"I'll be in a position to make sure you get into whatever law school you want and get you a job when you graduate. I've got contacts everywhere—corporate firms, the government, public welfare law, environmental law firms."

As a paralegal Taylor Lockwood had learned that the engine of law ran on many fuels and that it would seize and burn without the delicate web of contacts and networks and unspoken obligations that Reece was not so subtly referring to.

But she also knew that you could always take a higher path and, with luck, sweat and smarts make your own way in this world. She said stiffly, "I appreciate that, Mitchell, but my undergrad professors're writing me all the letters of recommendation I need."

He blinked and held up a hand. "Look, I'm sorry. That was out of line. I'm used to dealing with clients who're either crooks or greedy bastards." A sour laugh. "And I'm not sure which are my pro bono criminal clients and which are the white-shoe folks we wine and dine at the Downtown Athletic Club."

She nodded, accepting his apology but glad certain ground rules were clear.

Reece looked her over for a moment, as if he suddenly saw her differently. A faint smile bloomed on his face. "I'm kind of like you."

"How do you mean?" she asked.

"I get the sense that you *never* ask for help."

She shrugged.

"I don't either. Never. But now I *need* help and it's hard for me to ask. I don't even know how to.... So, let me try again." A boyish laugh. "Will you help me?" he asked in a voice filled with what seemed to be uncharacteristic emotion.

Taylor looked out the window. The pale sun went behind thick clouds and the sky became as dark as its reflection in the choppy harbor. "I love views," she said. "In my apartment, you can see the Empire State Building. Provided you lean out the bathroom window."

Silence. Reece brushed his hair aside then rubbed his eyes with his knuckles. The brass clock on his desk ticked softly.

Taylor mentally asked the opinion of Alice, the young

girl in the English countryside who decided out of summer boredom to follow a talking white rabbit down its hole to a world very different from her own. Finally Taylor said to the lawyer, "All right. I frankly don't have a clue what to do but I'll help you."

Reece smiled and leaned forward suddenly then stopped fast. There's a code of chastity within law firms. Whatever liaisons occurred in hotel rooms or attorneys' beds at home, when you were within the labyrinth of the office, cheeks were not kissed and lip never met lip. Even embracing was suspect. Reece's concession to gratitude was taking Taylor's hand in both of his. She smelled a mix of expensive aftershave and sweat in his wake as he sat back.

"So, first of all," she said, "what does it look like? The note."

"Nothing fancy. One piece of eight-and-a-half-by-eleven paper." He showed her a binder containing a copy of it.

She looked over the undistinguished document then asked, "Tell me what happened and when."

"The bank messengered the note to me at five in the afternoon on Saturday—they were closed on Sunday and since the trial started at nine on Monday I needed it early to make copies for pleadings. Well, I locked it in my file cabinet as soon as it came in. I made the copies about ten or eleven that night, put it back in the cabinet, locked it. I left at three on Sunday morning. I got some sleep, came back around nine-thirty. I noticed some scratch marks on the lock and opened it up. The note was gone. I spent the rest of Sunday looking for it. I appeared in court yesterday, got the continuance for a week from today and then came back here to find somebody to help me."

"Did you see anybody at the firm that night?"

"Not after five or six. Not a soul. But I was at my desk practically the whole time."

"Well." She sat back, reflecting. "You mentioned motive. Who has a motive to steal it? You said it was negotiable. Could somebody cash it in?"

"No, nobody in the world'd take paper like that. Too big

and too easily traced. I'm sure it was just to delay the case—to give Lloyd Hanover a chance to hide his assets."

"Who knew you had it?"

"The messenger didn't know what was in the bag but it was an armed courier service so they'd know it was valuable. At the bank, as far as I know, the only one who knew I took delivery was the vice president who worked on the deal."

"Could he have been bribed by Hanover?"

Reece said, "Anything's possible, but he's a career officer. Been with the bank for twenty years. I know him personally. He and his wife live in Locust Valley and they've got plenty of money on their own. Anyway, he's the point man on the deal. If the bank doesn't collect on this note, he'll be fired."

"Who here knew you were working on the case?"

Reece laughed. He slid a memo across to her.

> From: M. A. Reece
> To: Attorneys of Hubbard, White & Willis
> Re: Conflicts of Interest
>
> I am representing our client New Amsterdam Bank & Trust in a lawsuit against Hanover & Stiver, Inc. Please advise if you have ever represented Hanover & Stiver or have any other conflicts of interest involving these companies of which the firm should be aware.

"This is the standard conflicts of interest memo. To let everybody know who we're suing. If any lawyers here have ever represented Hanover we have to drop the case or do a Chinese wall to make sure there was no appearance that we were compromising either client. . . . So, in answer to your question, *everybody* here knew what I was doing. And by checking copies of my correspondence in the file room they could figure out when I'd be receiving the note."

Taylor prodded the conflicts memo with the fork of her fingers.

"What do you know about the executives at Hanover?"

"I've had murderers in the pro bono program who're more upright than the CEO—Lloyd Hanover. He's unadulterated scum. He thinks he's some kind of smooth operator. You know the kind—late fifties, crew-cut, tanned. Has three mistresses. Wears so much gold jewelry he'd never get through a metal detector."

"That's not a crime," Taylor said.

"No, but his three SEC violations and two RICO and one IRS convictions were."

"Ah."

Taylor glanced out the window: across the street was a wall of office windows, a hundred of them. And beyond that building were others with more office windows, and still more beyond that. Taylor Lockwood was, momentarily, overwhelmed by the challenges they faced. Needles and haystacks...She asked, "Are you sure we're looking for something that still exists?"

"How do you mean?"

"If nobody's going to cash the note why wouldn't they just burn it?"

"Good question. I've thought about that. When I was an assistant U.S. prosecutor—and when I do my criminal defense work now—I always put myself in the mind of the perp. In this case, if the note disappears forever that implies a crime. If it's just misplaced until Hanover's hidden his assets and then it resurfaces, well, that suggests, just legal malpractice on Hubbard, White's part; nobody looks any farther for a bad guy than us. That's why I think the note's still in the firm. Maybe in the file room, maybe stuck in a magazine in a partner's office, maybe behind a copier—wherever the thief hid it.

Thief....Lockwood felt her first uneasy twinge—not only at the impossibility of the task but that there was potential danger too.

In Wonderland the Queen of Hearts' favorite slogan was "Off with their heads."

She sat back. "I don't know, Mitchell. It seems hopeless. There're a million places the note could be."

"We don't have the facts yet. There's a huge amount of information at the firm about where people have been at various times and what they've been doing. Billing department, payroll, things like that. I guess the first thing I'd do is check the door key entry logs and time sheets to find out who was in the firm on Saturday."

She nodded at the lock. "But we think it was a pro, don't we? Not a lawyer or employee?"

"Still, somebody had to let him in. Either that or they lent him their key card—or one they'd stolen." Reece then took out his wallet and handed her a thousand dollars in hundreds.

She looked at the cash with a funny smile, embarrassed, curious.

"For expenses."

"Expenses." Did he mean bribes? She wasn't going to ask. Taylor held the bills awkwardly for a moment then slipped them into her purse. She noticed a sheet of paper on Reece's desk. It was legal-sized and pale green—the color of corridors in old hospitals and government buildings. She recognized it as the court calendar the managing attorney of Hubbard, White circulated throughout the firm daily. It contained a grid of thirty days beginning with today. Filling these squares were the times and locations of all court appearances scheduled for the firm's litigators. She leaned forward. In the square indicating one week from today were the words:

New Amsterdam Bank & Trust v. Hanover & Stiver.
Jury trial. Ten a.m. No continuance.

He looked at his watch. "Let's talk again tomorrow. But we should keep our distance when we're at the firm. If anybody asks tell them you're helping me with some year-end billing problems."

"But who'd ask? Who'd even know?"

He laughed and seemed to consider this a naive comment. "How's the Vista Hotel at nine-thirty?"

"Sure."

"If I call you at home I can leave a message, can't I?"

"I've got an answering machine."

"No, I mean, there won't be anybody else there to pick it up, right? I heard you lived alone."

She hesitated momentarily and said only, "You can leave messages there."

CHAPTER FOUR

███████ "I have a breakfast meeting in half an hour then the partnership meeting for the rest of the morning," Wendall Clayton said into the phone. "Get me the details as soon as possible."

"I'll do what I can, Wendall," Sean Lillick, a young paralegal who worked for Clayton regularly, replied uneasily. "But it's, like, pretty confidential."

"'Like' confidential. It is confidential or not?"

A sigh from the other end of the phone line. "You know what I mean."

The partner muttered, "You meant it *is* confidential. Well, find out who has the information and aristocratize them. I want the particulars. Which you might just have found out *before* you called. You'd know I'd want them."

"Sure, Wendall," Lillick said.

The partner dropped the phone into the cradle.

Wendall Clayton was a handsome man. Not big—under six feet—but solid from running (he didn't jog; he *ran*) and tennis and skippering the forty-two-foot *Ginny May* around Newport every other weekend from April through

September. He had a thick bundle of professorial hair and he wore European suits, slitless in the back, forgoing the burdened sacks of dark pinstripe that cloaked most of the pear-shaped men of the firm. Killer looks, the women in the firm said. Another three inches and he could have been a model. Clayton worked hard at his image, the way nobility worked hard. A duke had to be handsome. A duke enjoyed dusting his suits with pig-bristle brushes and getting a radiant glow on his burgundy-colored Bally's.

A duke took great pleasures in the small rituals of fastidiousness.

Aristocratize them....

Sometimes Clayton would write the word in the margin of a memo one of his associates had written. Then watch the girl or boy, flustered, trying to pronounce it. *Ar-is-TOC-ra-tize...* he'd made up the term himself. It had to do with attitude mostly. Much of it was knowing the law, of course, and much was circumstance.

But mostly it was attitude.

Clayton practiced often and he was very good at it.

He hoped Sean Lillick would, in turn, be good at aristocratizing some underling in the steno department to get the information he wanted.

By searching through the correspondence files, time sheets and limousine and telephone logs the young paralegal had learned that Donald Burdick had recently attended several very secretive meetings and made a large number of phone calls during firm hours that had not been billed to any clients. This suggested to Clayton that Burdick was plotting something that could jeopardize the merger. That might not be the case, of course; his dealings could be related to some private business plans that Burdick or his Lucrezia Borgia of a wife, Vera, were involved in. But Clayton hadn't gotten to his present station in life by assuming that unknown maneuverings of his rivals were benign.

Hence, his sending Lillick off on the new mission to find out the details.

The Tuesday morning light filtered into his office, the

corner office, located on the firm's executive row, the seventeenth floor. The room measured twenty-seven by twenty—a size that by rights should have gone to a partner more senior than Clayton. When it fell vacant, however, the room was assigned to him. Even Donald Burdick never found out why.

Clayton glanced at the Tiffany nautical clock on his desk. Nearly time. He rocked back in his chair, his throne, a huge construction of oak and red leather he had bought in England for two thousand pounds.

Aristocratize.

He ordered his secretary to have his car brought around. He rose, donned his suit jacket and left the office. The breakfast get-together he was about to attend was perhaps the most important of any meeting he'd been in in the past year. But Clayton didn't go immediately to the waiting car. Rather, he decided he'd been a bit harsh on the young man and wandered down to Lillick's cubicle in the paralegal department to personally thank the young man and tell him a generous bonus would be forthcoming.

████

"You ever been here, Wendall?" the man across the burnished copper table asked.

When Clayton spoke, however, it was to the captain of the Carleton Hotel on Fifty-ninth Street, off Fifth Avenue. "The nova, Frederick?"

"No, Mr. Clayton." The captain shook his head. "Not today."

"Thanks. I'll have my usual."

"Very good, Mr. Clayton."

"Well, that answers my question," John Perelli said with an explosive laugh. "How's the yogurt today, Freddie?"

"It's—"

"That's a joke," Perelli barked. "Gimme a bowl. Dry wheat toast and a fruit cup."

"Yessir, Mr. Perelli."

Perelli was stocky and dark, with a long face. He wore a navy pinstripe suit.

Clayton shot his cuffs, revealing eighteen-karat-Wedgwood cuff links, and said, "I feel, in answer to your question, right at home here."

Though this was not completely true. Recently Wendall Clayton had been coming to this dining room—where many of Perelli's partners breakfasted and lunched—to make inroads into Midtown. Yet this was not his natural turf, which had always been Wall Street, upper Fifth Avenue, his weekend house in Redding, Connecticut, his ten-room cabin in Newport.

Clayton had a stock portfolio worth around twenty-three million (depending on how the Gods of the Dow were feeling at any particular moment). Hanging on the oak paneling in his Upper East Side den were a Picasso, three Klees, a Mondrian, a Magritte. He drove a Jaguar and a Mercedes station wagon. Yet his wealth was of the hushed, Victorian sort: a third inherited, a third earned at the practice of law (and cautious investment of the proceeds), the rest from his wife.

But here, in Midtown, he was surrounded by a different genre of money. It was loud money. Acquired from new wellsprings. This money was from media, from advertising, from public relations, from junk bonds, from leveraged buyouts, from alligator spreads and dividend-snatching. Commission money. Sales money. Real estate money. Italian money. Jewish money. Japanese money.

Clayton's wealth was money with cobwebs and therefore it was, ironically, suspect—at least around here. In this part of town, when it came to wealth the slogan was: the more respectable, the less acceptable.

He tried not to give a damn. Yet here Clayton felt as if he were "without passport," the phrase whose acronym gave rise to the derisive term for Italians. Wendall Clayton in Midtown was an immigrant in steerage.

"So why the call, Wendall?" Perelli asked.

Clayton replied, "We need to move faster. I'm trying to accelerate the vote on the merger."

"Faster? Why?"

"The natives are restless."

Perelli barked, "What does that mean? I don't know what it means. That your people wanta go forward or that Burdick and his cronies're trying to fuck the deal?"

"A little bit of both."

"What's Donald doing? Setting up an office in D.C. and London to goose up your operating expense?"

"Something like that. I'm finding out," Clayton conceded with a nod.

The waiter set the plates on the table. Clayton hunched over the soft mounds of eggs and ate hungrily, cutting the food into small bites.

Perelli waited until the server was gone then examined Clayton carefully and said, "We want this to work. We've got labor clients we can parlay into your SEC base. We've got products liability cases that are gold mines. You've got corporate people and litigators who'd be a natural fit. Obviously we want your banking department and you want our real estate group. It's made in heaven, Wendall. What's Burdick's problem?"

"Old school. I don't know."

"The fact we've got Jewish partners? The fact we have Eye-talian partners?"

"Probably."

"But there's more to it, right?" the keen-eyed Perelli asked. "Cut the crap, Wendall. You've got an agenda that's scaring the shit out of Burdick and his boys. What?"

Okay, Clayton thought. This is it. . . . He reached into his jacket and handed Perelli a piece of paper.

Perelli read then looked up questioningly. "A hit list?"

Clayton tapped the paper dramatically. "Yep. That's who I want out within a year after the merger."

"There are—what?—twenty-five names here?" Perelli read. "Burdick, Bill Stanley, Woody Crenshaw, Lamar Fredericks, Ralph Dudley . . . Wendall, these men *are* Hubbard, White & Willis. They've been there for decades."

"They're deadwood, has-beens. This is the last piece of the deal, John. For the merger to work they have to go."

Perelli chewed some of his toast and washed it down with

coffee. "You said you wanted to accelerate the merger." He waved at the paper. "But if you're asking us to agree to *this* it'll only slow things up. I've got to run these names by the management committee. We'll have to review each one of their partnership contracts. Christ, they're all over forty-five. You know the kind of trouble they could make in court for us?"

Clayton laughed with genuine amusement. "John, with my connections you really think the EEOC would be a problem?"

"All right, maybe not. But these're still dangerous men."

"And they're the ones who're bleeding the firm dry. They have to go. If we want to the firm to succeed they have to go." He pushed aside his empty plate. "A week, John. I want the merger papers signed in a week."

"Impossible."

"Considering that you might have to move slightly more quickly," Clayton said, "we would be willing to alter our partnership share price."

"You—"

"If we ink the deal next week, Hubbard, White and Willis is willing to reduce our first-year share take by eight percent."

"Are you out of your fucking mind? You're talking millions of dollars, Wendall."

"*Thirteen* million dollars."

This meant that the Hubbard, White and Willis partners would in effect give the incoming partners a huge bonus simply for expediting the deal—and for ousting Burdick and his cronies.

Clayton continued, "We'll claim it has to be done by year end for tax reasons. That'll be our excuse."

"Just tell me: If I insisted that Burdick stay for, say, five years, would you still be willing to proceed?"

Clayton signed his name to the check. He offered no credit card.

"Let me tell you something, John. Twenty years ago Donald Burdick was asked by the President to head a special committee looking into abuses in the steel industry."

"The Justice Department was involved. I heard about that."

"Burdick was picked because he was known in both Albany and Washington. The executive committee at Hubbard, White—it was called a steering committee then—was ecstatic. Publicity for the firm, a chance for Burdick to do some serious stroking on the Hill. Afterward, a triumphant return. Well, Donald Burdick told the committee he'd accept the appointment on one condition. That when he returned he and a man of his choosing would be placed on the executive committee and three particular partners would be asked to leave the firm. Now, John, that was at a time when law firms did not fire partners. It simply was not done."

"And?"

"Three months later, a memo went around the office congratulating three partners who were unexpectedly leaving Hubbard, White and starting their own firm." Clayton pushed back from the table. "The answer to your question is this: The only way the deal works is without Burdick . . . and everyone else on that list. That's the quid pro quo. What do you say?"

"You really fucking want this, don't you?"

"Deal?" Clayton asked, sticking out his hand.

Perelli hesitated for a moment before pronouncing, "Deal," and shaking Clayton's hand but the delay was merely because he had to swallow the piece of bacon he'd snuck off Clayton's plate and wipe his fingers.

███

Who are these men and women?

What do I know about them other than the baldest facts of their wealth, their brilliance, their aspirations?

In the back of the massive sixteenth-floor conference room Donald Burdick heard the grandfather clock chime and begin its ringing climb toward 11 A.M. The partners were arriving. Most carried foolscap pads or stacks of files and their ubiquitous leather personal calendars.

Over the years I've seen men like this, women now too,

display stubbornness and brutality and brilliance and cruelty.

And generosity and sacrifice.

But those are the mere *manifestations* of their souls; what's truly in their hearts?

The partners took their places around the table in the dark conference room. Some, the less confident, the younger ones, examined the dings in the rosewood and traced the pattern of the marble with their fingers and eyes and made overly loud comments about their Thanksgivings and about football games. They wore jackets with their suits. Others, the veterans, were in shirtsleeves and had no time for chatter or the administrivia of meetings like this. They appeared inconvenienced. And why shouldn't they? Isn't the point of a law firm, after all, to practice law?

They're my partners . . . but how many are my friends?

Donald Burdick, sitting at the apogee of the table, however, understood that this was a pointless question. The real one was: How many of my friends will stab me in the back? If the tally that Bill Stanley had showed him earlier was accurate the answer to this question was one hell of a lot.

To Stanley, Burdick whispered, "Nearly fifteen'll be missing. That could swing it one way or another."

"They're dead," Stanley replied in a growl. "And we'll never find the bodies."

Wendall Clayton entered the room and took a seat in the middle of one leg of the U. He wasn't particularly far away from Burdick and not particularly close. He busied himself jotting notes and, smiling, chatting with the partner next to him.

At eleven-fifteen Burdick nodded for a partner to close the door. The lock mechanism gave a solid click. It seemed to Burdick that the pressure in the room changed and that they were sealed in, as if this were a chamber in the Great Pyramid.

Donald Burdick called the meeting to order. Minutes were read and not listened to, a brief report from the executive committee on staff overtime went ignored. Committee reports were recited at breakneck speed, with uncharacteristically few interruptions and little debate.

"Do you want to hear about the hiring committee's schedule?" asked a sanguine young partner, who had probably stayed up half the night to prepare it.

"I think we'll postpone that one," Burdick said evenly, and—seeing several partners smile—realized that the royal pronoun was an unfortunate slip.

There was silence in the room, punctuated by the popping of soda cans and papers being organized. Dozens of pens made graffiti on legal pads. Burdick studied the agenda for a moment and then it was time for Wendall Clayton to make his move. He slipped his suit jacket off, opened a file and said, "May I have the floor?"

Burdick nodded in his direction. In a rehearsed baritone Wendall Clayton said, "I'd like to make a motion relevant to the proposed merger of our firm with Sullivan & Perelli."

Burdick shrugged. "You have the floor."

Sipping had stopped. Doodling had stopped. Some partners—like the aging, oblivious Ralph Dudley—were confused because the final vote on the merger wasn't scheduled until January. They were terrified that they might have to make a decision without someone's telling them what to do.

"I'm moving to change the date of the ratification vote regarding the merger to November 28, one week from today."

Clayton's trim young protégé, Randy Simms III, whom Burdick detested, said quickly, "Second."

There was complete silence. And Burdick was mildly surprised that Clayton's bid caught some people off guard. But then Burdick and his wife were rumored to have the best intelligence sources on Wall Street and were often one step ahead of everybody else.

One voice called, "Can we discuss it?"

"The rules of order allow for debate," Clayton said.

And debate ensued. Clayton was clearly prepared for it. He met every objection, making a good case for the acceleration—the year-end tax planning, for instance, hinting that the merger would put significant money into the pockets of all the partners and that they needed to know before December 31 how much this might be.

More voices joined in and a tide of comments and tension-breaking laughter filled the room.

Clayton managed to insert into the discussion a comment on Sullivan & Perelli's income cap on the executive committee partners. Burdick observed that this was irrelevant to the immediate motion under consideration but would not go unnoticed by the younger, poorer partners: The gist of the comment was that after the merger the senior partners could earn no more than two million a year, leaving that much more to be distributed to the rest of the partners. Hubbard, White & Willis currently had no such cap, which was the reason that five partners on the executive committee—such as Burdick and Stanley—earned 18 percent of the firm's income and junior partners often earned less than they did as salaried associates.

"What is the cap?" one partner, obviously impressed, asked.

Goddamn socialism, Burdick thought, then he interrupted the youngster to say bluntly, "We're not here now to discuss the substantive issue of the merger. It's merely a procedural matter on *when* the vote should be. And my opinion is that it's impossible to review the material in one week. We need until January."

"Well, Donald," Clayton pointed out, "you've had everything for two weeks already. And I'd imagine you, like all the rest of us, read it as soon as they messengered the binders to us from Perelli & Sullivan."

He *had* read it, of course, and so had the team of lawyers he and Vera had hired.

A new partner at the end of the table made a comment. "I don't think we can debate this too much. It's not inappropriate to talk about the substance of the merger now, I think." His dialect put him within five minutes of the Charles River.

"Yes, it is inappropriate," Burdick said shortly, silencing him. Then to Clayton: "Go ahead with your vote. It makes no sense to me but if two thirds of the partners are in favor—"

Clayton gave a very minuscule frown. "A simple majority, Donald."

Burdick shook his head. A trace of confusion now crossed *his* face. "Majority? No, Wendall, I don't think so. The issue is the merger of the firm and that requires a vote of two thirds."

Clayton said, "No, we'd be voting simply on establishing an agenda and timetable. Under the partnership rules, Donald, that requires only a simple majority."

Burdick was patient. "Yes, but it's an agenda and timetable that *pertain* to a merger."

Each of the two partners pulled out a copy of the partnership documents, like dueling knights drawing swords.

"Section fourteen, paragraph four, subparagraph d." Clayton said this as if reading from the tome though everyone knew he'd memorized it long ago.

Burdick continued reading for a few moments. "It's ambiguous. But I won't make an issue of it. We'll be here all day at this rate. And I, for one, have some work to do for clients."

The senior partner knew, of course, that Clayton was absolutely correct about the majority vote on this matter. However, it had been vitally important to make clear to everyone in the room exactly where Burdick stood on the merger—how adamantly against it he was.

"Go ahead," Burdick said to Stanley.

As the rotund partner growled off names, Burdick sat calmly, pretending to edit a letter though he was keeping a perfect tally in his head of the fors and againsts.

Distraction on his face, agony in his heart, Burdick added them up. His mood slipped from cautious to alarmed to despairing. Clayton prevailed—and by almost a two-thirds majority, the magic percentage needed to win the entire war.

The list Stanley had shown Burdick earlier was not accurate. Clayton was *stronger* than they'd thought.

Clayton looked at Burdick, studying his opponent from behind the emotionless guise of the great. His gold pen danced on a pad. "If anyone needs any information from Perelli—to make a better-informed decision next week— just let me know."

Burdick said, "Thank you, Wendall. I appreciate the time you've spent on the matter." Looking around the room—at both his supporters and his Judases—with as neutral a face as he could muster, he added, "Now, any more issues we ought to discuss?"

CHAPTER FIVE

 "Dimitri." Taylor Lockwood's voice was a whisper. "Don't say 'satin touch' tonight. Please."

"Hey, come on," the man replied in a deep Greek-accented voice, "the guys in the audience, they like it."

"It's embarrassing."

"It's sexy," he replied petulantly.

"No, it's not, and all it does is get me moony looks from the lechers."

"Hey, they like to fantasize. So do I. You got the lights?"

She sighed and said, "Yeah, I got the lights."

From the amplifier his voice filled the bar: "Ladies and gentlemen, Miracles Pub is pleased to bring you the silky and oh-so-smooth satin touch of Taylor Lockwood on the keys. A warm round of applause please. And don't forget to ask your waitress about the Miracles menu of exotic drinks."

Oh-so-smooth satin touch?

Taylor clicked the switch that turned the house lights down and ignited the two overhead spots trained on her. Dimitri had made the spotlights himself—pineapple cans painted black.

Smiling at them all, even the moony lechers, she began to play Gershwin on the battered Baldwin baby grand.

It wasn't a bad gig. The temperamental owner of the club in the West Village—a lech himself—had figured that an attractive woman jazz pianist would help sell bad food, so he'd hired her for Tuesday nights, subject only to sporadic preemption by Dimitri's son-in-law's balalaika orchestra.

With her day job at the firm and this gig, Taylor had found a type of harmony in her life. Music was her pure sensual love; her paralegal job gave her the pleasures of intellect, organization, function. She sometimes felt like those men with two wives who know nothing of the other. Maybe someday she'd get nailed but so far the secret was safe.

A half hour later Taylor was doing the bridge to "Anything Goes" when the front door swung open with its familiar D to B-flat squeak. The woman who entered was in her mid-twenties, with a round, sweet, big-sister face framed by hair pulled back in a ponytail. She wore a sweater decorated with reindeer, black ski pants and, on her petite, out-turned feet, Top-Siders. She smiled nervously and waved broadly to Taylor then stopped suddenly, afraid of disrupting the show.

Taylor nodded back and finished the tune. Then she announced a break and sat down.

"Carrie, thanks for coming."

The young girl's eyes sparkled. "You are *so* good. I didn't know you were a musician. Where did you study? Like, Juilliard?"

Taylor sipped her Seagram's and soda. "Juilliard? Try Mrs. Cuikova's. A famous music school. Freddy Bigelow went there. And Bunny Grundel."

"I never heard of them."

"Nobody has. We were all in the same grade school. We'd go to Frau Cuikova's in Glen Cove every Tuesday and Thursday at four to be abused about arpeggios and finger position."

Several men in the audience were restless, about to make their moves, so Taylor did the lech maneuver—positioning her chair with her back to them—and turned her whole attention to Carrie.

Taylor had spent the day looking through documents on the *New Amsterdam Bank v. Hanover & Stiver* case, collecting the names of everyone who'd worked on it: partners, associates and all the paralegals, typists, messengers and other support staff. But the case had been in the works for months and the cast of characters at Hubbard, White who'd been involved totaled nearly thirty people. She needed to narrow down the suspects and to get the key entry logs and the time sheets, as Reece had suggested. But to do this, she'd found, you needed to be a registered user and to have a pass code. Carrie Mason, a friend of hers at the firm, was the paralegal who oversaw the billing and time recording system and so Taylor had asked the girl to meet her here after work.

Taylor now looked at the girl's Coach attaché case. "You've got what I asked for?"

"I feel like a, you know, spy," the girl joked, though uneasily. She opened the briefcase and pulled out stacks of computer papers.

"I wouldn't have asked if it weren't important. Are these the door key logs?"

"Yeah."

Taylor sat forward and examined the papers. On top was a copy of the computer key entry ledger for the firm's front and back doors. Like many Wall Street firms Hubbard, White had installed computer security locks that were activated with ID cards. To enter the firm you had to slide the card through a reader, which sent the information to the central computer. To leave, or to open the door for someone outside, you had only to hit a button inside the firm.

Taylor read through the information, noting who'd used their keys to get into the firm on Saturday and Sunday morning. There were fifteen people who'd entered on Saturday, two on Sunday.

"Where're the time sheet reports?"

More documents appeared on the table. It was on these

time sheets that lawyers recorded in exasperating detail exactly how they spent each minute at the firm: which clients they worked for and what tasks they'd performed, when they took personal time during office hours, when they worked on business for the firm that was unrelated to clients.

Taylor looked through papers and, cross-checking the owner of the key code with the hours billed, learned that fourteen of the fifteen who'd checked in on Saturday morning had billed no more than six hours, which meant they would have left by four or five in the afternoon—a typical pattern for those working weekends: Get the work done early then play on Saturday night.

The one lawyer who'd remained was Mitchell Reece.

Flipping to the Sunday key entries, she saw that Reece had returned, as he'd told her, later that morning, at 9:23. But there was an entry *before* that, well before it, in fact. Someone had entered the firm at 1:30 A.M. But the only lawyer for whom there were time sheet entries was Reece.

Why on earth would somebody come into the firm that late and not do any work?

Maybe to open the door for a thief who would steal a gazillion-dollar note.

She flipped through the key assignment file and found that the person who'd entered at 1:30 had been Thomas Sebastian.

"Sebastian." Taylor tried to picture him but couldn't form an image; so many of the young associates looked alike. "What do you know about him?"

Carrie rolled her eyes. "Gag me. He's a total party animal. Goes out every night, dates a different girl every week, sometimes two—if you want to call it a date. We went out once and he couldn't keep his hands to himself."

"Is he at the firm now, tonight?"

"When I left, maybe a half hour ago, he was still working. But he'll probably be going out later. Around ten or eleven. I think he goes to clubs every night."

"You know where he hangs out?"

"There's a club called The Space...."

Taylor said, "Sure, I've been there." She then asked, "Did you bring copies of the time sheet summaries from the *New Amsterdam v. Hanover & Stiver* case?"

Carrie slid a thick wad of Xerox copies to Taylor, who thumbed through them. These would show how much time each person spent on the case. Those more familiar with the case, Taylor was figuring, would be more likely to have been the ones approached by Hanover to steal the note.

Of the list of thirty people who'd been involved, though, only a few had spent significant time on it: Burdick and Reece primarily.

"Man," Taylor whispered, "look at the hours Mitchell worked. Fifteen hours in one day, sixteen hours, fourteen—on a Sunday. He even billed ten hours on Thanksgiving."

"That's why I love being a corporate paralegal," Carrie said, sounding as if she devoutly meant it. "You do trial work, you can kiss personal time so long."

"Look at this." Taylor frowned, tapping the "Paralegals" column on the case roster. "Linda Davidoff."

Carrie stared silently at her frothy drink. Then she said, "I didn't go to her funeral. Were you there?"

"Yes, I was."

Many people at the firm had attended. The suicide of the pretty, shy paralegal last fall had stunned everyone in the firm—though such deaths weren't unheard of. The subject wasn't talked about much in Wall Street law circles but paralegals who worked for big firms were under a lot of pressure—not only at their jobs but at home as well: Many of them were urged by their parents or peers to get into good law schools when they in fact had no particular interest in or aptitude for the law. There were many breakdowns and more than a few suicide attempts.

"I didn't know her too good," Carrie said. "She was kind of a mystery." A faint laugh. "Like you in a way. I didn't know you were a musician. Linda was a poet. You know that?"

"I think I remember something from the eulogy," Taylor said absently, eyes scanning the time sheets. "Look, in

September Linda stopped working on the case and Sean
Lillick took over for her as paralegal."

"Sean? He's a strange boy. I think he's a musician too. Or
a stand-up comic, I don't know. He's skinny and wears
weird clothes. Has his hair all spiked up. I like him, though.
I flirted with him some but he never asked me out. You ask
me, Mitchell's cuter." Carrie played with the pearls around
her neck and her voice flattened to a gossipy hush. "I heard
you were with him all day."

Taylor didn't glance up. "With who?" she asked casually
but felt her heart gallop.

"Mitchell Reece."

She laughed. "How'd you hear that?"

"Just the rumor around the paralegal pen. Some of the
girls were jealous. They're dying to work for him."

Who the hell had noticed them? she wondered. She
hadn't seen a soul outside his office when she entered or
left. "I just met with him for a few minutes is all."

"Mitchell's hot," the girl said.

"Is he?" Taylor replied. "I didn't take his temperature."
Nodding at the papers: "Can I keep them?"

"Sure, they're copies."

"Can I get any of this information myself?"

"Not if it's in the computer. You need to be approved to
go on-line and have a pass code and everything. But the raw
time sheets—before they're entered—anybody can look at.
They're in the file room, organized by the attorney assigned
as lead on the case or deal. The other stuff . . . just tell one of
the girls what you want and they'll get it for you. Uhm,
Taylor, can you, like, tell me what's going on?"

She lowered her voice and looked gravely into the eyes
of the young woman. "There was a mega mix-up on the
New Amsterdam bill. I don't know what happened but the
client's totally pissed. It was kind of embarrassing—with all
the merger talks going on and everything. Mitchell wanted
me to get to the bottom of it. On the Q.T."

"I won't say a word."

Taylor put the rest of the papers into her attaché case.

"Ms. Satin Touch?" Dimitri called from behind the bar in a singsongy voice.

"Brother." Taylor grimaced. "Gotta go pay the rent," she said and climbed back under Dimitri's homemade spotlights.

A trickle of fear ran through her as she began to play.

Who else had seen Mitchell and her together?

Taylor suddenly gave a brief laugh as she realized the title of the tune she found herself playing, selected by some subconscious hiccup.

The song was "Someone to Watch Over Me."

━━━━━

"Hey," the young man shouted over the music cascading from the club's million-decibel sound system, "I'm sorry I'm late. Are you still speaking to me?"

The blond woman glanced at the chubby man. "What?" she called.

"I can't believe I kept you waiting."

She looked over his smooth baby-fatted skin, the newscaster's perfect hair, the gray suit, wing tips, Cartier watch. He examined her right back: red angular dress, paisley black stockings, black hat and veil. Small tits, he noticed, but a lot of skin was exposed.

"What?" she shouted again. Though she'd heard his words; he knew she had.

"I got held up," he explained, hands clasped together in prayer. "I can't really go into it. It's an unpleasant story."

These were lines he used a lot in clubs like this. Cute lines, silly lines. As soon as the women realized that they'd never seen him before and that he was hitting on them in a major way, they usually rolled their eyes and said, "Fuck off."

But sometimes, just sometimes, they didn't. This one said nothing yet. She was taking her time. She watched him sending out Morse code with something in his hand, tapping it against the bar absently, while he smiled his flirts toward her.

Tap, tap, tap.

"I thought for sure you would've left. Would've served me right. Keeping a beautiful woman waiting," said this young man with a slight swell of double chin and a belly testing his Tripler's 42-inch alligator belt.

The process of scoring in a place like this was, of course, like negotiating. You had to play a role, act, be somebody else.

Tap, tap, tap.

The club was an old warehouse, sitting on a commercial street in downtown Manhattan, deserted except for the cluster of supplicants crowding around the ponytailed, baggy-jacketed doorman, who selected Those Who Might Enter with a grudging flick of a finger.

Thom Sebastian was never denied entrance.

Tap, tap, tap.

True, mostly the women roll their eyes and tell him to fuck off. But sometimes they did what she was doing now: looking down at the telegraph key—a large vial of coke—and saying, "Hi, I'm Veronica."

He reacted to the gift of her name like a shark tasting blood in the water. He moved in fast, sitting next to her, shaking her hand for a lengthy moment.

"Thom," he said.

The sound system's speakers, as tall as the six-foot-six, blue-gowned transvestite dancing in front of them, sent fluttering bass waves into their faces and chests. The smell was a pungent mix of cigarette smoke and a gassy, ozonelike scent—from the fake fog.

Tap, tap, tap.

He offered his boyish grin while she rambled on about careers—she sold something in some store somewhere but wanted to get into something else. Sebastian nodded and murmured single-word encouragements and mentally tumbled forward, caught in the soft avalanche of anticipation. He saw the evening unfold before him: They'd hit the john, duck into a stall and do a fast line or two of coke. No nookie yet, nor would he expect any. After that they'd leave and go

over to Meg's, where he was a regular. Then out for pasta.
After that, when it was pushing 3 A.M., he'd ask her with
mock trepidation if she ever went north of Fourteenth
Street.

A car-service Lincoln up to his apartment.

Your condom or mine . . .

And later, after a Val or 'lude to come down, they'd
sleep. Up at eight-thirty the next morning, share the shower,
take turns with the hair dryer, give her a kiss. She'd cab it
home. He'd down some speed and head to Hubbard, White
& Willis for another day of lawyering.

Tap, tap, tap. . .

"Hey," Thom said, interrupting her as she was saying
something, "how about—"

But there was a disturbance. Another incarnation of
Veronica appeared: a young woman walking toward them.
Different clothes but the same high cheeks, pale flesh, laces,
silks, a flea market's worth of costume jewelry. Floral
perfume. They were interchangeable, these two women.
Clones. They bussed cheeks. Behind Veronica II stood a pair
of quiet, preoccupied young Japanese men dressed in black,
hair greased and spiked high like porcupine quills. One
wore a medal studded with rhinestones.

Sebastian suddenly detested them—not because of the
impending kidnapping of his new love but for no reason he
could figure out. He wanted to lean forward and ask the
young man if he'd won the medal at Iwo Jima. Veronica
nodded to her other half, lifted her eyebrows at Sebastian
with regret and a smile that belied it and disappeared into
the mist.

Tap, tap, tap.

"*Quo vadis,* Veronica?" Sebastian whispered, pronouncing the v's like w's the way his Latin professor had in-
structed. He turned back to the bar and noticed that
somebody had taken Veronica's space. Someone who was
the exact opposite of her: homey, pretty, dressed conserva-
tively but stylishly in black. She was vaguely familiar; he

must've seen her here before. The woman ordered a rum and Coke, gave a laugh to herself.

She was hardly his type but Sebastian couldn't help raise an eyebrow at the laugh. She noticed and said in response, "That woman over there? She's decided I'm her soul mate. I don't know what she wants but I don't think it's healthy."

Instinctively he glanced where the woman was nodding and studied the gold lamé dress, the stiletto heels. He said, "Well, the good news is it's not a woman."

"What?"

"Truly. But the bad news is that I'm betting what he has in mind is still pretty perverse."

"Maybe I better head for the hills," she said.

"Naw, hang out here. I'll protect you. You can cheer me up. My true love just left me."

"The true love you just met four minutes ago?" the woman asked. "*That* true love?"

"Ah, you witnessed that, did you?"

She added, "Mine just stood me up. I won't go so far as to say true love. He was a blind date."

His mind raced. Yes, she *was* familiar. . . . She now squinted at him as if she recognized him too. Where did he know her from? Here? The Harvard Club? Piping Rock?

He wondered if he'd slept with her, and, if he had, whether he'd enjoyed it. Shit, had he called her the next day?

She was saying, "I couldn't believe it. The bouncer wasn't going to let me in. It took all my political pull."

"Political?"

"A portrait of Alexander Hamilton." She slung out the words and Sebastian thought he heard something akin to mockery in her voice, as if he wasn't quick enough to catch the punch line.

"Gotcha," Sebastian said, feeling defensive.

"This drink sucks. The Coke tastes moldy."

Now he felt offended too, taking this as a criticism of the club, which was one of his homes away from home. He sipped his own drink and felt uncharacteristically out of control. Veronica was easier to handle. He wondered how to get back in the driver's seat.

"Look, I know I know you. You're?"

"Taylor Lockwood." They shook hands.

"Thom Sebastian."

"Right," she said, understanding dawning in his eyes.

With this, his mind made the connection. "Hubbard, White?"

"Corporate paralegal. Hey, you ever fraternize with us folks?"

"Only if we blow this joint. Let's go—there's nothing happening here."

The tall gold-clad transvestite had begun a striptease in front of them, while ten feet away Tina Turner and Calvin Klein paused to watch.

"There isn't?" Taylor asked.

Sebastian smiled, took her hand and led her through the crowd.

CHAPTER SIX

The drapery man was having a busy night.

He pushed a canvas cart ahead of him, filled with his props—draperies that needed to be cleaned but never would be. They were piled atop one another and the one on top was folded carefully; it hid his ice-pick weapon, resting near to hand.

This man had been in many different offices at all hours of the day and night. Insurance companies with rows of ghastly gray desks bathed in green fluorescence. CEOs' offices that were like the finest comp suites in Vegas casinos. Hotels and art galleries. Even some government office buildings. But Hubbard, White & Willis was unique.

At first he'd been impressed with the elegant place. But now, pushing the cart through quiet corridors, he felt belittled. He sensed contempt for people like him, sensed it from the walls themselves. Here, he was nothing. His neck prickled as he walked past a dark portrait of some old man from the 1800s. He wanted to pull out his pick and slash the canvas.

The drapery man's face was a map of vessels burst in

fistfights on the streets and in the various prisons he'd been incarcerated in and his muscles were dense as a bull's. He was a professional, of course, but part of him was hoping one of these scrawny prick lawyers, hunched over stacks of books in the offices he passed (no glances, no nods, no smiles—well, fuck you and your mother)...hoping one of them would walk up to him and demand to see a pass or permit so he could shank them through the lung.

But they all remained oblivious to him. An underling.

Not even worth noticing.

Glancing around to make sure no one was approaching, he stepped into the coffee room on the main floor and took a dusty container of Coffee-mate from the back of a storage shelf. In thirty seconds he'd slid out the tape recorder, removed the cassette, put in a new one and replaced the unit in the canister. He knew it was safe in this particular container because he'd observed that the prissy lawyers here insisted on real milk—half-and-half or 2 percent—and wouldn't think of drinking, or serving their clients, anything artificial. The Coffee-mate tube had been here, untouched, for months.

Making sure the corridor was empty again, the drapery man walked across the hall to Mitchell Reece's office and, listening carefully for footsteps, checked the receiver of Reece's phone.

On Saturday night, when he'd been here to steal the promissory note, he'd placed in the handset of the phone unit an Ashika Electronics omnidirectional ambient-filtering microphone and transmitter. The device was roughly the size of a Susan B. Anthony silver dollar. It was, however, considerably more popular and was used by every security, private eye or industrial espionage outfit that could afford the eight-thousand-dollar price tag. This bug broadcast a razor-clear transmission of all of Reece's conversations on the phone or with anyone else in the office to the radio receiver and tape recorder in the Coffee-mate container across the hall. One feature of the transmitter was that it contained a frequency-canceling feature, which made it virtually invisible to most commercial bug-detecting sweepers. He checked the battery and found it was still good.

When he was finished he spent another three or four minutes arranging the drapes so they looked nice. This was, after all, his purported job.

He peeled off the gloves and walked out into the halls, which greeted him once again with their silence and their real, or imagined, disdain.

———

"I suffer from the fallacy of the beautiful woman."

The Lincoln Town Car limo crashed through the meat-packing district in the western part of Greenwich Village, near the river. Taylor leaned sideways to hear Thom Sebastian over the crackly sound of the talk show on the driver's AM radio.

He continued, "Which is this: that because a woman is attractive she can do no wrong. You think, Christ, the way she lights a cigarette is the right way, the restaurants she picks are the right restaurants, the way she fakes an orgasm—pardon my French—is the right way so *I* must be doing something wrong. For instance, we're now on our way to Meg's. The club. You know it?"

"Absolutely no idea."

"There, my point exactly. I'm thinking: Jesus, I'm doing something wrong. Taylor is a primo woman but she doesn't know about this club. *I've* fucked up. *I've* got it wrong."

Taylor smirked. "Does this usually work?"

Sebastian paused then slouched back in the cab seat and lit a cigarette. "What?"

"That line? The one you're using on me now?"

Sebastian waited a few more seconds and must've decided there'd be no recovery from her busting him. "You'd be surprised at some of the lines I've gotten away with." He laughed. "The thing is *women* suffer from the fallacy of the man who knows what he's doing. We never do, of course." He gave her what might pass for a sincere glance and said, "I like you."

They pulled up in front of nothing. A row of ware-houses and small factories, not a streetlight in sight, only the distant aurora borealis of industrial Jersey across the Hudson River.

"Welcome to my main club."

"Here?"

"Yep. I'm here six, seven nights a week."

Sebastian led them through an unguarded, unmarked door into what looked like a Victorian bordello. The walls were covered with dark tapestry. The tables were marble and brass. Oak columns and sideboards were draped with tooling and floral chintz. Tiffanyesque lamps were every-where. The uniform for men was tuxedo or Italian suits, for the women, dark, close-fitting dresses with necklines that required pure willpower to keep nipples hidden. The rooms were chockablock with high-level celebs and politicos, the sort that regularly make *New York* magazine and Liz Smith's columns.

Sebastian whispered, "The three little piggies," and pointed out a trio of hip young novelists whom a *Times* critic had just vivisected en masse in an article called "Id as Art: The Care and Feeding of Self-Indulgence." Skinny women hovered around the threesome. Sebastian eyed the women with dismay and said, "Why are they wasting time with those dudes? Didn't they see the article?"

Taylor said dryly, "You assume they can read." And bumped into Richard Gere. He glanced at her with a polite acknowledgment, apologized and continued on.

"Oh my God." She gasped, staring at the man's broad back. "*He's* here."

"Yes," Sebastian said, bored. "And so are we."

The music wasn't as loud as at the previous club and the pace was less frantic. Sebastian waved to some people.

"What're you drinking?" he asked.

"Stick with R&C."

They sipped their drinks for a few minutes. Sebastian leaned over again and asked, "What's your biggest passion? After handsome men like me, I mean."

"Skiing, I guess." Taylor was circumspect about telling people her second career—the music—and was particularly reluctant to give a robbery suspect too much information about herself.

"Skiing? Sliding down a mountain, getting wet and cold and breaking bones, is that it?"

"Breaking bones is optional."

"I did some exercise once," Sebastian said, shaking his head. "I got over it. I'm okay now."

She laughed and studied him in the mirror. The lawyer didn't look good. His eyes were puffy and red. He blew his nose often and his posture was terrible. The coke and whatever other drugs he was doing were taking their toll. He seemed deflated as he hunched over his drink, sucking his cocktail through the thin brown straw. Suddenly he straightened, slipped his arm around her shoulders and kissed her hair. "Does anyone ever get lost in there?"

She kept the smile on her face but didn't lean into him. She said evenly, "It's true that I had date failure tonight. But I still do things the old-fashioned way. Real slow." She eased away and looked at him. "Just want the ground rules understood."

He left his arm where it was for a noncommittal ten seconds, then dropped it. "Fair enough," he said with a tone that suggested: all rights reserved.

"You go out a lot?" she asked.

"Work hard and play hard. By the time I burn out at forty-five..." His voice faded and he was looking at her expectantly.

Tap, tap, tap.

She saw his hand swinging against the bar. A brown vial.

"You want to retire to the facilities with me? Build strong bodies twelve ways?"

"Not me. I have to keep in shape for breaking bones."

He blinked, surprised. "Yeah? You sure?"

"Never touch the stuff."

He laughed. Then put the bottle away.

Just then another man appeared from the crowd and walked up to Sebastian though his attention seemed fixed on Taylor. He resembled Sebastian some but was thinner, shorter, a few years younger. He wore a conservative gray suit but bright red sunglasses, from which a green cord hooked to the earpieces dangled down the back of his neck.

She noted Sebastian's surprise when the young man approached.

Sebastian said, "Hey, Taylor, meet my main man, Bosk. Hey, Bosk, Taylor." They shook hands.

"Will you marry me?" Bosk asked her in a slurred voice. He'd had a great deal to drink and she knew that beneath the silly Elton John sunglasses his eyes would be unfocused.

"Oh, gosh," she answered brightly, "I can't tonight."

"Story of my life." He turned back to Sebastian. "Hey, you never fucking called me back. We've gotta talk. He called and wanted to know where—"

Bosk suddenly fell silent and as Taylor reached for her drink she observed in the mirror behind the bar two very subtle gestures by Sebastian, a nod toward her and a wag of his finger, whose only possible meaning was that the topic Bosk was raising was not to be discussed in front of her.

Bosk recovered, though not very well, by saying, "What it is, I've still got some room on that New Jersey project if you're interested."

"How leveraged?"

Bosk said, "We'll need to come up with probably six five."

"No fucking way." Sebastian laughed.

"Sea Bass, come on. . . ."

"Three eight was the top, dumbo. I'm not going over three eight."

These figures might have referred to percentages or shares of stock or money, in which case, considering that the context was New York metro area business or real estate, they might be talking about hundreds of thousands or even millions of dollars.

And Alice thought Wonderland was topsy-turvy. . . .

"Don't be such a fucking wuss," Bosk muttered drunk-enly. Studying Taylor.

Sebastian grinned and grabbed Bosk, swung him into a neck lock then rapped him on the head.

Bosk broke away and shouted, laughing, "You're a fuck-ing cow chip, you know that?" He replaced his gaudy sun-glasses. "Hey, you want to come out to Long Island for dinner on Friday? My mother'll be out with her cook. Bunch of the gang. Brittany said she, like, forgives you for not calling."

An electronic pocket calendar appeared in Sebastian's pudgy hand. He studied it. "Can do, dude," he said at last. They slapped palms and Bosk vanished.

"Primo guy," Sebastian said.

"He's a lawyer?"

"Among other things. We go way back. We're doing some projects together."

Projects . . . as vague a euphemism as there was.

"Like real estate?" Taylor asked.

"Yeah." But she heard a lie in his voice.

Taylor turned back to her drink. "I'd like to do some in-vesting. But I got one problem. No money."

"Why's that a problem?" Sebastian said, frowning, gen-uinely perplexed. "You never use your own money. Use somebody else's. It's the only way to invest."

"Hubbard, White lets you work on your own? Don't you have to clear it with somebody?"

Sebastian laughed, a sharp exhalation of bitterness that surprised her. "We aren't on such good terms lately, Messrs. Hubbard, White and Willis and myself." He apparently de-cided to drop the fast-lane image. Deflated, he sighed and muttered, "They passed me over for partner." His lips tight-ened into a bleak smile and she got what she thought was her first real look at Thom Sebastian.

"I'm sorry." Taylor knew that this would have been a devastating blow to him. Partnership was the golden ring young associates strived for. They worked sixty or seventy hours a week for years for the chance to be asked to join the firm as one of the partners—the owners.

Taylor, on the trail of a thief, after all, sensed he might be revealing a motive to lift the promissory note—revenge—and wanted him to keep talking. She said, "Must've been tough."

"After they told me, I tried to convince myself I didn't really *want* to be partner. I mean, Christ, you can make more money at real estate or investment banking. I said, 'Fuck it. Who needs them? It's just a bunch of old men....' Well, that's what I told myself. But, damn, I wanted it bad. I've worked all my professional life to get my name on the letterhead of Hubbard, White & Willis. And this is what they do to me."

"Did they tell you why?"

His pale jaw, round with fat, trembled. "Bullshit. I mean, finances was what they said. 'Effecting economies,' if I may quote. But that wasn't the reason." He turned to her and said, "See, I don't fit the Hubbard, White mold."

"What's the mold?"

"Ha, that's the catch. They can't tell you; they just know whether you've got it or not. And that prick Clayton didn't think I had it."

"Wendall Clayton? What did he have to do with it?"

"I'm not one of his chosen few. Most of the partnership slots this year got filled with his boys and girls. Look at that asshole Randy Simms."

She had a vague memory of a young, square-jawed blond partner.

"Randy Simms III," Sebastian spat out. "The 'third,'" he mused bitterly. "But, hey, he's gotta be the end of *that* family line though. I'm sure the guy doesn't have a dick."

"But Clayton's not even on the executive committee," Taylor said.

He laughed. "What difference does *that* make? He's got ten times more power than Burdick or Stanley think. He's going to ramrod the merger through."

"The merger?" she said. "That's just a rumor. It's been going around for months."

Sebastian looked at her and detected no irony. He snorted. "Just a rumor? You think that, then you don't know Wendall Clayton. Two months from now, you won't be able to recognize our firm. . . ." His voice dwindled. "I should say, *your* firm. Ain't mine no more."

"What're you going to do?"

He was about to say something but grew cautious. She could sense he was selecting his words carefully. "Oh, I'll get a new job. Probably go in-house, become chief general counsel for a client. That's what happens to most senior associates after they cut your balls off."

Okay, Taylor told herself. Go for it.

"Then why're you working so hard?" she asked. "If I got passed over I sure wouldn't be working holiday weekends."

A brief hesitation. "Weekends?" he asked.

"Yeah, you were in the firm on Sunday morning, weren't you?"

He took a long sip of his drink then said, "Me? No. I was here all night. I left about three, when they were getting ready to close."

She frowned. "That's funny. I was doing some billing for . . . who was it? I don't remember. Anyway, I saw your key card number. You came in real early on Sunday." He looked at her for a long moment. His face was completely blank but she sensed that his thoughts were grinding hard and fast. Then he nodded in understanding. "Ralph Dudley," he said angrily.

"Dudley? The old partner?"

"Yeah, Grandpa. Yesterday he dropped my key off in my office. He said I left it in the library and he'd picked it up by mistake on Friday. He must've used it on Sunday."

She couldn't tell whether to believe him or not.

Agitated at this news, Sebastian fished in his pocket and found the little vial. He held it up. "You sure?" She shook her head and he looked toward the men's room. "Excusez-moi."

After he disappeared, Taylor motioned the bartender over to her and said, "You working last Saturday night?"

He normally didn't get questions like this. He polished glasses. But finally he said, "Yeah."

"Was Thom in here from one to three or so on Sunday morning?"

"I don't remember."

She slid two twenties toward him furtively. He blinked. This only happened in movies and the man seemed to be considering how his favorite actor would handle it. The bills disappeared into tight black jeans. "No. He left around one—without a girl. That *never* happens. If he's by himself usually he closes the place. He's even slept here a couple times."

When Sebastian returned he took Taylor's purse and slipped it around her—over one shoulder and under the other arm, the way paranoid tourists do. "Come on. I'm wound, I'm flying like a bird. I gotta dance. . . ."

"But—"

He pulled her onto the small floor. After fifteen minutes, her hair was down, streaming in thick, sweaty tangles. Her toes were on fire, her calves ached. Sebastian kept jerking away in time to the reggae beat, eyes closed, lost in the catharsis of the motion and music and the coke. Taylor collapsed on his shoulder. "Enough."

"I thought you were a skier."

"Exhausted." She was gasping.

His brow arched and the surprise in his eyes was genuine. "But we haven't eaten yet."

Taylor said, "It's one A.M. I've been up for nearly twenty-four hours."

"Time for penne!"

"But—"

"Come on. One plate of darling little squigglies of pasta in alfredo sauce with cilantro and basil, one teeny endive salad, one bottle of Mersault."

Taylor was weakening.

"*Belgium* endive! . . ." Then he lowered his head. "Okay."

Sebastian the negotiator was now speaking. "How's this for a deal? We have dinner and you can tell me about the Pine Breath Inn in Vermont or wherever the hell it is you ski and we'll call it a night. Or I can take you home now and you'll have to fight off my frontal assault at your door. Few women have been able to resist."

"Thom—"

"I take no prisoners."

She lowered her head on his shoulder then straightened up, smiling. "Does this place have spaghetti and meat balls with thick red sauce, à la Ragú?"

"I'll never be able to show my face there again. But if you want it I'll force the chef to make it."

She sighed, took his arm and together they made their way toward the door.

CHAPTER SEVEN

The alarm clock wailed like a smoke detector.

Taylor Lockwood opened one eye. Was this the worst headache of her life? she wondered.

She lay still for five minutes while the votes rolled in. Yes, no?

Sitting up decided the contest—a clear victory for the pain. She slammed her palm down on the alarm then scooted gingerly to the edge of the bed. She still wore her panty hose and bra; the elastic bands had cut deep purple lines into her skin and she was momentarily concerned that she'd have permanent discolorations.

Oh, man, I feel lousy....

Taylor's one-bedroom apartment was small and dark. It was located in the Fifth Avenue Hotel, a dark, Gothic building distinguished only by the prestige of the street it was located on and its reputation for being the place that New York's Judge Crater was supposedly on his way to when he disappeared seventy years before—still an open case on the NYPD books.

Her parents had offered to send her whatever furniture

she wanted from their eight-bedroom house in Chevy Chase or from one of their summer homes but Taylor had wanted this apartment to be exclusively hers. It was furnished post-collegiate—Conran's, Crate & Barrel, Pottery Barn. A lot of fake stone, Formica, black and white plastic. A huge pillow sofa. Canvas chairs that, looked at straight on, seemed to be grinning. A number of interesting pieces from the Twenty-sixth Street flea market on Sixth Avenue.

The bedroom was the homiest room in the place, decorated with lace tulle, art deco lamps and old furniture—battered but loaded with personality—a hundred books, souvenirs from the trips young Taylor took to Europe with her parents.

On the wall was a large poster—one of Arthur Rackham's sepia illustrations of Lewis Carroll's *Alice's Adventures in Wonderland*.

The picture wasn't like the Disney cartoon or the original Sir John Tenniel drawings but was a masterful work by the brilliant artist. It showed an alarmed Alice lifting her hands to protect herself as the Red Queen's playing card soldiers flew into the air.

The caption read:

> At this the whole pack rose up into the air,
> and came flying down upon her.

The framed poster had been a graduation present from her roommates at Dartmouth. Taylor loved the Carroll books, and Alice memorabilia were sure bets as birthday and Christmas presents. There were many other *Wonderland* and *Through the Looking-Glass* artifacts throughout her apartment.

Taylor sent her tongue around her parched mouth; she didn't enjoy the trip. She staggered into the bathroom, where she downed two glasses of water and brushed her teeth twice. She squinted at the clock. Let's see, Sebastian had dropped her off at about four. Do the math. . . . Okay, we're talking about three and a half hours' sleep.

And, more troubling, it turned out that she'd largely wasted her time. Thom Sebastian had denied being in the firm on Saturday or Sunday and had remained tight-lipped about his dealings with Bosk though he'd continued to talk bitterly about the firm's decision to pass him over. He'd had no response when she'd casually mentioned Hanover & Stiver, Inc.

She kneaded her belly, which swelled slightly over the top of her panties, recalling that there were a hundred fifty calories in each cocktail. . . . She squeezed her temples. Her vision swam.

A blinking red light across the room coincided with the throbbing in her head. It was her answering machine, indicating a message from last night. She hit the play button, thinking it might be a call from Mitchell Reece, remembering his asking her if it was okay to call her at home.

Beep.

"Hello, counselor."

Ah, her father, she realized with a thud in her turbulent stomach.

"Just wanted to tell you: You owe me lunch. Earl Warren was chief justice when the case was decided. Call when you can. Love you."

Click.

Shit, she thought. I shouldn't've bet with him.

Taylor didn't mind losing to him, of course; half the lawyers in Washington, D.C., had lost a case or motion or argument to Samuel Lockwood at one time or another in their careers. The *Washington Post* had called him "The Unbeatable Legal Eagle" (the article was framed and displayed prominently in their living room at home). No, it was that even though she could see clearly that he was testing her, she'd weakened and agreed to the pointless bet.

It was very, very difficult to say no to Samuel Lockwood.

He called her two or three times a week but unless he had something specific to ask her he usually picked "safe" times: During the day he'd call her home, at night he'd call the firm, leaving messages—fulfilling his parental duty and making his royal presence felt in her territory but making sure he didn't waste time actually talking to her. (She noted cynically that she might reasonably have been expected to be home last night when he'd phoned—because the purpose of that call had been to gloat.)

Well, she could hardly point fingers; Taylor did the same—generally calling home when she knew he was working so she could chat with her mother untroubled by the brooding presence of her father hovering near the receiver, a presence she could sense from even three hundred miles away.

She winced as the headache pounded on her again, just for the pure fun of it, it seemed. A glance at the clock.

Okay, Alice, you got twenty minutes to get yourself up and running. Go for it.

▄▄▄▄▄

Sitting before Mitchell Reece in the glaringly lit Vista Hotel dining room was a plate of scrambled eggs, hash browns, bacon and a bagel. Taylor was nursing a grapefruit juice and seltzer.

She'd already been stared down by her dry toast.

Reece said, "You feeling okay?"

"I was out dancing last night till four."

"All work and no play . . ."

Taylor grunted. "The good news is I've got us a suspect." The juice was reviving traces of rum lurking in her bloodstream. This resuscitation was not pleasant. "Thom Sebastian."

She explained to him about cross-referencing the computer key entries and the time sheets.

"Brilliant," he told her, lifting an eyebrow.

She nodded noncommittally and downed two more Advils.

"Sebastian?" Reece pondered. "In the corporate group, right? He's done work for New Amsterdam in the past. He

might even've done some of the work on the original loan to
Hanover. But what's his motive? Money?"

"Revenge. He was passed over for partner."

"Ouch." Sympathy crept into Reece's face, which revealed the fatigue-dulled skin and damp red eyes that Taylor
knew matched hers. Still, his suit of textured charcoal wool
was perfectly pressed and his shirt was as smooth and white
as the starched napkin that lay across his lap. His dark hair
was combed back, slick and smooth from either a recent
shower or some lotion. He sat comfortably upright at the
table and ate hungrily.

Taylor braved the toast again and managed to eat a small
piece. "And he acted real odd about something. He's got a
quote project going on with somebody nicknamed Bosk.
Another lawyer here in town, young kid. But he wouldn't
talk about it. He also claims he was in a club on Saturday
but the bartender there said he wasn't. He left about one. I
asked Sebastian about it and he claims Ralph Dudley took
his computer door key."

"Old Man Dudley? Working on Sunday at one-thirty?
No way. Past his bedtime." Reece then reconsidered. "Funny,
though, I heard Dudley had money problems. He's borrowed big against his partnership equity."

Taylor said, "How'd you find that out?" The individual
partners' financial situations were closely guarded secrets.

As if citing an immutable rule of physics Reece said,
"*Always* know the successful partners from the losers."

"I'll check out Dudley today."

"I can't imagine he was in the firm on legitimate business. Dudley hasn't worked a weekend in his life. But I also
can't see him as our thief. He's such a bumbler. And he's got
that granddaughter of his he's looking after. I don't see how
he'd risk going to jail and leaving her alone. She doesn't
have any other family."

"That cute little girl he brought to the outing last year?
She's about sixteen?"

"I heard that Dudley's son abandoned her or something.

Anyway, she's in boarding school in town and he takes care of her." He laughed. "Kids. I can't imagine them."

Taylor asked, "You don't have any?"

He grew wistful for a few seconds. "No. I thought I would once." The stoic lawyer's facade returned immediately. "But my wife wasn't so inclined. And, after all, it does take two, you know."

"When I hit thirty-eight I'm going to find a genetically acceptable man, get pregnant and send him on his way."

"You could always try marriage, of course."

"Oh, yeah, I've heard about that."

He looked at her eyes for a moment then started laughing.

She asked, "What?"

"I was thinking, we should start a group."

"What?"

"The Visine Club," he said.

"I can get by with seven hours' sleep. Less than that, no way."

Reece said, "Five's pretty much standard for me." He finished the bacon and held a forkful of eggs toward her. She smiled, fought down the nausea and shook her head. She noticed, behind the bar, a stack of wine bottles and felt her stomach twist. Reece ate some of his breakfast and asked, "Where you from?"

"Burbs of D.C. Chevy Chase in Maryland. Well, I was born on Long Island but my parents moved to Maryland when I was in middle school. My father got a job in the District."

"Oh, I read that article in the *Post* about him last month. His argument before the Supreme Court."

"Tell me about it," she grumbled. "I've heard the blow-by-blow a half-dozen times. He overnighted me a copy of his argument. For my leisure-time reading, I guess."

"So how'd you end up on Wall Street?" Reece asked.

"Very long story," she said with a tone that told him that this was not the time or place to share it.

"School?

"Dartmouth . . . music and poly sci."

"Music?"

"I play piano. Jazz mostly."

This seemed to intrigue him. He asked, "Who do you listen to?"

"Billy Taylor's my fave, I guess. But there's something about the fifties and sixties. Cal Tjader, Desmond, Brubeck."

Reece shook his head. "I'm mostly into horn. Dexter Gordon, Javon Jackson."

"No kidding," she said, surprised. Usually only jazzophiles knew these players. "I love Jabbo Smith."

He nodded at this. "Sure, sure. I'm also a big Burrell fan."

She nodded. "Guitar? I still like Wes Montgomery, I've got to admit. For a while I was into a Howard Roberts phase."

Reece said, "Too avant-garde for me."

"Oh, yeah, I hear you," she said. "A melody . . . that's what music's got to have—a tune people can hum. A movie's got to have a story, a piece of music's got to have a tune. That's my philosophy of life."

"You perform?"

"Sometimes. Right now my big push is to get a record contract. I just dropped a bundle making a demo of some of my own tunes. I rented a studio, hired union backup. The works. Sent them to about a hundred companies."

"Yeah?" He seemed excited. "Give me a copy if you think about it. You have any extra?"

She laughed. "Dozens. Even after I give them away as Christmas presents this year."

"How's the response been?"

"Next question?" she asked, sighing. "I've sent out ninety-six tapes—agents, record companies, producers. So far, I've gotten eighty-four rejections. But I did get one 'maybe.' From a big label. They're going to present it to their A&R committee."

"I'll keep my fingers crossed."

"Thanks."

"So," he asked, "how's the music jibe with the law school track?"

"Oh, I can handle them both," she said without really thinking about her response. She wondered if the comment came off as pompous.

He glanced at his watch, and Taylor felt the gesture abruptly push aside the personal turn their conversation had taken. She asked, "There is one thing I wanted to ask you about. Linda Davidoff worked on the Hanover & Stiver case, right?"

"Linda? The paralegal? Yeah, for a few months when the case got started."

"It struck me as a little curious that she quit working on the case pretty suddenly then she killed herself."

He nodded. "That's odd, yeah. I never thought about it. I didn't know her very well. She was a good paralegal. But real quiet. It doesn't seem likely she'd be involved," Reece said, "but if you asked me it if was likely somebody'd steal a note from a law firm, I'd say no way."

The waitress asked if they wanted anything else. They shook their heads. "You women, always dieting," Reece said, nodding at her uneaten toast.

Taylor smiled. Thinking: We women, always trying not to throw up in front of our bosses.

"What's up next?" he asked.

"Time to be a spy," she said.

███████

Taylor sat in her cubicle at the firm and dialed a number.

She let the telephone ring. When the system shifted the call over to voice mail she hung up, left her desk and wandered down the halls. Up a flight of stairs. She turned down a corridor that led past the lunchroom then past the forms room, where copies of prototype contracts and pleadings were filed. At the end of this corridor—in the law firm's Siberia—was a single office. On the door was a nameplate: *R. Dudley*. Most of these plates in the firm were plastic; this one, though it designated the smallest partner's office in Hubbard, White, was made of polished brass.

Inside the office were crammed an Italian Renaissance desk, a tall bookcase, two shabby leather chairs, dozens of prints of nineteenth-century sailing ships and eighteenth-century foxhunting scenes. Through a small window you could see a brick wall and a tiny sliver of New York Harbor. On the desk rested a large brass ashtray, a picture of an unsmiling, pretty teenage girl, a dozen Metropolitan Opera *Playbills,* a date book and one law book—a Supreme Court *Reporter.*

Taylor Lockwood opened the *Reporter* and bent over it. Her eyes, though, camouflaged by her fallen hair, were not reading the twin columns of type but rather Ralph Dudley's scuffed leather date book, opened to the present week.

She noticed the letters *W.S.* penned into the box for late Saturday evening or early Sunday morning, just before the time Dudley—if Sebastian was right—had used the associate's key to get into the firm.

The initials *W.S.* were also, she observed, written in the 10 P.M. slot for tomorrow. Who was this person? A contact at Hanover? The professional thief? Taylor then opened the calendar to the phone number/address section. There was no one listed with those initials. She should—

"Can I help you?" a man's voice snapped.

Taylor forced herself not to jump. She kept her finger on the *Reporter* to mark her spot and looked up slowly.

A young man she didn't recognize stood in the doorway. Blond, scrubbed, chubby. And peeved.

"Ralph had this *Reporter* checked out from the library," she said, nodding at the book. "I needed to look up a case." Taking the offensive, she asked bluntly, "Who're you?"

"Me? I'm Todd Stanton. I work for Mr. Dudley." He squinted. "Who are *you?*"

"Taylor Lockwood. A paralegal." She forced indignation into her voice.

"A paralegal." His tone said, Oh, well, that doesn't really count. "Does Mr. Dudley know you're here?"

"No."

"If you need anything, you can ask me for it. Mr. Dudley doesn't like"—he sought the least disparaging term—"anyone in his office when he's not here."

"Ah," Taylor said and then turned back to the book and slowly finished reading a long paragraph.

Stanton shifted then said with irritation, "Excuse me but—"

Taylor closed the book softly. "Hey," she said, offering a concerned glance. "Don't sweat it. You're excused." And walked past him back into the deserted corridor.

CHAPTER EIGHT

"Dactyloscopy," the man said. "Repeat after me: dactyloscopy."

Taylor did.

More or less.

"Good," the man said. "Now you know the first thing about fingerprinting. It's called dactyloscopy. The second is that it is a royal pain in the butt."

She sat in the office of John Silbert Hemming. His card explained that he was a vice president in the corporate security department at Manhattan Allied Security, Inc.

The man, in his mid-thirties, had been recommended by a friend from the music world who did word processing for Allied Security to support his addiction to the saxophone.

Taylor had spent most of the day at Hubbard, White, poring over records of the *New Amsterdam Bank v. Hanover & Stiver* case, trying to find a reference to anyone who might have shown unusual interest in the promissory note or who'd requested files on the deal when there didn't seem to be a reason for them to do so.

But after nearly eight hours of mind-numbing legal babble Taylor found not a shred of evidence to suggest that Ralph
Dudley or Thom Sebastian—or anyone else—was the thief.

She'd decided to give up on the subtle approach and try
a more traditional tack, à la *Kojak* or *Rockford Files*.

Hence, the tall shamus she was now sitting across from.

When Hemming had come to meet her in the reception
area she'd blinked and looked up. He was six feet ten. His
height had led, he had explained on their way back to his
office, to his becoming a backroom security man—the company technical and forensic expert.

"You've got to be unobstrusive in private detective work.
A lot of what we do is surveillance, you know."

She said, "Tailing."

"Pardon?"

"Don't you say 'tailing'? You know, like you tail somebody?"

"Hmmm, no, we say say 'surveillance.'"

"Oh."

"If you stand out like me that's not so good. When we
recruit we have a space on our evaluation form—'Is subject
unobstrusive?' We mean 'boring.'"

His hair was tawny and unruly and Taylor's impression
of Hemming was that he was a huge little boy. He had eyes
that seemed perpetually amused and that belied a face that
was dramatically long (what else could it be, given that it sat
atop a body like his?). Despite this quirky appearance there
was something rather appealing about him.

Now, John Silbert Hemming was aiming a startlingly
long finger at her and saying, "I hope you mean that, about
wanting to know everything. Because there's a lot, and here
it comes. Let's start with: What *are* fingerprints?"

"Uh—"

"I know. You paid the money, I've got the answers. But I
like people to participate. I like interaction. Time's up. No
idea? I'd suggest you avoid *Jeopardy!* Now: Fingerprints are
the impressions left by the papillary ridges of the fingers
and thumb, primarily in perspiration. Also called friction

ridges. There are no sebaceous glands in the fingertips themselves but people sometimes leave fingerprints in human oils picked up elsewhere on the body. Yes, in answer to the first most-often-asked question, they are all different. Even more different than snowflakes, I can say safely, because for hundreds of years people have been collecting fingerprints from all over the world and comparing them, and nobody—none of *my* close friends, I'll tell you—have been doing that with snowflakes. Go ahead, ask the next-most-popular question."

"Uh, do animals have fingerprints?"

"Primates do, but who cares? We don't give apes government clearances or put them on the ten-most-wanted list. That's not the question. The question is twins."

"Twins?"

"And the answer is that twins, quadruplets, duodeceplets—they all have different fingerprints. Now, who first discovered fingerprints?"

"I have a feeling you're going to tell me?"

"Guess."

"Scotland Yard?" Taylor offered.

"Prehistoric tribes in France were aware of fingerprints and used them as cave decorations. In the sixteen and seventeen hundreds they were used as graphic designs and trademarks. The first attempt to study them seriously was in 1823—Dr. J. E. Purkinje, an anatomy professor, came up with a crude classification system. Fingerprints became sexy in the late 1800s. Sir Francis Galton, who was a preeminent scholar in the field of . . ." He cocked his eyebrows at Taylor. "Daily Double?"

"Dactyloscopy?"

"Nice try but no. In the field of heredity. He established that all fingerprints are different and they never change throughout one's life. The British government appointed Edward Richard Henry to a commission to consider using fingerprints to identify criminals. By around the turn of the century Henry had created the basic classification system they use in most countries. His system is called, coincidentally, the Henry system. New York was the first state to start fingerprinting all prisoners. Around 1902."

While she found this fascinating the urgency of the Hanover case kept prodding her. When he came up for air she asked, "If one were going to look for fingerprints, how would one do it?"

"'One'?" he asked coyly. "You?"

"No, just . . . one."

"Well, it depends on the surface. You—excuse me, *one*—should wear cloth gloves—not latex. If the surface is light-colored one would use a carbon-based dark powder. On dark, one would use an aluminum-and-chalk mixture; it's light gray. One would dust on the powder with a very soft, long-bristle brush. Then one removes the excess—"

"How?"

"Flip a coin," the detective said.

"One blows it off."

"A lot of rookies think that. But you tend to spit and ruin the whole print. No, use a brush. Now, powders only work on smooth surfaces. If you've got to take a print from paper there are different techniques. If the print's oily maybe it'll show up in iodine vapor. The problem is that you have to expose it in an enclosed cabinet and take a picture of the print very quickly because the vapors evaporate right away. Sometimes latents come out with a nitrate solution or ninhydrin or superglue. But that's the big league, probably over your—one's—skill level.

"Now, once *one* has the print, he or"—a nod toward her—"*she* has to capture it. You lift it off the surface with special tape or else take a picture of it. Remember: Fingerprints are *evidence*. They have to get into the courtroom and in front of an expert witness."

"Now," she said, "just speaking theoretically, could someone like me take fingerprints?"

"If you practiced, sure. But could you testify that prints A and B were the same? No way. Could you even tell if they were the same or different? Not easy, mama, not at all. They squoosh out, they move, they splot. They look different when they're the same, they look identical except for some little significant difference you miss.... No, it isn't easy. Fingerprinting is an art."

"How 'bout a machine, or something? A computer?"

"The police use them, sure. The FBI. But not private citizens. Say, Ms. Lockwood?"

"Taylor," she prompted.

"Perhaps if you told me exactly what your problem is I could offer some specific solutions."

"It's somewhat sensitive."

"It always is. That's why companies like us exist."

"Best to keep mum for the time being."

"Understood. Just let me know if you'd like another lesson. Though I do recommend keeping in mind the experts." He grew serious and the charming banter vanished. "Should the matter become, let's say, more than *sensitive*—a lot of our people here have carry permits."

" 'Carry'?"

"They're licensed to carry weapons."

"Oh," she said in a soft voice.

"Just something to think about."

"Thanks, John." Then she said, "I do have one question."

The hand in which a basketball would look so at home rose and a finger pointed skyward. "Allow me to deduce. The inquiry is: Where you can get a Dick Tracy fingerprint kit?" Before she answered yes, he was writing an address on the back of his business card. "It's a police equipment supply house. You can buy anything but weapons and shields there."

"Shields?"

"Badges, you know. Those you can buy—*one* can buy—in Times Square arcades for about ten bucks. But you're not supposed to. Oh, not to be forward, but I did happen to write my home phone number on the back of the card. In case any questions occur to you after hours, say."

She decided she liked this guy. "This's been fascinating, John. Thank you." She stood and he escorted her toward the elevator, pointing out a glass case containing a collection of blackjacks and saps.

"Oh, and Miss Lockwood? Taylor?"

"Yes?"

"Before you leave I was just wondering: Would you like to hear the lecture I give to our new employees on the laws against breaking and entering and invading privacy?"

Taylor said, "No, I don't believe I would."

████████

She'll be moody today.

Ralph Dudley sat in his creaky office chair. The nape of his neck eased into the tall leather back and he stared at the thin slice of sky next to the brick wall outside his window. Gray sky, gray water. November.

Yes, Junie would be in one of her moods.

It was a talent, this intuition of his. Whereas Donald Burdick, to whom he constantly—obsessively—compared himself, was brilliant, Ralph Dudley was intuitive. He charmed clients, he told them jokes appropriate to their age, gender and background, he listened sympathetically to their tales of sorrow at infidelities and deaths and to their stories of joy at grandchildren's births. He told war stories of his courtroom victories with a dramatic pacing that only fiction—which they were, of course—permits. With his patented vestigial bow Dudley could charm the daylights out of the wives of clients and potential clients.

He had sense and feeling while Burdick had reason and logic.

And, sure enough, he was now right. Here came fifteen-year-old Junie, a sour look on her face, trooping sullenly into his office, ignoring the woman from the word processing pool who was handling a typing job for him.

The girl stopped in the doorway, a hip-cocked stance, unsmiling.

"Come on in, honey," Dudley said. "I'm almost finished."

She wore a jumper, white blouse and white stockings. A

large blue bow was in her hair. She gave him a formal kiss
on the cheek and plopped into one of his visitor's chairs,
swinging her legs over the side.

"Sit like a lady, now."

She waited a defiant thirty seconds then slipped on her
Walkman headset and swiveled slowly in the chair, planting
her feet on the lime-green carpet.

Dudley laughed. He picked up the handle of his dictat-
ing machine. "Look, I've got one, too—a recorder."

She looked perplexed and he realized she couldn't hear
what he was saying (and would probably have thought his
joke was idiotic if she'd been able to). But Dudley had
learned not to be hurt by the girl's behavior and he unemotionally proceeded to dictate a memo that gave the gist of
some rules of law he believed he remembered. At the end of
the tape he included instructions to Todd Stanton, his associate at the firm, who would rewrite the memo and look up
the law Dudley hoped existed to support his points.

Ralph Dudley knew they sometimes laughed at him, the
young associates here. He never raised his voice, he never
criticized, he was solicitous toward them. He supposed the
young men (Dudley had never quite come to terms with the
idea of women lawyers) held him in all the more contempt
for this obsequiousness. There were a few loyal boys, like
Todd, but on the whole no one had much time for Old Man
Dudley.

"Grandpa," he'd heard that the associates called him.
Partners, too, although somewhat more subtly, joined in the
derision. Yet though this treatment soiled his days here—
and obliterated whatever loyalty he had once felt for
Hubbard, White & Willis—he was not overly troubled. His
relation with the firm became just what his marriage to
Emma had been: one of respectful acknowledgment. He was
usually able to keep his bitterness contained.

Junie's eyes were closed, her patent-leather shoes sway-
ing in time to the music. My God, she was growing up. Fifteen. It gave him a pang of sorrow. At times he had
flashes—poses she struck, the way the light might catch her

face—of her as a woman in her twenties. He knew that she, abandoned in adolescence, carried the seeds of adulthood within her more fertilely than other children.

And he often felt she was growing up far too fast for him.

He handed the dictated tape to the typist, who left.

"So," he said to the girl, "are we going to do some shopping?"

"I guess."

That question she heard perfectly, Dudley observed. "Well, let's go."

She shrugged and hopped off the chair, tugging at her dress in irritation, which meant she wanted to be wearing jeans and a T-shirt—clothes that she loved and that he hated.

They were at the elevator when a woman's voice asked, "Ralph, excuse me, you have a minute?"

He recognized the young woman from around the firm but couldn't recall a name. It stung him slightly that she had the effrontery to call him by his first name but because he was a gentlemen he did nothing other than smile and nod. "Yes, you're . . ."

"Taylor Lockwood."

"Sure, of course. This is my granddaughter, Junie. Junie, say hello to Miss Lockwood. She's a lawyer here."

"Paralegal, actually." Taylor smiled and said to the girl pleasantly, "You look like Alice."

"Huh?"

"Alice in Wonderland. It's one of my favorite books."

The girl shrugged and returned to the oblivion of her music.

Dudley wondered what this woman wanted. Had he given her some work? An assignment?

"I'd like to ask you something."

"What's that?"

"You went to Yale Law School, didn't you?"

"That's right, I did."

"I'm thinking of applying there."

Dudley felt a bit of alarm. He hadn't quite graduated, despite what he'd told the firm, and so couldn't exactly send a letter of recommendation for her.

But she added, "My application and letters and everything're in. I just want to know a little about the school. I'm trying to decide between there and Harvard and NYU."

Relieved, Dudley said, "Oh, I went there before you were born. I don't think anything I'd have to tell you would be much help."

"Well, somebody here said you helped them decide to go to law school, that you were very helpful. I was sort of hoping you could spare a half hour or so."

Dudley felt the pleasure he always did at even minor adulation like this. "Tonight?"

She said, "I was thinking tomorrow night maybe. After work? I could take you out to dinner."

A woman taking a man out to dinner? Dudley was nearly offended.

The paralegal added, "Unless you have plans."

He did, of course—plans he *wouldn't* miss. But that was at 10 P.M. He said, "I'm busy later in the evening. But how would seven be?" A charming smile. "I'll take you to my club."

Junie of the selective hearing said, "Like, Poppie, you told me they didn't let women in there."

Dudley said to her, "That's only as members, honey." To Taylor he said, "Come by tomorrow at six, we'll take a cab uptown. . . ." Then, calculating the taxi fare, he added, "No, actually a subway would be better. That time of day, traffic is terrible."

"Now he's going after the clients."

Donald Burdick knotted the silk tie carefully with his long fingers. He liked the feel of good cloth, the way it yielded yet was tough. Tonight, though, the smooth texture gave him little pleasure.

"First he rams through the accelerated vote and now I hear he's targeting the clients."

"The clients," Vera Burdick repeated, nodding. "We should've thought of that." She sat at her dressing table in the bedroom of their Park Avenue co-op, rubbing prescription retin-A cream on her neck. She wore a red and black silk dress, which revealed pale freckled skin along the unzipped V in the back. She was leaning forward studiously, watching the cream disappear.

A resolute woman, in her early sixties, she'd battled age by making tactical concessions. She gave up tanning fifteen years ago and carefully gained a little weight, refusing to join in the dieting obsession of many of her friends, who were now knobby scarecrows. She let her hair go white but she kept it shiny with Italian conditioner and wore it pulled back in the same style as her granddaughter. She'd allowed herself one face-lift and had flown to Los Angeles to have a particular Beverly Hills surgeon perform the operation.

She was now as she'd always been: attractive, reserved, stubborn, quiet. And virtually as powerful as the two men who'd influenced her life—her father and Donald Burdick, her husband of thirty-two years. Arguably she was *more* powerful in some ways than each of these men because people were always on guard with the masters of Wall Street, like Donald Burdick, but tended to get careless around women and be too chatty, to give away secrets, to reveal weaknesses.

Burdick sat on the bed. His wife offered her back and he carefully zipped up the dress and hooked the top eyelet. The partner continued, "Clayton's moving against them. It's pretty clever, I have to admit. While Bill Stanley and Lamar and I've been taking on as much debt as we can to poison the merger Wendall's been spending time with the clients, trying to convince *them* to pressure the partners at the firm to support the merger."

Vera too felt admiration for what Wendall was doing. Although a firm's clients have no official vote in firm affairs they ultimately pay the bills and accordingly can exert astonishing influence over which way the partners vote. She'd often said that if clients unionized against law firms it would be time for her husband to find a new line of work.

"How's he doing it?" she asked, curious to learn his technique.

"Probably promising big discounts in legal fees if they support the merger. Those that still don't go along with him—my clients or Bill's, the ones who won't support the merger in any case—we're afraid he's going to sabotage."

"Sabotage. Oh, my. What's the vote so far?"

"It's closer than it should be."

"You've got the long-term lease with Rothstein, right?" Vera asked. "That should slow him up some. When are you signing it?"

"Friday or the weekend," he answered glumly.

"Not till then?" She winced.

"I know," he said. "The fastest they could get the papers together. But it's okay—Clayton doesn't know anything about it. Then I've been talking to Steve Nordstrom."

"At McMillan Holdings," Vera recalled. "Your biggest client. Steve's the chief financial officer, right?"

A nod. "I'm closer to him than I am to Ed Gliddick, the CEO. I'm going to get them to lobby some of the other partners against the merger."

"And Steve'll agree?"

"I'm sure he will. Gliddick's in charge. But he listens to Steve. Wendall doesn't know about that either. I've been excruciatingly discreet. I . . . ."

Burdick realized that he sounded desperate and hated the tone of his voice. Then he glanced at his wife, who was gazing at him with a savvy smile on her face. "We can do it," she said. "Clayton's not in our league, dear."

"Neither was that cobra on vacation last year. That doesn't mean he's not dangerous."

"But look what happened to it."

Hiking in Africa, Burdick had accidentally stepped on the snake in the brush. It had puffed out its hood and prepared to strike. Vera had taken its head off with a swipe of a sharp machete.

Burdick found his teeth clenched. "Wendall just doesn't understand what Wall Street law practice is. He's crude, he bullies. He has affairs."

"Irrelevant." She began on her makeup.

"Oh, I think it *is* relevant. I'm talking about the survival of the firm. Wendall doesn't have *vision*. He doesn't understand what Hubbard, White is, what it should be."

"And how do you define 'should be'?"

Touché, Burdick thought. He grinned involuntarily. "All right, what *I've* made it. Bill and Lamar and I. Wendall wants to turn the firm into a mill. Into a big merger-and-acquisition house."

"Every generation has its own specialties. That's very profitable work." She set down the blush. "I'm not justifying him, darling. I'm only saying we should stay focused. We can't make logical arguments against the nature of the legal work he wants the new firm to handle. We have to remember that the risk is that as part of the merger he's going to burn the firm to the ground and then sow the ashes with salt. *That's* why we have to stop him."

She was, as usual, right. He reached for her hand but the phone rang and he walked to the nightstand to answer it.

Burdick took the call and listened in dismay as Bill Stanley's gruff voice delivered the message. He hung up and looked at his wife, who stared at him, clearly alarmed by his drawn expression.

"He's done it again."

"Clayton?"

Burdick sighed and nodded. He walked to the window and gazed outside into the trim, windswept courtyard. "There's a problem with the St. Agnes case."

Donald Burdick's oldest and second-most-lucrative client was Manhattan's St. Agnes Hospital. It had recently been sued for malpractice and Fred LaDue, a litigation partner, was handling the trial, which was in its fourth day now.

The case was routine and it was likely that the hospital was going to win. Stanley had just reported, however, that the plaintiff's attorneys—from a tough Midtown personal injury firm—had found a new witness, a doctor whose testimony could be devastating to St. Agnes. Even though he was a surprise witness, the judge was going to let him testify tomorrow.

The judgment could be for tens of millions and a loss this big might mean that St. Agnes—which was self-insured—would fire Hubbard, White & Willis altogether. Even if the hospital didn't do so, though, the credibility of Burdick and his litigation department would be seriously eroded and the hospital might push to support the merger; John Perelli's firm was renowned for its brutal handling of personal injury defense work.

"Damn," Burdick muttered. "Damn."

Vera's eyes narrowed. "You don't think that Wendall slipped your client's files to the other side, do you?"

"It did occur to me."

Vera took a sip of scotch and set the Waterford glass down on the table. Burdick's eyes were distant, trying to process this news. His wife's, however, had coalesced into dark dots. "One thing I'd say, darling."

The wind rattled the leaded-glass windows. Burdick glanced at the sound.

She said, "With a man like Wendall, we have to hit him hard the first time. We won't have a second chance."

Burdick's eyes dropped to the Pakistani carpet on the bedroom floor. Then he picked up the phone and called the night operator at the law firm. "This is Donald Burdick," he said politely. "Please locate Mitchell Reece and have him call me at home. Tell him it's urgent."

CHAPTER NINE

Taylor Lockwood walked through the breezy evening streets of the East Village, the curbs banked with trash, and thought of a funeral she'd attended several months earlier.

She'd sat in the front pew of the church in Scarsdale, north of the city, a wood-and-stone building built, someone behind her had whispered, by contributions from tycoons like J. P. Morgan and Vanderbilt. Although Taylor had been in black, that color did not seem to be requisite at funerals any longer; any somber shade was acceptable—purple, forest green, even dusk-brown tapestry. She sat on the hard pew and watched the family members, lost in their personal rituals of grief, tears running in halting streams, hands squeezing hands, fingers rubbing obsessively against fingers. The minister had spoken of Linda Davidoff with genuine sorrow and familiarity. He knew the parents better than the daughter, that was clear, but he was eulogizing well.

Most attendees had seemed sad or bewildered but not everyone had cried; suicide makes for an ambivalent mourning.

The minister had closed the service with one of Linda's poems, one published in her college literary magazine.

As he'd read, images of Linda had returned and the tears that Taylor Lockwood had told herself not to cry appeared fast, stinging the corners of her eyes and running with maddening tickles down her cheeks, even though she hadn't known the paralegal very well.

Then the organ had played a solemn cue and the mourners had filed outside for the drive to the interment.

As she'd told Reece, nothing that she'd found suggested that Linda Davidoff had had any connection with Hanover & Stiver or the loan deal. But there was something suspicious to Taylor about the way the girl had worked such long hours on the case then stopped abruptly—and then committed suicide.

She felt she needed to follow up on this question. Alice, after all, had wandered everywhere throughout Wonderland—a place, however, in which you sure wouldn't find the disgusting six-story tenement she now stood in front of. In the foul entry foyer the intercom had been stolen and the front door was open, swinging in the breeze like a batwing door in a ghost town saloon. She started up the filthy steps.

■■■■■■

"It may look impressive, but the bank owns most of it," Sean Lillick said.

The young paralegal was sitting on the drafty floor, shirtless and shoeless, shoving a backpack under the bed as she walked in.

Taylor Lockwood, catching her breath from the climb, was surveying what Lillick was referring to: a wall of keyboards, wires, boxes, a computer terminal, speakers, guitar, amps. Easily fifty thousand dollars' worth of musical equipment.

Lillick—thin, dark-haired, about twenty-four—was smelling socks, discarding them. He wore black jeans, a sleeveless T-shirt. His boots sat in front of him. The only clue as to his day job at Hubbard, White & Willis were two dark suits and three white shirts, in various stages of recycling, hanging on nails pounded crookedly into the wall. He studied her for a moment. "You look impressed or confused. I can't tell."

"Your place is a little more alternative than I expected." The apartment was a patchwork. Someone had nailed pieces of plywood, plastic or sheet metal over cracks and holes. Joints didn't meet, plaster was rotting, floorboards were cracked or missing. In the living room: one hanging bare bulb, one floor lamp, one daybed, one desk.

And a ton of bank-owned musical instruments and gear.

"Have a seat."

She looked helplessly about her.

"Oh. Well, try the daybed. . . . Hey, Taylor, listen to this. I just thought it up. I'm going to use it in one of my pieces: You know what a preppy is?"

"I give up."

"A yuppie with papers."

She smiled politely. He didn't seem concerned about the tepid response and wrote the line down in a notebook. "So what do you do?" she asked. "Stand-up comedy?"

"Performance art. I like to rearrange perceptions."

"Ah, musically speaking," she joked, "you're a *re*-arranger."

He seemed to like her observation too and mentally stored it somewhere.

Taylor walked over to a music keyboard.

Lillick said, "You're thinking organ, I know. But—"

"I'm thinking Yamaha DX-7 synthesizer with a digital sampler, MIDI and a Linn sequencer that should store about a hundred sequences in RAM. You mind?"

He laughed and waved his hand. She sat on a broken stool and clicked on the Yamaha. She ran through "Ain't Misbehavin'."

Lillick said, "This machine cannot deal with music like that. I think it's having a breakdown."

"What do you play?" she asked him.

"Postmodern, post–New Wave. What I do is integrate music and my show. I call myself a sound painter. Is that obnoxious?"

Taylor thought it was but just smiled and read through some of his lead sheets. In addition to standard musical notation they included drawings of pans and hammers, lightbulbs, bells, a pistol.

"When I started composing I was a serialist and then I moved to minimalism. Now I'm exploring nonmusical elements, like choreography and performance art. Some sound sculpture, too. I love what Philip Glass does only I'm less thematic. Laurie Anderson, that sort of thing. I believe there should be a lot of randomness in art. Don't you think?"

She shook her head, recalling what she'd told Reece that morning: How she believed music should stay close to melodies that resonated within people's hearts. She said, "You're talking to Ms. Mainstream, Sean," and shut off the system. She asked, "Got a beer?"

"Oh. Sure. Help yourself. I'll take one, too, while you're at it."

She popped them and handed him one. He asked, "You perform?"

"You wouldn't approve. Piano bars."

"They serve a valuable function."

Irritated by his too hip, and too righteous, attitude, Taylor asked, "Are you being condescending?"

"No. I mean it. I like classics too." Lillick was up, hobbling on one boot to his rows of records and CDs and tapes. "Charlie Parker. I got every Bird record ever made. Here, listen." He put on an LP, which sounded scratchy and authentic. "Man, that was the life," Lillick said. "You get up late, practice a bit, hang out, play sax till three, watch the sunrise with your buddies."

Taylor, lost in one of Bird's solos, mused, "Man died young."

"Thirty-five," Lillick said.

"World lost a lot of music."

"Maybe it wouldn't have been so, you know, deep, so righteous if he'd lived longer."

Taylor said, "Maybe just the opposite. Hooked on smack's gotta affect you."

He nodded at his record collection, which did contain a lot of mainstream jazz. "See, I'm not a snob. We need people like that. If you don't have rules and traditions there's nothing to break."

If it ain't broke, don't fix it, Taylor thought. But she wasn't here to debate the philosophy of music with him.

Lillick retrieved a fat joint and lit it up. He passed it toward Taylor. She shook her head and, examining the musical armada of equipment, asked, "What're you doing at a law firm, you're so into artsy-fartsy?"

"Steady salary, what else. The way I look at it, Hubbard, White & Willis is supporting the arts." He seemed uneasy, as if the conversation was going down paths he didn't want to tread.

He suddenly pulled out a pad of music staff paper and a pencil. "Keep talking. I work best when I'm only using half my mind."

She asked, "What I came to ask you about . . . You took over for Linda Davidoff on the Hanover & Stiver case, right?"

"Yeah."

"What do you know about her?"

Lillick looked at his cracked plaster walls for a moment and wrote a measure of music. She sensed he was performing for her—playing the distracted artist.

"Linda Davidoff?" she repeated.

After a moment he looked up. "Sorry . . . Linda? Well, we went out a few times. I thought she was more interesting than most of the prep princesses you see around the firm. She wanted to be a writer. It didn't go very far between us."

"Why'd she stop working on the Hanover case?"

Silent for a moment, Lillick thought back. "I'm not sure. I think she was sick."

"Sick? What was wrong with her?"

"I don't know. I remember she didn't look good. She was—"

"—pale," Taylor recalled.

"Yeah, exactly. I saw her filling out insurance forms a couple of times. I asked her about it but she didn't tell me anything."

"Do you know why she killed herself?" Taylor asked.

"No, but I'll tell you I wasn't wildly amazed she did. She was too sensitive, you know? She took things too much to heart. I don't what she was doing working for a law firm." Lillick erased and rewrote a line. He hummed it. "Give me a B-flat diminished."

Taylor turned on the DX-7 and hit the chord.

"Thanks." He wrote some more musical notations.

"Where'd she live?"

"I don't know—in the Village somewhere, I think. What's up? Why're you so interested in Linda?"

"Screwup with the New Amsterdam bill, going way back. They were majorly underbilled and I'm supposed to check out what happened. When you took over for her did she say anything about the case?"

Lillick shook his head.

Taylor asked, "You're still billing time on the case, aren't you?"

"Some. But Mitchell's handling most of it himself." Lillick didn't seem to have any reaction to her questions.

"Anybody she was close to?"

"Her roommate, Danny Stuart. He's an editor or something. Lives in the West Village. Over on Greenwich Street, I think." He rummaged in a stack of papers. "I've got the number somewhere." He handed it to her. "Hey, back in a flash."

He ducked into the john.

Which gave Taylor the chance she'd been waiting for. She dropped to her knees and found the backpack that Lillick had been stashing when she'd entered. It had seemed to her that he'd hidden it just a little too quickly when she walked inside.

A fast unzip revealed cash. A lot of it. Taylor had only ten seconds for a fast estimate but figured the total would probably be something on the order of thirty or forty thousand dollars. An amount equal to his yearly salary at the firm—which didn't, of course, pay in greenbacks.

And, a regular of the Downtown performing circuit herself, Taylor knew that, to quote her father, there was no way in Satan's backyard that anyone would ever make any kind of serious money playing music in bars.

Which meant that, no, Sean, the bank *didn't* own most of your equipment.

She'd come here only for information but had found another suspect.

Taylor shoved the bag back a few seconds before the young man returned. "Better roll," she said. "Thanks for the beer."

"You like goat?"

"What?"

"I'm thinking of going over to this place on Fourteenth. The goat's the best in the city. It's a totally happening place."

The thought of another night partying was more than she could handle. Besides, she had a mission back at the firm.

"Not tonight."

"Hey, this place is mondo cool. Bowie hangs out there. It's so packed you can hardly get in. And they play industrial out of one set of speakers and the Sex Pistols out of the other. I mean in the same room! Like, at a thousand decibels."

"Kills me to say no, Sean. But I'll take a pass."

Wendall Clayton liked the firm at night.

He liked the silence, the jeweled dots of boat lights in New York Harbor, liked taking a mouthful of cigar smoke

and holding it against his palate, free from the critical
glances his secretary and some of the more reckless younger
lawyers shot his way when he lit up a Macanudo in the firm.

This after-hours atmosphere took him back to his days
just after law school, when he'd spend many of his nights
proofreading the hundreds of documents that make up typical business deals: loan agreements, guarantees, security
agreements, cross-collateralization documents, certificates
of government filings, corporate documents and board reso-
lutions.

Proofreading ... and carefully watching the partners he
was working for.

Oh, he'd learned the law, yes, because in order to be
good a lawyer must have a flawless command of the law. But
to be a *great* lawyer—that requires much more. It requires
mastering the arts of demeanor, tactics, leadership, extortion, anger and even flirtation.

Sabotage too.

He now looked over statements by a witness in a case
that Hubbard, White was currently defending on behalf of
one of Donald Burdick's prize clients, St. Agnes Hospital in
Manhattan. Sean Lillick and Randy Simms, Clayton's head
of the SS, had dug up the identity of a doctor who had firsthand knowledge of the hospital malpractice St. Agnes was
allegedly guilty of.

Clayton had slipped the identity of this man to the
plaintiff—in effect, scuttling the case against his firm's own
client.

This troubled him some, of course, but as he read
through the witness's statements and realized that the St.
Agnes doctors had indeed committed terrible malpractice,
he concluded that his sabotage was in fact loyalty to a
higher authority than the client or the firm: loyalty to abstract justice herself.

He rolled these thoughts around in his complex mind
for a few minutes and reached this conclusion: that he could
live with St. Agnes Hospital's extremely expensive loss in the
trial.

He hid these documents away and then opened another sealed envelope. Sean Lillick had dropped it off just before he'd left for the night. He read the memo the paralegal had written him.

Clayton's money was being well spent, he decided. Lillick had apparently aristocratized the right people. Or begged them or fucked them or whatever. In any case the information was as valuable as it was alarming.

Burdick was taking an extreme measure. The firm's lease for its present office space in Wall Street would be up next year. This expiration had been a plus for Clayton's merger because it meant that the firm could move to Perelli's Midtown office, which was much cheaper, without a difficult and expensive buyout of an existing lease.

The purpose of the secret talks Lillick had learned about between Burdick, Stanley and Harry Rothstein, the head of the partnership that owned the building, was to negotiate a new, extremely expensive long-term lease for the existing office space.

By entering the lease, the firm would take on a huge financial commitment that would cost millions to buy its way out of. This would make Hubbard, White a much less attractive target for a merger. The full partnership didn't need to approve the lease, only the executive committee, which Burdick's side controlled.

The lease agreement, Lillick had learned, wouldn't be signed until this weekend.

Son of a bitch, he raged. Well, he'd have to stop the deal somehow.

He put Lillick's memo away and began thinking about defensive measures. If Burdick learned what Clayton was up to, particularly with the St. Agnes case and the lease, he and his bitchy wife would strike back hard. Clayton began to worry about loose ends.

He picked up the phone and called Lillick.

The boy's cheerful voice drooped when he realized who the caller was.

"That information was . . . helpful."

This was one of Clayton's highest forms of compliments. *Helpful.*

"Like . . . I mean, I'm glad."

"I'm a little concerned though, Sean. You *are* being careful, aren't you?"

The boy hesitated and Clayton wondered if there was anything more to his uneasiness than a phone call from his boss.

"Of course."

"I'm aware of people asking questions around the firm, Sean. Anybody been asking you questions?"

"Uh, no."

"You are making sure you cover tracks? Being a good Boy Scout or nature guide or something?"

"Yeah, I'm not stupid, Wendall."

"No, of course you're not. Just make sure everything's covered up carefully, no way to trace what you and I've been up to. You know legal defense fees can be *so* expensive. They can eat up all one's savings in a flash."

The boy's silence told him that the threat had been received.

Clayton looked up into the doorway, where a young woman stood at attention. "Better go, Sean. Be in early tomorrow. Snip any ends, okay?"

"Sure."

The partner hung up, his eyes on the woman. She was one of the night stenographers from the word processing department. Her name was Carmen and she was slim and had a complexion like a week-old tan. She wore tight blouses and dark skirts that would be too short for the day, but on the evening shift the dress code was more relaxed.

"I got your call, Mr. Clayton. You need some dictation?"

Clayton looked at her legs then her breasts. "Yes, I do."

Carmen had a five-year-old son, fathered by a man who was currently in prison. She lived with her mother in the Bronx. She had a patch of stretch marks on her lower belly and a tattoo of a rose on her left buttock.

"Why don't you close the door," he said. "We don't want the cleaning staff to disturb us."

She waited until he'd taken his wallet from his suit jacket pocket and opened it up before she swung the door shut and locked it.

CHAPTER TEN

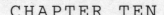It was nearly 8 P.M. but for some reason the closing of a corporate merger that had begun at 2 that afternoon ran into difficulties and was not yet completed—some delay in Japanese regulatory approvals.

The Hubbard, White & Willis lawyers and paralegals working on the case, clutching stacks of documents, scurried back and forth between the several conference rooms devoted to the closing like ants stealing bread crumbs from a picnic though with considerably more content faces than their insect counterparts—presumably because ants don't make a collective $4,000 per hour for carting around bits of soggy food. The clients, on the other hand—the *payers* of those legal fees—were nothing but frustrated.

Back from her trip to Lillick's apartment, Taylor Lockwood had learned many intimate details about the closing because she'd been dodging the lawyers and clients for the past hour. Like the clients in the delayed deal, Taylor had her own frustrations.

John Silbert Hemming had neglected to tell her that dactyloscopy powder didn't come off.

She'd just finished fingerprinting Reece's burglarized file cabinet and painstakingly transferring the sticky tape of the two dozen latents she'd found to cards. She thought back to what Hemming'd told her. Yes, he'd mentioned the different kinds of powders. He'd mentioned how to spread it around and how to brush, not blow, the excess away.

But he hadn't told her the stuff was like dry ink.

Once you—once *one*—dusted it onto the surface the damn stuff didn't wipe off. The smear just got bigger and bigger.

She wasn't concerned about the file cabinet that had contained the note. She was concerned about Mitchell Reece's coffee mug, emblazoned with "World's Greatest Lawyer," which she'd dusted to get samples of his prints to eliminate those from the ones she lifted off his cabinet.

Fingerprinting powder coated the mug like epoxy paint. She did her best to clean it then noticed she'd gotten some on her blouse. She pinched the midriff of the shirt and fluffed the poor garment to see if that would dislodge the powder. No effect. She tried to blow it away, and—as her tall private eye had warned—spit into the smear, which immediately ran the powder into the cloth. Permanently, she suspected.

Taylor sighed and pulled on her suit jacket to cover the smudge.

She hurried down to Ralph Dudley's office, where she lifted samples of his fingerprints, then on to Thom Sebastian's, where she did the same.

Finally, back in the paralegal pens, she took samples of Sean Lillick's prints from several objects in his cubicle. Then back in her own cubicle she put the fingerprint cards in an envelope and hid it under a stack of papers in the bottom drawer of her desk.

She found the phone number that Lillick had given her—Danny Stuart, Linda Davidoff's roommate—and called him. He wasn't in but she left a message asking if they could meet; there was something about Linda she wanted to ask him about.

She hung up and then happened to look down at her desktop and, with a twist in her gut, noticed the managing attorney's daily memo. In the square for Tuesday of next week were these words:

> New Amsterdam Bank & Trust v. Hanover & Stiver.
> Jury trial. Ten a.m. No continuance.

As she stared there was suddenly a huge explosion behind her.

Taylor spun around, inhaling a scream.

Her eyes met those of a young man in a white shirt. He was standing in the hall, staring back at her. He held a bottle of French champagne he'd just opened. "Hey, sorry," he said. Then smiled. "We just closed. We finally got Bank of Tokyo approval."

"I'm happy for you," she said and snagged her coat then started down the hallway as he turned his groggy attention to opening more bottles and setting them on a silver tray.

███

The drapery man watched her pull her overcoat on and step into the lobby, the door swinging shut behind her.

He patiently waited a half hour, just in case she'd forgotten anything, and when she didn't return he walked slowly down the corridor to Taylor Lockwood's cubicle, pushing the drapery cart in front of him, his hand near his ice-pick weapon.

Upstairs the firm was bustling like mid-morning—some big fucking business deal going on, dozens of lawyers and assistants ignoring him—but down here the place was dark and empty. He paused in the Lockwood woman's cubicle, checked the hallways again and dropped to his knees. In two minutes he'd fitted the transmitting microphone, like the one he planted in Mitchell Reece's phone, into hers.

The drapery man finished the job, tested the device, ran a sweep to make sure it wasn't detectable and walked to the entranceway of the paralegal cubicles.

Nearby was a conference room, in which he saw a half-dozen open bottles of champagne sitting on a silver tray. When he touched one with the back of his hand he found it was still cold. He glanced behind him, pulled on his gloves and lifted the first bottle to his mouth. He took a sip then ran his tongue around the lip of the bottle. He did the same with the others.

Then feeling the faint buzz from the dry wine—and a huge sense of satisfaction—he returned to the hallway and started pushing his cart toward the back door.

████

"Never take a job," Sean Lillick said pensively, holding the door open, "where you have to hold things in your teeth."

Carrie Mason, standing in the door of his shabby East Village walk-up, blinked. "Never what?" she asked, entering.

"That's a line from a piece I'm working on right now. I'm, like, a performance artist. This one's about careers. I call it 'W2 Blues.' Like your W2 form, the tax thing. It's spoken over music."

"Never take a job that..." Pained, she said, "I don't think I get it."

"There's nothing to get," he explained, a little irritated. "It's more of a social comment, you know, than a joke. It's about how we're defined in terms of what we do for a living. You know, like the first thing lawyers say when you meet them is what they do for a living. The point is we should be human beings first and then have a career."

She nodded. "So when you just said you were a performance artist, that was, like, being ironic?"

Now, *he* blinked. Then, even more irritated, he nodded. "Yeah, exactly. Ironic."

He examined her from the corner of his eye. The girl was hardly his type. Although on the whole Lillick preferred women to men (he'd had his share of both since he came to New York from Des Moines five years ago) the sort of women he wanted to fuck were willowy, quiet, beautiful and passed cold judgment on anyone they bothered to glance at.

Carrie Mason didn't come close to meeting his specifications. For one thing, she was fat. Well, okay, not fat, but round—round in a way that needed pleated skirts and billowy blouses to make her look good. For another, she was polite and laughed a lot, which was evidence that she would rarely pass moody judgments on anyone at all.

Lillick also suspected she blushed frequently and he couldn't see himself getting involved with anybody who blushed.

"You know," she said after a moment, "tailors hold pins and things in their teeth. Fashion designers too. And carpenters hold nails when they're building houses."

That was true. He hadn't thought of that. And her comment made him even angrier with her. "I meant more like, you know, maybe holding bits of tape or tools or something." Then he added quickly, "The point is, like, just to make people think about things."

"Well, it *does* make you think," she conceded.

Lillick took her coat. "You want a beer?"

She was studying the keyboards and computers. "Sure."

"Have a seat."

She ran her hand over the tie-dye bedspread and glanced at her fingers to make sure the coloring didn't come off.

Excuse me, your royal highness. . . .

She sat down. He opened a Pabst and handed it to her, thinking only after he did that he probably should have poured it into a glass. But to take it back and find a clean mug would now seem stupid.

"I was surprised when you called, Sean."

"Yeah?" Lillick punched on a Meredith Monk tape. "I've been meaning to. You know, you work with somebody and you think, I'm going to call her up, yadda, yadda, yadda, but you get caught up in things."

"That's sure true."

"Anyway, I was thinking of going over to this place for

goat...." But he stopped speaking fast, thinking what the hell would his buddies from the East Village say if they saw him at Carlos' with a fat preppy princess?

But he didn't need to worry; Carrie wrinkled her nose at the food. "Goat?"

"Maybe," he said, "we'll find someplace else. Whatta you like?"

"Burgers and fries and salads. Usual stuff, you know. I usually hang out at the bars on Third Avenue. They're fun. You know, sing along."

"When Irish Eyes Are Smiling..." God in heaven save me.

"You want me to ...," Carrie began.

"Huh?"

"Well, I was going to say: If you want me to iron your shirt I'm, like, way good at that sort of thing."

The garment was a tan shirt printed with tiny brown scenes of European landmarks. It was one of his favorites and the cloth was wrinkled as a prune.

He laughed. "You iron this poor thing, it'd curl up and die."

Carrie said, "I like ironing. It's therapeutic. Like washing dishes."

In his five years in Manhattan he'd never ironed a single piece of clothing. He *did* do the dishes. Occasionally.

Outside a man's scream cut through the night. Then another, followed by a long moan. Carrie looked up, alarmed.

Lillick laughed. "It's just a hooker. There's a guy turns tricks across the air shaft. He's a howler." He pointed to a machine. "That's a digital sampler. It's a computer that records a sound and lets you play it back through your synthesizer on any note you want."

Carrie looked at the device.

Lillick continued, "I recorded the screaming one night. It was totally the best!" He laughed. "I performed a piece from Bach's *Well-Tempered Clavier,* only instead of the harpsichord sound it's a gay hooker shouting, 'Deeper, deeper!'"

She laughed hard. Then looked out the window toward

the diminishing wails. "I don't get downtown as much as I'd like."

"Where do you live?"

"East Eighty-fourth."

"Ah."

"I know," she said, blushing, as he'd predicted. "It's not so cool. But I kinda ended up there and I've got a three-year lease."

"So, how's Mexican?" he asked. He glanced down at his shirt. It wasn't *that* fucking wrinkled. "There's a place around the corner. I call it the Hacienda del Hole. Kinda a dive but the food's good."

"Sure, whatever." Then she suggested, "Or we could just hang out here. Like, maybe order pizza, watch the tube." Carrie nodded at his dusty TV set. "I like *Cheers*," she said. "And *M*A*S*H*."

Lillick only watched TV to pick up on pop culture icons he could trash in his performance pieces. He had to admit, though, he liked *M*A*S*H*. Well, and *Lucy* reruns. And *Gilligan's Island* (though not a soul in the universe knew *that*).

"It's kinda broken. I mean, the reception's pretty shitty."

He walked over to his Yamaha keyboard and turned it on. The amps sent a moan of anticipation through the warm air. "I'll show you how the sampler works. I'll play something for you."

"Good, I'd like to hear it. Hey, got another beer?"

He went to the fridge. "Those were the last. How 'bout wine?"

"Sure."

He poured two large tumblers and handed one to her. They tapped glasses. She picked a piece of cork or lint or something out of hers and they both drank.

Then she slipped off her white plastic headband and lay back on the bed. She ran her hand over the middle part of the mattress. "What's this?"

"What?"

"This lump?"

"I don't know. A pillowcase, I think."

But Carrie was frowning. "No, it's, like, weird. You better check it out."

He stood up and sat on the bed next to her, rummaged under the covers to find the lump. It turned out to be not a pillowcase but a woman's red high-heel shoe.

"How'd that get there?" Carrie laughed, teasing.

"I used it in one of my pieces."

"Uh-huh," she said, not believing him.

It's true, goddamn it, he thought angrily. I'm not a fucking transvestite. . . .

She looked into his eyes and, without even thinking about it, he leaned forward and kissed her. He tasted lipstick and the Binaca she'd sprayed into her mouth when he was busy pouring the wine.

Then she lifted the red shoe away, dropped it on the floor and directed his hand to her breasts.

This is weird. . . .

Carrie reached up and turned off the skewed floor lamp. The only illumination in the room was from the display lights on the synthesizer.

Weird . . .

He began to kiss her hard, desperately, and she kissed him right back.

She pulled off her jeans and sweater. Lillick stared at the huge breasts defined by the netlike cloth of her bra, nipples dark circles.

He kissed her for a full minute.

Weird.

Lillick realized that he'd left the recorder on the sampler running; it would store every sound in the room for the next twenty minutes. He supposed he should shut it off but in fact he didn't really want to get up. Besides, he figured, you never knew when you could use some good sound effects.

CHAPTER ELEVEN

Taylor wasn't sure when the idea occurred to her—probably 4 or 5 A.M. as she lay in bed, listening to the sounds of the city. She was in a half-waking, half-dreaming state—in Wonderland or on the far side of the looking glass.

She'd been thinking about the evidence she'd gathered. A brief comparison of the prints on the safe with her suspects—Sebastian, Lillick and Dudley—wasn't conclusive but it was more likely than not that Sebastian had left several prints on the safe.

But was there any way to verify that he—or someone else—had been in the firm that Saturday night, other than through the time sheets and key card entry logs?

Sure, she realized, there was: The thief might've taken a cab or car service limo to the firm that late at night. And he might've just used his real name and employee number on the reimbursement or payment voucher.

And copiers too. If he'd been in the firm for some legitimate reason he might've used a copier—you had to use a special key, with your number on it, to activate the machine.

Or, she thought, excited about these leads, the thief might have logged onto one of the Lexis/Nexis computers.

Or used the phone.

Every service or function within the firm that can be charged to a client (plus a delightful 300 percent markup for overhead) is recorded in the firm computers.

She glanced at the clock: 7:40 A.M.

Brother.

Exhausted, she rolled out of bed. At least she didn't have a hangover—and she'd managed to change into boxers and a T-shirt last night, saving her skin from more stigmatas of Victoria's Secret.

Let's go, Alice.... This is getting curiouser and curiouser....

At 9 A.M. exactly Taylor was standing in the accounting department at Hubbard, White & Willis.

"I'm doing a bill for Mitchell Reece," she told the computer operator. "Can you let me see the copier card, taxi and car service voucher ledger, phone records and Lexis/Nexis log-ons for last Saturday and Sunday?"

"It's not the end of the month." The operator snapped her gum.

"Mitchell wants to give the client an estimate."

Snap.

"An estimate of disbursements? It couldn't be more than a thousand bucks. Who'd care?"

"If you don't mind," Taylor said sweetly. "Please."

Snap. "I guess." The woman hunched over the keys and typed several lines. She frowned and typed again.

Taylor bent over the computer screen. The screen was blank.

Snap, snap...

"I don't know what's going on. There's no taxi vouchers. There *always* are on Saturday." Taylor knew this very well. The rule was if you had to work on Saturday the firm paid for your taxi to and from your apartment or house.

Alarmed, Taylor said, "How about the copiers?"

The fingernails tapped. The operator squinted, tapped some more and stared at the screen. "Well, this's damn funny."

"Nobody made any copies either."

"You got it."

Snap.

"Phones? Lexis/Nexis?"

The clattering of keys. "Nothing."

Taylor asked, "You think the files were erased?"

"Hold on a minute." Her fingers tapped as noisily as her popping gum.

Snap, snap . . .

The young woman looked up. "That's it. Erased. Must've had a software hiccup or something. The disbursement and incidental expense files for the past week've been deleted. Taxis, meals, copiers, even the phones. All gone."

"Has that ever happened before?"

"Nup. Never."

Snap.

███

Sean Lillick stopped by Carrie Mason's cubicle to say good morning to her.

He could tell immediately how pleased she was to see him comply with the famous morning-after rule.

They talked for a few minutes and then he said how much he wanted a cup of coffee and, as he'd expected, she was on her feet immediately and asking him, "How do you want it?"

"Black," he answered because even though he liked a lot of sugar it was cooler to say "Black."

"Sure. I'll be right back."

"You don't have to—," he started to say.

"No problem."

She trotted off down the hallway.

Which gave him the chance to put her computer room access card back into her purse.

That's what'd been so weird last night.

The fact that the sex had been initiated by *her*.

Because the whole point of calling her up was to get her over to his place, get her drunk, seduce her and when she was dozing afterward steal her access card, which would allow him to erase the telltale files of expenses—like the taxi he'd taken from the firm to the office of the plaintiff's lawyer in the St. Agnes case, or the phone calls he'd made about the new lease with Rothstein. After he'd talked to Wendall Clayton earlier Lillick had realized that he *had* been pretty careless and needed to, as the partner had said, "snip some ends."

Hence, the grand seduction last night.

Weird . . .

Carrie now returned with the coffee and when she handed it to him their hands met and they looked into each other's eyes for a moment. It took perhaps two seconds for the guilt to prod him into looking away and he said quickly, "Got a big project. Better run. I'll call you."

■

Donald Burdick believed that bringing one's first client into a law firm was the most significant milestone in the career of a Wall Street lawyer.

Unlike graduation from law school, unlike admission to the bar, unlike being made partner—all of which are significant but abstract stages in a lawyer's life—hooking a money-paying client was what distinguished, in his metaphor, the nobility from the gentry.

Many years ago Burdick—a young, newly made partner at Hubbard, White & Willis—had just finished the eighteenth hole at Meadowbrook Club on Long Island when one of the foursome turned to him and said, "Say, Donald, I hear good things about you. Legal-wise, I'm saying. You interested in doing a little work for a hospital?"

That had been on a Sunday afternoon and two days later Burdick had presented to the executive committee of the firm his first signed retainer agreement—with the huge St. Agnes Hospital complex in Manhattan.

At nine-thirty this morning Donald Burdick sat in his office with the chief executive officer of St. Agnes, a tall, middle-aged, mild-spoken veteran of hospital administration. Also present were Fred LaDue, the senior litigation partner handling the malpractice case against the hospital, and Mitchell Reece.

Three of these four appeared very unhappy, though for different reasons. Burdick, because of what he'd learned last night—that with the new witness St. Agnes would probably lose the malpractice trial, which would make the hospital throw its support to Clayton and the pro-merger crowd. The CEO, of course, because his hospital now stood to lose millions of dollars. Lawyer LaDue, because Burdick had summarily ordered that he stand down today and that a young associate Mitchell Reece, take over the cross-examination of the new witness.

Reece, on the other hand, was calm as a priest though it was clear the man hadn't had more than a few hours' sleep. He'd been preparing virtually nonstop since Burdick and LaDue had briefed him last night around 9 p.m.

"Who is this guy?" the CEO asked. "The witness?"

"That's the problem. He was working at St. Agnes when they brought the plaintiff in. He didn't treat the patient himself but he was in the room the whole time."

"One of our own people? Testifying against us?" The CEO was dumbfounded.

"Apparently he was a visiting professor from UC San Diego."

"Can't we object?"

"I did," LaDue said plaintively. "Judge overruled me. The best he did was give us a chance to depose the witness before he goes on."

Reece said, "I'll do that in a half hour. The guy goes on the stand at eleven."

"How bad do you think his testimony's going to be?" the administrator asked.

"From what the other side's lawyer said," Reece explained bluntly, "it could lose you the case."

Burdick, who realized he had been squeezing his teeth together with fierce pressure, said, "Well, Mitchell, perhaps it isn't as hopeless as you're painting it."

Reece shrugged. "I don't think it's hopeless. I never said it's hopeless. But the plaintiff's lawyers've upped their settlement offer to thirty million and they're holding firm. That means that this witness is the smoking gun."

LaDue sat and stewed. The doughy man was as pale as always though at this particular moment his waxen complexion was largely due to the fact that he'd done a very clumsy job at the trial so far.

Burdick played with a manicured thumbnail. He was furious that Clayton had probably spent thousands of dollars to track down this witness and had anonymously sent his name to the plaintiff's attorney.

"What do you have in mind, Mitchell?" LaDue asked. "How're you going to handle the cross?"

Reece looked up and started to answer but then Burdick's secretary walked into the doorway. "Mr. Reece, your secretary said you've just got an important call. You can take it in the conference room there."

"Thank you," he said to her. Then glanced at his watch. "I'll be busy for the rest of the morning, gentlemen. I'll see you in court."

CHAPTER TWELVE

███████ If she hadn't been initiated, Taylor Lockwood would never have known she was watching a trial.

She saw a bored judge rocking back in his chair, distracted lawyers. She saw clerks walking around casually, no one really concentrating on what was going on. She saw dazed jurors and few spectators—a half dozen or so, retirees, she guessed, like the unshaven men who take trains out to Belmont or Aqueduct racetracks in the morning, just for a place to spend their slow days.

She'd found Reece in the hall at the firm earlier and wanted to update him on what she'd learned—the fingerprints and the erased files. But he was jogging from the library to his office, two huge Redweld folders under his arms. He paused briefly to tell her that he'd been called in to handle an emergency cross-examination and that he could see her at the courthouse on Centre Street later, around noon.

Taylor had decided to sit in on this portion of the trial and catch him in the hall afterward. Maybe they could have lunch.

She now looked around the courtroom in which *Marlow v. St. Agnes Hospital and Health Care Center* was being tried and located the plaintiff. Mr. Marlow sat in a wheelchair, pale and unmoving. Unshaven, his hair disheveled. His wife was nearby, with her hand resting on his arm. Taylor's father, a trial lawyer himself, had instilled enough cynicism in his daughter to make her believe that, while undoubtedly the man had suffered a serious injury, the wheelchair might just be a prop and there was no need for him to be looking as destroyed as he did here.

The door opened, and in walked a man she recognized from the firm. It took her a moment to place the name. Randy Simms—either the III or the IV. She recalled that he was a protégé of Wendall Clayton. He sat in the back row, by himself, putting away a cellular phone. He put his hands in his lap and sat perfectly still, perfectly upright.

She scanned the rest of the visitors and was surprised to find Donald Burdick himself in the gallery. He too glanced at Randy Simms, a faint frown on the old partner's face.

Finally, papers were sorted out and the judge pulled off his glasses. In a gruff voice he told the plaintiff's counsel that he could present his witness.

The lawyer rose and called to the stand a handsome, gray-haired man in his mid-fifties. He gazed pleasantly out at the jury. Under questioning from the plaintiff's counsel, he began his testimony.

Taylor Lockwood worked primarily for corporate lawyers at Hubbard, White & Willis but she knew the basics of personal injury law. This man's testimony was clearly devastating to St. Agnes.

Dr. William Morse's credentials were impeccable and, unlike many expert witnesses, who testify based only on what they've read in reports long after the accident, he was actually present at the hospital when the alleged malpractice occurred. The jury members took in his comments and looked at each other with lifted eyebrows, obviously impressed with the man's demeanor and by what he was saying.

"Let's reiterate what happened here," the plaintiff's lawyer said. "In March of last year a doctor at St. Agnes treated a patient—Mr. Marlow there in the wheelchair, the plaintiff in this case—who was suffering from arthritis and adrenal insufficiency with seventy milligrams of cortisone acetate in conjunction with one hundred milligrams of indomethacin."

"That's correct," Morse said.

"Did you observe him do this?"

"I saw the injection and then looked at the chart afterward and told him immediately the mistake he'd make."

"And why was that a mistake?"

"Mr. Marlow had a preexisting ulcerous condition. Everyone knows that such a patient should absolutely not be treated with the drugs he was administered."

"I'd object, sir," Reece said politely. "The witness can't speak for, quote, everyone."

Dr. Morse corrected, "The medical literature is quite clear that such a patient should not be treated with those particular drugs."

The plaintiff's lawyer continued, "What was this doctor's reaction when you told him that?"

"He said that I was not on the staff, I was a visiting physician and, in effect, I should mind my own business."

"Objection," Reece called again. "Hearsay."

The plaintiff's lawyer said, "I'll rephrase. Sir, after you called attention to what you perceived as a dangerous condition, did anyone take any steps to correct it?"

"No."

"What happened then?"

"I told a nurse to monitor the patient carefully and that I thought he might have serious adverse reactions. Then I went to see the chief of staff."

"That would be Harold Simpson?"

"Yessir."

"And what was his reaction?"

"Dr. Simpson was not available. I was told he was playing golf."

"Objection. Hearsay."

"He was not available," the witness corrected.

"What happened then?"

"I returned to Mr. Marlow's ward to see how he was doing but he was unconscious, comatose. The nurse I'd left to monitor his condition was gone. We stabilized his condition. But he remained comatose."

"Would it have been possible, when you called attention to the drugs that had been improperly prescribed, to administer an antidote—"

"Objection," Reece called. "He's suggesting that we poisoned the plaintiff."

"You *did*," Dr. Morse snapped.

"Your honor?" Reece asked.

"A more neutral term, counselor," the judge said to the plaintiff's lawyer.

"Yessir. Dr. Morse, would it have been possible to administer other drugs to counteract the damaging effects of the drugs that the St. Agnes staff doctor administered?"

"Absolutely. But it would have to be done immediately."

"And what happened then?"

"That was my last day at the hospital. I returned to California the next day and as soon as I arrived I called the hospital to check on the status of the patient. I was told that he'd come out of the coma but had suffered irreparable brain damage. I left messages for the chief of staff, the head of the procedures committee and the head of the department of internal medicine. No one ever called me back."

"No further questions."

A murmur from the peanut gallery at the deadly testimony. Taylor concurred with the apparent reaction. She thought, Okay, we just lost the case.

The judge rocked back in his chair and said, "Mr. Reece, cross-examination?"

Mitchell Reece stood and—in smooth motions—buttoned his jacket, straightened his paisley tie.

"Thank you, your honor. First of all"—he turned to the jury—"I'd like to introduce myself. I'm Mitch Reece. I work for Hubbard, White & Willis, along with my friend and colleague, Fred LaDue, who I think you know. And he's been gracious enough to let me visit with you for a few hours to-day." He smiled, creating a camaraderie with six men and women bored numb from days of medical testimony.

Hunkered down behind two octogenarian trial buffs, Taylor watched him pace back and forth slowly.

Reece said, "Now, sir, you know I'm getting paid for asking you questions."

The witness blinked. "I—"

Reece laughed. "It's not a question. I'm just telling you that I'm getting paid to be here, and I assume you're getting paid to testify. But I don't think it's fair to ask you how much *you're* getting, if I'm not prepared to tell you how much *I'm* getting. And I'm not. Lawyers're overpaid anyway." Laughter filled the room. "So we'll just let it go at the fact that we're both professionals. Are we all together on that?"

"Yessir."

"Good.

The plaintiff's lawyers grew wary at this. One of the first ways cross-examining lawyers attack experts is to make them sound like mercenaries.

"Now, Doctor," Reece said, "let me ask you, how often do you testify at medical malpractice cases like this one?"

"Rarely."

"How rare would that be?"

The witness lifted his hand. "I've probably testified three or four times in my life. Only when I feel a terrible injustice has been done and—"

Reece held up his hand and, still smiling, said, "Maybe if we could just stick to answering my questions, please."

"The jury will disregard the witness's last sentence," the judge mumbled.

"So it's safe to say that you spend most of your time *practicing* medicine. Not testifying against other doctors."

"That's right."

"That's so refreshing, Doctor. I mean that. It's clear you care about your patients."

"Helping patients is the most important thing in the world to me."

"I applaud that, sir. And I welcome your appearance here—I mean that. Because these are very tricky technical matters that my friends on the jury and I have to wrestle with, and cooperative witnesses like you can make the issues clearer."

The witness laughed. "I *have* had a bit of experience."

"Let's talk about that, sir. Now, you practice internal medicine, correct?"

"That's correct."

"You're board-certified in internal medicine?"

"I am."

"And you have occasion to administer various drugs?"

"Oh, yessir."

"Would you say you have great experience administering them?"

"I would say so, sure."

"Those ways of administering them would include sublingual—that's under the tongue, right?"

"That's right."

Reece continued, "And rectally as well as administering injected medicines, like the sort that the plaintiff received."

"That's true."

"I don't want you to think I'm up to anything here, sir. You've testified that my client did something wrong in administering certain medicines and all I want to do is make it clear that your observations about what my client did are valid because of your expertise. We're all together on that?"

"All together, yessir."

"Good."

Taylor could see that the jury had brightened up. Something was happening. Reece was being *nice* to the witness. Shouldn't they be screaming at each other? The jury was confused and because of that they'd started paying attention.

She noticed something else: Though she hadn't seen him change his appearance, Reece's jacket, at some point, had become unbuttoned and in lifting his hand to straighten his hair he'd mussed it. He looked boyish. She thought of him suddenly as a young Southern lawyer—a hero in a John Grisham book.

The witness too had relaxed. He was less stiff, less cautious.

Taylor, though, thought that Reece had gone too far with the good-old-boy approach. The witness was looking good in the eyes of the jury; the credibility of his testimony was improving. By now, she reflected, her father would've cut the balls off this doctor and had him cowering on the stand.

Reece said, "Now, let me quote from the record as best I can." He squinted and recited, " 'In March of last year a doctor from St. Agnes treated a patient—Mr. Marlow there in the wheelchair, the plaintiff—who has arthritis and adrenal insufficiency with seventy milligrams of cortisone acetate in conjunction with one hundred milligrams of indomethacin.' "

"That's right."

"And you testified that you wouldn't have done that."

"Correct."

"Because of his preexisting ulcerous condition."

"Yes."

"But I've looked through his charts. There's no record of his having an ulcer."

The witness said, "I don't know what happened with the charts. But he told the doctors he had an ulcer. I was there. I heard the exchange."

"He was in the emergency room," Reece said. "Generally a busy place, a lot of doctors trying to cope with all kinds of problems. I've been in them myself—cut my thumb bad last year...." Reece winced and smiled at the jury. "I'm a real klutz," he told them. Then back to the doctor: "So will you agree that it's *possible* that the person Mr. Marlow told about his ulcer wasn't the person who administered the drugs?"

"That doesn't—"

Reece smiled. "Please, sir."

"It's possible. But—"

"Please. Just the question."

Taylor saw that Reece was preventing the witness from reminding the jury that it didn't matter who knew before the injection because Dr. Morse had brought it to the staff's attention just *after* the injection, when there was still time to correct it, but the staff had ignored him.

"It's possible."

Reece let this sit for a moment. "Now, Dr. Morse, there's been a lot of talk in this trial about what is and is not an accepted level of medical treatment, right?"

Morse paused before answering, as if trying to figure out where Reece was going. He looked at his own lawyer then answered, "Some, I suppose."

"I'm thinking that if, as you say, you wouldn't've treated the patient with these medications then I assume you feel that St. Agnes's treatment was below the standards of proper medical care?"

"Certainly."

Reece walked to a whiteboard in the corner of the courtroom, near the jury, and drew a thick line horizontally across it. "Doctor, let's say this is the standard-of-care line, all right?"

"Sure."

Reece drew a thin dotted line an inch below it. "Would you say that the level of care St. Agnes provided in administering those drugs was this far below the standard level of care? Just a little bit below?"

Morse looked at his lawyer and was greeted with a shrug.

"No. It wasn't just a little bit below. They almost killed the man."

"Well." Reece drew another line, farther down. "This far?"

"I don't know."

Another line. "This far below?"

Dr. Morse said in a solemn voice, "It was very far below."

Reece drew another two lines then stopped writing. He asked, "Once you get below a certain level of the standard of care ... well, how'd you describe that?"

Another uncertain look at his lawyer then the witness answered, "I'd say . . . I'd guess I'd say it was malpractice."

"You'd characterize St. Agnes's treatment of Mr. Marlow," Reece said in a sympathetic voice, "as malpractice."

"Well, yes, I would."

A murmur of surprise from several people in the courtroom. Not only was Reece befriending the witness but his cross-examination was having the effect of making the witness repeat over and over again that the hospital had made a mistake. He had even gotten the witness to characterize the staff's behavior as malpractice—a legal conclusion that no defense lawyer in the world would have accepted from a plaintiff's witness. Yet it had been Reece himself who elicited this opinion.

What was going on here? Taylor glanced at Burdick and saw him sitting forward, clearly troubled.

A dozen rows behind him Clayton's representative, Randy Simms, sat immobile though with a slight smile on his face.

The judge looked at Reece, opposing counsel looked at Reece.

"I appreciate your candor, Doctor. Malpractice, malpractice." Reece walked back to the table slowly, letting the word sink into the jury's consciousness. He stopped and then added brightly, "Oh, Doctor, if you don't mind, I just have a few matters of clarification."

"Not at all."

Reece said, "Doctor, where are you licensed to practice?"

"As I said before, California, New Jersey and New York."

"No other state?"

"No."

Reece turned to look into Morse's eyes. "How about any other *country*?"

"Country?"

"Yessir," Reece said. "I'm just curious if you've ever been licensed to practice in any other country."

A hesitation. Then a smile. "No."

"Have you ever *practiced* medicine in another country?"

"I just said I wasn't licensed."

"I caught that, sir. But what I just asked was 'practiced,' Doctor, not licensed. Have you ever *practiced* medicine anywhere outside of the United States?"

The man swallowed, a look of horror in his eyes. "I've done some volunteer work...."

"Outside of the country."

"Yes, that's right."

"And would you be so kind as to tell us which country, if that isn't too much trouble, Doctor?"

"Mexico."

"Mexico," Reece repeated. "What were you doing in Mexico?"

"I was getting a divorce. I liked the country and I decided to stay for a while—"

"This was when?"

"Eight years ago."

"And you practiced medicine in Mexico?"

Morse was looking at his fingertips. "Yes, for a while. Before I moved back to California. I set up a practice in Los Angeles. I found Los Angeles to be—"

Reece waved his hand. "I'm much more interested in Mexico than Los Angeles, Doctor. Now, why did you leave Mexico?"

Dr. Morse took a sip of water, his hands trembling. The plaintiff's lawyers looked at each other. Even the poor plaintiff seemed to have sat up higher in his wheelchair and was frowning.

"The divorce was final.... I wanted to move back to the States."

"Is that the only reason?"

The witness lost his composure for a moment as a time-lapse bloom of anger spread on his face. Finally he controlled it. "Yes."

Reece said, "Did you run into some kind of trouble down in Mexico?"

"Trouble, like the food?" He tried to laugh. It didn't work and he cleared his throat again and swallowed.

"Doctor, what is Ketaject?"

Pause. Morse rubbed his eyes. He muttered something.

"Louder, please," Reece asked, his own voice calm and utterly in control of himself, the witness, the universe.

The doctor repeated: "It's the brand name of a drug whose generic name I don't recall."

"Could it be the brand name for ketamine hydrochloride?"

The witness whispered, "Yes."

"And what does that do?"

Morse breathed deeply several times. "It is a general anesthetic." His eyes were joined to Reece's by a current full of fear and hate.

"And what is a general anesthetic, Doctor?"

"You know. Everybody knows."

"Tell us anyway, please."

"It's a solution or gas that renders a patient unconscious."

"Doctor, when you were in Mexico, did you have a patient, a Miss Adelita Corrones, a seventeen-year-old resident of Nogales?"

Hands gripped together. Silence. He wanted water but was afraid to reach for the glass.

"Doctor, shall I repeat the question?"

"I don't recall."

"Well, I'm sure she recalls you. Why don't you think back to the St. Teresa Clinic in Nogales. Think back seven years ago. And try to recall if you had such a patient. Did you?"

"It was all a setup! They set me up! The locals—the police and the judge—blackmailed me! I was innocent!"

"Doctor," Reece continued, "please just respond to my questions." His tie was loose, his face was ruddy with excitement, and even from the back of the courtroom Taylor could see his eyes shining with lust.

"On September seventeenth of that year, pursuant to a procedure for the removal of a nevus—that is, a birthmark—from Miss Corrones's leg, did you administer

Ketaject to her and then, when you perceived her to be unconscious, partially undress her, fondle her breasts and genitals and masturbate until you reached a climax?"

"Objection!" Marlow's lead lawyer was on his feet.

The judge said, "Overruled."

"No! It's a lie," the witness cried.

Reece returned to the counsel table and picked up a document. "Your honor, I move to introduce Defense Exhibit Double G: a certified copy of a complaint from the federal prosecutor's office in Nogales, Mexico."

He handed it to the judge and a copy to the plaintiff's counsel, who read it, grimaced and said in disgust, "Let it in."

"So admitted," the judge intoned and looked back to the witness.

Dr. Morse's head was in his hands. "They set the whole thing up. They blackmailed me. I paid the fine and they said they'd seal the record."

"Well, I guess it's been unsealed," Reece responded. "Now, the report goes on to say that the reason Miss Corrones was aware you were molesting her was that you not only administered the wrong dosage of Ketaject but that you injected it improperly so that most of the drug didn't even reach her bloodstream. Is this what the prosecutor's report says?"

"I—"

"True or not true? Answer the question."

"They set me—"

"Is this what the report says?"

Sobbing, the man said, "Yes, but—"

"Wouldn't you say, sir, that you can hardly state my client is guilty of malpractice because of the improper administration of drugs when you can't even knock out a teenager enough to rape her?"

"Objection."

"Withdrawn."

"They set me up," the witness said. "Just to blackmail me. They—"

Reece turned on him. "Well, then, Doctor, did you at

any time contact the law enforcement authorities in Mexico City or in the United States to report that you were being blackmailed?"

"No," he raged. "I paid them the extortion money and they said I could leave the country and they'd seal the record. I—"

"You mean," Reece said, "you paid the *fine* for your *punishment*. Like any other criminal. No further questions."

Taylor found herself sitting forward on the edge of the pew. She now saw Reece's brilliant tactic. First, he'd gotten the jury's attention. Expecting petty bickering, they'd seen Reece befriend the witness, surprising them and getting them to sit up and listen. Then he got the man to say the magic word that, by rights, Reece or LaDue or anyone on the St. Agnes legal team would try never even to allow into testimony, let alone elicit themselves: "malpractice."

And then, in a masterful stroke, he'd linked that characterization—that one magic word—to the witness's terrible behavior and completely destroyed his credibility.

Taylor saw a gleam in Reece's face, a flushing of the cheeks, fists balled up in excitement.

Reece turned. He noticed Donald Burdick in the back of the courtroom. The two men looked at each other. Neither smiled, but Burdick touched his forehead in a salute of respect.

Taylor turned and looked at Burdick then behind him. Finally Randy Simms showed some emotion. His lips were tight and his eyes bored into the back of Donald Burdick's head. He rose and stepped out of the courtroom, which was utterly silent.

Except for the sobbing of the witness.

CHAPTER THIRTEEN

She stopped him in the hallway of the court.

Reece smiled when he saw her.

"How'd I do?"

"How do you think? I'd say you mopped up the floor with him."

"We'll see." Reece continued, "What most lawyers don't realize is that cross-examination isn't about being an orator. It's about having information. I called a private eye I've used out in San Diego and he dug up the dirt on the guy. Cost me—well, cost St. Agnes—fifty thousand. But it saved them a lot more than that."

"You enjoyed it, didn't you?"

"Handling the cross? Yep." He hesitated a moment, and finally spoke, though whether it was what he'd originally intended to say or not she couldn't tell. "I sometimes feel bad for them—people like that witness—when I tear apart their testimony. But in this case it was easy. He was a rapist."

"You believe he did it? What happened in Mexico?"

He considered. "I *chose* to believe he did something

wrong. It's a mind-set thing. Hard to explain but, yes, I believe it."

Taylor reflected: You could certainly argue that their
client, the hospital, had done something wrong too—destroying the plaintiff's life; and she wasn't sure if the rape, if
it had actually occurred, undermined the legitimacy of
Morse's opinion about that.

She said nothing about any of this though and, indeed,
she secretly envied Reece his fervent view of right and
wrong. For her, justice wasn't quite as clear as that. It was a
moving target, like the birds she'd watch her father hunt
every fall. Some he hit and some he missed and there was
no grand design as to which.

"Listen," she said. "I've got some leads. Have time for
lunch?"

"Can't. I'm meeting one of the vice presidents from New
Amsterdam. I've got to be at the Downtown Athletic Club
fifteen minutes ago."

He looked around. "Let's talk later. But tell you what:
Come over to my place for dinner."

"I'm playing Mata Hari tonight. What's tomorrow?
Friday—how's that?"

"Make it Saturday. I'm meeting with the bank people all
day tomorrow and I'm sure it'll go into dinner." He fell silent
as someone walked by, a sandy-haired man in coveralls,
who glanced at them quickly and then continued on.
Reece's eyes followed the man uneasily as he walked away.

"Paranoid," he muttered with a smile, gave her hand a
fast squeeze and then left the courthouse.

On her way back to the firm Taylor's willpower faded,
her lust for a fast-food burger won and she decided she'd get
something to eat.

This was how she found out that Mitchell Reece had
lied to her.

Instead of going back to the office she'd headed north,
to a Burger King, and as she turned the corner she saw
Reece ahead of her. But he was walking *away* from the

Downtown Athletic Club, where he'd said he was going for lunch. She slowed, stung at first, then thinking, No, he probably meant another athletic club: the *New York* Athletic Club on Central Park South in Midtown.

Only, if that was so, why was he disappearing into the Lexington Avenue subway stop? The train went uptown but there were no stops anywhere near the NYAC. And why was he taking a train in the first place? The rule on Wall Street was that if you went anywhere on firm business, you always took the car service or a cab.

Taylor had had four or five serious relationships in her life and one thing about men that irked her was that their fondness for the truth fell far short of other appreciations. Honesty was her new standard for love and she didn't think that it was too much to ask.

Reece, of course, was nothing more than her employer—but still the lie hurt; she was surprised at how much.

Well, maybe his plans had changed—maybe he'd checked his messages, found the witness had canceled and was on his way to Tripler's to pick up a couple of new shirts.

But on impulse she found herself pulling a token out of her purse and hurrying down the subway stairs.

Why? she wondered.

Because she was Alice. That was the only answer. And once you slip into the rabbit hole, Taylor Lockwood had learned, you go where fate directs you.

Which happened to be Grand Central Terminal.

Taylor followed the lawyer, climbing up the stairs, skirting a small colony of homeless. She watched Reece buy a train ticket and walk toward the gates. She stopped.

Squinting though the misty afternoon light that spilled across the huge cavern of the terminal, she caught a glimpse of him standing at a vending cart in front of a gate. A crowd of passengers walked between them, obscuring him.

She jockeyed aside to get a better view. Then she laughed to herself when she saw what he'd bought.

One mystery of Mitchell Reece had been solved.

He was walking to one of the commuter trains carrying a large bouquet of flowers.

He had a girlfriend after all.

Digging another token from her purse, she descended once more into the piquant subway to return to the firm.

████████

Sometimes he felt like a juggler.

Thom Sebastian was thinking of an off-Broadway magic show he'd seen some years ago.

Sebastian remembered the juggler most clearly. He hadn't used balls or Indian clubs but a hatchet, a lit blowtorch, a crystal vase, a full bottle of wine and a wineglass.

From time to time, Sebastian thought of that show, of the tension that wound your guts up as the man would add a new object and send it sailing up in an arc, a smile on his face, eyes at the apogee. Everyone waited for the metal to cut, the torch to burn, the glass to shatter. But nope, the man's no-sweat smile silently said to the audience: So far, so good.

Sebastian, sitting in his office this afternoon, feeling depleted, coked out, 'phetamined out, now told himself the same thing.

So far, so good.

When he had learned that Hubbard, White & Willis had chosen not to make him a partner Thom Sebastian had held a conference with himself and decided after considerable negotiation to cut back on his working hours; he was going to relax.

But that didn't work. Clients still called. They were often greedy, they were occasionally bastards, but a lot of times they were neither. And whether they were or not was irrelevant. They were still clients and they were scared and troubled and needed help that only a smart, hardworking lawyer could give them.

Sebastian found to his surprise that he was physically incapable of slowing down. He continued at a frantic pace, his hours completely absorbed by two refinancings, a leveraged buyout, a revolving credit agreement.

By his own real estate transactions, by his special project with Bosk, by his girlfriends, by arranging buys with his drug dealer, Magaly, by his family, by his pro bono clients, all in motion, all spinning, all just barely under control.

So far . . .

He desperately wanted sleep and that thought momentarily brought to mind another: The brown glass vial hidden in his briefcase. But it was no more than that—a passing image. Sebastian did not even consider slipping into the men's room to partake. He never did drugs within the walls of Hubbard, White & Willis. That would be a sin.

. . . so good.

He closed the door to his office then pulled a manila envelope out of his desk. He removed the computer printouts and began to read—all about Ms. Taylor Lockwood.

He found the information fascinating. He jotted a few notes and hid them under the blotter on the desk then fed the printouts themselves and the envelope through the shredder in his office.

Sweeping the phone from the cradle, Sebastian dialed her number from memory.

"Hello?"

"Hey, Taylor . . ."

He heard tension and anxiety in his own voice. This was bad. Take charge.

"Thom?"

"Yeah. How you doing?"

"Fine, but guilty. I'm finishing a Whopper."

With any other woman he'd have jumped on that line with both feet and flirted relentlessly. But he resisted and said casually, "Hey, you survived an evening with me. Not a lot of girls can make that claim. Oops, women. Meant to say 'women.' Have I offended you yet?"

"You're not even on the radar screen."

"I'll try harder." In fact he wasn't really in the mood to joke but he forced himself to maintain a certain level of patented Sebastian banter. "You realize that we're leaving for the airport in a half hour."

"And the 'we' would be who?"

"You and me."

"Ah. Our elopement. Your friend Bosk was first in line. You can be best lawyer."

Damn, she was fast. He'd run out of jokes. "Listen, speaking of your betrothed, I'm going out to dinner in the Hamptons tomorrow with him and a few other folks."

"I remember you mentioning that."

She had? That was interesting. Why'd she been paying attention to their offhand comments? "Hey, it's totally last-minute, I know, but any chance you'd like to come? It'll give me the chance to kill him so that I can move to the number one spot."

"Chivalrous."

He added gravely, "I have to warn you . . ."

"Yes?"

"It's not a stretch limo."

"That's not a deal-breaker. What's the occasion?"

"It's Take Someone to Dinner in the Hamptons Day. You *do* know about that, don't you?"

"I saw the card rack at Hallmark. I thought I'd have to celebrate by myself with popcorn and the tube."

"How 'bout it? Leave early, five-ish. We'll be back by midnight, one."

"Fair enough. Dress?"

"Business."

"Cool," she said. "I'll come by your office."

Sebastian set down the receiver and closed his eyes. He breathed deeply. He relaxed.

The motion of his imaginary juggler slowed. Unnecessary thoughts fell away. Projects that weren't immediate dissolved. The image of the Chinese-American girl he'd picked up last night and would be meeting at The Space tonight vanished. Some technical financial aspects of his project with Bosk rose then faded, as did a nasty, dark portrait of Wendall Clayton. Finally Sebastian was left with two thoughts, tossing them around slowly. One was the loan agreement he was working on, spread out on his desk before him.

The other was Taylor Lockwood.

He pulled the agreement toward him and looked at the words with a grave intensity. But ten minutes passed before he started to read them.

For Donald Burdick there was no square in New York City more beautiful than that at Lincoln Center.

The buoyant fountain, the soaring white rock architecture, the energetic Chagall...these all came together as a testament to the power of culture and moved him now, as they always did. It was especially stunning on fall nights like this, when the concert halls radiated their rich glow into the misty dimness of the city.

Burdick, his hands in his cashmere coat pockets, paced slowly in front of the fountain. It was chilly but waiting inside the Metropolitan Opera, where he and his wife had tickets for Stravinsky later that night, would undoubtedly require him to speak to any number of other box holders, who like him were major patrons of the arts and arrived early for dinner in the private dining room.

At the moment he didn't want to be distracted.

He glanced up and saw the Silver Cloud ease to the curb and Sergei leap out to open Vera's door. She stepped onto the pavement in her sable coat. He remembered how a few years ago, as Vera had waited for a light to change on Madison Avenue, an animal rights activist had sprayed her mink with orange paint. His wife had grabbed the young woman's arm and wrestled her to the ground, pinned her there until the police arrived.

They hugged and she took his arm as they walked to the private entrance that led to the club reserved for the most generous patrons. Burdick had once calculated that, even adjusted for the charitable deduction, each glass of champagne here cost him roughly two hundred dollars.

They let another couple go ahead of them so they could take an elevator alone.

"St. Agnes?" Vera asked abruptly.

"Mitchell won. Well, they dropped their settlement offer to five million. We'll pay one. That's nothing. Everybody at the hospital's ecstatic."

"Good," she said. "And the lease? Did you sign it up?"

"Not yet. It's on for Monday now. Rothstein...I *hate* dealing with him. And we have to keep everything hush-hush so Wendall doesn't find out."

"Monday," she said, troubled, then his wife glanced at her reflection in the elevator's metal panel. She turned back to her husband. "I made some calls today. Talked to Bill O'Brien's wife."

This was an executive of McMillan Holdings, which was Hubbard, White's biggest client. The company was Burdick's client alone and he took home personally about three million a year from McMillan.

"Trouble?" Burdick asked quickly.

"Apparently not. Wendall hasn't approached them about the merger."

"Good," Burdick said. "He doesn't even know the board's meeting in Florida this week or if he does he hasn't made any rumblings about going down there."

Burdick had assumed that Clayton wouldn't waste the time trying to sway McMillan since it was so firmly in the antimerger court.

"But the board's been talking among themselves. They're wondering if the merger'd be good or bad for them."

"Bill's wife knows that?"

Vera nodded matter-of-factly. "She's sleeping with one of the board members: Frank Augustine."

Burdick nodded. "I wondered who he was seeing."

Vera said, "I think you have to get down to Florida and talk to them. As soon as possible. Hold their hands, rally them against the merger. Warn them about Clayton."

"I'll go this weekend. It'll be a good excuse to miss

Clayton's party on Sunday. Last thing in the world I want to do is spend time in that pompous ass's house."

Vera smiled. "I'll go," she said cheerfully. "One of us should be there, I think. Just to keep him a little unsettled."

And, Burdick thought as the elevator door opened, you're just the woman to do it.

CHAPTER FOURTEEN

██████ *Ms. Lockwood:*

We cannot thank you enough for the opportunity to review your demo tape.

Taylor hurried to her apartment from her building's mailroom, clutching three return envelopes from three record companies. She'd called Dudley and told him that she wanted to change before seeing him for dinner at his club in Midtown and that she'd meet him there.

As she walked down the hallway she fantasized about the contents of the envelopes.

It so captivated the initial screener that he sent it to our A&R department, where it made the rounds in record (forgive the pun) time. Your masterly reinterpretations of the old standards in juxtaposition with your own works (masterpieces in fusion) make the tape itself worthy of production, but we would propose a three-record project of primarily original material.

Enclosed you will find our standard recording contract, already executed by our senior vice president, and, as an advance, a check in the amount of fifty thousand dollars. A limousine will be calling for you. . . .

Not able to wait until she got inside, she ripped the envelopes open with her teeth, all of them at once. The torn-
off tops lay curled like flat yellow worms on the worn carpet
behind her as she read the form rejection letters which were
a far cry from the one that her imagination had just com-
posed.

The one that said the most about the music business,
she decided, began with the salutation "Dear Submitter."

Shit.

Taylor stepped out of the elevator and tossed the letters
into the sand-filled ashtray next to the call button.

Inside her apartment, she saw a blinking light on her
answering machine, and pushed the replay button as she
stripped off her coat and kicked her shoes in an arc toward
the closet.

Her machine had a number of messages:

Ralph Dudley, giving her the address of his club again.

Sebastian, confirming dinner tomorrow.

Reece, confirming dinner on Saturday.

Danny Stuart, Linda Davidoff's roommate, apologizing
for not getting back to her but suggesting they meet for
lunch in the Village tomorrow.

Three dinners and a lunch. Damn, how *do* spies manage
to stay trim?

One more message remained. She hit play.

"Hello, counselor. Got some news. I'll be in town in a
week or so and I'm going to take my little legal eagle out to
dinner. Call me and we'll make plans."

Taylor instantly looked around her room to see how
straightened up it was—as if the phone contained a video
camera beaming the images directly to her father's law office.

She sat down slowly on the arm of the couch, Samuel
Lockwood's call reviving a question Mitchell Reece had
asked yesterday.

So how'd you end up in New York?

Taylor recalled perfectly sitting in front of her father two
years ago, the man of medium build, jowly and pale—by

rights, he should have broadcast an anemic image, but he filled the living room of their house in Chevy Chase, Maryland, with his powerful image.

She tried to gaze back at him.

But couldn't, of course.

Finally, the sound of spring lawn mowing from outside was broken by his asking, "You can simply try it, Taylor."

"I have other priorities, Dad."

" 'Priorities,' " the lawyer said quickly, pouncing. "See, that very word suggests that there are several directions you'd want to go in." A smile. "In the back of your mind you're already entertaining the possibility that you'd like to be a lawyer."

"I mean—"

What *had* she meant? She was too flustered to remember.

"My talent—"

"And you *are* talented, darling. I've always recognized that. Your grades...Honey, A's in every government, politics, philosophy course you've ever taken."

And in music composition, music theory, improvisation and performance.

"Music too," he added, with perfect timing, diffusing her anger. Then he laughed, "But there's no way in Satan's backyard that anyone would ever make any kind of serious money playing music in bars."

"I don't do it for the money, Dad. You know that."

"Look, you should pursue everything. Lord knows I do."

And he had. Law, business, golf, tennis, skydiving, sailing, teaching.

"It's just that it's easier to get your law degree now. Going back after you're older...it limits your opportunities."

Reduced to a child before him, Taylor could think of no logical retorts. Well, the best legal minds in the country had engaged in forensic battle with Samuel Lockwood and lost. She said weakly, "I just feel alive when I play music, Dad. That's all there is to it."

"And what a feeling that must be," he said. "But remember that we go through stages in life. What excites us now isn't necessarily what sustains us all forever. I pitched a dozen no-hitters in college. And I never felt higher than being on the pitcher's mound. What a thrill that was! But making that my life? A pro ball player? No, I had other things to do. And I found getting up in court gave me exactly the same thrill. Even better, in fact, because I was in harmony with my nature."

"Music isn't a sport to me, Dad." She believed she was whining and hated herself for it.

"Of course not. I know it's an important part of your life." He then tactically reminded, "I was at every single one of your recitals." A pause. "I'm only saying that it would be better to excel in a profession—doesn't have to be the law, not by any means."

Oh, right...

"And work at the music part-time. That way if the... you call them gigs, right? If they *don't* happen, well, you'd still have something. Or you could do both. Your music could come first and law could be second."

He seemed to have forgotten that he'd absolved her from the practice of law just a moment earlier.

Continuing, Samuel Lockwood said, "There's a whole different approach to practicing nowadays. There are part-time arrangements. A lot of women have other 'priorities'—families and so on. Firms are flexible."

"I'm supporting myself playing, Dad. Not a lot of people are." Not that the eighteen thousand a year she'd made in clubs and playing weddings and a few corporate shows last year could be considered supporting herself.

"And what a feather in your cap that is," he said. Then frowned. "I've got a thought. How about a compromise? What if you got a job as a paralegal at one of the firms in Washington, one of our affiliated firms. I'll get you in. You can try out law firm life, see if you like it. I'll put aside some funds for school."

She'd said no at first but Samuel Lockwood was relentless and she'd finally given in.

"But I'll get a job on my own, Dad. I'll support myself. If I like it I'll apply to law school. But I'll play music at nights. Nothing's going to interfere with that."

"Taylor . . ." He frowned.

"It's the best I can do. And not in D.C. I'll go to New York."

He took a breath and then nodded his concession to her victory over him. "You've got backbone, counselor."

And he gave her a smile that chilled her soul—because it unwittingly revealed that this "spontaneous" thought of his had been born some time ago and nurtured over many nights as he lay in his twin bed, three feet from his wife's, trying to figure out exactly how to manipulate her.

Taylor was furious with herself for letting her guard down. He'd never intended that she work in Washington, wouldn't have presumed to link her with him by getting her a job and would never have threatened her music directly— out of fear that he'd push her away completely.

In the end, even though she'd defiantly resisted him, it turned out that Taylor had played right into his hand.

"You understand I'm doing this because I love you and care for you," he said.

No, she thought, I understand you're doing this because the thought of being unable to control the slightest aspect of your life is abhorrent to you.

She'd said, "I know, Dad."

But, as it turned out, the paralegal life was not as bad as she'd anticipated. Smart, tireless, unintimidated by the culture of Wall Street money and Manhattan society, Taylor had made a reputation for herself at the firm, quickly becoming one of the most popular paralegals, always in demand. She found that she enjoyed the work and had considerable aptitude for it.

So when a cycle came around for applying to law schools and Samuel Lockwood asked her which schools she'd decided to apply to (not *if* she intended to apply), she said what the hell and plunged forward with a yes and basked in the sunlight of her father's approval.

Taylor, lost in this complex answer to Reece's simple question, now realized that she was still frozen in place, perched on a sofa arm, her hand floating above her answering machine.

Why exactly was her father coming here? Where could they eat? Would the place she picked please him? Would he want to come see her perform? They sure couldn't eat at Miracles or one of the other clubs she played at; he'd make a fuss about the menu. Want to know what kind of oil they cooked with, send food back if it wasn't prepared just right.

The electronic woman in the answering machine told her, "*To save this message, press two. To erase this message, press three.*"

She hit two and walked into the bedroom to dress for her Mata Hari date.

■

This is a Midtown club? she thought.

Taylor had expected that it would be more, well, spiffy. More of a power, platinum-card corporate watering hole and less of a tawdry college lounge. Well, maybe old money was allowed a little shabbiness. In any case, Taylor Lockwood looked at the fiercely bright lighting, the dusty moose head sprouting from the wall, the threadbare school banners and uncarpeted floor, and asked herself again, This is a club?

But Ralph Dudley was excited about the Knickerbocker Businessmen's Club. He was at home here and buoyant at showing off his nest to a stranger.

"Come along now," the partner said. And he ushered her into the club's dining room. He walked to what must've been his regular table and, amusing her beyond words, actually held the chair out for her and bowed after she'd sat.

"Have the steak, Miss Lockwood. They have chicken, too, but order the steak. Rare, like mine." The old partner's excitement was infectious, his eyes gleaming as if he were back in the arms of his alma mater.

They ordered. Dudley took instantly to his task as mentor and launched into a series of stories about his law school. It seemed an endless tumble of hard work, harmless collegiate pranks, chorale singers, respectable young gentlemen in suits and ties and tearfully inspiring professors.

All forty years out of date, if it wasn't complete fiction.

She nodded, smiled till she felt jowls and said "Uh-huh" or "No kidding" or "How 'bout that" every so often. She got good mileage out of "That's very helpful, just what I was wondering."

The waiter brought the steaks, charred and fatty, and although she wasn't particularly hungry, she found hers tasted very good. Dudley made sure she was looked after. He was a natural host. They ate in silence for a few minutes as Taylor took in the young men at the tables around them—recent grads, she assumed. In white shirts and striped ties and suspenders, they were just beginning the journeys that, in four decades, would take them to the destinations at which Donald Burdick and Ralph Dudley and Bill Stanley had arrived.

She looked at her watch. "You said you had some plans tonight. I don't want to interfere with them. I hope you're not working late?"

He gave her a charming smile. "Just meeting some friends."

The mysterious W.S.

Taylor took a sip of the heavy wine he'd ordered. "I'd rather work late than on weekends."

"Weekends?" He shook his head. "Never."

"Really?" she asked casually. "I was in on Saturday night. I thought I saw you. Actually I think it was early Sunday morning."

He hesitated a moment but there was nothing evasive about his demeanor when he answered. "Not I. Maybe it was Donald Burdick. Yes, that was probably it. I'm told we look alike. No, I haven't worked on a weekend since, let's see, '79 or '80. That was a case involving the seizure of foreign assets. Iranian, I think. Yes, it was. Let me tell you about it. Fascinating case."

Which it may very well have been. But Taylor wasn't

paying any attention. She was trying to decide if he'd been lying or not.

Well, looking at his frayed cuffs and overwashed shirt, she observed a motive for stealing the note: money. Dudley was a charming old man but he wasn't a player in Wall Street law and probably never had been. His savings dwindling, his partnership share decreasing as he made less and less money for the firm, he would have been an easy target when somebody from Hanover approached and asked him to let a man inside the firm—an industrial spy, they'd probably said.

Dudley finished his story and glanced at his watch.

It was nine-thirty and he was meeting W.S. in a half hour, she recalled.

He signed the bill and they wandered out of the club into the cold, damp ozone of a New York evening on the shag end of November.

Taylor hoped the cool air would wake her but it had no effect. The narcotics of red wine and heavy food numbed her mind. She groggily followed the partner down the front steps, half-wishing she partook in Thom Sebastian's magic wake-up powder.

She thanked Dudley for his insights and for dinner and said that his school had slipped into the front-runner spot.

This seemed to genuinely please him.

He said, "You all right, Taylor?"

"Fine, just a little tired."

"Tired?" Dudley said, as if he had never heard of the word. "I'll walk you to the subway." He started down the sidewalk in long, enthusiastic but gentlemanly strides.

CHAPTER FIFTEEN

"Wait."

Sean Lillick's voice was sufficiently urgent that Wendall Clayton stopped, frozen in the back entrance of the Knickerbocker Club.

"What is it?" the partner asked.

"There, didn't you see them? It was Ralph Dudley and Taylor Lockwood. They were going out the front."

Clayton frowned. It was a constant source of irritation that a has-been like Dudley belonged to the same club that he did. He resumed his aristocratic stride. "So?"

"What are they doing here?" Lillick wondered uneasily.

"Fucking?" Clayton suggested. He glanced toward the stairway, which led to the club's private bedrooms.

"No, they came out of the dining room, it looked like."

"Maybe he bought her dinner and *now* he's going to fuck her. I wonder if he can still get it up."

"I don't want them to see us," Lillick said.

"Why not?"

"I just don't."

Clayton shrugged. He looked at his watch. "Randy's late. What's going on?"

Lillick said, "I've got to leave about midnight, Wendall. If it's okay." His suit didn't fit well and he looked like a college boy out to dinner with Dad.

"Midnight?"

"It's important."

"What's up?" Clayton smiled. "Do you have a date?" He dragged the last word out teasingly.

"Just seeing some friends."

"I don't think it's 'okay.' Not tonight."

Lillick said nothing for a moment. Then: "It's pretty important. I've really got to."

Clayton examined the young man. Like most denizens of the East Village, he seemed damp and unclean. "One of your performances?"

"Yeah."

"Yeah," the partner mocked.

"Yes," Lillick corrected himself instantly though in a tone that approached rebellious.

"We've got so much to do. . . ."

"I mentioned it a week ago."

"And what a busy week it's been, don't you agree?"

"It'll just be a few hours. I'll still be at the office at six if you want."

Clayton had let him dangle enough. He said, "This once, I suppose, it's all right." He had plans of his own tonight and didn't give a rat's rosy ass what Lillick did after they were finished here.

"Thanks—"

Clayton waved him off and gave a reserved smile to Randy Simms, who now walked through the revolving door of the club.

Ignoring Lillick, as he always did, Simms said, "I saw Ralph Dudley outside. With a woman."

Piqued again by the reference to the old partner, Clayton snapped, "Appreciate the weather report, Randy."

Simms was six feet three, thin and solid. Ralph Lauren might have designed a line of Connecticut sportswear around him. A mother and her teenage daughter entered the lobby. They eyed the young lawyer with similar degrees of desire.

"How'd they get the lowdown on our witness?" Clayton was referring to the evisceration of Dr. Morse on the witness stand in the St. Agnes Hospital case.

"Reece used some private eye in San Diego."

"Fuck, that was good," Clayton said with admiration. He didn't know Reece well but he'd make sure the associate was guaranteed a partnership slot next year or the year after.

"When's our guest arriving?" Clayton asked him.

"Any minute now."

"Give me the details."

"His name's Harry Rothstein. Senior partner in the general partnership that owns the firm's building. He's got full authority to go forward or pull the plug. He and Burdick are planning to sign the new lease on Monday. Rothstein doesn't seem to have any mistresses but I found some accounts in the Caymans. Son's got two drug convictions."

"What kind?"

"Cocaine."

"I mean what kind of *convictions*?"

"Felony. One sale, one possession."

"Is he a good friend of Burdick's?"

Simms's face eased into a faint smile.

"What's that supposed to mean?" Clayton snapped again.

"How can he be a friend of Donald's?" Simms asked. "Rothstein's a Jew."

A tall, bald man walked through the door and looked around.

"That's him," Simms said.

Clayton's face broke into a huge smile as he strode forward. "Mr. Rothstein. I'm Wendall Clayton," he called. "Come join us, my friend."

At the corner of Madison Avenue and Forty-fourth Street Taylor and Ralph Dudley paused and shook hands.

He inclined his head toward her in a Victorian way she found quaint and said, "Which train're you taking?"

"I'll walk."

"I'll cab it, I suppose. Good luck to you. Let me know how you fare with Yale." He turned and walked away.

Taylor had thought she'd have to do a private-eye number: *Hey, follow that cab; there's a fiver in it for you.* But no: Dudley didn't flag down a taxi at all. He was on foot, going to meet the mysterious W.S., whom he had visited the night the note was stolen.

When he was a half block away, Taylor followed. They moved west through the eerie illumination of a city at night—the glossy wetness of the streets and storefront windows lit for security. Still plenty of traffic, some theaters letting out now, people leaving restaurants en route to clubs and bars. Taylor felt infused with the luminous energy of New York; she found that she'd sped up to keep pace with it and had nearly overtaken Dudley. She slowed and let him regain a long lead.

Out of the brilliant, cold, fake daylight of Times Square. Only now did Taylor feel the first lump of fear as she crossed an invisible barrier, into pimp city. The public relations firms hired by New York developers called this area Clinton; almost everyone else knew it by its historical name—the more picturesque Hell's Kitchen.

Taylor continued her pursuit even when Dudley hit Twelfth Avenue, near the river, and turned south, where the streetlights grew sparser and the neighborhoods were deserted, abandoned even by the hookers.

Then Dudley stopped so suddenly, catching Taylor in mid-thought, that she had to jump into a doorway to avoid being seen.

The concrete reeked of sour urine. Hugging the shadows,

she felt nauseous. When she looked again Dudley was gone. Taylor waited for five minutes, breathing shallow gasps of cold air, listening to the sticky rush of traffic on the West Side Highway. Then she walked toward the spot where Dudley had disappeared: the doorway of a small two-story building. There were no lights radiating from the windows; she saw they were painted over. An old sign, faded, read, *West Side Art and Photography Club*.

W.S. on his calendar. So, a place, not a person.

He'd come here on Saturday night and then—possibly—gone to the firm around the time the note had disappeared.

But was there a connection?

Or was this just his hobby? Taking pictures or attending lectures on Ansel Adams and Picasso?

She cocked her head and listened. She thought she heard something. Wait, wait. Taylor tried to block out the rush of the cars and trucks and believed she heard music, something syrupy, full of strings, like Mantovani. Standing in the doorway, her feet stinging from the unaccustomed exercise in very unsensible Joan and David heels, she leaned against the stone and watched a cluster of intrepid rats browse through a garbage pile across the street.

He goes in, she figured, he's got to come out.

Forty minutes later he did.

The door swung wide. Taylor caught an image of pink and lavender. Soft music and softer light spilled out into the street. A radio cab—owned by the company that the firm used—pulled up. Dudley vanished immediately into the car, which sped away.

The question was, what would Mitchell do?

No, that wasn't the question at all. She *knew* what he would do. The question really was, did she have the guts to do the same thing?

The grapevine says you've got balls.

Yeah, well . . . Taylor walked to the front door and pressed the buzzer.

A handsome black man, large and trapezoidal, opened the door. "Yes?" he asked, poised and polite.

Taylor said, "Um, I'm here. . . ." Her voice clogged.

"Yes, you are."

"I'm here because a customer—"

"A member?"

"Right, a member referred me."

The bouncer looked past her and then opened the door. Taylor stepped inside.

It was like the lobby of an exclusive hotel. Smoky pastels, brushed copper, leather furniture, a teak bar. Three Japanese men, all in dark suits, sat on a plush couch, smoking furiously. They looked at Taylor briefly—hopefully—then, when she met their gaze with chill defiance, looked away fast.

A woman in her forties, wearing a conservative navy suit and white blouse, walked silently up to her. "How may I help you?" The smile of a maitre d'.

"I had a little time free tonight. I thought I'd check the place out."

"Well," the woman said, now playing tour director, "the West Side Art and Photography Club is one of the oldest art appreciation clubs in the city. Here's some literature." She handed Taylor a glossy brochure. There were programs of music, art shows, classes.

But how could she find out who Dudley met here?

Taylor nodded. "Ralph can't say enough good things about you."

"Ralph?"

"Ralph Dudley's a friend. I was going to meet him here earlier but—"

"Oh," the woman said quickly, "you just missed him. You should've said you knew him." She took back the brochure and tossed it in a drawer. "Sorry. I didn't know he'd referred you. ID, please."

"I—"

"Driver's license or passport."

What was Alice to do?

Play by the rules of topsy-turvy, what else?

She handed the license over and crossed her arms as the woman compared face and picture then went to a computer and typed in some information.

Apparently favorable results came back and the woman returned the license. "Can't be too careful, you know. Now, our membership fee is one thousand, and the hourly fee is five hundred per model. If you want a man, he'll have to wear a condom. Oral sex is completely up to the individual model; most do, some don't. Tipping is expected. The fee includes any standard toys but if you want something special it can probably be arranged. Will that be cash or charge?"

"Uh, American Express?"

"It'll show up as art instruction on your statement. One hour?"

"One hour, sure."

The woman took the card and asked, "Do you have any special requests?"

Taylor said, "Actually, I was thinking about something a little unusual. Could I have the, uh, model that Ralph Dudley sees?"

The hostess, trained to be unflappable, didn't look up from the charge voucher but hesitated for a millisecond. "You're sure?"

Thinking she'd never been less sure about anything in her life, Taylor Lockwood gave a slight smile and said, "Positive."

"There's a premium. Double."

"No problem." Smiling, Taylor took the credit card slip and a pen.

See the steadiness of my hand as I sign for the *two thousand Jesus Christ what am I doing dollars....*

The hostess disappeared into the back room. Muzak played quietly, a guitar rendition of "Pearly Shells." She returned a moment later with a key. "I've talked to her. She hasn't been with too many women but she's game to try."

"Good."

"I think you'll find her quite nice. Up the stairs, last room on the right. Liquor's free. Coke we can give you at cost."

"That's okay." Taylor walked into the cool corridor.

Topsy-turvy...

She knocked on the door. A voice called, "Come on in."

Taylor took a deep breath, exhaled and pushed into the room. She stopped, total shock in her eyes—an expression that perfectly matched the one on the face of the girl who stood, topless, in the center of the room.

It was the teenage girl she'd met in Dudley's office, Junie. His granddaughter.

The garter belt in the girl's hand fell to the floor with a dull clink. She said, "Oh, shit. Like, it's you."

CHAPTER SIXTEEN

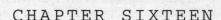 "You gotta, like, close the door," Junie said, regaining some composure. "It's a rule. Johnny, he's the bouncer, comes around and gets pissed, you don't."

Taylor stepped into the room, shut the door.

Junie said darkly, "Like, Ralph isn't going to be so happy this happened, you know."

Taylor whispered, "You're his granddaughter?"

"Like, helloooo. Whatta you think? Of course not. That's only what he tells people."

The girl was heavily made up, with dark streaks of brown and blue eye shadow that made her face sleek and serpentine. She retrieved the garter and began untangling it. "What it is, he's one of my oldest customers." Then she laughed. "I mean one of the dudes I've been seeing for the longest time. But, you know, he's one of the oldest, too. Probably, like, *the* oldest."

Taylor looked at a plush armchair. "Can I sit down?"

"It's your hour. Have a drink, you want."

Taylor poured sparkling wine into a crystal champagne glass. "You want any?"

"Me?" Junie looked horrified. "I can't drink. I'm under-age, you know."

Taylor blinked.

The girl laughed. "That's, like, a fucking joke. Of *course* I drink. Only they don't let us when we're working."

Taylor said, "You mind?" as she eased her shoes off. A swell of pain went through her feet then slowly vanished.

"Mind? Usually people take off a lot more than their shoes."

"So tell me about you and Ralph."

"I guess I oughta ask why."

"He could be in trouble. I need to find out whether he is or not."

The girl shrugged, meaning: That's not a good enough answer.

"I'll pay you."

This was a better response.

"I guess I oughta see the duckets."

"The what?"

The girl held her palm out.

Taylor opened her purse. She hadn't brought much of Reece's bribe money. She wadded together about two hundred dollars, keeping twenty for herself for cab fare home.

"I get that as a tip for a blow job," Junie said. "If the son of a bitch's cheap."

Taylor handed her more money. "That's all I have."

Junie shrugged and put the money in a dresser drawer. She pulled out a T-shirt and worked it over her head. "So, Poppie—that's what I call him—he likes girls my age. He came to the house last year and we had a date. It was like to-tally bizotic but we kind of hit it off, you know?" She whispered, "We started meeting outside the club. They get really pissed, they find out. But we did it anyway. He brought me some totally def clothes. Nice shit, you know. From the good stores. Anyway, we did some weird things, like, he took me to this art museum, which was a real bore. But then we went to the zoo.... Like, I've never been there before. It was way wild. We just kept hanging out more and more. He's lonely. His wife died and his daughter is a total bowhead."

"Junie . . . is that really your name?"

"June. I like June."

"June, last Saturday night, was Ralph here?"

"Yeah."

"When?"

"Around ten or eleven, I guess. We had our regular appointment, you know. I'm his on Saturday night. Sorta a tradition."

"Then what?"

She fell silent. Shrugged.

"Another two hundred."

The girl said, "I thought you don't have any more money."

"I can give you a check."

"A check?" Junie laughed.

"I promise it won't bounce."

"That was, what, five hundred, you said?"

Taylor hesitated. "You have a good memory." She wrote the check out and handed it to her. Mitchell, you're going to see a very weird expense account for this project.

Junie slipped the check into her purse. "Okay, but he didn't want me to tell anybody. . . . He went to your company."

"The law firm?"

"Yeah."

"What was he doing?"

"That's the thing: He wouldn't say. I'm, like, what're you going there for this time of night? I mean, it's midnight or whatever. He said he had to—something about a lot of money. But he wouldn't tell me what. And he told me never tell anybody."

At least anybody who didn't pay her seven hundred dollars.

Taylor asked, "Has he ever mentioned a company called Hanover & Stiver?"

"Naw, but he don't talk—I mean, he *doesn't* talk about his business too much. He's always correcting what I say. It's so mundo-boring."

Taylor stood slowly, slipped her swollen feet back into her shoes. She walked painfully to the door. She paused.

"How old are you?"

"Eighteen. And I've got a driver's license."

"I've had fake ones too, honey."

"Okay, I'm sixteen. But I tell Ralph I'm fifteen. He likes it that I'm younger."

"Do you go to school or anything?"

A laugh. "Where're you from? I made sixty-eight thousand dollars last year and have a hundred Gs in a, you know, retirement fund. Why the fuck would I want to go to school?"

Why indeed?

Taylor let herself out into the hallway, through which echoed a cacophony of voices and sounds very different from those she was used to at Hubbard, White & Willis.

■

At lunchtime the next day, her feet only marginally recovered from their abuse the day before, Taylor Lockwood was sitting across from a diminutive young man in a West Village diner: Danny Stuart, Linda Davidoff's former roommate.

The menu of the place, which had been Stuart's choice, was heavy on foods that had swayed in the wind when alive, and light on main courses that had walked around on two or four legs, the latter being by far Taylor's favorite.

"So," she asked, "you know Sean Lillick too?"

"Not at all really. I met him through Linda and went to some of his shows. But he's a little avante-garde for me."

"You're an editor?"

"That's mostly a hobby. Some of us put together an alternative literary magazine. I'm a computer programmer by profession."

Taylor yawned and stretched. A joint popped. The walls of the place were badly painted, swirls of dark paint didn't cover the lighter enamel underneath. The decorations were à la *Mother Jones* and Woodstock. But the space, she knew, had been a Beat club in the fifties. William Burroughs and Allen Ginsberg had hung out here—the ancient floor felt spongy under the chairs and the wooden columns were carved with the initials of hundreds of former patrons. What these walls have heard, she thought.

Danny ordered sprouts and nuts and yogurt; Taylor, a garden burger. "Bacon?"

"No bacon," the waitress replied through her pierced lips.

"Ketchup," Taylor tried.

"We don't have ketchup."

"Mustard?"

"Sesame-soy paste or eggless mayo."

"Cheese?"

"Not your kind of cheese," the waitress responded.

"Plain'll be just fine."

The woman vanished.

Stuart said, "I think I remember you from Linda's funeral."

Taylor nodded. "I didn't know many people there, except the ones from the firm."

"You a lawyer?" he asked.

"Paralegal. How did you meet her?"

"Just a fluke. You know, your typical New York story. You come to New York from a small town, look for a place to live, you need a roommate 'cause the rents are so high. The guy I was rooming with got AIDS and moved back home. I needed to split the rent and Linda'd been staying at some residence hall for women. She hated it. We roomed together for, I guess, about nine or ten months. Until she died."

"Did you know her well?"

"Pretty well. I read some of her pieces and did some editing for her. She wrote reviews for us and I was hoping eventually to publish some of her poems."

"Was she good?"

"She was young; her work was unformed. But if she'd kept at it I know she would've gone someplace."

"What was her style like? Plath?" Taylor had read some of Sylvia Plath's poetry and recalled that she too had committed suicide.

Stuart said, "Her poetry was more traditionally structured than Plath's. But her personal life? Yep, just as turbulent. The wrong men, always heartbroken. Too stoic. She needed to scream and throw things more. But she kept it all inside."

The food came and Danny Stuart dug eagerly into his huge mass of rabbit food. Taylor started working on the sandwich, which she decided should be named not the garden but the cardboard burger.

"How did it happen, the suicide?" she asked.

"She was up at her parents' summer house in Connecticut. The back deck was above this big gorge. One night, she jumped. The fall didn't kill her but she hit her head and got knocked out. She drowned in a stream."

Taylor closed her eyes and shook her head. "Did she leave a note?"

He nodded. "Well, it wasn't really a note. It was one of her poems. When you called and said you were curious about her I thought you'd like to see it. I made you a copy. It's dated the day before she died. It talks about leaving life behind her, all the cares. . . . I was going to publish it in my magazine but, you know, I haven't had the heart."

He handed her the Xerox copy. Taylor read the title: "When I Leave."

She looked at Danny and said, "I hope I can ask you something in confidence. Something that won't go any further."

"Sure."

"Do you think Linda killed herself because of something that happened at work?"

"No."

"You sound pretty certain."

"I am. I know exactly why she killed herself."

"I thought no one knew."

"Well, I did. She was pregnant."

"Pregnant?"

"I don't think anybody knew except me. She got an EPT kit? It was just a couple of weeks before she died. I saw the kit in the bathroom and asked her about it. You know, we were like girlfriends. She confided in me."

"But why would she kill herself?"

"I think the father dumped her."

"Who was the father?"

"I don't know. She was seeing somebody but never talked about him or brought him around the apartment. She was real secretive about him."

"Breaking up . . . that upset her so much she killed herself?"

Stuart considered. She thought, studying his face: poet's eyes, artist's eyes. Unlike Sean Lillick, this was the real thing. He said, "There's more to it. See, Linda had no business working at that law firm. She was too sensitive. The business world was way too much for her. She got thrown too easily. Then when her personal life came crashing down I think it pushed her over the edge."

"But you don't know if there was anything specific at the firm that upset her? Anything she might've felt guilty about?"

"Nope. She never mentioned a word about that. And she probably would have. As I said, she and I were like, well, sisters."

So, the rabbit hole of Wall Street had proved too much for poor Linda Davidoff.

Without the heart to read the girl's suicide poem, Taylor put it in her purse and continued to eat her bland lunch while she and Danny talked about life in the Village.

Her face broke into another major yawn. She laughed and Stuart joined her.

"Not getting enough sleep lately?" he wondered.

"The problem," she explained, "is that I've been living an after-hours life when I'm not an after-hours person. I'm a during-hours person."

CHAPTER SEVENTEEN

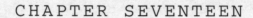Alice was on another trip through the looking glass.

This time, in a limo.

Taylor and Thom Sebastian were speeding down the Long Island Expressway Friday after work. The driver's eyes flicked to the radar detector needle as often as they glanced at the highway.

"I'm totally psyched you came," Sebastian said with apparent sincerity. "I thought you were going to boogie in with the Big E."

"E?"

"Excuse, you know. I—"

"Get that a lot?" she filled in.

"Yeah." He grimaced. "Now let me tell you about Bosk."

"What's the story behind the name?"

"His real handle's Brad Ottington Smith. B-O-S. Bosk. I'm Sea-bastian. Sea Bass. Get it? Okay. His father and mother have been separated practically since he was born. She has a house in Boston and his father has an apartment on the Upper East Side. They kept the summer place in the

Hamptons and have it on alternate weeks. They—that's the parents they—can't talk to each other without bloodshed so they have their lawyers schedule the visits to the house."

"And we're the mother's week."

"Right."

"Sounds like it's going to be a bucket of kicks and giggles. What is she, a wicked witch?" Taylor asked.

"All I'll say is she's more powerful than his father."

"What does *he* do?"

"Dad? What he does is he's rich. He's a senior partner at Ludlum Morgan, the investment bank."

"Bosk." She laughed. "I feel like I want to give him a Milk-Bone when I call him that. What firm does he work at?"

As he'd done the other night, though, he grew reluctant to give much away about Bosk professionally.

"Little shop in Midtown." Sebastian busied himself opening a Budweiser, handed it to her. Popped another.

"The mother?"

"Ada travels, entertains, does what any fifty-five-year-old sorority sister does: manages her portfolio. It's about a hundred million." Sebastian sipped the beer and let his hand stray—accidentally on purpose—to her knee. "Ho, boy, Taylor. This's gonna be primo. Good food, good drink, good people."

She lifted his pudgy fingers off her skirt. "And good behavior."

Sebastian moaned, then sat back in silence, and they gazed out the dim windows as dusk enveloped the flat, sandy landscape.

The Ottington Smith family manse was a three-story Gothic Victorian house, white with dark blue trim, about a hundred miles east of New York on the South Shore of Long Island. Two towers rose to widow's walks, which overlooked a huge yard and three connected outbuildings. The house itself was covered with skeletons of vines and wisteria. A spiked, wrought-iron fence surrounded a labyrinth of grounds. Much of the property had been reclaimed by tangles of forsythia, which sported sparse tags of brown and yellow leaves.

"Addams Family," Taylor said.

The circular driveway was full of cars. The limo paused and they got out. "God, more German cars than in Brazil," Sebastian said.

"Porches. I love porches," Taylor said. She sat on a wooden swing and rocked back and forth. "Wish it were thirty degrees warmer."

He rang the bell. A woman in her mid-fifties came to the door. Her dry, blond hair swept sideways Jackie Kennedy–style and was sprayed firmly into place. She wore a lime-green silk dress woven with pink and black triangles that pointed feverishly in all directions. Taylor bird-spotted Chanel.

The woman's face was long and glossy, the high bones holding the skin like a taut sail. Her jewelry was large. A blue topaz on her tanned, wrinkled finger was easily fifty carats.

"Thomas." They pressed cheeks and Taylor was introduced to Ada Smith—introduced, then promptly examined: the dynamics of the eyes, the contour of skin. The mouth especially. The review was mixed and Taylor believed she understood why: Bosk's little girlfriends—age twenty-three or twenty-four—could be forgiven their youth. Taylor had broken the three-oh barrier and yet had hardly a crow's foot or defining jowl.

She hates me, Taylor thought.

Yet Ada's smile and charm didn't waver; she'd been brought up right. "Call me Ada, please. I don't know where Bradford is. The others are in the den. Bradford's the cocktail and cigar director. I'm in charge of dinner. That will be at eight."

Then she was gone.

From the back hallway, a bellowing voice: "Sea Bass, Sea Bass!"

Sebastian ran toward him and grunted. "Bosk-meister! Yo!"

They slapped fists, reminding Taylor of bull rams smacking horns.

Their host was in chinos, Top-Siders and a green Harvard sweatshirt. His hands and face were red, his eyes watering from the cold. "We've been chopping wood for the fire."

A girl giggled at the apparent lie.

"Well," Bosk said, "carting it in. Same as chopping it. Just as much work."

Bosk leaned forward, his arm on Sebastian's shoulders. He whispered, "Jennie's here and she brought Billy-boy, you can believe it."

"No way! Is she totally fucked, or what?" Sebastian looked around uneasily. "And how 'bout Brittany?"

"Couldn't make it."

The lawyer's eyes were immeasurably relieved and Taylor remembered something from the club about unreturned phone calls.

Then Bosk's eyes danced to Taylor. " 'Lo. You're . . .?"

"Taylor Lockwood."

"Right, you're the one who won't marry me."

"True, but you're in good company." She nodded at Sebastian. "I won't marry him either. You have a nice place here."

"Thanks. I'll show you around later. Come on inside. We've got a fire going."

After she'd washed up she joined the crowd in the den. They were mostly in their twenties. Names went past—Rob and Mindy and Gay-Gay and Trevor and Windham and MacKenzie (the latter both female), clusters of contemporary syllables more distinct than the faces of the handsome men and pretty women they identified.

Taylor smiled and waved and forgot the names instantly. They were friendly but reserved and Taylor wondered what they were thinking of her—a woman with more wop and mick in her than Brit, with a mass of kinky black hair, not a pert ponytail, and wearing a long paisley skirt and a black blouse, not a J. Crew stitch upon her body.

Suspicion . . . That was the message from the women.

From the men there was something very different. Something between casual flirtation and a knee-jerk invitation to hump. Taylor supposed that soon there'd be a lot of female fingers twining possessively through the belt loops of their men.

Bosk made martinis for the crowd but Taylor stuck with beer.

"Are you a lawyer?" one blonde asked.

"A paralegal."

"Oh," the woman said, blinking. "That's interesting."

"We need you folks," one handsome young man said as he tinkered nervously with his Rolex. "You save our butts every day." It seemed he wasn't being condescending; he was simply embarrassed for her and trying to salvage her pride.

"Where're you from? Boston, right? I detect Bostonian."

"Born on the North Shore."

"Oh, Locust Valley?" a pretty blond woman asked. The residence of the crème de la crème. J. P. Morgan's home.

"No, Glen Cove." A pleasant but strip-malled city. "But we moved to Maryland when I was twelve."

"Is your father or mother in the business?"

"Which business would that be?" Taylor asked innocently.

"Law, banking?" As if no other businesses existed.

"He manages a convenience store," she replied.

Sebastian, who'd already commented about her father and his renowned law practice, glanced at her with a cryptic look.

"Well, retail," one girl finally said, nodding with robust approval. "Good margins in retail lately."

"Very good," somebody else added.

And to her relief, Taylor Lockwood ceased to be a human being as far as they were concerned and their own conversation—the real and important conversation—resumed.

███

Dinner was Ada's jurisdiction.

She presided with the quiet authority of someone

for whom social propriety is statutory. Somewhere, in a three-decades-old volume of Emily Post, this very layout of Waterford and Wedgwood was represented. Though the clothing was supposed to be casual, Ada's appearance in a rustling silk dress, black-velvet headband and necklace gripping a lemon-colored stone the size of a fat thumb made it clear that, whatever happened in the frat dining halls or eating clubs these youngsters were accustomed to, dinner in this particular house would be governed by a respectable modicum of formality.

Taylor tried a vain end run around the seating ("Oh, I'm sorry, was I supposed to sit there?"); Ada smilingly steered her away from Bosk's girlfriend (a potential source of information about the "project"), scolding, "Boy, girl, boy, girl ..."

Lobster bisque, a pear-and-Camembert salad, tiny veal chops surrounded by a yin-yang swirl of pureed peas and carrots, a green salad. A real butler served the meal.

Between polite words with the young man on her right Taylor tried to overhear the conversation between Bosk and Sebastian but Ada's voice was too loud—she was a lock-jawed caricature of Long Island money. She touched the men's arms with her dark, bony fingers and flirted fiercely. Yet their hostess knew this game as well as she knew the proper wording for bread-and-butter notes. She had no intention of seducing these boys; the only organ at play here was her ego—though sex was a strong undercurrent of the meal and crude jokes, some of them really disgusting, flew back and forth. (The upper class, Taylor remembered, had by and large not been Puritans.)

Halfway through the profiteroles and espresso with anisette, the doorbell rang. Bosk rose and a few minutes later returned with a man of about forty-five. He was introduced as Dennis Callaghan.

Taylor disliked him at once.

She wasn't sure why. What she might in fairness have read as groomed, discerning and charming she believed was vain (spun, sprayed hair combed forward, a close-fitting suit with shot cuffs, gold bracelet), pompous (a disdaining look at the children around him) and dishonest (a broad smile he could not have felt).

He was also insulting: He ignored Taylor while he studied the bloused or sweatered breasts of every woman younger than herself at the table before turning a flattering smile on Ada with the respect due a matriarch.

Taylor then noticed that the climate at the table had changed considerably. Sebastian's expression was one of anger. He shot a dark, mystified glance at Bosk, who shrugged with a look that meant, It wasn't my fault. When she saw that, Taylor's interest immediately perked up. Perhaps Callaghan had some connection with the "project."

The visitor, whose beach house was apparently nearby, announced that he'd played hooky from Wall Street today to hold a couple of meetings out here and happened to notice the cars as he was driving back to the city. He thought he'd stop in and see Bosk and Sebastian.

The man glanced at Sebastian, and Taylor saw another finger wag, just like the other night. Callaghan nodded subtly.

And so the conversation remained social. As he sat down at the table and took a glass of wine—he'd eaten already—they talked about problems in finding groundskeepers and the advantages and risks of helicoptering into Manhattan. Sebastian remained nervous as hell and when Taylor asked Callaghan what he did for a living the young lawyer answered for the businessman, offering quickly, "Wall Street, darling. *Everybody* out here's on Wall Street. Well, you've got an artist or two from time to time—Taylor's a musician, by the way."

"Really?"

The conversation turned back to her momentarily and before she could ask anything more about Callaghan, dinner was over and Sebastian had quickly shepherded Bosk and the businessman downstairs, explaining that they were going to check out Bosk's cigar cellar.

No one else was invited but the herd of preppies didn't

take any offense. Ada nodded toward the port, sherry and liqueur and, armed with yet more alcohol, this contingent ambled into the panoramic living room for more gossip.

It was then that Taylor recalled: She hadn't told Sebastian that she was a musician.

███████

Soon several people lit up cigarettes, Ada among them.

The smoke gave Taylor an excuse to drain her Grand Marnier and say she was going to step outside to get some air. Whether anyone thought this was rude, or suspicious, didn't matter; they all seemed relieved that the 7-Eleven heiress was leaving and they could spend some time dishing in earnest.

She took her leather jacket from the closet and walked out the front door, then strolled around the house until she spotted a four-foot-deep window well. She climbed down into it. A piece of glass was loose and she worked it free. She could not see the three men downstairs but their words, carried on the warm air, streamed up to her with the awkward-sounding hesitancies of conversations overheard but not witnessed.

"Got to be more careful," Sebastian said. "Jesus, I shit when I saw you here."

Callaghan said, "We've still got some details to work out. And you're impossible to get ahold of, Thom."

"Well, we can't just fucking waltz into each other's office and take a meeting now, can we? We've got to be careful about it, set it up ahead of time, keep everything secret."

Callaghan sighed. "I've been doing this sort of thing a lot longer than you have, Thom. We're going to get away with it. Stop worrying so much."

"I'm thinking about the phones," Bosk said. "You really think they're bugged?"

Sebastian said, "Of course they're fucking bugged. Jesus, don't be so naive.

Bosk: "Well, I can't run downstairs to make a call from a

pay phone every time I want to talk to you. Somebody sees me doing that a couple of times and what're they going to think?"

Sebastian: "Well, that's what you're going to have to do. You can pick up cell phone transmissions even easier than landlines."

Callaghan: "What we could do—I've done this before— what we could do is get an answering service. You call and leave messages. I'll call on a separate line and pick them up. We'll have a second answering service going the other way."

Clever, Taylor Lockwood thought, though being truly clever, Thom, would have meant wearing gloves when you check out the file cabinet you're about to break into so you don't leave fingerprints.

Suddenly she felt a curious thrill. What was it? The excitement of the pursuit, she supposed, getting closer to her quarry. What Reece felt in the courtroom yesterday. What her father undoubtedly felt—in court, on the golf course, with his beloved shotgun out in the fields.

When she was young her father would take her with him when he'd go hunting on Saturday mornings in the fall. She'd hated those times, wanted to be back home in bed, watching cartoons or playing on her upright piano, shopping with her mother. But Samuel Lockwood, eyes keen and hungry for a kill, had insisted she come along. He'd carried the tiny, still-warm corpses of the birds back to the car, where came the moment she dreaded: To make her understand that the dead birds couldn't hurt her, he had her touch each one with her index finger.

There, that wasn't so bad, was it? Didn't hurt. They can't bite when they're dead, Taylie, remember that.

Dennis Callaghan now said, "Look, yeah, we have to be careful but we can't let this paralyze us."

"We're fucking thieves," Sebastian said. "Am I the only one taking this seriously?"

Bosk's laugh was flinty. "Well, whatta you want, Thom? You want to get walkie-talkies and scramblers? Disguises?"

"I'm just a little paranoid, okay? There was a weird fuckup."

"What?"

"Well, last Saturday night, when I was in the firm?"

"Right," Callaghan offered.

"I made sure nobody knew I was there—on Friday I taped the back door latch down so I could get in without leaving any record I was in. But what happens is this old asshole, a partner, cops my key and uses it to get in early Sunday morning. So now I'm in the system."

Gotcha, thought Taylor Lockwood. John Silbert Hemming, her tall private eye, would be proud of her.

"Shit," Bosk said. "Why'd he do it?"

"How the fuck do I know? Alzheimer's."

Callaghan said, "Not the end of the world. They don't know what you were doing there, right?"

"I don't think so."

"Well, relax. You've covered up everything real well, Thom. . . . Oh, here. Got a present."

"Ah, nectar of the gods," Sebastian said.

"Sure," Bosk said. A long pause.

Then a sniff. Another.

The magic powder boosted Sebastian's spirits considerably. When he spoke next he said with a laugh, "I like this—fucking the firm that fucked me and getting rich in the process."

"You want a Lamborghini?" Callaghan asked.

Bosk said seriously, "I don't like the ride. Rough, you know."

Sebastian: "I live in Manhattan. What'm I gonna do, alternate-side-of-the-street parking with a two-hundred-thousand-dollar car?"

"Keep it out at your summer house, Thom, like we all do."

"I don't have a summer house. And I don't want one."

The wind was dicing her face and ears. She closed her eyes against the cold. Her legs and thighs, the last stronghold

of heat, were going numb. She touched the glass that separated her from a room that was fifty degrees warmer, where
she heard the sounds of two chubby, spoiled boys sniffing the
residue of cocaine into their nostrils.

Bosk said, "So what's with this Taylor cunt? She put out?"

"Fuck you," Sebastian said unemotionally.

"No, does she fuck *you*? That's what I'm asking."

Callaghan sniffed his white powder then said, "You've
got gonads for brains, Bosk. Is that all you think about? Sex?"

"Money, too. I think a lot about money but mostly I
think about sex. Tell me about Taylor."

"I don't want to talk about her," Sebastian said menac-
ingly.

"Does she have big tits? I couldn't tell. . . . Hey, chill, will
you, man? That's a fucking scary look. I was just curious."

There was a pause. And with an ominous tone in his
voice Sebastian said, "Well, don't get too interested in her.
You hear me?"

Taylor felt a ping of fear at that.

"I'm just—"

"You hear what I'm saying?"

"Hey, chill. . . . I hear you, Sea Bass, I hear you."

Then the conversation turned to sports and, stinging
with cold, Taylor left them to their banter. She walked inside and rejoined the crowd in front of the fireplace, observing how the conversation grew sedate when she entered the
room. She nudged herself into the center of the group and
sat on the hearth with her back to the fire until the pain
from the cold became a fierce itch and then finally died
away.

███

Around 10 P.M. the drapery man walked through
Greenwich Village under huge trapezoids of bruise-purple
clouds, lit from the perpetual glow of the city.

He was concentrating on the buildings and finally arrived at the address he sought.

At the service entrance, which smelled of sour garbage,

he inserted his lock gun and flicked the trigger a dozen times until the teeth of the tumblers were aligned. The door opened easily. He climbed to the fourth floor and picked another set of locks—on the door of the particular apartment he sought.

Inside, he slipped his ice-pick weapon into his belt, handle up, ready to grab it if he had to, and began to search. He found a bag of needlepoint (one a Christmas scene that sure wouldn't be finished in time for the holiday), a box of Weight Watchers apple snacks, a garter belt in its original gift box, apparently never worn, cartons of musty sheet music. An elaborate, expensive-looking reel-to-reel tape recorder. Dozens of tape cassettes with the same title: *The Heat of Midnight. Songs by Taylor Lockwood.*

Inside the woman's briefcase, in addition to sheet music, he found time sheets, key entry logs and other documents from Hubbard, White & Willis. He looked through them carefully and memorized exactly what they contained.

He found and read through the woman's address book, her calendar and her phone bills. He listened to her answering machine tapes. His client had hoped that she'd have a diary but very few people kept diaries anymore and Taylor Lockwood was no exception.

The drapery man continued his search, walking slowly through the apartment, taking his time. He knew his client would grill him at length about what he'd found here and he wanted to make sure he overlooked nothing.

CHAPTER EIGHTEEN

Taylor dropped into the chair in her cubicle.

It was six-thirty, Saturday morning. The gods of the furnace had decided that not even Type A attorneys would be in the office yet and so Hubbard, White & Willis was cold as Anchorage.

She shivered both from the temperature and from exhaustion too. She and Thom Sebastian had arrived back in the city late last night. The lawyer had been subdued. She'd sensed that he was worried she'd ask about Callaghan and he wouldn't be able to come up with a credible story. But there was something else troubling him. His jokey self was gone. And once she caught him looking at her with an odd, troubled expression on his face.

She had an image of herself as a condemned prisoner and him as a prison guard, distancing himself from someone about to die.

Ridiculous, she thought. Still, she could hear his words in her head:

Well, don't get too interested in her.

What did *that* mean?

And how the hell had he known she was a musician?

She noticed a flashing light on her phone, indicating that she had a message. She picked up the receiver to check voice mail.

Reece had called again to remind her about dinner at his place that night.

There was one other message.

Beep.

"*Hey, counselor, how you doing? Saw an article about your shop in the* Law Journal. *About the merger. You've probably seen it but I'm faxing it to you. Always stay on top of firm politics. . . .*"

If you only knew, Dad, she thought.

"*We're planning Christmas dinner and we've got an RSVP from a Supreme Court justice; I'll let you guess who. I'm putting him next to you at the table. Just keep your more liberal views to yourself, counselor. I'm serious about that. Okay, I'll be in town week after next. Your mother says hi.*"

Supreme Court? Samuel Lockwood never did anything without a purpose. What did he have in mind? Was the dinner table placement intended to help her career? she wondered.

Or *his?* she appended cynically.

Taylor found the fax her father had sent about the merger of the firms, scanned it quickly. It described the vicious infighting among the partners at Hubbard, White & Willis—Burdick v. Clayton—and how, despite the animosity, the merged firms would probably succeed much better in the new business climate than if they remained separate. The picture featured Burdick and his wife.

An idea occurred to her.

She wrote on the top, "Thom, FYI." And signed her name.

Using this as an excuse, she hurried to his office, propped the article on his chair and, with a glance into the deserted corridor, proceeded to search the room like an eager rookie cop on crime scene detail.

In his desk she found: condoms, Bamboo paper, an unopened bottle of Chivas Regal, matches from the Harvard

Club, the Palace Hotel and assorted late-night clubs around town, dozens of take-out menus from downtown restaurants, chatty letters from his brother and father and mother (all neatly organized, some with margin notes), brokerage house statements, checkbooks (Jesus, where'd he get all this *money*?), some popular spy and military paperbacks, a coffee-stained copy of the *Lawyer's Code of Professional Responsibility,* assorted photographs from vacations, newspaper articles on bond issues and stock offerings, the *Pennystock News,* candy bars, crumbs and paper clips.

Nothing about the note, no information linking him, Bosk or Callaghan to Hanover & Stiver.

On Sebastian's bookshelves were hundreds of huge books, bound in navy and burgundy and deep green. They'd contain copies of all the closing documents in a business transaction that Sebastian had worked on. They would be great places to hide stolen promissory notes and other incriminating evidence. But it would take several days to look through all of them. She saw Sebastian's name embossed in gold at the bottom of each one.

It was then that she noticed the corner of a piece of paper protruding from beneath Sebastian's desk blotter. Another glance into the corridor—still no signs of life—and she pulled the paper out.

The jottings were brief and to the point.

Taylor Lockwood. 24 Fifth Avenue.

Her age, schools attended. Home address in Chevy Chase. Phone numbers at the firm and at home. The unlisted one too.

Father: Samuel Lockwood. Mother: housewife. No siblings. Applied to law school. Employed by HWW for two years. Merit raises and bonuses at top levels.

"*Musician. Every Tuesday. Miracles Pub.*"

The son of a bitch, she whispered. Then replaced the sheet exactly where she'd found it.

She left his office and returned to the chilly corridor, hearing echoes of footsteps, hearing the click of guns being cocked and the hiss of knives being unsheathed.

And hearing over and over Thom Sebastian's words:
Well, don't get too interested in her.

In the firm's library she logged on to several of the computer databases that the firm subscribed to, including the
Lexis/Nexis system, which contains copies of nearly all
court decisions, statutes and regulations in the United
States, as well as articles from hundreds of magazines and
newspapers around the world.

She spent hours trying to find information about Dennis
Callaghan, Bosk and Sebastian.

There wasn't much that was helpful. Bradford Smith
had been admitted to the New York and federal bars and
currently practiced at a Midtown firm, which didn't, however, seem to have any connection to Hanover & Stiver or
New Amsterdam Bank.

Dennis Callaghan wasn't a lawyer but a businessman.
He dabbled in dozens of different activities and had been
under investigation for stock fraud and real estate scams
though he'd never been indicted. He was currently connected with about twenty different companies, some of
which were incorporated offshore and which, she guessed,
were fronts.

But still no connection between any of them and
Hanover & Stiver.

The information about Sebastian—found in alumni
magazine archives and legal magazines he'd contributed articles to—wasn't incriminating either, though she found, in-
terestingly, that the Upper East Side preppy image was fake.
Sebastian had grown up outside of Chicago, his father the
manager of a Kroger grocery store (hence, she realized, another reason for the funny look when he'd heard her tell the
youngsters at Ada's that Dad managed a convenience store).
Sebastian did have an undergrad degree from Harvard but it
had taken him six years because he'd gone part-time—
presumably while working to support himself.

The Yale Law School certificates she'd noticed on his

wall must have been for continuing education courses; he'd gotten his law degree from Brooklyn Law at night while working as a process server during the day—serving subpoenas in some of the toughest parts of the outer boroughs.

So, there was a different Thom Sebastian beneath the jokey party animal. One who was driven, ambitious, tough. And, Taylor knew, recalling the conversation in Ada's downstairs den, also a thief—fucking the firm that fucked him.

More associates were filing into the library now and she didn't want anybody to see what she was doing so she logged off the computer and went to the administrative floor.

There she walked into the file room Carrie Mason had told her about, a large, dingy space filled with row upon row of cabinets. It was here that the billing department kept the original time sheets that lawyers filled out daily.

Making certain the room was empty, Taylor opened the "D" drawer—where Ralph Dudley's sheets would reside— and found the most recent ones. They were little blue slips of carbon paper filled with his imperial scrawl, describing every ten-minute period during working hours. She read through and replaced them and then did the same in the "L" drawer for Lillick and the "S" for Thom Sebastian.

Taylor rose to leave but then paused.

The "R" cabinet was right next to her.

She rested her fingers on the handle and after a moment's hesitation, pulled it open and looked inside. She stared in astonishment at the booklets with Mitchell Reece's name on them. There were hundreds of them. Christ Almighty . . . nearly twice as many as for most other lawyers.

She pulled one out at random—September—and thumbed through it, looking at a typical day in the life of Mitchell Reece:

> *New Client relations—½ hour.*
> *New Amsterdam Bank & Trust v. Hanover & Stiver—4½ hours (depositions).*
> *Westron Electronic et al. v. Larson Associates—3¼ hours (motion to quash subpoena, J. Brietell).*

> *State of New York v. Kowalski*—½ hour *(conference
> with DA's office; pro bono).*
> *State of New York v. Hammond*—½ hour *(meeting
> with defendant; pro bono).*
> *In re Summers Publishing*—2½ hours *(research,
> briefing Chapter 7 bankruptcy issue).*

She skimmed ahead.

> *Lasky v. Allied Products...Mutual Indemnity of
> New Jersey v. New Amsterdam Bank...State of
> New York v. Williams.*

She totaled the hours: Sixteen were billed to clients.
That was sixteen hours of *productive* work, not commuting
time, lunch, trips to the rest rooms and the water fountain.

Sixteen hours in one day!

And every day was pretty much the same.

*Arguing motion, arguing motion, on trial, writing brief, on
trial, on trial, settlement conference, arguing motion, on trial,
pro bono meetings with criminal clients and prosecutors.*

On trial on trial on trial...

He never stopped.

A thought occurred to her and she smiled to herself.
Yes, no?

Go for it, Alice.

She opened the binder containing the most recent of his
sheets. She flipped through them until she found the day
that she'd followed him to Grand Central Station.

For the three hours he was out of the office he'd marked
the time Code 03.

Which meant personal time.

The time you spend at the dentist's office.

The time you spend at PTA conferences.

The time you spend in Westchester, with your girlfriend.

Taylor felt her skin buzzing with embarrassment as she
flipped through other lunch hours over the past several

months. In September he'd done the same—taken long lunches—only usually it was two or three times a week. Recently, in the month of November, for instance, he'd done so only once a week.

Three hours in the middle of the day for a workaholic like Reece?

Well, Taylor Lockwood understood; she'd had lovers herself.

She put the time sheets back and closed the drawer.

Outside, the air was cold but the city was ablaze with Christmas decorations and she decided to walk home. She slipped her Walkman headset on, then her earmuffs, and began to walk briskly, thinking about the evening ahead, dinner with Mitchell Reece—at least until the hiss of the cassette grew silent, Miles Davis started into "Seven Steps to Heaven" and the rest of the world was lost to Taylor Lockwood.

CHAPTER NINETEEN

Well, look at this.

Mitchell Reece could've been a professional interior designer.

Taylor would have thought he'd have no time for decor—or interest in the subject. So when he opened his door and ushered her into the huge loft, she exhaled a sharp, surprised laugh.

She was looking at a single room, probably twenty-five hundred square feet. There was a separate elevated sleeping area with a brass railing around it, containing an oak armoire and a matching dresser—and a bed, which caught her attention immediately. It was dark mahogany, with a massive headboard that would have dwarfed any smaller space. The headboard was carved in a Gothic style and the characters cut into the wood were cracked and worn. She couldn't tell exactly what they were—perhaps gargoyles and dragons.

She thought of the mythical creature in *Through the Looking-Glass*.

Beware the Jabberwock, my son!
The jaws that bite, the claws that catch!

Around the loft were plants, sculpture, antiques, tall bookshelves, tapestries. Pin spots shot focused streams of light onto small statues and paintings, many of which looked ugly enough to be very valuable. The walls were brick and plaster, painted mottled white and gray and pink. The floors were oak, stained white.

If this boy cooks, she joked to herself, I may just reconsider my baby-by-mail plan and marry him.

"You did this just to impress me, I know."

He laughed. "Let me take your coat." Reece wore baggy pants and a blousy white shirt. Sockless slippers. His hair was still damp from a shower.

Taylor had chosen noncommittal vamp. Black stockings but shoes with low, functional heels. A black Carolina Herrera dress, tight but high-necked. (Cleavage? A roommate had once bluntly assessed, *Forget boobs, Taylor: Avoid low-cut. But the rest of your bod—it's to die for. Wear short and tight. Remember that. Short and tight.*)

Taylor noted the sweep of Reece's eyes all along her body. He was subtle, but not subtle enough; she caught him in reflection in one of the mirrors near the Jabberwock bed.

Okay, Ms. Westchester, she thought to Reece's mysterious girlfriend, can *you* shoehorn into a dress like this?

She followed him across an oriental rug. The dinner table had feet, and on the side, carved faces of the sun. They were solemn.

"Your table looks unhappy."

"He gets bored. I don't have much company. He'll be happy tonight."

As Reece took the wine she'd brought she looked at him carefully and decided he wasn't very happy either. His eyes were still bloodshot and he seemed to be forcing himself to relax, to push the intruding distractions of the law firm away.

He walked into the kitchen area and put the chardonnay into a refrigerator. She looked inside; it contained nothing but wine. "You should try groceries sometime," she said. "Lettuce, oranges. You can even get chicken, I'm told, ready to cook."

"Wine cellar," Reece said, laughing. He pulled out a bottle of white, a Puligny-Montrachet. Her father's favorite Burgundy, Taylor recalled. Reece added, "The fridge's over there." He pointed to a tall Sub-Zero then took two crystal goblets in one hand and carried the wine and a ceramic cooler out into the living area.

Man, she thought, he's really slick at this.

He poured and they touched glasses. "To winning."

Taylor held his eye for a moment and repeated the toast. The wine was rich and sour-sweet, more like a food than a drink. The goblet was heavy in her hand.

They sat and he told her how he'd found the loft. It was raw space when he'd moved in and he'd had it finished himself. The project had taken nearly a year because he'd had three full-fledged trials that year and had been unable to meet with the contractors. "I slept in sawdust a lot," he explained. "But I won the cases."

"Have you ever lost a trial?" she asked.

"Of course. Everybody loses trials. I seem to win a few more than most people. But that's not magic. Or luck. Preparation is the key. And will to win."

"Preparation and Will. That could be your motto."

"Maybe I should get a crest. I wonder what it'd be in Latin."

Taylor rose and walked toward a long wooden shelf. "My mother," she said, "would call this a knickknack shelf. I used to think 'knickknack' was French for 'small, ugly ceramic poodle.'" He laughed.

She found herself looking at an army of metal soldiers.

"I collect them," Reece said. "Winston Churchill probably had the biggest collection in the world and Malcolm Forbes's wasn't too shabby either. I've only been at it for twenty years or so."

"What are they, tin?"

"Lead."

Taylor said, "One year my father got the idea that I should get soldiers, not dolls, for Christmas. I must've been eight or nine. He gave me bags and bags of these green plastic guys. He gave me a B-52 too so I nuked most of them and went back to Barbie and Pooh. You have other things, too? Like cannons and catapults?"

"Everything. Soldiers, horses, cannons, and caissons..."

She sipped the wine and was thinking: Sometimes in life this craziness falls right on top of you and you find yourself almost floating up and away from your body like a guru or psychic, looking down at yourself, and all you can say is, Shit a brick, this is *so* weird. I mean, here I am, Alice in Wonderland, in a fab loft, next to a handsome man I'm playing detective with, drinking hundred-dollar wine and talking toy soldiers.

Taylor told herself not, under any circumstances, to get drunk.

Reece played with some of the figures. "I have a British Square. I made it when I was sixteen."

"Like a park? Like Trafalgar Square?"

Reece was laughing. "Taylor, British Square? A fighting formation? You know, *Gunga Din.*"

"Kipling," she said.

He nodded. "The ranks divided into two lines. One stood and reloaded, the other knelt and fired. The fuzzy-wuzzies were the only warriors to break through the square."

"The, uh..."

"Zulus. African tribal warriors."

"Ah. Boer War."

"That was twenty years later."

"Oh, sure," she said seriously, nodding in recognition.

"You're laughing at me, aren't you?"

She shook her head but couldn't keep a straight face and said through the grin, "Definitely."

He hit her playfully on the arm and let his hand pause on the thin cotton of her blouse for a moment.

He put on some music jazz.

"Any word about your demo tapes?"

"The responses ain't been jim-dandy."

"It only takes one record company."

She shrugged. And glanced at an antique clock. Eight-thirty. She could smell nothing simmering. Well, scratch one: He can't cook. Maybe they were going out. But—

The door buzzer sounded.

"Excuse me."

He let a young man into the loft. He nodded politely to Taylor and, from a large shopping bag, took out plates wrapped in stippled foil. Reece set the table with bone china plates, silver and a candlestick.

The portable butler said, "Would you like me to pour the wine, Mr. Reece?"

"No, thank you anyway, Robert." Reece signed the proffered slip of paper. A bill changed hands.

"Then good night, sir."

███████

Dinner turned out to be blini with beluga caviar and sour cream, veal medallions with slivers of fresh truffles in a marsala sauce, braised endive and cold marinated green beans.

No fake burgers and sprouts for this boy...

They sat at the table and began to eat. Reece said, "Now, tell me what you've found out about the note."

Taylor organized her thoughts. "First, somebody got into the computer and erased all the disbursements, expenses and phone call logs for Saturday and Sunday."

"All of them?" He winced.

She nodded. "All last week, actually. Everything that'd link a particular person to the firm—except the door card keys and the time sheets."

"Okay." He nodded, taking this in. "Who can get into the system?"

"It's not that hard. You need an access card but it'd be

easy to steal one." More of the wonderful wine—he'd opened a second bottle. "Let me go through the suspects. First, Thom Sebastian."

He nodded. "Go ahead."

"Well, I fingerprinted your safe and found his on the top and side."

He laughed. "You did what?"

"I got a private-eye kit—deerstalker cap and decoder ring, the works. I dusted the scene of the crime and came up with twenty-five latents—that's prints, to you. Fifteen completely unrecognizable. The other ten, most were partials but seven seem to be the same person—you, I'm pretty sure. I dusted your coffee cup—I owe you a new one, by the way; the powder didn't come off too well. I threw it out."

"I wondered what happened to it."

"And three others. A couple of prints are unidentified but there are a dozen or so that're smooth smudges, as if somebody'd worn gloves. Thom's're pretty clear."

"Thom?" Reece frowned. "Son of a bitch."

She said, "I don't think he actually broke into the safe; from the position on the metal it looks like the guy who did that was the one wearing the gloves—the pro. But Sebastian may have checked it out before—or tried to open it that night and when he couldn't called in an expert. Is there any reason why he'd've been going through your files?"

"He's worked for New Amsterdam in the past though not on the Hanover & Stiver deal—not that I've *heard* about. Anyway, he'd have no business going through any-body's office without asking." He laughed and looked at her admiringly. "Fingerprints . . . That never occurred to me."

She continued, explaining to him that Sebastian had lied about how late he'd stayed at the club on Saturday night and that she'd confirmed he was in fact in the firm. She told him too about Bosk and Dennis Callaghan. How they'd talked about stealing something from the firm and how they were going to spend their money.

She asked, "You ever hear the name Callaghan in connection with the Hanover & Stiver case?"

"No." Reece shook his head. "But what about Sebastian's motive? He's risking prison just to get even with the firm?"

"Why not? The firm was his entire life. Besides, he's got a dark side to him. He was a process server in Brooklyn and Queens."

Reece nodded. "Yeah, those guys are tough."

Sebastian's implicit threat echoed in her mind again.

She said, "I think he wants revenge. But mostly I think he looks at the money Hanover'd pay him to lose the note as something the firm owes him—for not getting made partner. Think about it: He's a product of Hubbard, White—which's been training him for six or seven years to go for the throat, look only at the bottom line. He's also been checking me out."

"You?"

She nodded. "He's got a little dossier on me."

"Why?"

"Know your enemy?" She then continued, "Remember I mentioned Dudley? Well, are you ready for this?"

She told him about Junie and the West Side Art and Photography Club.

"Whoa," Reece blurted. "That little girl's a hooker? Dudley's mad. They'll put him away forever for that. Statutory rape, contributing to the delinquency."

"And it looks like he's paying a thousand bucks a week cash for her. You told me he's got money problems to start with. That's *his* motive. And as for being in the firm on Saturday I know he was there and he told Junie that some project he was working on was going to mean a lot of money. I checked his time sheets and he didn't bill any time Saturday or Sunday. So whatever he was doing at the firm then was personal. . . ."

Taylor added, "Now, we've got a third-party candidate."

"Who?"

"Sean Lillick."

"The paralegal? Hell, he's been working for me on the case—he knows all the details about the note. But what's his motive?"

"Also money. I found thousands of dollars hidden in his apartment. He didn't get it from a paralegal's salary. And he *sure* didn't make it doing that performance art crap of his."

"But he wasn't in the firm when the note was stolen, was he?"

"I'm not sure. He did come in Saturday morning, according to his key entry card. I assumed he left, because he only billed a few hours to a client. But he might've stayed all night."

Reece had a thought. "Something interesting . . . Lillick hangs around with Wendall Clayton a lot."

She nodded. She'd seen them together.

"But you know what's curious?" Reece mused. "Lillick's assigned to the litigation department. Not corporate. Why'd he be working for Clayton?"

"I don't know."

A frown on the lawyer's face. "Lillick'd be familiar with the St. Agnes files too. He might've fed Clayton some information that led him to that surprise witness from San Diego."

"You think *Clayton's* behind that?" she asked.

Reece shrugged. "St. Agnes is Donald's client and so's New Amsterdam Bank. All Clayton cares about is getting the merger through, and sabotaging Burdick's clients is a pretty efficient way to do it."

He stood, walked into the kitchen and returned with two glasses of cognac. He handed one to Taylor, the liqueur leaving thin, syrupy waves on the glass. "Tomorrow, Wendall's having a party at his Connecticut place. Why don't you come along. You might be able to find something."

"Oh, I couldn't go. I'm just a paralegal."

"It's a *firm* function; they just have it at his house. A party for the new associates, an annual thing. You can come with me."

"We shouldn't be seen together."

"We'll split up once we get inside. We'll get there late and just slip in." He tipped his glass to her. "Good job, counselor."

They clinked glasses but she must've winced a bit.

"What?"

"'Counselor.'"

"You don't like that?"

"My father's pet name for me. Fingernails on the black-board."

"Noted," he said. "I can imagine it's tough being Samuel Lockwood's child."

If you only knew, she thought, echoing the words she'd just directed to her father's phone message earlier that day.

They sipped the cognac and talked about the firm, part-ners, affairs, who was gay, who was on partnership track and who was not. She supplied most of the information and was surprised he knew so little about the gossipy side of the firm and its politics.

It was more astonishing to her that he knew so little about the merger. Although the lawyers and staffers of Hubbard, White spent more hours debating the merger than billing time for clients, Reece seemed oblivious to the whole thing. She mentioned the rumor that Clayton had a German lawyer inquire about accounts Burdick might have opened in Switzerland.

"Really?" Reece asked with what seemed unsophisti-cated surprise.

"Aren't you worried about it?" Taylor asked. "About what'll happen if Wendall wins?"

He laughed. "No. Doesn't make a bit of difference to me—as long as I can try cases, good cases, that's all I care about. Whether it's Donald in charge or Wendall or John Perelli, doesn't matter."

Together they cleared the dishes. He nodded toward the leather sofa and they walked over to it, sitting and sinking into the deep, supple piece of furniture.

There was a moment of quiet. The ticking clock. A siren far away. A distant shout.

That was when he kissed her.

And she kissed him back.

They embraced for a moment, his right hand sliding down the side of her face but coming to rest, ambiguously, at her collarbone.

His palm started downward but it stopped.

Perhaps because he sensed something coming from her—the reserve, the caution, that she in fact suddenly felt.

"Sorry," he said. "I'm impulsive and pushy. Tell me to go to hell."

"I would if I wanted to."

If you only knew...

He sat back and after a moment said, "There's something I wanted to say."

"Sure."

"It's nothing really. But it's been bugging me. Remember when I said I couldn't have lunch after the cross? Yesterday?"

"Right." She found her heart beating hard.

"I didn't have a meeting."

She pictured the three-hour lunch reference on the time sheet. The flowers.

"I went up to Westchester."

Taylor nodded, said nothing.

He continued. "There's something I don't talk about too much. My mother's in a home up there."

"Oh, I'm sorry, Mitchell."

He was stoic but she believed she could see pain somewhere behind his eyes. "Schizophrenia. It's pretty bad. I go to see her a couple times a week. Sometimes she remembers me." He smiled. "Yesterday she was pretty good. I took her some flowers and she went on and on about them for a long time."

"She's on medication?"

"Oh, yeah. And the nurses at the home are real good to her. The thing is, it's hard for me to talk about it. In fact, you're the only one I've told."

She felt a burst of pleasure at this confidence, even more than being singled out by Reece to help him find the promissory note. "I won't say anything. . . . If there's anything I can do—"

"Hey, how 'bout just a kiss to forgive me for not being honest."

She laughed and squeezed his arm. And leaned forward. Kissed him quickly.

Then eased her arms around his neck and kept kissing him.

Hard.

Where are we going with this? she wondered.

As she kissed and was kissed, as she touched and was touched, her mind counted her marriage proposals (two), the live-in boyfriends (three), the men she'd slept with (thirteen).

She thought of the ones she felt mere fondness for who'd claimed they were madly in love with her. And the flip side: the ones she'd lusted or pined for who hadn't cared she existed.

But maybe *this* time would be different, she thought. Maybe getting older, maybe simply getting by, *surviving* in this world had changed her, made her more discerning, given her better judgment.

Maybe she'd broken into a different place—that Wonderland where her father and Mitchell Reece resided. Where she was their equal.

But be careful, she thought. Remember Thom Sebastian's myth of the beautiful woman? Well, beware the myth of the absolute moment, a moment like this—when we sit, or lie, close together, muscles ticking, limbs at their most relaxed, bathed in the certainty of love. The absolute moment, when conversation soars, confidences are shared, coincidences between you and your lover pop up like crocuses in April.

The absolute moment—when we forget that most loves aren't forever, that most words are mere vibrations of insubstantial air, that most unions are a nest of comic and aching differences that no other animal in the world would tolerate, let alone desperately pursue.

She eased back slightly, wiped the war paint of lipstick off his cheek. He glanced down at her empty glass. He stood up and filled both of theirs again and returned, sat down, slouching back into the leather, playing with the top button of his shirt. His hair was mussed. He tried to brush it back but the thick comma stayed put.

"Know what?" he asked.

"What's that?"

"I'm glad."

"About what?" Taylor felt it then, that unwinding feeling within her. Despite the keen warning to herself a moment ago, the spring had been set loose.

Was it going to be good or bad? The time was coming soon, quick as a wet-leaf skid. Okay? Decide, good or bad? Decide fast, Alice; you've got about three minutes.

"I'm glad we haven't caught our thief yet. I like working with you." His voice was husky.

Reece held his glass up.

Come on, this is the moment. Now. You going, or staying? You've still got the power. It hasn't tipped yet. You can do it easy, diffuse the whole thing. Thank him for dinner. Stand up. That's all it would take.

One way or another, decide: In the end, is this good or bad?

She lifted her glass too and tapped but as he sipped, some of the cognac spilled onto the front of his shirt.

"Oh, hell," he muttered.

Come on, good or bad? Make it your decision. Choose. . . .

"Here, let me clean it up," she said.

Good or bad?

She thought that question to herself a dozen times in the space of five seconds or maybe two seconds or maybe just one but it never got answered; his mouth closed on hers and his hands—surprisingly large and strong for a bookish man—were covering her breasts and she felt the heat in his fingers as they then slid inside her dress, probing for fasteners.

Taylor in turn sought the smooth cloth of his shirt, gripped it hard and pulled him down on top of her.

Good or bad, good or bad...

███████

This Saturday night, late, Donald Burdick and Bill Stanley sat beside each other in tall-backed leather chairs and looked into the valet room of their private club on Broad Street.

It was in that room that every morning one of the club employees would iron the *New York Times, International Herald Tribune* and *Wall Street Journal* for the members. This had been a perk ever since the club had been founded in the mid-1800s. At that time, of course, when New York City boasted more than a dozen papers, the valet was busy all day long. Now, however, with no evening papers of worth, the room was used at night only for its junction box, to which telephones on long wires were connected. When a call came in these phones were carried to members; cellular phones were, of course, forbidden in the club.

Burdick and Stanley watched the poised black man, in a dinner jacket, now carrying one of these phones to Burdick, who took it with a nod of thanks.

The conversation lasted only four minutes.

Burdick absorbed the information, closed his eyes and, thinking that in Roman days the messenger would have been killed had he delivered news like this, nonetheless politely thanked the caller.

He dropped the receiver into the cradle. The valet appeared instantly and removed the phone.

"What the hell was that?" Stanley asked.

"The lease," Burdick said, shaking his head.

"Oh, no," Stanley grumbled.

Burdick nodded. "He did it. Somehow Clayton deep-sixed the lease."

The caller had been an underling of Rothstein's, the head of the real estate syndicate that owned the building where Hubbard, White & Willis was located. The syndicate had suddenly withdrawn from the negotiations for the expensive long-term lease and was going to let the current lease lapse.

This meant that it would now make much more financial sense to merge the firm with Perelli and move into the Midtown firm's space.

Damn... Burdick clenched his fist.

"*Clayton's* telling *Jews* what to do with their Manhattan real estate?" Stanley barked. There was no need to lower his voice. The only non-Protestant sect represented in the club was Papist and none of the three Catholic members was here tonight. "How the hell did he do it?"

Burdick didn't know and didn't care but, as his wife had admitted not long ago, he couldn't help but admire Clayton. He hadn't thought that the partner even *knew* about the negotiations, let alone that he could put together some bribery—or extortion—plan to sabotage the lease this quickly.

Now, with the lease gone, all Burdick had left to use as leverage was urging McMillan Holdings to take a stand against the merger.

"I'm going down to Florida tomorrow," he said.

"McMillan?" Stanley asked.

Burdick nodded. "Their board meeting. I'll do whatever I have to to make sure they let Perelli know where they stand."

"That'll help some, I guess." Then Stanley muttered something that Burdick couldn't hear.

"What was that?" the partner asked him.

"I said, 'Remember the days when all we had to do was get clients and practice law?'"

"No," Burdick replied sourly. "That must've been before my time."

CHAPTER TWENTY

 The law professor and legal philosopher Karl Llewellyn wrote a book called *The Bramble Bush*. The foliage in his title was a metaphor for the study and practice of law and his meaning was that this field, in all its many incarnations, is endless. In that book he wrote that "the only cure for law is more law," by which he was suggesting that you cannot dabble at the profession. When you are overwhelmed by the case, the business deal, the jurisprudential study, when you are exhausted, when you cannot bear the thought of proceeding one more moment, you can find salvation only by pushing forward, deeper into the tangle.

The law, he was suggesting, is an infinitely complex, uncompromising mistress.

Wendall Clayton thought of Professor Llewellyn's writing now as he sat across his desk from Randy Simms, late Sunday morning at the firm.

The smarmy young lawyer had just delivered troubling news. They had managed to sabotage the long-term lease that Burdick had been trying to put into place. But some of the old-guard partners at the firm were refusing to vote in favor

of the merger. Burdick's win in the St. Agnes trial had heartened them and a bit of cheerleading on Bill Stanley's part had
gotten them to switch their votes back to Burdick's camp.

Which meant that there was now some doubt that
Clayton would have enough votes, come Tuesday, for the
merger to be approved.

"How close is it?" Clayton asked.

"Pretty evenly balanced. Right down the middle, more
or less."

"Then we have to make it less 'pretty even.'"

"Yessir."

"Stay on call. I'll be right back." Clayton rose and walked
down the stairs to the paralegal pen.

To his surprise he found Sean Lillick was not alone.

The pretty boy was standing with a girl, another paralegal in the firm.

Clayton didn't understand what Lillick saw in her. She
seemed shy, timid, unassertive. A bit, well, rotund too.

A consolation fuck at best.

When they saw him coming they stepped apart and
Clayton noticed, though he pretended not to, that they'd
been fighting about something. The girl's eyes were red from
crying and Lillick's otherwise pasty face was flushed.

"Sean," the partner said.

The boy nodded. "Hi, Wendall."

"And you are? . . ."

"Carrie Mason."

"Ah."

"I hope I'm not interrupting anything," Clayton said.

"No. Not at all."

Carrie said quickly, "We were just talking."

"Ah. Talking. Well, if you'll excuse us, Carrie. Sean and I
have some business."

Neither of them moved. Lillick looked at the floor.
Carrie cleared her throat and said, "We've got some documents to copy. For the SCI deal."

Clayton didn't say anything. He just stared from one to
the other.

Lillick said to her, "Why don't you get started."

She hesitated then hefted an armful of papers and walked moodily down the hall on her solid legs.

Clayton said, "You'll be at my party tonight, won't you, Carrie? My place in Connecticut."

The girl looked back and said to the partner, "Yeah, I'll be there."

"I'm so pleased," the partner said, smiling.

When she'd vanished, Clayton said to the young man, "We've got some problems. About the vote. I need some information. Good information. And I need it fast. The vote's day after tomorrow."

It was, of course, the paralegals—and the support staff—who had the best access to information at the firm. As with the butlers and maids on *Upstairs, Downstairs,* the higher echelons of the firm babbled like schoolgirls in front of the hired help at Hubbard, White & Willis. This is why Clayton had swooped down on poor Lillick last year and began bribing him for information.

Lillick swallowed and looked down. "I think I've already done enough."

"You've been very helpful," the partner agreed smoothly.

"I don't want to help you anymore." He looked in the direction Carrie had disappeared.

Clayton nodded. There were times to push and times to placate. "I know it's been tough for you. But everything you've done has been for the good of everybody who works here." He rested his hand on the boy's shoulder. "We're very close, Sean, close to winning. And if we win, well, that'll be . . . rewarding for the whole firm, you included."

When the paralegal said nothing more Clayton said, "There've been some defections. I need any unusual phone calls that Burdick might've made. Travel plans. Anything like that. He's a desperate man and desperate men are his enemy's best friends. Know why? Because they make mistakes. You understand that?"

"Yessir."

"You're grasping it, you're committing it to memory?"

"Yes."

"Good. Find something and it'll be worth a lot of money. I mean five-figure money."

Clayton said nothing further but just leveled his eyes at the boy. After thirty seconds Lillick said slowly, "Let me look around. See if I can find something sort of helpful."

"Ah, wonderful," Clayton said. "Actually, though, it really has to be *very* helpful. I don't have any time left for subtleties."

███████

Every color clashed.

Taylor Lockwood looked over the apparel of the crowd milling in the living room of Wendall Clayton's country home in Redding, Connecticut. She saw plaid. She saw lemon yellow with orange. She saw lime shirts with red slacks.

She saw madras!

Her mother had told her about madras: In the ancien régime of the sixties, star-burst tie-dye marked the hippies; madras flagged the nerds.

To be fair, the collision of hues was almost exclusively on the frames of the older lawyers. The younger crowd of associates were in chinos and Izod shirts or skirts and sweaters. A lot of pearls, a lot of blond hair, a lot of pretty faces.

It was Sunday, around five-thirty, and Reece and Taylor had cruise-controlled their way here along the wide parkway in a car he'd rented. They had found Clayton's place after asking directions twice and, after they'd parked, had walked into the house without knocking. They stood, unnoticed, in the entrance foyer.

"We're overdressed," she observed.

Reece pulled his tie off and stuffed it in his pocket. "How do I look?"

"Like an overdressed lawyer who lost his tie."

He said, "I'll take the first floor. You take the second."

"Okay," she said quickly. Then she hesitated.

"What's wrong?" Reece asked.

"We're kind of like burglars, aren't we?"

He recited quickly, "Burglary is entering a dwelling without permission with the intention of committing a felony." He gave her a fast smile. "We've got permission to be here. Therefore, it's not burglary."

If you say so . . .

Reece disappeared and Taylor found the bar. The bartender was doing a big business with mugs of sweet, mint-laced Southsiders. Taylor shook her head at the offered drink and got a glass of Stag's Leap Chardonnay. Before the first sip a man was right beside her, gripping her arm.

Thom Sebastian.

She shivered, hearing in her mind's ear Sebastian's comment to Bosk, his warning not to get too interested in her, the dangers it implied.

"Hey," the pudgy associate said, "you recovered okay?"

"Recovered?"

"From a night out with me."

"Nothing to report to any official governmental bodies."

"Excellent." His eyes were evasive, almost as if he had something he wanted to confess to her. After a glance around the room he asked casually, "You doing anything tomorrow night?"

What was on his mind?

"I think I've got some time free."

"Maybe dinner?"

"Sure," she said.

"Great. I'll call you." He gazed at her, expressionless, for a moment and she believed suddenly, as she looked into his cryptic eyes, that if he *was* the thief he wanted to come clean with her.

And if he confessed and produced the note? What then? she wondered.

Reece or her father . . . well, they would, of course, destroy Sebastian's life: force him into leaving the practice of law in New York. But *her* inclination would be to reward a confession with anonymity and to let him go.

But, as she watched him walk down a corridor in search of more liquor, she realized that she was getting ahead of herself.

Find the note first, then we'll consider justice. . . .

Taylor made her way through the hallway. As she did she noticed an older woman scrutinizing her carefully, with a look of almost amused curiosity. The woman reminded her of Ada Smith, Bosk's mother. Taylor tried to avoid her but once their eyes met and held, she felt the power of a silent summons and she remained where she was as the woman approached.

"You're Taylor Lockwood," the woman said.

"Yes."

"I'm Vera Burdick, Donald's wife."

"Nice to see you," Taylor said recalling the name from the newspaper article her father had just faxed to her. They shook hands. The woman must have seen the surprise in Taylor's face—surprise that the Burdick camp would be represented in enemy territory. Vera said, "Donald had business tonight. He asked me to come in his stead."

"It's a nice party," Taylor said.

"Wendall was kind enough to donate his house for the evening. He does the same for the summer associates in July. It's a sort of fresh-air outing for lawyers."

Silence filled the small space between them.

Taylor broke the stalemate with "Well, I think I'll mingle a little."

Vera Burdick nodded, as if her examination of Taylor had produced all the information she needed. "A pleasure seeing you again, dear. And good luck."

Taylor watched the partner's wife join a cluster of associates nearby. *Good luck?* As the woman's voice rose in laughter Taylor started again for the stairs. She'd gotten halfway across the hall when she heard another voice—a man's voice, soft, directed at her. "And who are you again?"

Her neck hair bristled.

Taylor turned to look into the face of Wendall Clayton.

She was, at first, surprised that he was only a couple of inches taller than she. Then she noticed that he was much more handsome up close than he seemed from a distance.

And then her mind went blank. For three or four seconds she was utterly without a conscious thought. Clayton's eyes were the reason. They were the eyes of a man who knew how to control people, a man to whom it would be excruciating to say no, even if he made his demands with silence.

A man exactly like her father.

"Pardon?" Taylor asked.

He smiled. "I asked who you were again?"

She thought: The same person I've always been, no "again" about it, hotshot. Then she got lost in his eyes once more and didn't try a snappy comeback. She said, "Taylor Lockwood."

"I'm Wendall Clayton."

She said, "Yes, I know. I'd thank you for inviting me, Wendall, but I'm afraid I crashed. Are you going to kick me out?" She found a smile somewhere and slipped it on, reminding herself to resist the urge to call him "Mr. Clayton."

"On the contrary, you're probably the only person in this crew worth talking to."

"I don't think I'd go that far."

He took her arm. She had never been touched in this way. His grip wasn't a disciplinarian's or a friend's or a lover's. In the contraction of the muscles was a consuming pressure of authority. As if he'd squeezed her soul. After a moment he lowered his hand.

Clayton said, "Would you like a tour of the house?"

"Sure.

"It's an authentic 1780s. I—"

"Taylor! You're here!" Carrie Mason trotted up to them.

"Hello, Carrie."

"Welcome." Clayton took Carrie Mason's hard-pumping hand. "Sean's not here?"

Carrie hesitated and said, "No, he had something else to do." It seemed there was a darkness in her face.

"Ah, maybe one of his performances."

"Carrie," Taylor said, "Wendall was just going to give me a tour of his house. Join us."

"Sure," the chubby girl said.

Clayton didn't appreciate that they were now a threesome but his reaction vanished as Vera Burdick walked past.

The woman stopped and extended a hand to Clayton.

He smiled and shook it graciously, clasping hers in both of his. "Vera. How good to see you again. Donald made it, I hope."

"Unfortunately not. That fund-raiser at City Hall?"

"When the mayor summons you—" Clayton said.

"The governor actually," she corrected.

"—you better go."

Taylor felt the tension between them like sparking wires. Vera Burdick clearly detested the partner, and while Clayton obviously returned the feeling, it was she who easily held his eye and the lawyer who looked defensively away as he made trivial conversation.

In this tableau Taylor recognized a truth about Clayton: While the partner knew men and how to handle them, he was only comfortable with women he could sexualize or control as his lessers.

She was nearly queasy, observing a man like this feeling threatened—a powerful man and, considering that he might have engineered the theft of the New Amsterdam note, one who was quite dangerous.

"I'll leave you to your friends," Vera said, the disdain visible like breath on a cold spring day. A glance at Taylor and Carrie. A meaningless smile.

Clayton said, "I hope Donald enjoys the fund-raiser."

■

"Donald, you're white as snow. Damn it, man, you've got to get more fresh air. Brought your racket, I hope?"

Burdick leaned against the railing of the penthouse suite in the Fleetwood Hotel in Miami Beach and looked at the cool disk of the setting sun. "More business than pleasure today, I'm afraid, Steve."

Burdick was tired. The firm's private Canadair jet hadn't been available—some maintenance problem—and he'd had to fly down to Miami in a commercial airliner. First class, of course, but he'd still had to stand in lines and then there'd been a delay on the runway that put him an hour off schedule.

He'd arrived exhausted but had ordered the car service to bring him directly here before checking in to a room.

Steve Nordstrom, shaking martinis like an ace bartender, was the president of McMillan Holdings. He was thick and square, with gray hair trimmed so impeccably it might have been injection-molded in the company's Teterboro plant, and was wearing a purple Izod shirt and white slacks.

"Drink?"

Burdick didn't want alcohol but he knew he would take the offered glass from Nordstrom, a man of fifty, whose face was already in bloom from the damaged blood vessels.

"How's the board meeting going?" Burdick asked.

Nordstrom licked martini off his finger. He grinned happily. "We're cutting a melon this year, Donald. Three sixty-three a share."

"Ah," Burdick said approvingly.

"You read the *Journal,* you read the *Times*—everybody's cratering but us. Hey, tomorrow, we're meeting on the new industry association. You want to sit in?"

"Can't. But tell your people to watch what they say. I told you that Justice is heating up again and Antitrust is looking at price-fixing. Don't even mention dollars. No numbers at all. Remember what happened in '72."

"Always looking out for your client, Donald?" Nordstrom's question contained the silent modifiers "biggest" and "most lucrative."

They sat down at a table. The bellboy, who had been waiting patiently, brought out lobster salads in half pineapples and set them on the balcony table. The men ate the salad and raisin rolls—the lawyer struggling to down the food, which he had no appetite for—while they talked about vacations and family and house prices and the administration in Washington.

When they were finished eating, Burdick accepted another martini and pushed away from the table. "Which of our boys is down here helping you with the board meeting, Steve?"

"From Hubbard, White? Stan Johannsen is here and Thom Sebastian did most of the advance work last week. He's covering the front in New York. I understand he didn't make partner. What happened? He's a good man."

Burdick looked out over the flat scenery at a line of cars shooting flashes of glare from the expressway. After a moment he realized he had been asked a question and said, "I don't remember exactly about Thom."

He wished Bill Stanley were with him. Or Vera. He wanted allies nearby.

Nordstrom frowned. "But that's not what you're here for, is it? About the board meeting."

"No, Steve, it's not...." Burdick stood and paced, hands clasped behind his back. "Hubbard, White's been doing your legal work for, let's see, thirty-five years?"

"About that. Before my time."

"Steve, I'd ask you to keep what I'm going to tell you between you and me and Ed Gliddick. For the time being, at least. No bullshit between us."

"Never has been." The businessman looked the partner over coyly. "This's about the merger, I assume?"

"Yes. And there's more to it than meets the eye." Burdick explained to him about Clayton and his planned massacre after the merger was completed.

Nordstrom said, "So you'd be out? That's crap. You've made the firm what it is. You *are* Hubbard, White."

Burdick laughed. "I hate to put it this way, Steve, but McMillan is our largest single source of revenue."

"Well, you give us good service. And we're happy to pay for it."

"So when you or Ed talk, partners at the firm listen."

"And you want me to talk against the merger."

"It'd be bad for you and bad for dozens of other clients. Wendall Clayton has no vision of what a law firm should be. He wants to turn us into some kind of assembly line. Profit's all he thinks about."

Nordstrom picked up a fat piece of lobster and sucked it clean of dressing, then chewed and swallowed it slowly. "What's the time frame?"

"Clayton ramrodded the merger vote through early. It'll be this Tuesday."

"Day after tomorrow? Fuck me," Nordstrom said. "That man is crazy." He probed for more lobster. He settled for raisins. "Ed's in a dinner meeting right now but he should be free in an hour or so. I'll have him call and we'll have after-dinner drinks. About ten or so? By the pool over there. Don't worry, Donald. We'll work *something* out."

CHAPTER TWENTY-ONE

Clayton moved them quickly through his old manse like a tour guide goosed by a tight schedule.

It was a rambling house—big, though the rooms themselves were small and cockeyed. Beams were uneven, floorboards sprung. Much of the furniture was painted in drab Colonial colors. The gewgaws were of hammered tin and wicker and carved wood.

He led them upstairs. Taylor pretended to be studying portraits of horses, Shaker furniture and armoires while in fact she looked for places where he might have hidden information about Hanover & Stiver or the note. She glanced into a small room that seemed to be an office and saw a desk.

"Are you with us, Taylor?" Clayton asked and she hurried to join them. He continued the tour. "...Mark Twain's house, the house he died in, isn't far from here."

"Are you a Son of the American Revolution?" Carrie asked.

Clayton spoke with a feigned indignity that rested on real pride. "The Revolutionaries? They were *newcomers*. My family was one of the original settlers of Nieuw Nederlandt. We came over in 1628."

"Are you Dutch?"

"No. My ancestors were Huguenots."

Taylor said, "I always got those mixed up in school—the Huguenots and the Hottentots."

Clayton smiled coldly.

Ooooh, doesn't like potshots into the family tree.

"The Huguenots were French Protestants," he explained. "They were badly persecuted. In the 1620s Cardinal Richelieu ordered a siege of La Rochelle, a large Huguenot town. My family escaped and settled here. New Rochelle, New York, by the way, is named after La Rochelle."

Carrie asked, "What did your ancestors do when they got here?"

"There was considerable prejudice against the Huguenots, even here. We were barred from many businesses. My family became artisans. Silversmiths mostly. Paul Revere was one of us. But my family were always better merchants than craftsmen. . . . We moved into manufacturing and then finance though that field had largely been preempted by . . . other groups." For a moment he looked wily and Taylor suspected he was suppressing an opinion about early Jewish settlers.

"My family," he continued, "ended up in Manhattan and stayed there. Upper East Side. I was born within a five-block radius of my father's and grandfather's birthplaces."

That touched Taylor. "You don't see that much anymore. Today, everybody's spread all over the world."

"You shouldn't let that happen," Clayton said sincerely. "Your family history is all you have. You should keep your ancestry and be proud of it. This year I'm steward of the French Society. . . ."

Carrie, of the front row in law school, blinked. "Oh, I've heard of that. Sure."

Clayton said to Taylor, "After the Holland Society it's the most prestigious of the hereditary societies in New York."

The chubby paralegal was impressed but another need intruded. "Say, Mr. Clayton, where's the little girls' room?"

Oh, honey, don't fail me now. . . . Taylor wanted Carrie to keep Clayton busy, giving her a chance to take a look in the office.

But he said, "We've been having problems with the one up here. Why don't you go downstairs. We'll meet you there in a bit."

Carrie trotted off, and it was then that Taylor realized they had ended the tour at Clayton's bedroom. The room was dramatic, filled with Ralph Lauren rust and red florals, English-hunt green, brass. This was the room of a nobleman.

Beware the Jabberwock, my son. . . .

Clayton closed the door. "You're very attractive."

Taylor sighed. Doesn't go much for subtlety, does he? She said, "I should be getting downstairs."

He took her hand. To her astonishment she let him and the next thing she knew some undefinable pressure overwhelmed her. She found herself sitting on the bed next to him.

"Wendall . . ."

"Look at me."

Taylor did, feeling a growing power from the partner, a magnet tugging at her soul—and at everything around her. It seemed to Taylor that her hair actually stirred in this invisible wind.

She thought of the playing-card soldiers swirling around Alice. *Beware the . . .*

"Wendall—"

"I want to tell you one thing," he said calmly. "This has to be completely clear. Whatever happens—or doesn't happen—has no affect on your career at Hubbard, White. Is that understood?"

She pulled her arm away. "I don't even know you. I've never even spoken to you before." But she was shocked to hear that her words seemed weak, as if she were wavering.

He shrugged. "Spoken to me? I don't want to have a discussion. I want to make love to you."

There was no physical impediment to her leaving. He wasn't even standing in her way. One foot, then the other, and she could troop right out the door. Yet she didn't.

Clayton crossed his legs. He brushed the tassel of his hair off his forehead.

"I have commitments," she explained.

No, no, no . . . Don't say that. You're meeting his argument. It's like making excuses to your father. Tell him to fuck off. Forget who he is. Forget the case. Just say it now: Fuck off. Fuck. Off.

Say it!

"Well, Taylor, we all have commitments. That's not really the issue."

She felt her throat thicken.

Don't swallow. It's a weakness.

She swallowed. "We don't even know each other."

Clayton smiled, shaking his head. "Hey, look, I don't want to marry you. I want to make love to you. That's all. Two adults. I'm telling you that you're an attractive woman."

"I have to go."

"It's not a compliment," he continued. "It's an observation. I know how to make love to women. I'm good at it. Don't you find me attractive?"

"That's not the point—"

"So you do?" he said quickly. He stroked the bed and repeated, "I want to make love with you. Harmless and simple."

Taylor smiled. "You don't want to make love at all. You want to fuck me."

"No!" he whispered harshly. Then he smiled. "I want us to fuck *together.*"

Mistake, girl. He likes dirty talk.

"Look." He waved his hand in front of his crotch like a magician. He was erect. "You did this. Not everybody does."

She found herself leaning back, first her palms on the rich bedspread, then her elbows.

"Do you know the first thing I noticed about you?" Clayton whispered, touching a renegade strand of her hair. "Your eyes. Even from across the room."

She rolled onto her side. She glanced down between his legs and said, "You're a pretty gifted man, Wendall. I would have thought that with all the excitement at the firm you'd be more distracted."

He hesitated then asked, " 'Excitement'?"

"The merger."

He didn't move for a moment. She'd thrown him off stride. He laughed seductively. "I've got a pretty big appetite."

Taylor scanned his face, which was no more than twelve inches from hers. "I read somewhere that hunters make love before the hunt," she said. "Sex is supposed to steady the hand." She shook her head. "Me, I think it's dissipating."

"Ah, dissipate me, dissipate me. . . ." But the words fell short of their intended playfulness and he sounded like a college boy making an inappropriate joke. And suddenly the balance of this contest shifted—barely—to her.

He whispered, "Lie down, put your head on the pillow." He spoke in a mesmerizing voice and Taylor was suddenly aware of his penis pressing through layers of cloth against her leg. Clayton said, "I have some toys."

"Do you?"

"I can make you feel very, very good. Like you've never felt before."

She laughed and more power slipped to her side of the board. When the spell wasn't working, his lines began to sound silly. She asked, "Why do you hate Donald Burdick?"

"I'm not interested in talking about him. Or about the merger."

"Why not?"

"I'd rather make love to you."

"The merger is all everybody's talking about."

"Are you worried about your job? You won't have to be. I promise you that," he said.

"I haven't worried about a job for years. I'm mostly just curious why you dislike Donald Burdick so much."

She sat up. Clayton seemed befuddled. The evidence of his passion hadn't diminished but he seemed uncertain—as if he had met and overcome all types of reluctance in seducing women over the years yet had suddenly run into a new defense: a barrage of questions.

"Go on," she said. "Tell me why."

"Well," Clayton finally offered, "I don't dislike Donald personally. He's one of the most charming men I know. Socially, I admire him. He's a fine representative of old money."

"The rumor is that you want to destroy him."

Clayton considered his answer. "I hear lots of rumors at the firm. I suspect those that I hear aren't any more accurate than the ones you hear. The merger is solely business. Destroying people is far too time-consuming. . . ."

Finally the partner's spell broke completely.

Taylor Lockwood rolled off the bed and ran her fingers through her hair. "You should go downstairs, I think. You are the host, after all."

Clayton tried one last time. "But . . ." His hand strayed across the bulging front of his slacks.

"You know, Wendall," Taylor said, smiling, "that's the best compliment I've had in months. Does a girl's heart good. But if you'll excuse me."

███████

After leaving the bedroom Taylor walked into the upstairs bathroom (which, she noticed, seemed to be in perfect working order). There she waited until Clayton was out of sight. Then she slipped into his office.

Inside, in addition to the desk, were an armchair, a Victorian tea serving table, several floor lamps, two large armoires; there were no closets. She turned on a lamp and pushed the door partially closed.

The desk was unlocked. Its cubbyholes were filled with hundreds of slips of paper. Bank statements, canceled checks, memos, notes, personal bills, receipts. Taylor sighed at the volume of material she'd have to look through then sat in the red-leather chair and started going through the items one by one.

She'd been doing this for fifteen minutes when she heard a voice in the doorway say, "Ah, here you are...."

The man speaking was Wendall Clayton.

CHAPTER TWENTY-TWO

 Taylor spun around and stood up, knocking a stack of papers to the floor. The sheets spread like spilled water.

Wendall Clayton was outside the door, talking to someone else. Just out of his line of sight, she reached toward the papers then heard Clayton say, "Let's go inside here for a minute, shall we?"

Desperately she kicked the papers under the desk; they disappeared—except for the corner of one letter. She reached down for it but the door was swinging open. Taylor leapt behind the largest armoire. She pressed herself flat against the wall, her head pressing painfully into the hard, cold plaster. Another voice spoke. A man's voice, one she recognized. Ralph Dudley asked, "What is it exactly you wanted to see me about, Wendall?"

The door closed. Clayton said, "Have a seat."

"Is something wrong?"

Clayton's voice was curious. "I don't remember this light being on."

Taylor eased back harder against the wall.

Silence. What were they doing? Could they see the tips of her shoes, the corner of the paper under the desk? Was the chair she'd sat in still warm?

Clayton said, "Ralph, you're part of, I guess I'd call it, the old guard, the old-boy network at the firm."

"I go back a ways, that's true."

"You and Donald started at about the same time, didn't you?"

"Bill Stanley, too. And Lamar Fredericks."

"I see you at the DAC with Joe Wilkins and Porter quite a bit, don't I?"

"Yes, we go there often. What do you—"

"Enjoying yourself tonight, are you?"

"Quite, Wendall." The old partner's voice was filled with anxiety as Clayton asked these pleasant questions with a slightly sadistic edge.

Silence. Feet shifting.

Clayton continued. "Young people here tonight. Lots of young people. It's funny, isn't it, Ralph? When I was their age I was making . . . fifty, seventy-five dollars a week. These youngsters make ninety thousand dollars a year. Amazing."

"Wendall, is there something you want?"

"Ralph, I want you to vote in favor of the merger on Tuesday. That's what I want."

A long pause. The old man's voice was trembling when he said, "I can't, Wendall. You know that. If the merger goes through I lose my job. Donald loses his; a lot of people do."

"You'll be well provided for, Ralph. A good severance."

"I can't. I can't afford to retire."

"No, of course not. You've got expenses."

Dudley sounded very cautious now. "That's right. It costs a lot to live here."

"Manhattan . . . most expensive city on earth."

"I'm sorry, Wendall. I'll have to say no to the merger."

Silence again. Taylor imagined Dudley's thoughts racing to catch up with Clayton's. Taylor's, however, had already arrived at their sad destination.

"You don't mind blunt talk?" Clayton asked.

"Of course not. I appreciate candor and—"

"If you don't vote in favor of the merger I'll go public with your affair with a sixteen-year-old girl."

The choked laugh didn't mask the despair. "What are you talking about?"

"Ralph, I respect your intelligence; I hope you'll respect mine. The little whore, the one you dress up and parade around as your granddaughter, which makes it all the more disgusting. You—"

Taylor heard the slap of a blow, a laugh of surprise from Clayton, feet dancing in the awkward shuffle of wrestling. Finally: a sad, desperate groan from Dudley—a sound filled with pain and hate and hopelessness.

Clayton laughed again. "Really, Ralph...Are you all right? There, sit down now. Are you hurt?"

"Don't touch me," Dudley said, his voice cracking. The sounds of the older man's sobbing echoed softly in the room.

Clayton said patiently, "Let's not be emotional. There's no reason for me to tell anyone. Let's negotiate a little bit. You're the firm's charmer, aren't you? You're suave, debonaire. You're a holdout from the days when a lawyer's manners were as important as his intelligence. So, now, how's this? You and three of your cronies switch your votes in favor of the merger and I won't share your secret."

"Three others?"

"Say, Joe, Porter, pick somebody else. But—here's the good part—you bring me any *more* and I'll kick in fifty thousand each to your severance package. That should keep you in teenage pussy for another year or so."

"You're vile," Dudley spat out.

"More vile than you?" Clayton asked. "I wonder. The vote's day after tomorrow, Ralph. Why don't you think about it." Clayton's was the voice of luxurious moderation. "Just think about it. It's your decision. Come on, go downstairs, have a drink. Relax."

"If you only understood—"

Clayton's voice cut through the room like a knife. "Oh, but that's the point, Ralph. I can't understand. And no one else will either."

The door opened. Two pairs of feet receded. Both slowly. One pair in triumph, one in despair, but the sound they made was the same.

███████

Still in the quiet den Taylor was concentrating on a single noise.

Rhythmic and soft.

She had stayed here, hiding behind the armoire, after the partners had left because Clayton had remained upstairs; she'd heard his voice from nearby.

Then after five minutes or so the sound began. What is that?

A voice chanting? Primitive music?

She couldn't place it at first. It seemed very familiar but she associated it with an entirely different place.

Rhythmic and soft.

No, couldn't be. . . .

She walked to the far wall and pressed her head against the plaster again. The sound was coming from the other side—Clayton's bedroom.

Oh, Taylor realized. *That's* the sound. Of course. Not one voice, but two.

The nature of the activity didn't surprise Taylor much, considering what she now knew about Wendall Clayton. What did surprise her, however, was that the other participant was Carrie Mason, who was contributing half of the sound effects.

"Fuck me, fuck me, fuck me. . . . I'm almost there. . . . Yeah, yeah, yeah. . . ."

Carrie may have finished quickly but it took Clayton considerably longer. Long enough, in fact, for Taylor to go through the partner's desk carefully. The sound track conveniently helped her gauge how much time she had.

She found only one thing that interested her: an invoice

for a security firm. The bill was for ongoing services, which had begun last month. The job description was "As directed by client."

She debated stealing it. What would her detective friend John Silbert Hemming do? He'd use a spy camera, she guessed. But ill-equipped Taylor Lockwood did the next best thing: She carefully copied all the information and put the invoice back.

Downstairs she noticed the crowd had dwindled considerably, as you'd expect for a Sunday night party. Only the hard-core partyers remained. Thom Sebastian, for instance, who swooped in for another sloppy bear hug. She ducked away from it. He said good-bye and reiterated his dinner invitation for tomorrow. Taylor ambled through the house, aiming toward the buffet and listening to the snatches of muted, often drunken, conversation.

He's going to do it. For sure. Next month, we're going to be Hubbard, White, Willis, Sullivan & Perelli.

You're out to lunch, dude. No way'll Burdick let it happen.

Do you realize the vote is Tuesday? Day after tomorrow.

You hear about the detective that was going through Burdick's Swiss accounts?

You hear Burdick had somebody check Clayton's law review article to see if he plagiarized?

That's bullshit.

You want to talk bullshit, this merger is bullshit. Nobody's getting any work done.

Where's Donald?

He doesn't need to be here. He sent Himmler instead.

Who?

His wife. See, Burdick would charm a man out of his balls; Vera'd just cut 'em off. You know the stories about her, don't you? Lady Macbeth . . .

Taylor noticed that Burdick's wife was no longer here.

She then surveyed the long table where there'd once sat mounds of caviar, roast beef, steak tartare and sesame chicken. All that now remained was broccoli.

Taylor Lockwood hated broccoli.

On the patio deck of the Fleetwood Hotel's penthouse on the Miami Beach strip Ed Gliddick sent a golf ball near the putting cup embedded in the roof's AstroTurf.

"Hell," he said of the miss and looked at the trim young man near him, who watched the shot without emotion. Standing ramrod-straight, he offered Gliddick no false compliments and said only, "I play tennis, not golf."

The man was Randall Simms III, Wendall Clayton's protégé. It was he who'd pirated the Hubbard, White & Willis chartered jet to beat Donald Burdick down to Florida to meet with the executives of McMillan Holdings.

While Burdick himself was cooling his heels with the second-in-command of the company, Steve Nordstrom, Simms had been meeting with Gliddick, the chairman of the board and CEO of McMillan.

McMillan was a company that did nothing but own other companies, which either manufactured obscure industrial parts or provided necessary though obscure services to other businesses or in turn owned other companies or portions of them. The vagaries of this structure and function, however, were not to suggest that Gliddick didn't know how to satisfy a market need when he saw one. McMillan was consistently in the top twenty of the most profitable companies in the world.

At sixty-five, Gliddick was stooped and paunchy amidships. His ruddy skin was wrinkled from years of sun on golf courses and tennis courts around the world. Sparse gray hair, a hook of a nose.

So he said to Simms, "Wendall didn't come down to see me. He sent you instead."

Simms said nothing.

Gliddick held up a hand. "Which means only one thing. You're the muscle, right?"

Unsmiling, Simms folded his arms and watched Gliddick miss another easy putt. "Wendall wanted a little distance between himself and what I'm going to say to you."

"This's all about that fucking merger, isn't it?"

"I'd suggest we go inside," Simms said. "Somebody could have an antenna trained on us. They really make those things, you know. They're not just in the movies."

"I know."

Gliddick walked into the room, shut the window and drew the curtains. Simms mixed whiskey sours for them both. Gliddick wondered how this man, whom he'd never met, had known that this was his drink.

The chairman sipped the sweet concoction. "You know Donald Burdick's meeting with Steve Nordstrom right now."

"We know."

We.

"So what is it that you want, I mean, Wendall wants?"

"We want you to let it be known around the firms—ours and John Perelli's—that you want the merger to go through."

"Why would we *not* want it to go through?"

Simms said bluntly, "Donald and his cronies won't be there afterward."

"Ah." Gliddick nodded. "I see."

"You might feel some loyalty to him," Simms said.

"Fuck, I do feel loyalty to him."

"Of course you do. You've been friends for years. But putting that aside for a moment, let's talk about why you *would* want the firms to merge," Simms said.

This is one slick boy—I like him, Gliddick thought, but immediately gave up the idea of trying to wrest him away from Hubbard, White to work for McMillan. Wendall Clayton was not somebody you stole employees from.

Simms continued, "We've gone over your billings, Ed. Burdick's robbing you blind. Your legal costs are totally out of control. You're paying two hundred bucks an hour for first-year associates who know shit. You're paying for limo deliveries when messengers can take public transportation. You're paying premium bonuses for routine legal work. If you help the merger along we'll pare your expenses by an easy five million a year."

"Five?"

"Five. And if the merger goes through, Perelli can take over your labor law work. Right now you've got Mavern, Simpson handling it and, frankly, they're idiots. They didn't do shit to keep the unions out of your subs' Oregon and Washington State operations. Perelli's the toughest labor lawyer in New York. He'll fuck your unions in the ass."

Gliddick shook his head. "Donald was on our board for I don't know how long. He's got friends all over the company. There're a lot of people won't take it kindly that we've sold him out."

"'Kindly'?" Simms said the word as if it were in a foreign language. "Well, loyalty's important. But it works both ways. I'd think you'd have to *earn* loyalty. And do you think a lawyer who misses a takeover plan against his client deserves it?"

"A . . . What're you talking about?"

"There's a rumor. . . . Only a rumor but Wendall and I think it's valid."

"We're always hearing that. Hell, we beat projections every quarter last year. Everybody'd love to acquire us."

"But does everybody contact your institutional investors on the sly?"

Gliddick's glass froze halfway to his mouth. "Who?"

"GCI in Toronto."

"Weinraub, that fucking Jew prick." A glance to Simms to see if the young man was Semitic but the results of the scan came back reassuringly Aryan. "I saw him just last week in London. He gave me the great stone face."

Simms continued, "We're thinking four months till a tender offer. If you wait you'll pay a takeover firm a million or two to defend. Perelli can preempt it for a quarter of that. And he can handle it in a way that your stockholders and key employees won't get nervous and bail out. That's what he does best."

"Donald doesn't know about it?"

"Nope. We found out through Perelli.

He finished his drink. Simms poured another.

"Randy, I don't know. I can't argue with what you're say-ing, with the numbers. It's a moral decision. I don't like moral decisions. Maybe—"

There was a knock on the door. A young woman. Blond, about five-two, wearing a short leather miniskirt and tight white blouse, walked into the suite.

"Mr. Simms, I've got the file you asked for."

"Thank you, Jean." He took a thick manila folder. "Jean, this is Mr. Gliddick."

They shook hands. Gliddick's eyes skimmed the white silk over her breasts, the lacy bra clearly visible beneath.

"Jean's an assistant with a firm we use down here occa-sionally."

"Nice to meet you, Jean."

Simms tapped the folder. "There's a lot of other material in there about how the merger'd be good for your company, Ed." He looked at his watch. "Say, I've got a conference call scheduled now. I'll make it from my room so I don't bother you. Look over that stuff, think about what I'm saying."

"Sure," Gliddick said, eyes still scanning Jean's figure. She smiled broadly at the paunchy businessman.

"Say, Jean," Simms said, "you know Miami, right?

"Well, now, I've lived here all my life" came the lilting accent.

"Then maybe you could help Mr. Gliddick figure out a place where he and I could go listen to some music. Jazz or Cuban or something."

"I'd be happy to." The young woman sat on the bed and picked up an entertainment guide. Her skirt hiked up high. "If that's all right with him."

"I'd appreciate your input," Gliddick said.

Simms said, "We're off-duty now, Jean, how 'bout you fix yourself a drink. And another one for Mr. Gliddick too."

"Thanks, Randy. I believe I will."

"I'll be back in about an hour," Simms said.

"That'd be fine," Gliddick replied, setting the file on the table and watching Jean scoot pertly off the bed and walk to the bar. Somehow her shoes had come off in the process.

Moral decision...

As Simms was about to step through the door, Gliddick said, "One thing, Randy?"

The tall lawyer turned.

"Maybe you could call first—before coming back to the room?"

"Not a problem, Ed."

At 10 P.M., as Reece was accelerating south onto the highway that would take them from Clayton's Connecticut home back to the city, Taylor stretched out in the reclining seat of the rented Lincoln.

She was listening to the moan of the transmission. The flabby suspension swayed her nearly to sleep. She'd told him about Clayton's blackmailing Dudley and then about the invoice she'd found.

"'Client-directed' security services?" Reece asked. Then he nodded. "A euphemism for industrial espionage. Good job, finding that. How much was it for?"

"Two thousand a month."

"That's pretty low for stealing a note. Maybe it's for spying on people for the merger."

"Did you hear the talk at the party? My God, these are first-year associates and all they were talking about was the merger. Wendall's out on a limb. If he doesn't get it through he's lost a lot of credibility...."

Reece laughed. "Ha, if he doesn't get the merger through he's lost his *job*...." He looked over and caught her in the midst of another huge yawn. "You okay?"

"I used to sleep."

"I tried it once," Reece said, shrugging. "It wears off."

He reached over and began massaging her neck.

"Oh, that's nice...." She closed her eyes. "You ever made love in a car?"

"Never have."

"I never have either. I've never even been to a drive-in movie."

Reece said, "One time when I was in high school, I— Jesus!"

A huge jolt. Taylor's eyes snapped open and she saw a white car directly in front of them. It'd veered into their lane. Reece swerved onto the shoulder but the Lincoln slipped off the flat surface and started down a steep embankment.

"Mitchell!" Taylor screamed and threw her arms up as trees and plants raced at them at seventy miles an hour. The undercarriage scraping and groaning, metal and plastic supports popping apart. Then brush and reeds were flashing past the car's windows.

Reece called, "That car, that car! He ran us off the road! He ran us—"

He was braking, trying to grip the wheel as it spun furiously back and forth, the front tires buffeted by rocks and branches. The car slowed as it chewed through the underbrush, the buff-colored rushes and weeds whipping into the windshield.

Taylor's head slammed against the window; she was stunned. She felt nausea and fear and a huge pain in her back.

Then they were slowing as the slope flattened out. The car was still skewing but the wheels started to track, coming under control. . . . She heard Reece say reverently, "Son of a bitch," and saw him smile as the car started a slow skid on the slippery vegetation. Thirty miles an hour, twenty-five . . .

"Okay, okay . . .," Reece muttered to himself. He steered carefully into the skids, braking lightly, regaining control, losing and then regaining it. "Okay, come on," he whispered seductively to the huge Lincoln.

The car slowed to ten miles an hour. Taylor took his arm and whispered, "Oh, Mitchell." They smiled at each other, giddy with relief.

But as she looked at his face his smile vanished.

"God!" He shoved his foot onto the brake with all his weight. Taylor looked forward and she saw the brush disappear as they broke out of the foliage and dropped over a ridge, onto a steep incline that led down to the huge reservoir, a half mile across, its surface broken with choppy waves. The locked wheels slid without resistance along the frost and dewy leaves.

"Taylor!" he called. "We're going in, we're going in!"

With a last huge rocking jolt, the scenery and the distant gray horizon disappeared. A wave of black oily water crashed into the windshield and started coming into the car from a dozen places at once.

CHAPTER TWENTY-THREE

At eleven that night, in Miami, the phone in Donald Burdick's hotel room rang.

The partner had been waiting for Ed Gliddick all evening and had fallen asleep, fully dressed, on the couch in his room.

"Yes, hello?" he asked groggily.

"Mr. Burdick?" a woman's voice asked.

"That's right. Who's this?"

"My name's Jean. I'm calling for Mr. Gliddick."

Jean? Burdick wondered. Who was this? Ed Gliddick had had the same secretary, Helen, for twenty years and never traveled anywhere without her.

"Yes, Jean, well, I've been waiting to see Ed all night. Is he all right?"

"Mr. Gliddick asked me to call you and apologize. He won't be able to see you, I'm afraid."

Burdick was angry and disappointed but he said, "Well, it's late anyway. We can meet for breakfast. I'll—"

"Actually, sir, I'm afraid he won't be able to see you at all this trip. He's got meetings nonstop for the next two days and then he's got to get home to Battle Creek."

Burdick closed his eyes and sighed. So, ambushed by Clayton yet again.

"I see. By any chance was there another attorney from Hubbard, White & Willis in town tonight?"

"I wouldn't know, sir."

"Okay," Burdick said wearily, realizing it would be pointless to call Steve Nordstrom—the coward wouldn't even pick up the phone. "If you could deliver a message to Ed for me."

"I'd be happy to."

" 'And you too, Brutus?' Do you have that?"

"Uhm, I do, sir. Will he know what it means?"

"I'm sure he will." Burdick dropped the phone in the cradle then picked it up once more to call his wife.

███

In front of them the huge reservoir extended in faintly lapping waves to the trees on the opposite shore. The moon reflected off the water, broken into a thousand crescents on the textured surface. It would've been quite romantic if they hadn't been wet and freezing.

Taylor Lockwood and Reece sat in the front seat of the rental Lincoln, legs crossed to keep their feet out of the six inches of water that filled the bottom of the car's interior.

After the skid to the bottom of the hill, with its dramatic conclusion—a braking splash like a Disneyland ride—the Lincoln had settled into about eighteen inches of water and stopped sinking.

The reservoir was huge but here, apparently, very shallow.

They'd laughed—edgy and a bit hysterical—but then the humor wore off quickly when they realized that while they could open the door, they'd have a thirty- or forty-foot trek through freezing water up to a deserted road, where they'd have to wait for help with no way to keep warm.

Reece called the police on his cell phone and then they curled their legs up and huddled in their coats.

The dispatcher had assured them that a squad car and rescue truck would be there in ten minutes. But that had been some time ago and, since Reece had been unable to tell them exactly where they'd run off the road, he guessed their rescue might not be imminent even now.

"Who was it?" Taylor asked.

"The thief, I assume. I didn't get a good look at him. Middle-aged guy, white, hat, collar turned up. I didn't even see what kind of car it was. Just a white streak."

"An accident?"

"No way," Reece answered. "He was steering for us."

"Who was at the party—who'd know we were there?"

Reece shrugged. "Thom Sebastian, Dudley. And most of Clayton's little goose-stepping clones, except Randy Simms." Then he fell silent for a moment, finally saying, "I'm thinking it's time to tell the police what happened. Tell them everything."

"No." She shook her head.

"I didn't think this was going to happen, Taylor. I never thought it could turn violent."

She said, "It wouldn't make sense to kill us. That'd bring the police in for sure, and he doesn't want that any more than we do. He didn't know we'd go off the road. He was just scaring us."

Reece considered.

Taylor scooted closer to him. "We're almost there. I can feel it. The trial's day after tomorrow. Let's just hold out until then." She took his head in both her hands. "Just until then?"

"I don't know."

But he was weakening. She repeated, "Just until then," though when she said the words this time, they were not spoken as a question but as a command. He opened his mouth to protest, but she shook her head and touched his lips with her finger.

He leaned close, following the motion of her finger to

her own lips. They kissed hard and their arms wound around each other.

A moment later this embrace was interrupted by several probing flashlights, their fierce halogen beams converging on the car. As Reece and Taylor leapt apart they could hear a laugh and an amused voice. "Whoa, lookit that car! Looks like it's floating. Hank, lookit! I mean, you ever seen anything like that?"

To which another voice replied, "I surely haven't. Not in a month of Sundays."

███████

At lunch on Monday, the day before the New Amsterdam trial, Taylor Lockwood sat in Mc Sorley's Old Ale House in Manhattan and watched John Silbert Hemming down a mug of ale.

He may not've been the traditional private eye who tossed back Scotch on the job but this boy loved his beer. The tall man finished his sixth mug of dark brew and called for three more. "They're small."

True, they were, though Taylor was having trouble with her second. She'd drunk more wine than she'd intended at Clayton's and had not gotten much sleep, thanks to the dip in the reservoir—and Reece's presence in bed next to her.

She told Hemming about the Supreme Court case that required the pub to allow women in; for many years it had been a men-only establishment.

"Some achievement," Hemming muttered, looking at the carved-up bare wood tables, the wishbone collection growing a dark fur of dust and the crowds of young frat boys shouting and hooting. He glowered at a drunk, beer-spilling student stumbling toward them. The boy caught the huge man's gaze and changed direction quickly. With some true curiosity in his voice the detective asked Taylor, "Are we having a date?"

"I don't think so."

"Ah," he said and nodded. "How did the fingerprints work out?"

"Not bad. I'll send you a postcard."

"If you want I'll show you how to do plantars."

"Vegetable prints?"

"Very good but no—feet, Ms. Lockwood."

"Taylor."

"Feet."

Taylor handed him the piece of paper with the information from the invoice she'd found in Wendall Clayton's desk. "John, have you ever heard of this company?"

He read, "Triple A Security? They're not around New York. But we can assume it's a sleazy outfit."

"Why's that?"

"It's an old trick to get in the front of the phone book— to have your listing first. Name your company with a lot of A's. You want me to check it out?"

"Can you?"

"Sure." A waiter carrying fifteen mugs in one hand swooped past and dropped two more, unasked-for.

"Would somebody from a security service—say, this disreputable Triple A outfit—commit a crime?"

"Jaywalking?"

"Worse."

"Stealing apples?"

"That category. More valuable than fruit."

He sat up and towered over her for an instant then hunched forward again. "At the big security firms, like our place, absolutely not. You commit a crime, you lose your license and your surety bond's invalidated. But these small outfits"—he tapped the paper—"there's a fine line between the good guys and the bad guys. I mean, somebody's got to *plant* the bugs that my company finds, right? And planting bugs is illegal."

"Any funny stuff?"

"That's not a term of art in my profession."

"Say, hypothetically, trying to run somebody off the road."

"Run somebody off . . ."

Taylor whispered, " . . . the road."

Hemming hesitated a moment and said, "This sort of

place—Triple A Security—yeah, you could possibly find somebody there who might be willing to do that. Worse too."

Taylor finished the bitter dark ale. She opened her purse, pulled out a twenty and signaled the waiter.

"Is there a Mr. Lockwood?" Hemming asked.

"Yes, but you wouldn't really like my father."

"Well, anything in the fiancé-boyfriend category. You know, those pesky fellows that tend to get there first?"

"Not exactly."

John Silbert Hemming said, "How about dinner?"

"Can't."

"I was going to let *you* take *me* out so you could deduct it."

She laughed and said, "I've got plans for the immediate future."

"Plans are what contractors and shipbuilders use."

"Some other time?" she asked. "I mean it."

"Sure," Hemming said. Then, as she started to stand, he held up a finger, which returned her to her seat. "One thing...there's this friend I have. He wears a badge and works at a place called One Police Plaza and I was thinking maybe it's time you gave him a call. Just to have a chat."

Taylor replayed the drive through the foliage down to the reservoir last night and thought Hemming's was an excellent idea.

But she answered, "No."

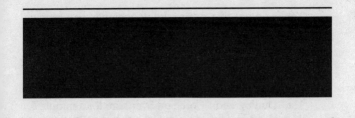

CHAPTER TWENTY-FOUR

They walked together through Battery Park.

Ralph Dudley's eyes were on the Statue of Liberty, rising from the harbor like a sister of the figure of blind justice. Junie walked silently beside him. He wanted to hold her hand but of course he did not. Like tourists, they were on their way to see the monument up close.

Dudley wondered how many people Junie's age knew the lines carved on the base of the statue, knew they were from a poem called "The New Colossus" by Emma Lazarus.

> *Give me your tired, your poor,*
> *Your huddled masses, yearning to breathe free,*
> *The wretched refuse of your teeming shore....*

Hardly any.

But, he also wondered, how many Wall Street lawyers knew it?

Not many of them either.

"Is it, like, cold on the boat?"

"You're saying 'like' again a lot. Remember, you were going to watch it."

"Whatever."

"I'm sure we can sit downstairs where it's warm. We'll get some hot chocolate."

"Or a beer," she muttered.

"Ha," Dudley said. "Come on over here for a minute."

He nodded to a bench and they sat down, Dudley wondering, as he had for a thousand times that year, why he was so taken with this little creature.

"Yo, so wassup?" she said. Sometimes she talked black and there was nothing he could say to get her out of this mode. He'd learned that it was best to ignore her affectations. They went away sooner or later.

"I've got some papers here. For you to sign. We couldn't do it in the firm."

She put her Walkman headsets on. He took them off her and smoothed her hair. She wrinkled her face.

"You've got to sign them."

"Like, okay."

He dug them out of his briefcase and handed them to her.

"Okay," she said, snapping her gum. "Gimme a pen."

Dudley reached into his jacket pocket and found that he'd accidentally picked up his Cross mechanical pencil. "Damn, I forgot mine."

"I, like, have one." She reached into her purse and pulled it out. But as she did a piece of paper fell to the ground. Dudley had picked it up and started to hand it back when he looked at the check.

He saw Junie's name.

He saw Taylor Lockwood's name.

His hand froze in midair between them.

Dudley looked at her with rage in his face. "What is this? I—"

"What the hell have you done?"

"Poppie?" she asked, dropping her Walkman. It broke apart on the asphalt.

"How could you?" he whispered. "How could you?"

The going rate to get Alice into the rabbit hole of a Manhattan apartment was a sob story.

I feel so stupid, Ralph Dudley's my uncle? And my aunt— that's his wife—passed away two years ago today and he was feeling really lousy. I wanted to make him dinner, just to cheer him up.

She held up the Food Emporium bag as evidence.

Here's fifty for your trouble. Don't say anything, okay? It's a surprise.

Taylor Lockwood had dressed in her business finest, to allay the doorman's concerns. He looked her over, pocketed the money, slipped her a spare key and turned back to a tiny television.

She knew Dudley wouldn't be here. She'd run into him in the halls and he'd told her that he was taking the afternoon off to show Junie the Statue of Liberty. The sullen girl had been in the lobby, waiting for him. Taylor shivered at the thought of the two of them together. For the girl's part, she looked from Dudley's face to Taylor's and back again. And just seemed bored.

Taylor now walked inside and found that Dudley's apartment was much smaller and more modest than she'd expected.

Although she knew about his financial problems, she'd assumed that an elderly Wall Street law firm partner like Dudley would be living at least in simple elegance, jaded though it might be. In fact, the four rooms in the prewar building didn't not have much more square footage than her own apartment. The walls were covered with cheap paint, which blotched where it was thin and peeled where the painters had bothered to apply several coats. There was no way the windows would ever open again.

She gave a cursory once-over to the living room, which was filled with old furniture, some of whose tattered, cracked arms and legs were tied together neatly with twine. She saw chipped vases, lace that had been torn and carelessly

resewn, books, afghans, walking sticks, a collection of
dented silver cigarette cases. Walls were covered with old
framed pictures of relatives, including several of Dudley as a
young man with a large, unfriendly-looking woman. He was
handsome but very thin and he stared at the camera with
solemn introspection.

In his bedroom, beside a neatly made bed, she found
what looked like a wooden torso with one of Dudley's suit
jackets hanging on the shoulders. A clothes brush rested on
a small rack on the torso's chest and on the floor in front of it
was a pair of carefully polished shoes with well-worn heels.

His fussiness made her job as burglar easy. Each of the
pigeonholes in his oak rolltop desk contained a single, well-
marked category of documents. Con Ed bills, phone bills,
letters from his daughter (the least-filled compartment),
business correspondence, warranty cards for household ap-
pliances, letters from his alumni organization, receipts. He
separated opera programs from symphony programs from
ballet programs.

Taylor finished the desk in ten minutes but could find
nothing linking Dudley to the note or to Hanover & Stiver.
Discouraged and feeling hot and filthy from the search, she
walked into the kitchen, illuminated with pallid light from the
courtyard that the room's one small window looked out on.

Taylor leaned against the sink. In front of her was
Dudley's small kitchen table, on either side of which were
two mahogany chairs. One side of the table was empty. On
the other was a faded place mat on which sat an expensive,
nicked porcelain plate, a setting of heavy silverware, a wineglass—all arranged for his solitary dinner that evening. A
starched white napkin, rolled and held by a bright red napkin ring, rested in the center of the plate. The gaudy ring was
the one item glaringly out of place. Taylor picked up the
cheap plastic, the kind sold at the bargain stores in Times
Square where tourists buy personalized souvenirs—cups,
dishes, tiny license plates.

She turned it over; the name sloppily embossed in the
plastic was *Poppie*.

A present from June, the object of his perverse desire.

Her hour was up. Book on outta here, Alice....

Nothing, she thought angrily. I didn't find a thing. Not a single hint as to where the note might be. She stuffed the grocery bag, which had been filled only with wadded-up newspapers, into the trash chute and left.

So, can we eliminate Dudley? she wondered.

No, but we can put him lower on the list than Thom Sebastian.

Well, don't get too interested in her....

She'd charm the young lawyer, interrogate him—the prick who'd been collecting information on her. She remembered his troubled expression yesterday. Maybe a confession *would* be forthcoming at dinner tonight. She still held out that hope.

Outside, she paused for a moment, rubbed her eyes.

Tomorrow, she thought in alarm, the trial was tomorrow.

Taylor stepped into the street to flag down a cab.

Thom Sebastian sat at the bar of the Blue Devil on the far edge of West Fifty-seventh, near the Hudson River.

An excellent place, he assessed, it had a mostly black audience, dressed super-sharp. He was working on a vodka gimlet, imagining his juggler and thinking, So far, so good.

But also thinking *goddamn,* I'm nervous.

He was considering what was about to happen tonight.

Was this a way-major mistake?

For a while he'd thought so. But now he wasn't so sure. Had no idea.

But it *was* going to happen; the die had been cast, he thought, phrasing the situation in a cliché that he found unworthy of a lawyer of his caliber.

He found himself coolly considering partnership at Hubbard, White & Willis and he remembered—almost with amusement—that he'd always considered achieving partnership a matter of life and death.

Death...

After Wendall Clayton had called him into his office and told him in that soft voice of his that the firm had concluded it would be unable to extend the offer of partnership to him, Sebastian had sat motionless for three or four minutes, smiling at the partner, listening to the man describe the firm's plans for Sebastian's severance.

A smile, yes, but it was really a rictus gaze, what to Clayton—had the fucking prick even noticed—must have seemed like a grin of madness: teeth bared, eyes crinkling in a psychotic squint.

"We'd like to make you a partner, Thom—you're respected here—but you understand that economies have to be effected."

Meaning simply that Sebastian was not a clone of Wendall Clayton and was, therefore, expendable.

Effecting economies... Oh, how that term—pure corporatespeak—had inflamed him like acid.

Listening to Clayton, he'd lowered his head and had seen something resting on the partner's desk: an inlaid dish of Arabic design. Sebastian's eyes had clung to the dish as if he could encapsulate the terrible reality in the cloisonné and escape, leaving his sorrow trapped behind him.

And now he thought about the problem of Taylor Lockwood.

But he tried as hard as he could to push her away, put her out of his mind, and replaced her with the image of the juggler once more.

He glanced at his watch.

Okay, let's do it. He stood up from the bar, told the bartender he'd be back in five.

So far...

■

Without really thinking about it, the man in the Dodge reached over to the passenger seat and felt the breakdown—a Remington automatic 12-gauge shotgun.

Six shells in the extended magazine. Six more wedged into the seat, business end down.

He wasn't concentrating on the hardware, though; his eyes were on the woman walking down the street toward the fat boy, Thom Sebastian, who waved at her, smiling a weird smile. Looking all shit-his-pants.

All right, so this bitch was the one.

The man in the Dodge watched her, wondering what kind of body she had underneath the overcoat. He would've liked it if she'd been wearing high heels. He liked high heels, not those stupid black flat shoes this broad wore.

The man in the Dodge checked for blue-and-whites and pedestrians who might block the shot.

Clear street, clear shooting zone.

He eased the car forward then braked slowly to a halt twenty feet from the woman. She glanced at him with casual curiosity. Her eyes met his and, as he lifted the gun, she realized what was going down. She screamed, holding up her hands.

Nowhere for her to run . . .

He aimed over the bead sight and pulled the trigger. The huge recoil stunned his shoulder. He had a fast image of the woman as she took one load of buckshot in the side, a glancing hit. He fired two more toward her back but the way she fell, it seemed that only one cluster struck her and even that wasn't a square hit.

Well, if she wasn't dead yet she probably would be soon. And at the very worst she'd be out of commission for months.

People screamed and horns wailed as cars screeched to a halt, avoiding the pedestrians who dived into the street for safety.

The man in the Dodge accelerated fast to the next intersection, skidded through the red then slowed and, once out of sight of the hit, drove carefully uptown, well within the speed limit, diligently stopping at every red light he came to.

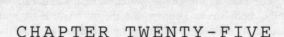

CHAPTER TWENTY-FIVE

Thom Sebastian, hands cuffed, was led into the precinct house by two uniformed cops.

Everybody stared at him—the cops, the drunk drivers, the hookers, a lawyer or two.

"Man," somebody whispered.

It was the blood, which covered Sebastian's jacket and white shirt. Nobody could figure out how somebody could be covered with this much blood and not have a dozen stab wounds.

The chubby lawyer slumped on a bench, waiting for the booking officer to get around to him, staring at his brown wing tips. A girl sat next to him, a tall black hooker with a tank top and hot pants under her fake fur coat. She looked at the blood then shook her head quickly, a shiver.

"Jesus," she whispered.

Sebastian felt a shadow over him; someone walking close. He looked up and blinked.

Taylor Lockwood said, "Are you all right? The blood . . ."

Sebastian nodded then closed his eyes and lowered his head again slowly. "Nosebleed," he muttered.

The desk sergeant said gruffly to her, "Who're you?"

Taylor said, "What happened?"

He looked over her black nylons, short black skirt and leather jacket. "Get outta here, lady. He's missin' his date for the night."

A bit of her father's temper popped within her. "And I'm making the trip down here to meet with my client. So I guess I'm missing mine too. Anything else you'd like to put on the record?"

The man's face reddened. "Hey, I didn't know you was a lawyer."

She had no idea what had happened. She'd shown up at the restaurant and found a crime scene investigation under way. Somebody'd been shot and Sebastian had been arrested.

She barked, "What's he been booked on?"

"Nothing yet. The arresting's on the phone to the medical examiner." He turned back to a mass of papers.

Man, that was a lot of blood.

A uniformed officer came up, a thin man, slicked-back hair, gray at the temples. He looked over Taylor and was not pleased. His would be a joint prejudice: against defense lawyers in general (who spent hours tormenting cops on the witness stand and reducing them to little piles of incompetence) and women defense lawyers in particular (who had to prove they could torment more brutally than their male counterparts).

Taylor Lockwood cocked her head and tried to look like a ballbuster. "I'm Mr. Sebastian's lawyer. What's going on?"

Suddenly a roar of a voice filled the station house. "Hey, Taylor!"

She froze. Oh, brother—why now? It was one of those moments when the gods get bored and decide to skewer you just for the fun of it. Taylor gave an inaudible sigh and turned toward the voice, now booming again, "Taylor Lockwood, right?"

A huge cop, a faceful of burst vessels, tan from a vacation in Vegas or the Bahamas, stalked across the room. He was off-duty, wearing designer jeans and a windbreaker. Early forties, thirty pounds overweight. Trim, razor-cut blond hair. A boyish face.

There was nothing to do, she decided, but go all the way. Her father's advice: If you're going to bluff, bluff like there's no tomorrow.

"Hey," she said, smiling.

"It's Tommy Blond. Don'tcha remember? Tommy Bianca, from the Pogiolli case."

"Sure, Tommy. How you doing?" She took his massive, callused hand.

The man was looking down at Sebastian. "He okay?"

"Nosebleed is all," the arresting said. "We thought he'd taken one, too. EMS looked him over, said he'll be okay, he keeps an eye on his nostrils."

Tommy Blond looked at the arresting and the desk sergeant. "Hey, treat this lady right. She's okay. She was working with the lawyer got off Joey, youse remember—Joey Pogiolli from the Sixth? Got him off last year some asshole sued him, said Joey worked him over on a bust. . . . Hey, Taylor, you was a paralegal then. What, you go to law school?"

"Nights," Taylor said, grinning and wondering if the nervous sweat that had gathered on her forehead would start running down to her chin and carrying her makeup with it.

"That's great. My kid's applying to Brooklyn. Wants to be FBI. I told him agents don't got to have law degrees anymore but he wants to do it right. Maybe sometime he could talk to you about school? Got a card?"

"None with me. Sorry."

She glanced at Sebastian, staring at the floor.

Tommy Blond said, "Whatsa story, Frank?"

The arresting said, "We got a vic got took out outside the Blue Devil, name of Magaly Sanchez. Upscale coke dealer moving into the wrong territory. We think whoever did her wasn't sure what she looked like and was using him"—he nodded toward Sebastian—"to ID the hit. Or maybe they wanted to whack her in front of a customer. Send a message, you know. She had about ten grams on her, all packaged and ready for delivery. And Mr. Sebastian had a quarter gram.... That's why we brought him in."

Taylor rolled her eyes. "A quarter gram? Come on, you guys."

"Taylor, I know what you're asking...." Tommy Blond said, then: "That's a lot of blood. You're sure it's just a nose-bleed?"

She remembered a buzzword. "What was your probable cause for search?"

"Probable cause?" The arresting blinked in surprise. "He was waving at a known drug dealer who got whacked right in front of him? That's not probable cause—that's for-damn-fucking-sure cause."

"Let's talk." She walked over to the bulletin board. Tommy Blond and the arresting looked at each other and then followed her. She stood with her head down and whispered harshly to the arresting, "Come on, he's never been arrested before. Sure, the guy's an asshole, but a quarter gram? You and I both know a collar like that's optional."

Taylor was making this up.

The arresting: "I don't know.... Everybody's pissed off about these assholes from Wall Street think they can buy and sell blow and we're not going to do anything about it."

"Let's cut a deal," Taylor continued. "Tell you what. Give him back to me and he'll give you a statement about the late Miss Sanchez and her friends—as long as it's anonymous and he never has to testify in court against anybody. And I'll make him promise to get off the stuff."

"Whatta you say?" Tommy Blond said to the uniformed officer.

"Look," Taylor pushed, "he works for the same firm got your buddy Joey off. That oughta count for something."

Joey, Taylor remembered, was the patrolman who maybe *did* get a little carried away with his nightstick on that black kid who maybe lifted a wallet but maybe didn't. And who maybe reached for that tire iron, even though, funny thing, it was found twenty feet away from the scuffle. Took the ER fifty-eight stitches to repair Officer Joey's handiwork on the kid's face.

The arresting gave Taylor a look that's shorthand in law enforcement. It translates to: I don't need this shit.

"Okay, get him out of here. But tell him to clean up his act. I mean, like really. Next time they won't leave *nobody* around. Have him down to Narcotics at the Plaza next week and give 'em a statement." He wrote a name on a card. "Ask for this detective here."

Taylor said, "Thanks, gentlemen."

Tommy Blond shook her hand again. "Proud of you, little lady. A lawyer. That's all right." He walked off toward the locker room.

Taylor walked back to Sebastian, who'd been slumped in his seat, out of earshot of the bargaining. He didn't yet know he was free.

She knelt down next to him, looked at the blood on his face and shirt. It was quite brilliant. She said, "Thom, I may be able to help you out. But I've got to ask you something. I need an honest answer. . . . Look at me."

Boy's eyes. Indignant, hurt, scared boy's eyes.

"You went through Mitchell Reece's file cabinet sometime recently. Why?"

A furrow ran through his bloody forehead as he frowned. He sniffed. "What are you talking about?"

Taylor said brutally, "Fuck it, Thom, I can get you out of here or I can make sure they book you. That'll be the end of your life in New York. Now, it's your call."

He wiped tears from his cheeks. "Mitchell does trial work for New Amsterdam. I handle a lot of their corporate work. I probably needed some files he had."

"You've been in his safe file?"

Sebastian frowned again. "That thing he's got in his office with the locks on it? Yeah, a few months ago I got some files out of it, some settlement agreements from a secured-loan suit a couple of years ago. I needed them. It wasn't locked and Reece was out of town on business. What's this all about?"

"You know New Amsterdam pretty well?"

"What's this—"

"Answer me," she snapped.

"Know them?" He wiped his face with a tissue and looked at the blood. He laughed bitterly. "I've worked for them for years! I baby-sit them! I hold their hands and walk them through the deals. While Burdick's collecting their fucking check *I'm* the grunt doing all the work for them. While Fred LaDue takes 'em out to dinner and plays tennis with them *I'm* the one who's up till three A.M. doing the documents. *I'm* their lawyer." He sighed. "Yeah, I know them pretty well."

Taylor looked into his eyes and she believed him. But she persisted. "You were in the firm on Saturday night, a week ago. You lied to me about it. You snuck in through the back door."

"How did you know that?" he asked. But his voice faded as he noticed her gaze grow cold again. "I'm sorry. Yeah, I was there. I did lie . . . but I had to. Look, when I got passed over for partner I decided to start my own firm. That's what Bosk and I're doing. Dennis Callaghan's doing the real estate for us, brokering some office space downtown. I just don't want anybody at Hubbard, White to know yet. That's why I lied."

"Prove it."

Numb, he pulled out his cell phone and placed a call. "Dennis? It's Thom. I'm putting somebody on the line. Tell her exactly what you're doing for Bosk and me."

She took the phone and said simply, "Go ahead."

Callaghan hesitated a moment then told her the same thing Sebastian had. "Okay, thanks." She disconnected and handed Sebastian back the phone.

"Why'd you get all that information about me? The stuff under your desk blotter."

Another blink. Another dip of the head. "You showed

up in my life all of a sudden. You were just *there* and I didn't know why. You were ... interesting. I liked you. I was trying to find out about you. That's what I do—I'm a lawyer. That's how I work."

She looked over the miserable fat boy and knew he was innocent. He glanced at her once but had to look away quickly as if he were frightened by what he saw.

An odd feeling swept through her. Her face burned; she felt queasy. And she understood that for the first time in her life she'd done what her father would have done, what Mitchell Reece would have done: She'd been brutal in victory.

Power.

That was what she sensed. Sebastian, defeated in front of her, bloody and fearful as a child, was hers. The cops were hers. The sensation was exhilarating.

"Can you tell me what's going on?" he asked.

"No," she replied firmly. "I can't." She stood up. He looked uneasily at the cops.

"It's okay," she said. "You can go home."

"I can—"

"You can leave. It's all right."

Sebastian rose to his feet slowly and she took his arm to steady him. They started toward the door.

The hooker watched them leave and said cynically, "My, my, this be some justice system we got ourselves. Anybody gotta ciggie?"

███

Late Monday evening—the merger vote a mere fifteen hours away—Wendall Clayton sat in a conference room across across from John Perelli.

Fatigue had settled on Clayton like a wet coat. But, unlike Perelli, Clayton had not loosened his tie or rolled up the sleeves of his white, Sea Island cotton shirt. He sat the way he had been sitting for the past four hours: upright, only occasionally lowering his head to rub his bloodshot eyes or to stretch.

Beside him sat Randy Simms and another of Clayton's young partners. Perelli too had several of his lieutenants here.

Simms and the other young man were on the executive committee of Hubbard, White. Burdick had rallied hard to keep them off but Clayton had maneuvered their elections through, though Burdick had retained control. Before them were drafts of a document, the merger agreement, spread out like a patient under a surgeon's careful eyes.

Clayton glanced outside the door at a young woman, a secretary from a freelance legal services staffing firm. The woman knew every major word processing system in the United States, could take dictation and could keyboard 110 words a minute. These skills were fetching her forty-two dollars an hour though at the moment she was being paid that fee solely to sip coffee and read a battered paperback called *Surrender, My Love*.

He wondered if he'd still have the energy to fuck her in an hour or two, after the final negotiations were completed. Clayton thought it might be dicey; he was utterly exhausted.

Perelli wore half-rim glasses, low on his nose. He looked up and stared into Clayton's eyes. "I should tell you—my people aren't happy about your demand. About ousting Burdick. Even with the giveback."

"What're you saying?" Clayton asked coolly.

"He could sue. Older man, EEOC. He could make a mess."

"We're lawyers. Our job is to make messes go away."

"We'd prefer to keep him for a while. Say, a year. Phase him out."

Clayton laughed. "You don't phase people like Donald Burdick out. Either he's in charge or he's gone completely. That's his nature."

Perelli pulled off his glasses and rubbed the bridge of his nose.

The gesture explained that there'd been considerable rebellion in the ranks at Perelli's firm over Burdick. And Clayton knew that he had to act immediately.

"If you want Hubbard, White—Burdick has to go," he continued casually. He gestured in an aristocratic way toward the window, outside of which Wall Street at night glistened. "If you want Burdick, John, go find yourself another firm."

"You'd walk?"

"And not look back."

Perelli's assistants shifted uncertainly in their chairs.

A moment passed and not a cell in Wendall Clayton's face revealed the electric tension he felt.

Finally Perelli laughed. "Goddamn, you and I're going to make some serious fucking money together." He and Clayton shook hands with finality.

Perelli stood and stretched. "You going to use a special pen to sign the merger agreement, Wendall? Like the President does?"

"No, I'll just use this old thing."

He displayed a battered Parker fountain pen, one he had used for years. Not long after Clayton had started at Hubbard, White he found himself at a closing without a pen. Donald Burdick had shot him a gruff glance and slid this very pen to him. "You should always be prepared, Wendall. Keep that one as a reminder."

Wendall Clayton put the pen away and helped the other men organize the documents while he dictated instructions for the copying and assembly of the execution copies to the *Surrender, My Love* woman. After the firm approved the merger tomorrow, these papers would be brought into the large conference room for the signing of the agreement with Perelli's partners itself. Since so many people had to sign, the logistics of closing the deal were massive.

A half hour later, walking back toward his office, Clayton stopped and turned quickly, aware of someone approaching fast from down a dark corridor.

The person was making right for him.

For a moment he actually thought that Donald Burdick had lost his mind and was about to assault him.

But, no, it was Sean Lillick.

The red-eyed paralegal raged at Clayton. "You fucked her! You son of a bitch!"

"Quiet, you little shit!" Clayton whispered. John Perelli hadn't left yet.

"You fucked her!"

"Who?"

"Carrie Mason."

Clayton regarded the young man with some amusement. "And?"

"How could you do it?"

"Last time I looked, Sean, that girl was over eighteen and unattached." He lifted an eyebrow. "Was she wearing your Art Carved engagement ring? A tasteful but small solitaire? I didn't notice one."

"I don't want your fucking sarcasm, Wendall."

So, the puppy has some teeth. He'd never seen them bared before.

"Calm down, Sean. What the hell is she to you? She's a fat little inbred preppy and you're the point man of the avant-garde. Capulets and Montagues. You have nothing in common except gonads engorged by your differences."

"How could you treat her like that?"

"I treated her very well. Besides, the word 'consensual' comes to mind."

"She was drunk. She thinks you used her."

"She's an adult. What she thinks is her business. Not yours or mine." Clayton glanced back toward the conference room. He lowered his face and asked, "What? Did you think you two were going to move to Locust Valley and have babies? For God's sake, Sean. You're not crazy. Go find some girl with a crew cut, pierced labia and dirty fingernails."

"I hate you."

"No you don't, Sean. But even if you did your hatred is irrelevant. What is relevant is that you need me. Now, the merger vote's tomorrow and I don't have time for this. Learn a lesson, son: If somebody fucks your girlfriend the question isn't who did it and how can I get even—it's *why* did she want to? Think about that."

The boy fell silent.

Clayton could still see the anger and bitterness in his face. In a calmer tone he said, "It happened once. She was drunk, I was drunk. I have no intention of ever seeing her again." This was as close to a sincere apology as Wendall Clayton would ever come.

Lillick seemed to realize this. He wasn't pleased but Clayton saw that he'd pulled the rug out from underneath his rage.

"I'll tell her," Clayton joked, "what a wonderful human being you are."

"I—"

Clayton held up an finger. He said, "Tomorrow, early— in my office? We've got a big day tomorrow. We've got a thousand documents to get ready. The phalanxes will be marching through Rome."

CHAPTER TWENTY-SIX

North of Fourteenth Street, where Taylor Lock-wood had risen from the hot, pungent subway on her way to Mitchell Reece's, the broad sidewalks were sparse.

After she'd put Thom Sebastian into a cab Taylor had returned to her apartment, changed and was now on her way to report to Reece that one suspect had been eliminated—but that she still had no clue where the note might be, the note that he'd need in court tomorrow morning, a little over twelve hours from now.

She zigged around patches of ice, remembering how her music teacher taught her to think of footsteps as musical beats. As she walked she'd break the spaces between the tap of the steps into half notes, quarter notes, eighths, triplets, dotted quarters and eighths, whispering the rhythms.

One two and uh three four . . .

A noise behind her, footsteps on the gritty concrete.

She turned quickly but saw no one.

A block farther. Now the streets were completely deserted. This area, Chelsea, near Sixth Avenue, contained some residential lofts and cavernous restaurants. But this particular street was the home of professional photographers, printers, warehouses and Korean importers. At night it was empty, a gloomy, dark, functional place, and she felt another chill of uneasiness.

One and two and three and—

Suddenly the scenery vanished as the arm went around her chest and a hand clamped over her mouth.

She screamed.

The man started to drag her into the alley.

Goddamn, no . . .

She struggled to free herself but managed only to force her attacker to fall, still clutching her fiercely around the neck. They landed on some boxes and tumbled to the slick cobblestones. The man ended up on top of her and knocked the breath from her body. Choking, gasping, she threw her hands over her face, unable to call for help.

The man rose to his knees. Taylor took this chance to twist away, smelling rotting bean sprouts and chicken bones and garlic from restaurant trash. She saw a fist rise up, about to come plunging down toward her face.

But anger detonated within her and, still breathless, she pushed hard with her legs, slamming into the man's hip and knocking him against a wall. Taylor grabbed the first thing she could find as a weapon—a piece of jagged concrete—and staggered to her feet, about to swing the sharp stone.

Her hand paused as she heard the man's sobbing. The raspy voice wheezed between the sobs. "Why, why, why? . . ."

"You!" she whispered.

Ralph Dudley wiped his face and stared at her at her in raw hatred. He didn't pay any attention to the rock in her hand. He stiffly rose, walked to an overturned trash drum and sat on it, gasping for breath. "Why did you do it?"

"Are you out of your mind?" She pitched the rock away and began brushing her coat off, rubbing at the oil and grease stains. "Look at this! Are you crazy?"

The old partner stared blankly at the ground. "I followed you from your apartment. I don't know what I wanted to do. I actually thought about killing you."

"What are you talking about?"

"You followed me. You bribed my ... You bribed Junie to find out about me. Then I asked an associate if he'd seen you in my office and he said you had."

Taylor shrugged. "You lied to me, Ralph. You lied about being in the firm a week ago Saturday."

"So?" He smoothed his mussed hair, examined his damaged coat.

"What were you doing in the firm?"

"It's not any of your business."

"Maybe not. But maybe it is. What were you doing?"

"I love that girl."

Taylor said nothing.

"She makes me feel so alive. I hate it that she's in that business. She does too, I know she does. But she doesn't have any choice."

In her mind she saw the cheap red plastic napkin ring. *Poppie...*

Taylor's fear had changed into pity. The desires to flee, to slap him, to put her hand on his shoulder and comfort him were balanced.

He lifted his head; the cold light, shining down from above, hit his narrow face and made him look deranged and cadaverous. He started to speak then lowered his face into his hands. A dozen cars crashed over a pothole in the street next to them before he spoke. "Why did you do it?"

"Do what, Ralph?"

"Tell Wendall Clayton about us."

"I didn't tell Clayton anything."

"Somebody..." He wiped his face again. "Somebody told him."

"Oh, please..." Taylor laughed. "That law firm is like Machiavelli's villa. Everybody's got spies."

"But why did you go to the West Side Club? Why did you follow me?"

"There are problems at the firm. I needed to know where some people were at a certain time. I got the feeling you were lying to me so I followed you after dinner. Now, tell me what you were doing at the firm."

He shook his head.

Just as she had with the cop who'd arrested Sebastian, Taylor now lowered her head and said, "Ralph, I can put you in jail for a long time—because of that girl. And I'll do it if you don't cooperate. No bullshit. Tell me what you were doing in the firm."

The look of hatred in his face chilled her but he finally said, "Junie's father died two years ago and left her some money. But her mother and stepfather're keeping it all tied up. They're trying to get it for themselves. I've been spending every weekend and half my nights at the firm, learning trusts and estates and fiduciary law. I'm going to get the money back for her." He wiped tears. "I couldn't tell anybody at the firm because they'd find out she's not my granddaughter and then . . . they might find out the real situation. Besides, I've borrowed against my partnership draw so much the firm'd fire me if they knew I was spending my time on a project that wasn't making Hubbard, White any money."

He looked up, wretched and lost. "I'm really not a very good lawyer. I can charm people, I can entertain clients . . . but this is the only real law I've done in years."

"Prove it to me."

He said stiffly, "I don't think I owe you anything more."

Once again the same dark power she'd felt before filled Taylor Lockwood's heart and she whispered harshly, "Prove it to me or I go to the cops."

A wounded animal, Dudley hesitated. Then he glanced down, opened his briefcase. Shoved it toward her.

She knew little about trusts and estates law but it was clear that these documents—petitions to the Surrogate's Court, copies of cases and correspondence—bore out what he'd told her.

"You were in the firm early Sunday morning after Thanksgiving."

"Yes" he answered as if he were a witness under cross-examination.

"You used Thom Sebastian's key?"

"Yes. I didn't want anybody to know I was in that night. I got there about one-thirty. After I'd been to the West Side Club."

She asked, "Where *were* you in the firm?"

"Just the library and my office. The rest room. The canteen—for some coffee."

"Did you see anyone else there?"

Dudley rocked slowly back and forth on the trash can, under the rain of harsh streetlight. His breath popped out in small puffs as he worried the tear in his coat. "As a matter of fact," he answered, "I did."

———

The loft door was open. She paused in the hallway, seeing the trapezoid of ashen light fall into the corridor. Taylor felt a jab of panic. In a burst of frightening memory she remembered the white car driving them off the road and, though at the time she believed the thief had intended only to scare them, she thought for an instant that the man had come back and killed Mitchell. She ran to the door and pushed inside.

He was lying on the couch, wearing blue jeans and a wrinkled dress shirt. His hair was mussed and his arms lolled at his sides. His eyes stared unmoving at the ceiling.

"Mitchell?" she asked. "Are you all right?

He turned on his side slowly and looked at her. A faint smile. "Must've dozed off."

Taylor crouched next to him and took his hand. "I thought . . . you were hurt or something."

She felt the slight pressure of his hand on hers. He looked at her jacket and jeans. "What happened to you?"

Taylor laughed. "Little wrestling match."

"Are you all right?"

"You should see the other guy." Then she said, "I know who the thief is."

"What?" His eyes returned to life. "Who?"

"Wendall Clayton."

"How do you know?"

"I eliminated Thom and Dudley." She told him about Sebastian's adventure with the police and the old partner's attack on her. Then she said, "Clayton let the thief in that night."

"But he wasn't in the firm," Reece said.

"Yes he was. Dudley saw him. And Clayton's key entry didn't show up because he got to the firm on *Friday.*"

Reece nodded, eyes closing at the obvious answer. "Of course. He was there all weekend, working on the merger. He didn't leave until Sunday. He stayed two nights. Must've slept on the couch. I should've thought about that."

Taylor continued. "I just went back to the firm and checked his time sheets. We would've seen that he'd ordered food in and made phone calls and photocopies but all those records were erased, remember?"

Reece's smile faded. "That doesn't mean he stole the note though."

"But Dudley told me something else. About three-thirty or four on Sunday morning he saw this man, like a janitor, walking through the firm with an envelope. Dudley thought it was odd that he was carrying something like that. He noticed he went into Clayton's office with the envelope but came out without it. Dudley didn't say anything to him—or to anyone else about him—because he was working on something unrelated to firm business.

"I talked to my private detective. He said there is a Triple A Security—the receipt I found in Wendall's desk— and he checked the grapevine. It's in Florida. He said they're a firm that has a reputation for doing labor work. Which he tells me is a euphemism for rough stuff, like stealing documents and bugging offices and even driving people off the road. That's who Dudley saw. Clayton let him into the firm and he stole the note after you went home."

Reece said, "And you think the note's in that envelope?"

"I think so. Like you said, he probably hid it in a stack

of documents in his office. I'm going to search it. Only we have to wait. He was still at his desk when I left the firm and it didn't look like he was going to leave anytime soon. I'll go back to the firm and wait till he leaves for the night."

"Taylor ... What can I say?" He hugged her, hard, and she threw her arms around him. Their hands began coursing up and down each other's backs and suddenly it was as if all the compressed tension they'd felt over the past week had been converted into a very different kind of energy ... and now suddenly erupted.

The room vanished into motion: his arms around her, under her legs, sweeping her up. Reece carried her to the huge dining room table and lay her upon it, books falling, papers sailing off onto the floor. He eased her down onto the tabletop, her blouse and skirt spiraling off and away, his own clothes flying in a wider trajectory. He was already hard. He pressed his mouth down on hers, their teeth met and he worked down her neck, biting. Pulling hard on her nipples, her stomach, her thighs. She tried to rise up to him but he held her captive, her butt and leg cut by the sharp corners of a law book: The pain added to the hunger.

Then he was on top of her, his full weight on her chest, as his hands curled around the small of her back and tugged her toward him. She was completely immobile, her breath forced out of her lungs by his demanding strokes.

Taylor felt a similar hunger and she dug her nails into his solid back, her teeth clenched in a salivating lust for the pain it was causing.

They moved like this for minutes, or hours—she had no idea. Finally she screamed as she shuddered, her toes curling, her head bouncing against the table. He finished a moment later and collapsed against her.

Taylor lifted her hands. Two nails were bloody. She shoved the law book out from underneath her; it fell with a resonant thud. She closed her eyes and they remained locked this way for a long time.

She dozed briefly.

When she awoke a half hour later she found that Reece

was at his desk, dressed only in a shirt, scribbling notes, reading cases. She watched his back for a moment then walked to him, kissed the top of his head.

He turned and pressed his head against her breasts.

"It's up to you now," he said. "I'm going to proceed with the case as if we can't find the note." He nodded at the papers surrounding him. "But I'll hope for the best."

At three in the morning, wearing her cat burglar outfit of Levi's and a black blouse, Taylor Lockwood walked into Hubbard, White & Willis.

Her black Sportsac contained a pair of kidskin gloves, a set of screwdrivers, a pair of pliers, a hammer. The firm seemed empty but she moved through the corridors in complete quiet, pausing in darkened conference rooms, listening for voices or footsteps.

Nothing.

Finally she made it to Wendall Clayton's office and began her search.

By four-thirty, she'd covered most of it and found no sign of the note. But there were still two tall stacks of documents, on the floor beside his credenza, that she hadn't looked through yet.

She continued searching. She finished one and found nothing. She started on the second one.

Which was when jaunty footsteps sounded on the marble floor in the corridor nearby and Wendall Clayton's voice boomed to someone, "The merger vote's in six hours. I need those fucking documents now!"

CHAPTER TWENTY-SEVEN

He didn't truly live anywhere but here.

In murky, echoing rotundas of courthouses like this.

In marble corridors lit by milky sunlight filtering through fifty-year-old grimy windows, in oak hallways smelling of bitter paper from libraries and file rooms.

At counsel tables like the one at which he now sat.

Mitchell Reece studied the courtroom around him, where the opening volley in *New Amsterdam Bank & Trust, Ltd. v. Hanover & Stiver, Inc.* would be fired in a short while. He studied the vaulted ceilings, the austere jury box and a judge's bench reminiscent of a conning tower on a warship, the dusty flag, the pictures of stern nineteenth-century judges. The room was unlit at the moment. There was a scuffed, well-worn aspect to the place; it reminded him of old subway cars. Well, that was appropriate; after all, justice was just another service provided by government to its citizens, like public transportation and trash collection.

He sat for a few minutes but grew restless; he stood suddenly and began to pace.

And what, he speculated, would happen if Taylor *didn't* find the note?

He supposed he could find alternatives. But because Mitchell Reece was so very driven, because he was someone who, as Taylor had once said, had left behind reason and logic and even safety in this mad sojourn, he felt a fierce desperation to find that tiny piece of paper.

He wanted to win this one oh-so-badly.

He rose and walked to the soiled window, through which he watched men and women hurrying along Centre Street: attorneys and judges and clients. Everyone was wearing a suit but making the distinction among them was easy. Lawyers carried big litigation bags, clients carried briefcases and judges carried nothing.

He wandered to the judge's bench then to the jury gallery.

Theater.

Winning is about theater, he reflected.

The revelation had come to him early in his career—he was representing a young boy blinded in one eye when a lawn mower fired a rock out of the grass chute and into the child's face. The boy's father had used a hacksaw to cut off the safety deflector panel, believing the motor labored harder with the deflector in place and used more gas. Reece sued the manufacturer, claiming that the unit was defective because there was no warning that users should *not* cut the panel off.

It was understood by virtually everyone that—because the proximate cause of the injury was the father's removal of the device—Reece had absolutely no chance of winning. The bored judge knew this, as did the arrogant lawyer for the defendant and the complacent lawyer for the defendant's insurance company.

Seven people did *not* know the impossibility of the suit, however. One was Mitchell Reece. The others were the six members of the jury, who awarded the snotty, self-pitying little kid one point seven million bucks.

Theater.

That was the key to litigation: a dab of logic, a bit of law, a lot of personality, and considerable theater.

He glanced at the door to the courtroom, willing it to open and Taylor Lockwood to hurry inside, the note in hand.

But of course it remained closed.

After he'd heard nothing more from her after she left to go to the firm at 3 A.M. He'd gotten a few hours' sleep, shaved and showered then dressed in his finest litigation Armani. He'd gathered his documents, called the clients to have them meet him at the courthouse then limoed downtown, where he slipped into the cavernous domed cathedral of New York State Supreme Court.

Well, the matter was out of his hands, he now reflected. Either Taylor would find it and life would move in one direction, or she would not and an entirely different set of consequences would occur.

Mitchell Reece had not prayed for perhaps thirty years but today he addressed a short message to a vague deity, whom he pictured looking somewhat like blind Justice, and asked that she keep Taylor Lockwood safe and to please, please let her find the note.

You've done so much, Taylor; now do just a little more. For both of us. . . .

■

Taylor Lockwood stood in Wendall Clayton's private bathroom.

The time was now 9 A.M. and she'd hidden here for hours, waiting for the partner to take a break so that she could continue going through the remaining stack of papers.

But Clayton had never even stood up to stretch. In this entire time he'd remained rooted at his desk, reading, picking up the phone and calling partners and clients. The news he was receiving was apparently good for his side; it was clear to her that the merger would be approved and that both firms would sign it up later in the day.

Reece would be in court by now, probably despairing that he hadn't heard from her.

But there was nothing she could do other than wait.

Ten minutes passed. Then ten more. And finally Clayton rose.

Thank God. He was going to check on something.

She would grab the remaining stack and flee with it to her cubicle, looking through it there. Then—

Her gut jumped hard. Clayton wasn't leaving the office at all. He needed to use the rest room and was walking directly toward where Taylor Lockwood now hid, a room without a single closet or shower stall where she might hide.

———————

"Bench conference, your honor?" Mitchell Reece asked. He was standing in front of the plaintiff's table.

The judge looked surprised and Reece could understand why. The trial had just started. The opening statements had been completed and it was rare that a bench conference—a brief informal meeting between lawyers, out of earshot of the jury—should occur at this early stage; nothing had happened so far that the two attorneys could argue about.

The judge raised his eyebrows and Hanover & Stiver's slick, gray-haired lawyer rose to his feet and walked slowly to the bench.

The courtroom was half empty but Reece was distressed to see some reporters present. He didn't know why they were here; they never covered cases of this sort.

Someone's political hand? he wondered.

At the defendant's table sat Lloyd Hanover, tanned and trim, his hair combed forward in bangs, his face an expression of blasé confidence.

The two lawyers stood at the bench. Reece said softly, "Your honor, I have a best-evidence situation. I'd like to move to introduce a copy of the promissory note in question."

Hanover's lawyer turned his head slowly to look at Reece. It was the judge, however, who was more astonished. "You don't have the note itself?"

No one in the jury box or elsewhere in the courtroom could hear this exchange but the surprise on the jurist's face was evident. Several spectators looked at each other and a reporter or two leaned forward slightly, sharks smelling blood.

The Hanover lawyer said tersely, "No way. Not acceptable. I'll fight you on this all the way, Reece."

The judge said, "Was it a negotiable instrument?"

"Yes, your honor. But there is precedent for admitting a copy at this stage, as long as the original is surrendered before execution of the judgment."

"Assuming you *get* a judgment," the Hanover lawyer countered.

"Bickering pisses me off, gentlemen." When the jury wasn't listening the judge could curse to his heart's delight.

"Sorry, sir," Hanover's lawyer murmured contritely. Then he said, "You prove to me the note's destroyed—I mean, show me ashes—and then you can put a copy into evidence. But if not, I'm moving for dismissal."

"What happened to the original?" the judge asked.

"We have it at the firm," Reece said casually. "We're having some technical failure accessing it."

"'Technical failure accessing it'?" the judge blurted. "What the fuck does that mean?"

"Our security systems aren't functioning right, as I understand it."

"Well, wouldn't that be convenient, to have the note disappear just now?" the Hanover lawyer said. "Especially since we intend to call into question certain aspects of the execution of the note."

Reece gave a bitter laugh. "Let me get this right—you're saying that you gladly took my client's money but now you're not sure they executed the loan agreement correctly so you don't have to pay it back?"

"Our thinking is that the bank tried to give itself an out because interest rates turned and they want to invest the capital elsewhere."

"Your client missed six months of interest payments,"

Reece said, raising his voice just loud enough for the jury to hear. "How exactly—"

"Was I not making myself goddamn clear? No bickering, no fucking comments on the merits of the case in a bench conference.... Now, Mr. Reece, this is very unusual. A suit on a note, especially a negotiable note, requires the original document. Under the best-evidence rule if you can't explain the note's destruction, you're precluded from entering a copy into evidence."

Reece said calmly, "I'd like to make a motion to submit other evidence of the existence of the note."

"Your honor," opposing counsel said, "I would point out that it is Mr. Reece's client that sued on the note it alleges is properly executed. It is his responsibility to present that note. A copy won't show that there's been tampering on the part of Mr. Reece's client."

Reece countered, "Your honor, it is very important that the administration of justice not get bogged down in technicalities. The note is merely *evidence* of the debt owed—and remaining unpaid, I should point out—by Hanover & Stiver. It is true that the best-evidence rule generally requires the original but there are exceptions. We're all familiar with the rules of civil procedure, I'm sure."

"But this isn't a bill of sale, Mr. Reece," the judge said. "It's a negotiable instrument worth hundreds of millions of dollars."

"With all due respect to Mr. Reece," the Hanover lawyer said, "I am reminded of a case once in which a similar claim of a missing note was made and it turned out that the document in question had been sold by the bank to a third party. I would never suggest that New Amsterdam Bank was guilty of such wrongdoing but ... we can't take that chance."

Reece walked to the counsel table and returned with some documents. He handed one copy to the lawyer and one to the judge. "Motion papers. I move to allow the introduction of secondary evidence of the note. I've briefed the issue in here. If you would like to recess for twenty-four hours to allow my opponent here to respond—"

"No more delays," the judge snapped. "This case has fucked up my calendar enough."

The other lawyer shook his head. "You lost the note, Reece, I'm ready for trial. Your honor, I move for a directed verdict in my client's favor."

The judge flipped through the lengthy brief that Reece had prepared then lifted an impressed eyebrow. "Good work, Mr. Reece. Brilliant analysis." Then he tossed the brief aside. "But it doesn't cut it. No secondary evidence will be allowed."

Reece's heart sank.

"On the other hand, I won't grant a directed verdict for Hanover. What I will do is grant a motion to dismiss *without* prejudice. That will allow Mr. Reece to bring his case in the future. However, given the nature of defendant's financial condition, I doubt they'll have much money for your client to collect, Mr. Reece. You'd better talk to your malpractice carrier. I think your client may look to you for restitution in this matter. And that's to the tune of two hundred and fifty million dollars."

The opposing counsel began the formalities: "Your honor, I move for dismissal of—"

"Mitchell!" a woman's voice called from the back of the courtroom.

The judge looked up, glaring at the intrusion. Everyone in the gallery and the jury box swiveled to watch Taylor Lockwood hurry down the aisle.

"It's customary to ask permission before shouting in my courtroom, young lady," the judge snapped sarcastically.

"Forgive me, sir. I need to speak to plaintiff's counsel for a moment."

Hanover's lawyer said, "Your honor, I—"

The judge waved him silent and nodded Taylor forward.

CHAPTER TWENTY-EIGHT

■■■■■ "I *am* sorry, your honor," Taylor Lockwood said.

Judges were public servants, catering to the will of the people, but as her father had reminded from a young age, you could never be too deferential to jurists or, as he put it even to grade-school Taylie, you could never kiss too much judicial ass.

She walked to Reece and handed him an envelope. Inside was the promissory note, looking as mundane and matter-of-fact as the copy he'd showed her at their first meeting.

Mitchell Reece took out the document and exhaled slowly.

"Your honor, at this time the plaintiff would like to introduce Exhibit A." He handed it to the opposing counsel, who looked at Taylor with a gaze of distilled hate. "No objection." He returned the note to Reece's unsteady hands.

Reece walked back to his favorite space, in front of the jury box. "Your honor, before continuing with my case, I first must apologize to the court and to the jury for this delay." He smiled contritely. The six men and women smiled or nodded back and forgave him; the interruption had added an element of drama to the case.

"Fine, fine, Mr. Reece, let's move this along," the judge grumbled, his chances for a fast escape to golf or tennis ruined.

"One moment, your honor." The Hanover & Stiver attorney bent toward one of his clients, probably Lloyd Hanover, Taylor guessed, to judge from his slick, tanned appearance, which matched what Reece had told her of him. After a bit of conversation the attorney stood up. "Approach the bench again? With opposing counsel?"

The judge gestured them up. The defense lawyer said, "Your honor, my clients would like to present a settlement offer to the plaintiff."

The judge lifted an eyebrow to Reece. Taylor's father had also taught his daughter that settlement was the Holy Grail of judges. Burdened by an endless workload, they infinitely preferred the parties' agreeing to work out their differences rather than slugging it out at trial. The judge might even be able to get in nine holes today.

"We'll entertain it," Reece said stiffly.

The lawyer moved closer to Reece and whispered, "Look, you can get a judgment entered for the face value of the note plus interest but there's no way there'll be enough cash left in the company to collect that much by the time you enforce it. Not to mention your legal fees' eating up a lot of the rest."

"A number," Reece said. "Just give me a number."

"I—"

The judge: "Give him a number."

"Sixty-five cents on the dollar."

Reece said, "Eighty cents on the dollar. U.S. cash, not negotiable instruments or assets or tangible property, even gold."

"We're trying to be cooperative. But we have to be realistic," Hanover's lawyer said. Then he added ominously, "The money just won't be there in a few months."

"Then we'll just have to go a-lookin'," Reece said

cheerfully. "Now, Lloyd Hanover personally guaranteed the debt. I'm ready to interrogate—excuse me, *depose*—every one of his relatives and every business associate of his for the past ten years to find out where he hid the money."

"He didn't hide—"

"We'll look into every deal he's ever been involved in, every charity he ever gave money to, his kid's college funds."

"He's completely innocent of secreting funds if that's what you're suggesting."

Reece shrugged. "Dismissal without prejudice. Eighty cents on the dollar. Cash. And we close within one week. If not, then Lloyd Hanover and everybody he's ever known won't have a minute's peace."

The lawyer held his eye for a moment and strode back to his client, who listened, gave a searing look to Reece then whispered something to the lawyer.

When the man returned he said, "Agreed."

Reece nodded and said, "We'll execute the stipulation now."

"We don't want to take the court's time. I suggest—"

"I think his honor would prefer to spend a few extra minutes now rather than risk being back here in a few weeks for a full-fledged trial. Am I right about that, your honor?"

"You are, Mr. Reece. Write out the stipulation by hand and we'll get it signed up."

The defense lawyer sighed and scurried back to give the bad news to the client.

After the paperwork was completed hands were shaken among comrades, glares delivered between opponents and the courtroom emptied.

In the courthouse rotunda, the New Amsterdam vice presidents and executives clustered together, enjoying their relief. Taylor followed Reece to a small vestibule that contained public phones, which unlike most in the city were in old-fashioned booths with closing doors. He pulled her inside one and kissed her hard. After a moment he released her and leaned back. "What on earth happened? Where were you?"

"I was almost through searching Clayton's office but he came in early to take care of some last-minute things for the merger. I hid in the bathroom."

"Jesus. What happened then?"

"About nine or so he had to use the john. But I unscrewed the lightbulbs before he got there. So he went up the hall. When he did I grabbed the last stack of paper and ran down to my cubicle with them. I found all of this in the envelope the note was in."

Reece took the sheets of paper that Taylor offered. Shaking his head, he looked at them closely. A copy of a letter to the *National Law Journal*. "Re: Careless Security Costs Firm Client." The letter blamed Burdick and the executive committee. There was also a typewritten list with the names of several other clients and cases that Clayton was going to sabotage while, presumably, shifting the blame to Burdick.

From her purse Taylor then took a small tape recorder and held up a tiny microcassette. "This was in the envelope too." She inserted the cassette into the player and hit a button. They heard Reece's voice, thick with static, talking to her about the promissory note. She shut it off.

"Son of a bitch," Reece said. "He bugged my office. That's how he knew we were after him. He's known all along. He..." Then Reece paused and looked at his watch. "Oh, no."

"What?

"The firm's voting on the merger any minute now. We've got to tell Donald about this. It'll change everything."

He grabbed the phone and dug in his pocket for some change.

Perpetual motion does exist.

In business, in fact, where the mere laws of science

mean zip compared with the power of greed and ambition, it's one of the essential principles.

Donald Burdick sensed the undercurrent of this energy surrounding each partner as he or she entered the big conference room. Mostly they were uneasy. They lingered at the door, pretending to leave messages with the conference room secretary, pretending to wait for comrades so they might enter with human shields, or at least with allies to deflect the glare of the partners representing the other side of the merger issue from theirs.

As always, few of the younger partners would make eye contact with Burdick but this morning he felt this evasion was due not to distance in social station but to hostility on the part of his opponents and shame in the hearts of those who had betrayed him.

The Danish pastries on the Limoges china, the coffee in the sterling urn were practically untouched. Burdick, looking down, reviewed a loan document that did not need reviewing. He heard conversations about the Jets and Giants, about concerts, about vacations, about closings, about the faux pas of opposing counsel, about the Supreme Court's latest excursions to Olympus, about rumors of other law firms breaking up.

Finally, at eleven o'clock, Burdick started to call the meeting to order. He was about to ask for a quorum vote when:

"Excuse me," said Randy Simms, whom Donald Burdick couldn't help but picture as a handsome leech.

"Yes?" Burdick drew the word out threateningly.

Simms said, "We're not all present."

Eyes coursing leisurely around the table, Burdick said, "But we have a quorum."

"Well, Mr. Clayton isn't here."

"Either we have a quorum, in which case the meeting proceeds, or we do not, in which case it doesn't. Whom that quorum is made up of is not, to my memory, an issue of any concern in *Robert's Rules of Order.*"

"I'm just thinking that it might be appropriate—"

But the slick young sycophant's words were interrupted by a bold knock. The door opened and Burdick's secretary walked inside with a sealed envelope. Ignoring everyone in the room, the older partner took it, slit the seal open with his gold pen and read the note. He handed it to Bill Stanley, who blinked in surprise.

Burdick said, "If you'll excuse us for a moment please. There's something that needs attending to. We'll adjourn for fifteen minutes. Bill, you come too."

███

Donald Burdick was as angry as Taylor had ever seen him. He glanced at her and she looked away from his towering fury.

They sat in Burdick's office. Bill Stanley was on the couch, a fat ankle resting on a fat knee, and read over the papers Taylor had found in Clayton's office.

Stanley muttered, "What a stupid, stupid thing to do."

But Burdick was venting at Reece. "Why the hell didn't you tell me about the note?"

Reece said, "It was a judgment call. I didn't want word to get out. I had my own way of handling it."

"You almost lost the case," Burdick spat out. "You almost got yourselves killed."

Reece withstood the anger easily. "Clayton wasn't going to hurt us. I'm sure the car incident was just to scare us. As far as losing goes, well, yes, I took that chance."

"You risked our client because you were afraid you'd lose your job."

The associate fired back, "Of course that was one reason. But it was also because if word got out it would be bad for the firm. In my assessment we had to act covertly."

"'Covertly.' You sound like a damn spy." Burdick took the papers and the tape recorder from Stanley. "He wanted the merger so badly, he'd do this?" Burdick's anger was giving way to astonishment.

Stanley considered something. "You introduced the note into evidence, right?"

Reece nodded. "Hanover's agreed to settle. We're going to close in Boston next week."

"Well, then Clayton will've heard you found it. He'll know he's in trouble."

Burdick nodded. "That's why he's not at the meeting." The old partner rubbed his eyes. "What a mess."

"Fucking scandal," Stanley growled. "Last thing we need."

"Give me some thoughts on the damage assessment," Burdick said to the rotund partner.

"Probably not terrible." He nodded at Reece and Taylor. "They didn't tell anyone." A piercing glance at Taylor. "Right? You didn't mention it to anybody?"

"No, of course not. When I found those things in Clayton's office I took them right to Mitchell at the courthouse. I didn't even call—because I thought the phones might be bugged. Nobody else knows what I was doing."

Stanley nodded and continued, "The problem's going to be talking him into leaving. He knows we're afraid of publicity so we're not going to go to the police or going to sue him. Fucking clever when you think about it. He arranges to misplace a note, nearly loses our client and when we catch him red-handed he's practically got immunity from the liability."

Burdick was shaking his head. "We'll find a way to oust him. That man has to . . ." His voice faded as there was an urgent knock on the door.

"Come in."

The door opened fast and one of Burdick's secretaries stood there. Her face was white and her eyes were red from crying.

"What is it, Carol?"

Oh, no, Taylor thought: Just what they were afraid of had happened—word had gotten out that Clayton had stolen the note.

But the tragedy was of a somewhat different order.

The woman gasped, "Oh, Mr. Burdick...it's terrible. They just found Wendall Clayton in the garage downstairs. In his car...He's..."

"What, Carol?"

"He shot himself. He's dead."

TWO

Men of Most Renowned Virtue

"You will observe the Rules of Battle, of course?" the White Knight remarked, putting on his helmet....

"I always do," said the Red Knight, and they began banging away at each other with such fury that Alice got behind a tree to be out of the way of the blows.

—Lewis Carroll, *Through the Looking-Glass*

CHAPTER TWENTY-NINE

Only a few hours had elapsed since Clayton's suicide. But it seemed to Taylor Lockwood that days had passed—given all the conjuring that Donald Burdick had done in the wake of the tragedy.

First, he'd appeared at the merger vote meeting and delivered the news to the partners. Then, leaving the stunned men and women to make what they would of the man's death, he'd returned immediately to his office, where Reece and Taylor had been ordered to remain.

The senior partner had handled an endless stream of phone calls and meetings with his cronies. So far he'd talked to the mayor's and the governor's offices, the medical examiner's office, the police, the Justice Department, the press.

Taylor was startled to see Burdick's wife make an appearance, walking into her husband's office unannounced, without the least acknowledgment of Reece or Taylor. The woman apparently knew all about the suicide and she and her husband retired to the small conference room off his office and closed the door. Five minutes later Burdick returned alone.

He sat down, leaned back in the chair and then asked Reece and Taylor, "Do you have anything else that has to do with Wendall or the theft? Anything at all?"

Reece shook his head and looked at Taylor, who said numbly, "I didn't think this would happen."

Burdick looked at her blankly for a moment then repeated, "Anything else?"

"No," she said.

He nodded and took an envelope out of his pocket. "There was that suicide note in the car, the one the police found. Talking about pressures at work, being despondent." Burdick looked at both Reece and Taylor. He added, "But he wrote another one. It was on his desk, addressed to me."

He handed a sheet of paper to Reece, who read it and then passed it on to Taylor.

> *Donald, forgive me. I'm sending this to you privately to keep my theft of the note out of the news. It will be better for everyone.*
>
> *I want you to know that I truly believed the merger would save the firm. But I lost sight of how far I should go. All I'll offer is this from Milton: "Men of most renowned virtue have sometimes by transgressing most truly kept the law."*

Burdick took the letter back and locked it in his desk. "I'm going to try to keep this note quiet." He nodded at the drawer. "I'll talk to the police commissioner and I don't think he'll have a problem with it. This is Hubbard, White's dirty laundry and no one else's. Publicity would be bad for everyone. Bad for the firm. Bad for Clayton's widow too."

"Widow?" Taylor asked suddenly.

Burdick replied, "Yes, Wendall was married. Didn't you know?"

"No," she said. "She wasn't in Connecticut the other day.

I've never seen her at any of the firm functions. He never wore a ring."

"Well, I guess he wouldn't now, would he? Given his extracurricular activities."

His widow . . .

The words stung. Before his death Clayton the man had been hidden beneath Clayton the ruthless aristocrat. That he had a wife—and maybe children or living parents, siblings—was a shock.

"The newspapers'll get a watered-down story," Burdick continued. "I've called the public relations company. Bill Stanley's with them now. They're preparing a statement. If anybody asks we'll refer questions to them." He lowered his head and looked into Reece's eyes, then Taylor's. She had the same sense as when she met Reece's gaze, or Clayton's. Or her father's. They drew you in, made you forget who you were, forget your own thoughts. In Burdick's eyes she saw will and confidence, strong as bronze. Her mind went blank. He asked, "Will you back me on this? If I thought there was anything to be gained by a full disclosure I wouldn't hesitate to reveal everything. But I can't see any upside to it."

Men of most renowned virtue.

Reece said, "I won't perjure myself, Donald. But I won't volunteer anything."

"Fair enough." The partner looked at Taylor.

She nodded. "Sure. I agree."

The hairs on the back of her neck stirred.

Widow . . .

Taylor looked into the conference room, inside which Vera Burdick, her gray hair piled on her head in a stately bun, was on the telephone. She glanced back and caught Taylor's gaze. The woman half-rose and swung the door closed.

Burdick's phone rang and he took the call. He mouthed something about its being from someone at City Hall but Taylor was preoccupied. She was seeing in her mind's eye the real suicide note, tucked away in Burdick's desk. She vaguely heard Burdick speaking to the caller in a low, reassuring tone. She watched his long, jowly face, carefully shaved, his sparse gray hair brushed into precise alignment.

And Taylor Lockwood thought: What the hell had she been doing all along? What did she *think* would happen when she fingered the thief? Had she ever considered the consequences?

Never once.

Renowned virtue.

Burdick hung up the receiver and nodded with satisfaction. "I think we'll get away with it."

Taylor tried to figure out what he meant.

"The Medical Examiner's office is going to rule the death suicide. The AG agrees. And we can keep our other suicide note private."

Reece blurted an astonished laugh. "The ME ruled *already*?"

Burdick nodded then looked at Taylor and Reece with a vaguely ominous gaze, which she interpreted as: Don't be too curious about this.

The partner looked at his watch. He held out his hand to Reece, then to Taylor, who first wanted to wipe her palm. It was damp as a washcloth; Burdick's was completely dry.

"You two get some rest. You've been through a hellish week. If you want any personal time I'll arrange it. Won't come out of your vacation or sick leave. Are you busy now?"

Reece walked toward the door. "I've got the Hanover settlement closing in Boston next week. That's the only thing on the front burner."

"You, Ms. Lockwood?"

"No, nothing," she replied, still numb.

"Then take some time off. In fact, I'd urge you to. Might be best."

Taylor nodded and began to speak but hesitated. She

was waiting for some significant thought to arrive, some
phrase that neatly summarized what had just happened.

Nothing occurred; her mind had jammed.

Get away with it?

"Oh, Mitchell," Burdick said, smiling, as if the suicide
no longer occupied even a portion of his thoughts.

Reece turned.

"Congratulations on the Hanover settlement," the partner said. "I myself would have settled for seventy cents on
the dollar. That's why you're a litigator and I'm not."

He rose and walked to the small conference room,
where his wife awaited him. Burdick didn't open the door
right away, though. He waited, Taylor noticed, until she and
Reece had left the office.

■

They walked in silence to the paralegal pen.

Everyone in the corridors seemed to be staring at her. As
if they knew the part she'd played in the partner's death.

Near her cubicle, in a place where the hall was empty,
Reece took her by the arm. He bent down and whispered, "I
know how you feel, Taylor. I know how *I* feel. But this
wasn't our fault. There's no way we could've anticipated
this."

She said nothing.

He continued, "Even if the police'd been involved the
same thing would've happened."

"I know," she said in a soft voice. But it sounded lame,
terribly lame. Because, of course, she didn't know anything
of the kind.

Reece asked, "Come over for dinner tonight."

She nodded. "Okay, sure."

"How's eight?" Then he frowned. "Wait, it's Tuesday . . .
you're playing piano at your club, right?"

Was it Tuesday? The thought of the leches in the audience and Dimitri's reference to her satin touch suddenly re-
pulsed her. "Think I'll cancel for tonight."

Reece gave a wan smile. "I'll see you later." He seemed to be looking for something to add but said nothing more. He looked up and down the hallway to make sure it was empty then hugged her hard and walked away.

Taylor called Ms. Strickland and told her she was taking the rest of the day off. She couldn't get the supervisor off the line, though; all the woman wanted to do was talk about Clayton's suicide. Finally she managed to hang up. Taylor avoided Carrie Mason and Sean Lillick and a half dozen of the other paralegals and snuck out the back door of the firm.

At home she loaded dirty clothes into the basket but got only as far as the front door. She stopped and set the laundry down. She turned on her Yamaha keyboard and played music for a few hours then took a nap.

At six that night she called Reece at home.

"Look," she said. "I'm sorry, I can't come over tonight."

"Sure," he said uncertainly. Then he asked, "Are you all right?"

"Yeah. I've got the fatigues. Bad."

"I understand." But he sounded edgy. "Is this ... Come on, tell me, is what happened going to affect us?"

Oh, brother ... you can hardly *ever* get men to talk seriously. And then, at the worst possible time, you can't stop them. "No, Mitch. It's not that. I just need some R&R time."

"Whatever you want," he said. "That's fine. I'll be here. It's just ... I guess I miss you."

" 'Night."

"Sleep well. Call me tomorrow."

She took a long bath then called home. Taylor was troubled to hear her father answer.

"Jesus, Taylie, what the hell happened at your shop?"

No "counselor" now. They were regressing to her grade-school nickname.

"I just heard," her father continued. "Was that somebody you worked for, this Clayton fellow?"

"I knew him, yeah. Not too well."

"Well, take some advice: You keep a low profile, young lady."

"What?" she asked, put off by his professorial tone.

"You keep your head down. The firm's going to have some scars from a suicide. We don't want any of it to rub off on you."

How can scars rub off? Taylor thought cynically. But of course she said nothing other than: "I'm just a paralegal, Dad. Reporters from the *Times* aren't going to be writing me up."

Although, she added to herself, if they'd told the whole story by rights they *should*.

"Killed himself?" Samuel Lockwood mused. "If you can't stand the heat stay out of the kitchen."

"Maybe there was more to it than standing the heat, Dad."

"He took the coward's way out and he hurt your shop."

"Not mine," Taylor said. But her voice was soft and Samuel Lockwood didn't hear.

"You want to talk to your mother?" he asked.

"Please."

"I'll get her. Just remember what I said, Taylie."

"Sure, Dad."

Her mother, who'd clearly had a glass of wine too many, was happy to hear from her daughter and, to Taylor's relief, wasn't the least alarmist about what had happened at the firm. Taylor slipped into a very different mode with her—far less defensive and tense—and the women began chatting about soap operas and distant relatives and Taylor's Christmas trip home to Maryland.

The woman was so cheerful and comforting in fact that Taylor, on a whim, upped the length of her stay from three days to seven. Hell, Donald Burdick wants me to take some time off? Okay, I'll take some time off.

Her mother was delighted and they talked for a few minutes longer but then Taylor said she had to go; she was afraid her father would come back on the line.

She put a frozen pouch of spaghetti into a pot of water.

That and an apple were dinner. Then she lay on her couch, watching a *Cheers* rerun.

Mitchell Reece called once but she let her answering machine do the talking for her. He left a short message, saying only that he was thinking of her. The words shored her up a bit.

But still, she didn't call back.

Taylor Lockwood, curled on the old sofa, the TV yammering mindlessly in front of her, thought about when she was a teenager and her Labrador retriever would pile into bed next to her and lie against an adjacent pillow until she scooted him off. She'd then lie still, waiting for sleep, while she felt, in the warmth radiating from the empty pillow, the first glimmerings of understanding that the pain that solitude conjures within us is a false pain and has nothing to do with solitude at all.

Indeed, being alone was curative, she believed.

She thought about Reece and wondered if he was different, if he was like her father, who sought company when he was troubled—though it was not the presence of his family Samuel Lockwood had ever needed but that of business associates, politicians, fellow partners and clients.

But that's a different story, she thought wearily.

She lay back on the couch and ten hours later opened her eyes to a gray morning.

She took the next day off and spent much of the morning and early afternoon Christmas shopping. When she returned home, in the late afternoon, there was another call from Reece and a curious one from Sean Lillick. He seemed drunk and he rambled on for a few minutes about Clayton's death, an edge to his voice. He mentioned that Carrie Mason wasn't going to Clayton's memorial service with him and asked if Taylor wanted to go.

No, she thought. But didn't call him back.

Thom Sebastian too had left a message, asking her to phone back. She didn't call him either.

She rummaged through the mail she'd picked up downstairs and found, mixed in among the Christmas cards, a self-addressed envelope from a music company. Her heart sank as she felt the thick tape inside and realized what it contained. Ripping the envelope open, she upended it and let her demo tape clatter out onto the table.

This wasn't the last of the tapes she'd sent out for consideration—there were still about a half dozen out at various companies—but it was the important one, the only tape that had made it to a label's Artists and Repertoire committee.

There was no response letter; someone had simply jotted on her own cover note, "Thanks, but not for us."

She tossed it into a Macy's box with the rest of them and, finally, opened that morning's *New York Times*. She read the article she'd been avoiding all day, headlined:

WALL STREET LAWYER KILLS SELF
PRESSURE AT WHITE-SHOE FIRM
CITED IN DEATH OF PARTNER, 52

Burdick apparently had indeed gotten away with it.

His artistry was astonishing. Not a word about the Hanover & Stiver case, nothing about the theft of the promissory note. Nothing about her or Mitchell or the merger.

Burdick was quoted, calling the death a terrible tragedy and saying that the profession had lost a brilliant attorney. The reporter also quoted several members of the firm—Bill Stanley mostly (well, the PR firm)—discussing Clayton's huge workload and his moodiness. The article reported that in the past year Clayton had billed over twenty-six hundred hours, a huge number for lawyers of his seniority. There was a sidebar on stress among overworked professionals.

She sighed and threw the newspaper away then washed the ink off her hands as if it were blood.

At five-thirty the doorbell rang.

Who could it be? Neighbors? Thom Sebastian assaulting her to beg for a date?

Ralph Dudley simply assaulting her?

She opened the door.

Mitchell Reece, wearing a windbreaker, walked inside and asked her if she had a cat.

"What?" she asked, bewildered by his quick entrance.

"A cat," he repeated.

"No, why? Are you allergic? What are you doing here?"

"Or fish, or anything you have to feed regularly?"

She was so pleased to see him in a playful mood—so different from the shock in his face after Clayton's death—that she joked back, "Just occasional boyfriends. But none at the moment, as I think you know."

"Come on downstairs. I want to show you something."

"But—"

He held his finger to his lips. "Let's go." She followed him out to the street, where a limo awaited, a black Lincoln. He opened the door and pointed inside, where she saw three large bags from Paragon Sporting Goods and two sets of new Rossignol skis propped across the seats.

Taylor laughed. "Mitchell, what are you doing?"

"Time for my lesson. Don't you remember? You were going to teach me to ski."

"Where? Central Park?"

"You know of someplace called Cannon? It's in New Hampshire. I just called the weather number. Four inches of new powder. I don't know what that means but even the recorded voice sounded excited so I assume it's good."

"But when?"

"But now," he said.

"Just like that?"

"The firm's jet's on the ramp at La Guardia. And they bill us by the hour so I suggest you hustle your butt. Go pack."

"This is crazy. What about work?"

"Donald called—he or his wife found out you like to ski so he ordered us to take some time off. He's giving us the trip all-expenses-paid. He called it a Christmas bonus. I've bought everything we need, I think. The store told me what to get. Skis, poles, black stretch pants, boots, bindings, sweaters, goggles. And ..." He held up a box.

"What's that?" Taylor asked.

"That? The most important thing of all."

She opened it. "A crash helmet?"

"That's for me." He shrugged. "Maybe you're a good teacher." He smiled. "And maybe you're not."

CHAPTER THIRTY

 The helmet wasn't a bad idea. Reece had been on the bunny slope at the Cannon ski resort in New Hampshire for only fifteen minutes when he fell and jammed his thumb.

One of the resort doctors, a cheerful Indian, had taped it.

"Is it broken?" Reece had asked.

"No, is no fracture."

"Why does it hurt so much?"

"Lots of nerves in fingers," the doctor said, beaming. "Many, many nerves."

Afterward, they sat in the small lounge in the inn.

"Oh, Mitchell, I feel so bad," she said. "But you did a very respectable first run."

"My thumb doesn't feel too respectable. Is it always this cold?"

"Cannon's got the coldest, windiest runs in New England, dear," she said, pulling his head against her neck. "People have frozen to death not far from here."

"Really? Well, we wouldn't want to have too much fun now, would we?"

Reece actually didn't seem too upset about either the accident or the weather. And she soon learned why: He preferred to sit out the day with what he had smuggled with him—files from the Hanover settlement closing. Taylor too didn't mind; she was eager to get out onto the double-diamond trails and kick some ski butt, not baby-sit him on the beginner slopes or worry about him on the intermediates.

She kissed him. "Sit in the lodge and behave yourself."

As she crunched her way toward the lifts, he called, "Good luck. I assume you don't say, 'Break a leg.'"

She smiled, stomped into her skis and slid down the slight incline to the bottom of the lift.

At the top of the mountain, she eased off the chair and braked to a stop just past the lift house. She bent down and washed her goggles in snow. The White Mountains were, as she'd told him, son-of-a-bitch cold and the wind steadily scraped across her face. She pulled silk hand liners on and replaced her mittens, then poled her way into position and looked down the mountain. Her impression had always been that most runs never look as steep from the top as they do from the bottom but as she gazed down toward the lodge, over a half mile straight below her, she saw a plunge, not a slope. Her pulse picked up and immediately she realized how right Mitchell had been to arrange the trip. How important it was to get away from the city, to distance herself from Hubbard, White & Willis, from Wendall Clayton's ghost.

She pushed off the crest of the mountain.

It was the best run of her life.

Suddenly there was nothing in her universe but speed and snow and the rhythm of her turns.

Speed, speed, speed . . .

Which was all she wanted. Her mouth was open slightly in the ellipse that suggests fear or sexual heights. Her teeth dried and stung in the frigid slipstream but the pain only added to her surge of abandon.

Taylor danced over moguls the way girls skip double-Dutch jump rope on playgrounds. Once, her skis left the ground and she landed as if the snow had risen timidly to stroke the bottom of the fiberglass. Trees, bushes, other skiers were a swift-ratcheting backdrop sweeping past, everyone hushed, it seemed, listening to the cutting hiss of her Rossignol.

She was sure she was hitting sixty or seventy miles an hour. Her hair was whipping her shoulders and back. She wished she'd borrowed Reece's helmet—not for safety, but to cut the wind resistance of the tangled mass of drag.

Then it was over. She brodied to a stop near the base of the run, her thighs in agony but her heart filled with a glorious rush of fear and victory.

She did four runs this way, until on the last one, on a big mogul, she lost control and had to windmill her arms to re-gain her balance.

It sobered her.

Okay, honey, one suicide a week is enough.

At the bottom of the mountain, she kicked out of her skis and loosened her boot clasps. A tall, thin man came up to her and said in a Germanic accent, "Hey, that was a, you know, pretty okay run. You feel maybe like another one?"

"Uh, no, not really."

"Okay, okay. Hey, how about a drink?"

"Sorry." She picked up her skis and walked toward the cabin. "I'm here with my boyfriend."

And she realized suddenly that, by God, she was.

■

Taylor returned to find Reece in great spirits, the tiny room cluttered with papers and documents delivered by FedEx or DHL. He was on the phone but he motioned her to him and kissed her hard then resumed his conversation.

She sat on the bed, wincing as she pulled off her sweater

and stretch pants, and began massaging her thighs and calves.

It was around that time that Reece hung up the phone and stacked the files away in a corner.

When they awoke in mid-afternoon they went to several antique stores, which weren't the precious collections of cheese dishes and brass surveying instruments you find in Connecticut or New York. These were barns packed with furniture. Rows of dusty chairs and tables and dressers and pickle jars and canopy beds and armoires. Very rustic and practical and well cared for.

None of the shopkeepers seemed to expect them to buy anything and they didn't.

That night they ate in one of the half-dozen inter-changeable inns in the area, their menus virtually the same, they'd found: veal chop, steak, chicken, duck à l'orange, salmon or trout. Afterward, they had a drink in the common room in front of a huge fireplace.

After they made love that night and Reece had fallen asleep, Taylor Lockwood lay under the garden patch quilt of a hundred hexagons of cotton and felt the reassuring pressure of a man's thigh beside her. She smelled the cold air as it streamed through the inch-open window and gathered on the floor. She tried to forget about Wendall Clayton, about Hubbard, White & Willis, about life on the other side of the looking glass.

At 4 A.M. she finally fell asleep.

On Thursday morning Taylor was first in the lift line.

She skied her first run fast, smelling the clean electric scent of snow, the biting perfume of fireplace smoke, hearing the sharp hiss of her turns in the granular snow.

Today, however, the speed had none of the cleansing effect that it'd had on her first day out. She felt alone, frightened, vulnerable. Like the first time her father made her ride her bike without training wheels. He'd put her on the tall Schwinn, aimed it down a hill and pushed. (She'd refused to scream until the wobbly front wheel hit a curb and she'd gone over the handlebars onto the sidewalk.)

She made mistakes, skied too defensively and nearly wiped out bad.

At the bottom of the mountain she loaded her skis and boots into the rental car.

No, Dad, I'm *not* getting back on the fucking horse, she thought now.

She drove to their inn and went back to the room, where Reece was taking a shower. She poured coffee from the pot he'd ordered and dropped into the musty armchair.

Thinking:

Where and for a first cause of action, Taylor Lockwood did willfully . . .

Outside she could see other skiers heading down the mountain, some fast, some timidly.

. . . and with full knowledge of the consequences, without a warrant or other license, enter the office of one Wendall Clayton, the decedent, and . . .

She sipped the coffee.

Where and for a first cause of action, Taylor Lockwood did willfully ascertain and make public certain facts about one Wendall Clayton, the decedent, that caused . . .

Taylor sat back in the chair, closed her eyes.

. . . that caused said decedent to blow his fucking brains out.

Mitchell Reece, wrapped in a towel, opened the bathroom door and, smiling with pleasant surprise, walked up to her. Kissed her on the mouth.

"Back early. You okay?"

"I don't know. Wasn't fun. Thumb still hurt?" she asked.

"A bit. I tell you I'm no good at this sort of thing. . . . I'm much better with simpleminded, safe sports. . . ." He seemed to be groping for a joke, something cute about sex probably, but he sensed that she was upset. He sat down on the bed opposite her.

"So what's up, Taylor?"

She shook her head.

"What is it?" he persisted.

"Mitchell, you know history?"

He motioned with an open palm for her to continue.

She asked, "You know what the Star Chamber was?"

"Just that it was a medieval English court. Why?"

"We learned about it in my European history course in college. It came back to me last night. The Star Chamber was a court without a jury, run by the Crown. When the king thought the regular court might decide against him he'd bring a case in the Star Chamber. You got hauled up before these special judges—the king's privy counselors. They'd pretend to have a trial but you can guess what happened. If the king wanted him guilty he was guilty. Very fast justice, very efficient."

He looked at the coffee, swirled it. He set it down without drinking any more. His face was somber.

She blurted, "Christ, Mitchell, the man is dead."

"And you think it's your fault."

A spasm of anger passed through her. Why can't he understand? "I was so stupid." Taylor looked at him briefly. Wondering how Clayton had felt lifting the gun. Had it been heavy? Had there been pain? How long had he lived after pulling the trigger? What had he seen? A burst of yellow light, a second of confusion, a wild eruption of thoughts, then nothing?

"Taylor," Reece said with measured words, "Clayton was crazy. No sane man would've stolen the note in the first place and no sane man would've killed himself if he'd been caught. You can't anticipate people like that."

She gripped his arm firmly. "But that's the point, Mitchell. You're thinking the problem is that Wendall outflanked us—that our fault was we weren't clever enough. But the *fault* was that we shouldn't've been playing the game in the first place. That firm's like Wonderland—it's got its own set of rules, which don't even make sense half the time but you never think about that because you're so deep in the place. Topsy-turvy. . . . Everything's topsy-turvy."

"What're you saying?"

"That we *should've* gone to the police. And we should've

let the chips fall wherever. So New Amsterdam would've left the firm. Well, so what? And you? You're one of the best lawyers in New York. You would've landed on your feet."

He rose and walked to the window.

Finally he said softly, "I know, I know. . . . You think I haven't been living with exactly what you're talking about?" He turned to face her. "But if I don't lay part of the blame at Clayton's feet, it undermines all my beliefs as a lawyer." He touched his chest. "It undermines all that I am. You know, this is something I'm going to have to live with too. I mean, you did what I asked you to do. But ultimately it was my decision."

So here was another aspect of Mitchell Reece—not all-powerful, not in control, not immune to pain.

She walked next to him, lowered her head onto his shoulder. His hand twined through her hair. "I'm sorry, Mitchell. This is very odd for me. It's not the sort of thing *Ms.* or *Savvy* prepares the working girl for."

He rubbed her shoulders.

"Can I ask a favor?" she said.

"Sure."

"Can we go back?"

He was surprised. "You want to leave?"

"I've had a wonderful time. But I'm in such a funky mood. I don't want to spoil our time together and I think I'd be a drag to be with."

"But I haven't learned to ski yet."

"Are you kidding? You're a graduate of the Taylor Lockwood School of Skiing Injury. You can go out now and break arms and legs all by yourself. With that kind of education there's no telling how far you can go."

"Let me see when I can get the jet."

CHAPTER THIRTY-ONE

Thursday afternoon, Taylor Lockwood stood in front of the Metropolitan Museum of Art on Fifth Avenue, looking up at a brown brick apartment building across the street, about as far from the wilderness of New Hampshire as you could get, conceptually speaking.

She checked the address again and verified that she had found the right building. Inside, a solemn doorman regarded her carefully and then called upstairs to announce her.

She was approved and he nodded toward the elevator.

"Sixth floor," he said.

"Which apartment?" she asked.

He looked confused for a moment then said, "It's the whole floor."

"Oh."

She stepped into the leather-padded elevator and was slowly transported to a private entryway. She smoothed her hair, looking into a brass mirror, a huge thing. The foyer was in dark red and filled with Georgian yellow and white dovetail trim. The pictures were old English hunting scenes.

Plaster scrolls and cherubs and angels and columns were everywhere.

An ageless, unsmiling woman in a plain navy shift answered the door, asked her to wait then disappeared down the hallway. Taylor glanced through the doorway. The rooms were larger versions of the foyer. She looked back into the mirror and stared at herself, at a person who was thinner than she'd expected. Thinner and...what else? More drawn, gaunter, grimmer? She tried smiling; it didn't take.

A shadow passed across her and Mrs. Wendall Clayton stood in the doorway: a middle-aged woman, wearing the stiff, straight-cut, big-patterned clothes that people who learned style in the sixties still sometimes favor. Her straight hair was swept back and sprayed perfectly into place. Her thin face was severe. The foundation makeup had been applied thickly but her skin wasn't good and Taylor could see red patches beneath the pancake.

They shook hands and made introductions.

Taylor followed the woman into the living room. Why the hell am I doing this? she wondered suddenly. What possible point could it have?

I'm here to give you my deepest sympathy.

I'm here to say I worked with your husband.

I'm here to say that even though he's dead don't feel too bad because he tried to seduce me.

Mrs. Clayton sat upright in an uncomfortable satin wingback, Taylor in a spongy armchair.

I'm here because I helped kill your husband....

The widow asked, "Tea? Coffee?"

"No, thank you," Taylor said. And then realized that the woman's dress was red and that this was hardly a household in mourning—the room was festooned with antique Christmas decorations and there was a faint but rich scent of pine in the air. Classical Christmas music played on the stereo. Taylor looked at the woman's cocked eyebrow and her expression, which wasn't one of bitterness or sorrow. It was closer to curiosity.

"I worked with your husband, Mrs. Clayton."

"Yes."

"I just came to tell you how sorry I was."

And Taylor understood then, only at that moment, that uttering those words was all she could do. Watching this stolid, lone woman (Taylor couldn't picture her as one half of the Claytons) light a cigarette, she understood that the spirits of Donald Burdick and Vera Burdick and Messrs. Hubbard, White and Willis themselves had accompanied her here and were laying cold fingers on her lips. She could not, even here, in Clayton's home, do what she desperately wanted to do: explain.

Explain that she'd been the one who'd uncovered the terrible secrets about her husband, that she was the cause— the proximate cause, the law would say—of his death. No, there'd be no confession. Taylor knew what bound her. In this joint venture Hubbard, White & Willis had secured her soul.

"That's very kind of you." After a pause the woman asked: "Did I see you at the funeral? There were so many people."

"I wasn't there, no." Taylor eased back in the chair, uncomfortable, and crossed her arms. Wished she'd asked for coffee to keep her hands busy.

Now she looked around the room, aware of its size. The ceilings were twenty feet high. It reminded her of National Trust mansions and palaces in England. Taylor said, "He was an excellent lawyer. . . ."

Clayton's widow said, "I suppose." She was examining a tabletop. It seemed to be a dust inspection. "But then we didn't talk much about his career."

Taylor was counting the squares in the carpet. Trying to figure out the designs. Finally: St. George and the dragon, she believed.

Beware the Jabberwock . . .

The widow paused. "The truth is, Ms. Lockwood, I'm a little bewildered. I don't know you—though we may have met before. But you seem genuinely upset by my husband's death and I can't quite figure out why. You're not like the little sycophants who've come by since he died—the associates at the firm. They thought they were covering it up but I could see through them—in their eyes you could tell that they were amused at his death. I know they'd chuckled about it over their beers when they were alone. Do you know why they were here?"

Taylor was silent.

"They came because they thought word would get back to the firm that they'd done their duty. They'd made an appearance that might earn them another point or two, get them a step closer to being partner." She pressed out her cigarette. "Which is so ironic, of course, because they didn't grasp the situation at all. They should've been avoiding this house as if it were a leper colony. If word gets back to Burdick that young Samuel and Frederick and Douglas were paying respects to me, well, then, my God, they're in Dutch. At worst, they'd had the bad judgment to pick the wrong side; at best, they were displaying an oblivion about law firm politics.

"So you see, Ms. Lockwood, I am a little perplexed by your sympathy call." A smile. "That sounds appropriately Victorian, doesn't it? Sympathy call. Well, you aren't here to toady. You aren't here to gloat. Your dress and demeanor tell me you couldn't care less about what the Donald Burdicks and Wendall Claytons of the world think of you. You're clearly not one of the little malleable things he picked for his, dare I use the euphemism, girlfriends. . . . No, you're genuinely upset. I can see that. Well, you may have respected my husband as a lawyer and an ambitious businessman. But I doubt very much if you respected him as a human being. And I know without a doubt that you didn't like him."

"You had a loss in your life and I'm sorry," Taylor said evenly. "I didn't mean anything more or less than that." She fell silent, watching this shrewd woman light another cigarette with bony, red hands. It seemed as if the smoke that floated out of her nose and mouth had over the years taken with it her weight and softness.

Mrs. Clayton finally laughed. "Well, I appreciate that, Ms. Lockwood. Forgive my cynicism. I hope I haven't offended you. But don't feel sorry for me. Heavens, no. You're young. You don't have any experience with marriages of convenience."

Well, let's not go that far, Taylor thought, replaying many images: her parents' twin beds, her mother with her glass of wine sitting alone in front of the television, her father calling at midnight saying he was staying at his club. Night after night after night...

Clayton's widow said, "I guess you'd say our relationship wasn't even a marriage. It was a merger. His assets and mine. A certain camaraderie. Love? Was there any love between Williams Computing and RFC Industries when they consolidated? To name just one of the deals that took so much of Wendall's time..." She looked out over the park, spindly with branches, the residue of snow faintly surviving in shadows. "And that's the irony, you see."

"What?"

"Love—there was never any between us. And yet I'm the one he was most content with. Cold, scheming Wendall, the power broker. The master of control. But once outside of our life, he was at sea. Vulnerable. That's why he killed himself, of course. For love."

"What do you mean?" Taylor heard herself ask, her heart pounding fast.

"He killed himself for love," the widow repeated. "That's the one thing Wendall didn't understand and couldn't control. Love. Oh, how he wanted it. And as with so many beautiful, powerful people it was denied him. He was an alcoholic of love. He'd go off on his benders. With his chippies. His little sluts. And there were plenty of them— women would flock to him. A few of the men, too, I should tell you. How they all would want him!

"He'd spirit them away on carriage rides, buy them roses, have a breakfast tray put together at Le Perigord and sent to their apartments. Wendall goes a-courting. They were all disasters, of course. The girls never quite lived up to what he wanted. The older ones . . . they turned out to be every bit as superficial and material and cold"—she laughed again, dropping a worm of ash in the ashtray—"as cold as I was. Or he'd pick a young puppy, some ingenue, who'd cling to him desperately, rearrange her life around him. Then he'd feel the arms around his neck, dragging him down. Someone *relying* on him. My Lord, we couldn't have that, could we? Then he'd dump them. And back he'd come to me. To nurse his wounds."

Taylor jumped in to steer the conversation back on course. "What do you mean about his suicide? Killing himself for love?"

"It's the only thing that makes sense. He must've fallen madly in love with somebody and he was sure she was the one. When she told him no it must've devastated him."

"But the note he left said he was under pressure at work, stress."

"Oh, he wrote that for my benefit. If he'd mentioned a girlfriend, well, it would have embarrassed me." She laughed. "The idea of Wendall killing himself because of pressure? Why, he lived for pressure. He wasn't happy unless he had ten projects going at once. I've never seen him happier than over the past few months working on the merger, doing deals for his clients . . . and then planning the other firm."

"What other firm?"

She looked at Taylor cautiously then pushed out her cigarette. "I suppose it doesn't matter anymore. In case the merger didn't go through, he was going to leave Hubbard, White & Willis, take his boys and a couple of dozen partners and open his own firm. It was his alternative plan. I think he almost preferred that to the merger. Because he'd be a named partner. He always wanted to have his name on the letterhead. Clayton, Jones & Smith, or whatever."

Another firm? Taylor wondered.

The widow resumed her examination of Central Park flora. Then smiled. "That note . . . He could have said in the note how unhappy he was with me as a wife. With our life together . . . But he didn't. I was very touched."

Rising, Mrs. Clayton looked at her watch. "I'd like to talk to you longer." She picked up her Dunhill cigarette case. "But I have bridge club in ten minutes."

———

Aristocratize.

Taylor Lockwood was sitting at Wendall Clayton's desk.

It was late afternoon and a yellow-gray illumination lit the room from the pale sun over New York Harbor. The office lights were out and the door closed.

She looked at the jotting on a faded piece of foolscap.

Aristocratize.

Was that a word? Taylor glanced at the brass, the carpets, the vases, the tile painting, the wall of deal binders, the stacks of papers like the one that had held the note and tape recordings of her conversations with Mitchell Reece. The huge chair creaked as she moved.

Men of most renowned virtue . . .

Spinning around once more to face the window, she decided that, whether it was real or not, "aristocratize" certainly described the essence of Wendall Clayton.

There was no reason for her to be in the firm. Technically she was still on vacation, courtesy of Donald Burdick. She could leave at any moment, smile at Ms. Strickland and walk out of the front door with impunity. She was, in fact, due at Mitchell Reece's loft right about now. (It turned out that he could cook after all and was planning to make them a tortellini salad for dinner; he was currently baking the bread himself!) She wanted to lie in his huge bathtub, a wonderful bathtub that had claw feet, to luxuriate in the water holding a thin-stemmed glass of wine and smell him cooking whatever went into a tortellini salad.

Instead, Taylor slouched down in Clayton's chair and spun slowly in a circle, 360 degrees, once, twice, three times.

Alice spinning as she fell down the rabbit hole, Alice buffeted on the ocean of tears, Alice arguing with the Queen of Hearts. . . .

Off with their heads, off with their heads!

Taylor stopped spinning. She began what she'd come here for: a detailed examination of the contents of Wendall Clayton's desk and filing cabinets.

A half hour later, Taylor Lockwood walked slowly downstairs to the paralegal pen. She made certain that no one was in the cubicles surrounding hers then looked through her address book and found the number of her favorite private eye, John Silbert Hemming.

■

He stopped suddenly, jolted, as he watched her slip out of Wendall Clayton's office, looking around carefully as if she didn't want to be seen.

Sean Lillick ducked into a darkened conference room where Taylor Lockwood couldn't see him. It had scared the hell out of him, as he was walking toward Clayton's office, to see the sudden shadow appearing in the doorway. For a split second all his chic, retro-punk East Village cynical sensibilities had vanished and he'd thought: Fuck me, it's a ghost . . .

What the hell had she been doing in there? he now wondered.

Lillick waited until she was gone and the corridor was empty. Then he too ducked into the dead partner's office and locked the door behind him.

■

It was excellent tortellini salad—filled with all sorts of good things only about half of which she recognized. The bread was lopsided but Reece had propped it up in a cute way. Whatever its shape, it tasted wonderful. He opened a cold Pouilly-Fuissé.

They ate for ten minutes, Taylor nodding as he told her about the impending settlement conference in Boston during which Hanover & Stiver would transfer the bulk of the principal of the loan back to New Amsterdam. He told anecdotes about some of Lloyd Hanover's shady business dealings. Normally, she liked it when he talked about his job because, although she didn't always understand the nuances, the animation and enthusiasm that lit up his face were infectious.

Tonight, though, she was distracted.

He finally caught on that something was wrong and his voice faded. He looked concerned. But before he could question her, Taylor set her fork down with a tap. "Mitchell."

He refilled their glasses and cocked an eyebrow at her.

"There's something I have to tell you."

"Yes?" he asked cautiously, perhaps suspecting some personal confession.

"I've been looking into a few things. About Wendall Clayton."

Reece sipped his wine. Nodded.

"He didn't kill himself." Taylor picked a lopsided bit of bread crust off the table and dropped it on her plate. "He was murdered."

CHAPTER THIRTY-TWO

Mitchell Reece smiled, as if waiting for a punch line.

Then: "Why do you think that?"

"I went to see his widow," Taylor said. Then she added quickly, "Oh, I wasn't going to tell her what happened— about the note and everything. But..." She paused. "Well, you know, I'm not sure why I went. It was something I just had to do."

He said, "I hear she's a bitch."

Taylor shrugged. "She was civil enough to me. But you know what she told me? That if Wendall couldn't get the merger through he was going to start his own firm."

"What?" Reece frowned.

Nodding, she said, "He had it all planned out. I went through his desk at the firm. I found business plans, bank loan applications. He even had the firm name selected. Clayton, Stone & Samuels. He had a sample letterhead printed up and he'd been talking to a broker about space in the Equitable Building."

Reece too had put down his utensils. "But if he was ready to start his own firm it makes no sense for him to risk his career to push the merger through."

"Exactly. Stealing the note? He'd be disbarred if he got caught. And he'd probably be prosecuted." Taylor held up a finger. "Another thing. Think about the gun."

"The gun he used?"

"Right. I called my detective, my private eye, and he talked to some buddies of his at the police department. The gun he used was a .38 Smith & Wesson knockoff, made in Italy. No serial number. It's one of the most popular street guns there is. 'It's like your McDonald's of firearms' is what John said. But if you're going to kill yourself why buy an untraceable gun? You go to a sporting goods store, show a driver's license and buy a twelve-gauge shotgun."

"Or," Reece said, sitting forward, "why even shoot yourself? It's messy, unpleasant for your loved ones. I'd think you'd park your car in the garage with the engine running."

She nodded her agreement. "What I think is that somebody else stole the note and planted it in Clayton's office. Then when we found it he murdered Clayton to make it look like suicide."

"Who's the 'he'?" Reece asked.

"At first, I wondered if his widow might've done it. I mean here she was hosting a bridge party right after he died. She knew about the affairs he'd had. So she certainly had a motive."

"And she must have inherited some bucks from him."

"True. But then I got to thinking and it seems that the killer'd need to know about the firm and have access to it. Clayton's widow isn't like Vera Burdick, who's there all the time. Besides, Mrs. Clayton didn't seem that upset with all his affairs."

"Well," Reece suggested, "what about one of them? A lover? Somebody Clayton dumped?"

"Sure. That's a possibility. Or the husband or wife of

somebody he'd had an affair with. But," Taylor added, smiling, "what about some of the people we thought were suspects: Ralph Dudley. Clayton had found out about Junie and was blackmailing him."

"And Thom Sebastian. Clayton was the main reason he didn't make partner."

"He occurred to me, too. . . . And one other possibility."

Reece frowned, shaking his head.

Taylor pointed upward. "Go to the top."

"Donald Burdick?" Reece laughed. "Look, I know the motive's there. But Donald? I can't believe it. Whoever stole the note risked not only my career but risked losing a client as well—if we lost the case. There's no way Donald would've put New Amsterdam at risk."

Taylor countered, "But there *was* no risk. At the very worst, if we hadn't found the note, Donald would've sent his thief to get the note back from Clayton's office and it would've shown up on the file room floor or someplace in time for you to introduce it at trial."

Reece nodded, considering this. "And look how well Burdick covered everything up. The medical examiner, the prosecutor, the press . . . Nobody knows about the promissory note theft. And everything else—the evidence we found in Clayton's office, the real suicide note—I'm sure Burdick's shredded it by now." But then Reece shook his head. "Let's think about this. If it *is* Burdick remember that he's real tight with City Hall and Albany. We can't trust the police. We'll go to the U.S. attorney's office; I've still got friends there. I'll call them—"

"But didn't Donald call somebody in the Justice Department?" she asked. "After they found the body?"

Reece paused. "I don't remember. Yeah, I think he did."

Taylor said, "You're going to Boston tomorrow for the settlement closing. Do you know anybody in Justice up there?"

"Yeah, I do. I haven't talked to him for a while. Let's see if he's still there." He walked to his desk and found his address book and picked up the phone. But he looked at it warily.

"Bugs?" Taylor asked.

"Let's not take any chances—we'll go downstairs."

On the street they found a pay phone and Reece made a credit card call.

"Sam Latham, please.... Hey, Sam, Mitchell Reece."

The men apparently knew each other well and Taylor deduced from the conversation that they'd both been prosecutors in New York some years ago. After a few whatever-happened-to's, Reece told him their suspicions about Clayton's death. They made plans to meet at the U.S. attorney's office in Boston the next day, after the Hanover settlement closing. He hung up.

"He's getting his boss and an FBI agent to meet with me."

Taylor felt a huge weight lifted from her. At last the authorities were involved. This was the way the system was supposed to work.

They returned upstairs. Reece closed the front door and latched it then walked up behind her, enfolded her in his arms. She leaned her head back and slowly turned so that they were face-to-face.

He glanced at the table, where the meal sat unfinished: the exceptionally good tortellini salad, the cold wine, the sagging bread. She smiled and, with her fingertips, turned his head back to face her.

She kissed him hard.

Without a word they walked to Reece's bed.

███████

So far, not so good . . .

Thom Sebastian sat back in his office chair, pushing aside the documents he'd been working on all morning, a revolving credit agreement for New Amsterdam Bank.

He should have been comfortable, should have been content. But he was troubled.

Wendall Clayton, the man who'd destroyed his chances for partnership at Hubbard, White, was gone—as dead as a shot pheasant in one of the hunting prints hanging in the partner's office.

Good.

But his life didn't really *feel* good. He had a brooding sense that his entire world was about to be torn apart. And this terrified him.

Three times he reached for the phone, hesitated, put his hands flat on his thick thighs and remained where he was.

He peeked under his blotter and saw the notes he'd gathered on Taylor Lockwood over the past ten days or so.

Taylor Lockwood . . . the sole reason that things weren't so good.

Come on, Mr. Fucking Negotiator, make a decision.

But ultimately, he knew, there was no decision at all. Because there was only one thing to do.

The problem was finding the courage to do it.

■

The next morning Reece called Taylor from Boston.

She was at her apartment; she'd decided it was safest to stay away from the firm. He called to report that the settlement had gone well. The money from the Hanover settlement had been safely wired into a New Amsterdam account and he'd endured Lloyd Hanover's relentless glare and potshots at lawyers throughout the closing.

Reece was on his way to meet with his friend in the U.S. attorney's office.

"I miss you," he said.

"Hurry home," she told him. "Let's get this behind us and go back and ski for real."

"Or," he joked, "go back and shop and eat dinner at the inns."

"I'll get you on black diamond slopes sooner or later."

"What the hell? I've still got one thumb and eight fingers left."

After some Christmas shopping Taylor stopped at a coffee shop on Sixth Avenue, around the corner from her apartment, for some lunch.

Sitting at the counter, she wondered what to get Reece for Christmas. He had all the clothes he needed. Wine was too impersonal.

Then she recalled his collection of lead soldiers.

She'd find one that was perfect for him—just one. A special one, antique, expensive. But where? Well, this was New York, the city that boasted neighborhoods devoted to special interests: the garment district, the flower district, even the sewing machine district. There was probably a cluster of stores somewhere in Midtown selling antique toys.

A man sat down next to her, a large workman in gray coveralls, wearing a baseball cap. There was something vaguely familiar about him and she wondered if he worked in her apartment building; the structure was old and there were always people renovating and repairing.

He pulled out a book and began reading.

Taylor's chicken soup came and as she was sprinkling Tabasco on it the man next to her took a sip of coffee. When he replaced the cup his elbow knocked his book to the floor. It dropped at her feet.

"Oh, sorry," he said, blushing.

"No problem," she said and bent down to retrieve the book. When she handed it to him he smiled his thanks and said, "I like this place. You come here a lot?" A trace of some accent from one of the outer boroughs.

"Some."

"With your boyfriend?" he asked, smiling, ruefully.

She nodded, and let the small lie do double duty: let him know she wasn't interested and save his ego from a flat-out rejection.

"Ah, well," he sighed and returned to his book.

When she left he was working on a double cheese-burger. He waved to her and called, "Merry Christmas."

"You too," she said.

Back at home, she pulled the phone book out from under her bed and looked up toy stores.

Well, let's start at the beginning.

As she stood to get the phone she realized she felt achy, as if a cold were coming on. Her head was hurting a bit too. She went into the bathroom to get some aspirin, swallowed them down and returned to the bedroom to start calling the stores in search of Reece's Christmas present.

Feeling tired . . .

She reclined on the bed and picked up the cordless phone.

She'd dialed the first digit when she gasped and sat up fast. A churning pain struck somewhere deep within her abdomen. Her face burst out in sweat.

"Oh, man," she whispered. Not the flu, not now. . . .

Recalling that she often got sick around Christmas when she was young. A therapist she'd seen for a while had wondered if it wasn't her dread of a holiday presided over by a domineering father.

"Oh . . ." She moaned again, pressing the skin above the pang hard with both her hands. It ceased for a moment then exploded in another eruption of agony.

Taylor stood up, adding nausea to the sensation. The room began to spin and she tried to control her fall to the parquet floor. Her head hit the dressing table and she blacked out.

When she opened her eyes she saw claws.

The Jabberwock's claws, disemboweling her, tearing her stomach, throat, the back of her mouth, shredding her flesh . . .

She squinted. No, no, they were just the claws on the legs of her bed. She—

The pain stunned her again and she moaned, a low, animal sound.

Sweat filled her eyes and ran down her nose. She wrapped her arms around herself and drew her legs up, trying to stop the pain. Every muscle hard as rubber, she tried to will the pain away but this had no effect. Then the nausea overwhelmed her and Taylor crawled to the toilet, opened the seat and held herself up on one arm while she vomited and retched for what seemed like hours.

Her hands shook, her skin was inflamed. She stared at the tiny hexagonal tiles in front of her until she fainted again. Consciousness returned and she struggled for the phone. But her muscles gave out and she dropped again to the floor. From a distant dimension she heard a thunk—the sound of her head hitting the tiles.

She understood now that she'd been poisoned.... The man at the restaurant. The workman in the coveralls and baseball cap. *He* was the one who'd stolen the note, the one who'd run them off the road, the one who'd killed Wendall Clayton.

That was why he'd seemed familiar—because she must've seen him in the firm or following her and Reece earlier. Maybe he'd overheard her conversation with John Silbert Hemming. Maybe he'd put a tap on *her* phone at the office or even in her apartment.

She—

Then the poison began to churn again and she started to retch in earnest, unable to breathe, trying to scream for help, slamming her hand on the dresser so that somebody might hear and come to her aid. Perfume bottles fell, makeup, an Alice in Wonderland snowball crashed to the floor and broke, the water and sparkles spattering her.

She began to pummel the floor—until she realized she had no feeling in her hand; it was completely numb. Taylor Lockwood began to cry.

She crawled to the phone, dialed 911.

"Police and fire emergency."

She couldn't speak. Her tongue had turned to wood.

The air was becoming thinner and thinner, sucked from the room.

The voice said, "Is anyone there? Hello? Hello? . . ."

Taylor's hands stopped working. She dropped the phone. She closed her eyes.

CHAPTER THIRTY-THREE

"What happened?" Carrie Mason asked.

The doctor was a woman in her mid-thirties. She had straight blond hair and wore no makeup except for bright blue eye shadow. The medico's badge said Dr. V. Sarravich.

The woman said, "Botulism."

"Botulism? Food poisoning?"

"I'm afraid she ate some severely tainted food."

"Is she going to be okay?"

"Botulism's much more serious than other types of food poisoning. She's unconscious, in shock. Severely dehydrated. The prognosis isn't good. We should get in touch with her family, if she has any. She lived alone and apparently the police couldn't find her address book or any next-of-kin information. We found your name and number on a card in her purse."

"I don't know where her parents live. I'll give you the name of someone who can get in touch with them. Can I see her?"

"She's in the Critical Care Unit. You can't visit now," Dr.

Sarravich said. Medical people were all so serious, the girl thought.

Carrie asked, "Is it really bad?"

She hesitated—a concession to delicacy—and said, "I'm afraid it may be fatal and even if it isn't there could be some permanent damage."

"What kind of damage?"

"Neuromuscular."

"To her hands?" Carrie asked.

"Possibly."

"But she's a musician," the paralegal said, alarmed. "A pianist."

"It's too early to tell anything at this point." A pen and paper appeared, and the doctor asked, "Now, whom should I contact?"

Carrie wrote a name and phone number. The doctor looked at the pad. "Donald Burdick. Who is he?"

"The head of the firm she works at. He can tell you everything you want to know."

■■■■■

Taylor's eyes opened slowly. Her skin stung from the sandblasting of fever. Her vision was blurred. Her head was in a vise of fiery pressure. Her legs and arms were useless, like blocks of wood grafted to her torso. The nausea and cramps were still rampaging through her abdomen and her throat was dry as paper.

There was a young woman in a pale blue uniform making the bed next to hers.

Taylor had never been in such pain. Every breath brought pain. Every twitch was a throb of pain. She assumed that the nerves in her hands and legs had short-circuited—she couldn't move her limbs.

Taylor whispered.

No reaction from the young woman.

She screamed.

The attendant cocked her head.

She screamed again.

No reaction. Taylor closed her eyes and rested after the agonizing effort.

Several minutes later the bed was made. As the attendant walked toward the door, she glanced at Taylor.

Taylor screamed, "Poison!"

The aide leaned down. "Did you say something, honey?" Taylor smelled fruity gum on her breath and felt like gagging.

"Poison," she managed to say. "I was poisoned."

"Yes, food poisoning," the girl said and started to leave.

Taylor screamed, "I want Mitchell!"

The girl held up the watch on her pudgy wrist. "It's not midnight. It's about six."

"I want Mitchell. Please..."

Taylor tried fiercely to hold on to consciousness but it spilled away like a handful of sugar. She had an impression of struggling to leap out of bed and calling Mitchell in Boston but then she realized that her legs and arms had started to spasm. Then a nurse was standing over her, staring in alarm and reaching for the call button, pushing it fiercely over and over.

And then the room went black.

■

At 7:30 P.M. the telephone in Donald Burdick's co-op rang.

He was in the living room. He heard Vera answer it then mentally followed her footsteps as they completed a circuit that ended in the arched entrance near him. Her calm face appeared.

"Phone, Don," Vera said. "It's the doctor."

The *Wall Street Journal* crumpled in his hand. He rose and together they walked to the den.

"Yes?" he asked.

"Mr. Burdick?" a woman's matter-of-fact voice asked. "This is Dr. Vivian Sarravich again. From Manhattan General Hospital? I'm calling about Ms. Lockwood."

"Yes?"

"I'm afraid I have bad news, sir. Miss Taylor has gone into a coma. Our neurologist's opinion is that she won't be coming out of it in the near future...if at all. And if she does she's certain to have permanent brain and neuromuscular damage."

Burdick shook his head to Vera. He held the phone out a ways so that she too could hear. "It's that bad?"

"This is the most severe case of botulism I've ever seen. The infection was much greater than usual. She's had two respiratory failures. We had to put her on a ventilator. And a feeding tube, of course."

"Her family?"

"We've told them. Her parents on on their way here."

"Yes, well, thank you, Doctor. You'll keep me posted?"

"Of course. I am sorry. We did everything we could."

"I'm sure you did."

Burdick hung up and said to his wife, "She probably won't make it."

Vera gave a neutral nod and then glanced at the maid who'd silently appeared beside them. "They're here, Mrs. Burdick."

"Show them into the den, 'Nita."

███

Donald Burdick poured port into Waterford glasses. His hands left fingerprints in a slight coating of dust on the bottle, which, he noticed, had been put up in 1963.

The year that a Democratic President had been killed.

The year he made his first million dollars.

The year that happened to be a very good one for vintage port.

He carried the glasses to the guests: Bill Stanley, Lamar Fredericks, Woody Crenshaw—all old fogies, his granddaughter might say, if kids still used that word, which of course they didn't—and three other members of the executive committee. Three young partners to whom Burdick was making a point of being kind and deferential.

Three partners who were in absolute terror at the moment—because they had been picked and polished by Wendall Clayton and then leveraged by him onto the executive committee.

The men were in Burdick's study. Outside, wet snow slapped on the leaded glass windows.

"To Hubbard, White & Willis," Burdick said. Glasses were raised but not rung together.

The Reconstruction had began swiftly. Only one of Clayton's lackeys had been fired outright—tall, young Randy Simms III, a fair-to-middlin' lawyer but one hell of a scheming nazi sycophant, Vera Burdick had observed. It had been her delightful task to transmit, through her own social network, rumors of various types of illegal scams the young partner was guilty of. By the time she was through he'd been thoroughly blackballed and was a pariah in the world of New York law and Upper East Side society.

As for the other pretty young men and women associates on Clayton's side . . . they weren't asked to leave, the theory being they'd work even harder to rid themselves of the contamination. These secessionists and collaborators were given the shaved-head treatment then kicked onto the summer outing and hiring committees.

These three Nameless were the last order of business in the Purge.

One of them said, "Your wife, Donald, is a charming lady."

Burdick smiled. They had of course met Vera before this evening though she had never served them dinner, never entertained them, never told them stories of her travels and anecdotes about her famous political friends; never, in short, grilled them like an expert interrogator.

He set the assassination-year bottle in the middle of the tea table.

He said, "Bill knows this but for the rest of you, I have some news. I'm meeting tomorrow with John Perelli. We have a problem, of course. Perelli's position is that Wendall's discussions with him suggest an implicit agreement to go forward with the merger—even though the whole firm's never approved it."

One of the Nameless nodded. Impressed that the man returned his gaze, Burdick continued, "His thinking is that we agreed to negotiate in good faith. The firm has now decided that we do not want to go forward simply because we do not want to go forward. That is *not* good faith. We have an implied contract problem. Look at Texaco and Pennzoil."

Another Nameless: "I know the law, Don." This was a little brash, as the youngster understood immediately; he continued more contritely, "I agree they'd have an argument but I think we hedged well enough so that with Wendall gone the basic deal has changed."

Vera asked bluntly, "Was Clayton's presence a condition precedent to going forward?"

Two of the Nameless blinked, hearing the charming woman nail the legal situation perfectly with one simple question.

"No."

Her husband, smiling, shrugged. "Then, I submit, we still have our problem."

The first Nameless said, "But what would they want as a remedy? Specific performance?"

Burdick decided the man was an idiot and made a mental note to give him only scut work for the rest of his time at Hubbard, White. "Of course not. The courts can't *make* us merge."

Bill Stanley said, "They want money. And what do *we* want?" When no one answered he answered himself, "Silence."

Burdick said, "No more publicity. Under any circumstances. A senior partner kills himself? Bad enough and we're going to lose clients because of that, my friend. Then a suit from Perelli? No, I want to preempt them."

Lamar Fredericks, round, bald and roasted from two weeks of golf on Antigua, said, "Preempt? You mean bribe. Cut the crap and tell us what it's going to cost."

Burdick looked at Stanley, who said to the group, "We'd pay Perelli twenty million. Up to, that is. We'll start lower, of course. Full release and agreement not to say anything to the press. If they do, liquidated damages of a double re-fund."

Crenshaw snorted. "What does that do to our partner-ship shares?"

Burdick snapped, "It'll be a cut out of operating profits. Take a calculator and figure it out yourself."

"Will they buy into it?"

Burdick said, "I'll be as persuasive as I can. The reason you're all here is that it would be an expenditure out of the ordinary course. I don't want to present it to the firm. So to authorize it we need a three-quarters vote of the executive committee."

None of them had assumed that this was solely a social dinner, of course, but it was not until this moment that they understood the total implications of the invitation. They were the swing votes and were being tested; Burdick had to know where they stood.

"So," Burdick said cheerfully, "are we all in agreement?"

This was the final exorcism of Wendall Clayton. In these three trim, handsome lawyers resided what was left of his ambitious spirit.

Was his legacy, Burdick wondered, as powerful as the man?

Gazes met. No one swallowed or shuffled. When Burdick called for the vote they each said an enthusiastic "In favor."

Burdick smiled and, when he poured more port, gripped one of them on the shoulder—welcome to the club. He was the foolish partner, the one whose professional life would be a living hell from that day on.

Then Burdick sat down in his glossy leather wingback chair and reflected on how much he despised them for not having the mettle to take Clayton's fallen standard and shove it up his—Burdick's—ass. He then grew somber. "Oh, just so you know: We have another problem, I'm afraid."

"What do you mean?" Stanley's voice was a harsh whine.

"One of the paralegals is in the hospital," Vera Burdick explained. "It's quite serious. I have a feeling she won't survive."

"Who?" a Nameless dared to ask.

"Taylor Lockwood."

"Taylor? Oh, no, not her. She's one of the best assistants I ever had on a closing. What happened?"

"Food poisoning. Nobody knows exactly how she got it."

"Should we—" one of the Nameless began to ask.

But Vera Burdick interrupted. "I'm on top of it. Don't worry."

Bill Stanley shook his head. "God, I only hope it wasn't anything we catered. Could you pass that port, Donald?"

CHAPTER THIRTY-FOUR

███████ Mitchell Reece closed his litigation bag and slid it under the seat of the shuttle from Boston as they approached La Guardia early the next morning.

Still no call from Taylor Lockwood and he hadn't been able to reach her at the firm. He'd gotten only her voice mail.

He wondered what was going on.

But as he stared at the brown and gray expanse of the Bronx beneath him his thoughts returned to Wendall Clayton's funeral, held in an Episcopalian church on Park Avenue. The minister's words came clearly to mind.

I recall one time when I happened to meet Wendall; it was a Saturday evening, late. We happened to be strolling up Madison Avenue together, he returning from the firm, I from some function at my congregation....

The minister had foresaken the pulpit and, like a talk show host, walked down into his audience.

...and we passed a few moments in idle conversation. Though we were in very different places in our lives I saw that there were striking similarities between his profession and mine.

He voiced some concern for a young man or woman, a lawyer at his firm, who was suffering from doubts. Wendall wanted to inspire this protégé to be the best lawyer they might be . . .

Hundreds of people. Most of the partners from Hubbard, White & Willis, many associates, many friends had attended.

. . . just as I in my own way deal with spiritual doubt in our young people. . . .

Quite a church, Reece recalled. Huge, pointy, Gothic, solid. All the joists and beams met in perfect unison—high in the air. It was a fitting place for an aristocratic man to be eulogized.

Then he thought back to another death at the firm—Linda Davidoff's. Her funeral, Reece decided, had been much better. The church was tamer, the minister more upset. It seemed to Reece preferable to get more tears and fewer words from men of the cloth at times of mourning.

Clayton's Upper East Side minister had been correct about one thing, though: He and Clayton had indeed been cut from the same bolt—noblemen and medieval clergy. In tarot cards pentacles would be their suit. Choose this sign for dark men of power and money.

Aggressive men.

The minister was seizing an opportunity to preach, just as Clayton had seized a chance of his own—and had died as a consequence of his reach.

The sudden grind and windy slam of the plane's wheels coming down interrupted Reece's thoughts. And as he glanced out the window, Reece decided it was ironic that he saw below him the huge cluster of dense graveyards in Queens—a whole city of a graveyard. He watched until it vanished under the wing and they landed.

As he walked down the ramp toward the terminal Reece saw his last name on a card being held up by a limo driver.

"Is that for *Mitchell* Reece?" he asked.

"Yes, sir. You have luggage?"

"Just this."

The man took his bags.

Reece gave him the address of the firm.

"We're supposed to stop someplace else, sir."

"What do you mean?"

"I'm afraid there's some kind of problem."

Reece climbed into the back of the Lincoln. "What kind of problem?"

"An emergency of some kind."

Forty minutes later the driver pulled up in front of yellow-painted doors at an annex to Manhattan General Hospital. It was deserted, except for some big blue biohazard containers and a bloody gurney sitting by itself. It seemed as if a body had just been pulled from it and hauled off to a pauper's grave.

Inside, Reece stopped at a reception desk and was directed down a long, dim corridor.

He found the basement room he sought and pushed open the door.

Gray-faced and red-eyed, Taylor Lockwood blinked in surprise at his entrance and shut off the soap opera she was watching.

She smiled. "Mitchell, it's you! Kiss me—it's not contagious—then see if you can scarf up some food. I'm starving to death."

███

Suck on ice," Reece said when he returned a few minutes later.

Taylor frowned.

"I asked them what you could have to eat. They said you should suck on ice."

She nodded at the IV. "Glucose. It's pure carbohydrates. I'm dying for a hamburger."

Reece gave her a Life Saver. "You look, well, awful."

"'Awful' is a compliment, considering how I did look. The nurse tells me I've recovered incredibly well."

"What happened?"

Taylor nodded. "I was stupid. I'm sure *my* phone was bugged too, either at my apartment or cubicle. I should've thought about that. Anyway, we got busted—somebody overhead us. And then at lunch yesterday this guy sits down next to me. He drops a book—I mean, *pretends* to drop a book—and when I bent down to pick it up for him I think he squirted botulism culture into my soup."

"Jesus, botulism? The most dangerous food poisoning there is."

She nodded. "I think he got it from Genneco Labs."

"Our client?"

"Yep."

"I was talking to a pathologist here. He told me Genneco does a lot of research into antitoxins—you know, like antidotes."

"So whoever killed Clayton stole some culture—or told the killer about Genneco and *he* stole it?"

She nodded.

"I was feeling a lot better last night but I called Donald and told him I was almost dead, in a coma."

"You what?"

"I wanted word to get around the firm that I was almost dead. I was afraid the killer would try again. I called and pretended I was my doctor." She gave a faint laugh. "I called my parents and told them that whatever they heard I was fine—although I have to say I was inclined to let my father stew a bit more. Carrie Mason's the only one who knows I'm okay."

Reece stroked her cheek. "Botulism . . . that could've killed you."

"The doctor told me that, 'luckily,' I ingested too *much* of the culture. I got sick immediately and, well, the word they used was, quote, *evacuated* most of the bacteria. Man, it was unpleasant. I'm talking Mount Saint Helens."

He hugged her hard. "We're not going to have to worry about anything like this happening again. I talked to Sam, my friend at the U.S. attorney's office, yesterday afternoon. He's coming down tomorrow with a special prosecutor from Washington. We're going to meet with him at the federal building at three—if you feel up to it."

"I'll feel up to it. Whoever's behind this . . . we're going to stop them. . . ." Her voice faded. "What's wrong, Mitchell?"

"Wrong?" His eyes were hollow and troubled. "You almost got killed. . . . I'm so sorry. If I'd known—"

She leaned forward and kissed him. "Hey, I lost those five pounds I gained at Thanksgiving and then some. Call it an early Christmas present. Now, go on, get out of here. Next time you see me I promise I won't look like Marley's ghost."

CHAPTER THIRTY-FIVE

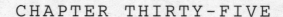 The girl walked sheepishly into the hospital room, hiding behind a bouquet of exotic flowers that she'd probably hand-selected from an Upper East Side florist.

"Whoa," Taylor told Carrie Mason, laughing at the massive arrangement. "Anything left in the rain forest?"

The chubby girl set the vase on the bedside table and sat in the functional gray chair near Taylor's bed, studying her carefully.

"You're looking a thousand times better, Taylor," Carrie said. "Everybody's like, ohmagod, she's dying. I wanted to tell them but I didn't. Not a soul—like you said."

Taylor gave her a rundown on her condition and thanked the girl for staying with her just after she'd been admitted.

"It's, like, no problem, Taylor. You looked...You were pretty sick."

Attempted murder does that to you.

"Well, I'll be getting out soon. May not eat for a week or so but it'll be good to get vertical again."

The girl avoided Taylor's eyes. She stood and arranged the flowers and it was this compulsive activity that told Taylor that she was troubled by something.

"What is it, Carrie?"

The girl paused, her back to Taylor, then sat down again. Tears were running down her cheeks. She wiped her face with the back of her fleshy hand. "I . . ."

"Go ahead. Tell me. What's the matter?"

"I think I know why Mr. Clayton killed himself. I think it was my fault."

"Your fault?" Taylor said. "What do you mean?"

"Well, okay . . . You know Sean."

One of the firm's busier spies. Taylor nodded.

"Well, what it was . . . see, last week Sean asked me out. I went over to his place. And I thought he wanted to go out with me and I was really, really excited about it. 'Cause I've had this crush on him for, like, a while. But it turned out . . . I mean, the thing was he just wanted to go through my purse."

"Why?"

"To get my log-on pass code for the firm computers. One of the operators told me he went on the system with my user name."

Taylor remembered the gum-snapping computer operator and the blank screen that should have had information about taxis and computer time and phone records. This was interesting. She nodded for the girl to continue and listened carefully.

"When I found out what he did I got totally mad. I asked him how could he do that? I mean, he way used me. Anyway he got all freaked out and apologized. But I was so mad. . . . Well, I wanted to get even with him and . . ." She again attended to the stalks of weird flowers. "And when I was in Connecticut with Mr. Clayton and you . . . Well, afterward, he came on to me, Mr. Clayton, you know and . . . well, we sort of slept together."

Taylor nodded, recalling that she'd overheard the tryst

from Clayton's den. The poor girl, suckered in by the vortex of the partner's eyes and charm.

"So, Sean found out and he had this big fight with Clayton. It was really vicious. I think Sean threatened to go to the executive committee about what happened and Clayton was afraid he'd get fired and he killed himself."

Taylor was frowning. So he and Lillick had had a fight. It had never occurred to her that *Lillick* might have killed Clayton.

Then she focused on the distraught Carrie once more. She couldn't, of course, say anything about Clayton's death but she could reassure the girl. "No, Carrie, that had nothing to do with it." A woman-to-woman smile. "Wendall Clayton slept with half the firm and he couldn't care less if anybody knew about it. Besides, I talked to Donald. I know why Clayton killed himself. I can't tell you but it had nothing to do with you or Sean."

"Really?"

"Promise."

"Despite what happened, I really kind of like him— Sean, I mean. He's weird, but underneath he's not as weird as he seems to be. We kind of patched things up. I think he likes me."

"I'm glad to hear that."

Taylor decided it was time to get out of the hospital. She feigned a yawn. "Listen, Carrie. I'm going to get some sleep now."

"Oh, sure. Feel better." Carrie hugged her. Then she asked, "Oh, one thing—do you know where the United Charities of New York general correspondence file is?"

"No idea. I never worked for them."

The girl frowned. "You didn't?"

"No. Why?"

"I was down in the pen this morning and I saw Donald Burdick's wife in your cubicle."

"Vera?"

"Yeah. She was looking through your desk. And I asked what she needed and she said she was doing a fund-raiser for the UCNY and needed the file. She thought you had it. But we couldn't find it."

"I've never checked out any of their files. Must be a mistake."

Carrie glanced at the TV and her face lit up. "Hey, look, it's *The Bold and the Beautiful*.... That's my favorite! I used to love summer vacations so I could watch all the soaps. Can't do that anymore. Things sure change when you start working."

Well, that's the truth....

Taylor's eyes strayed absently to the screen, watching the actors lost in their own intrigues and desires. When she turned to the doorway to say good-bye to Carrie, the paralegal had already left.

Taylor felt uneasy. Lillick, Dudley, Sebastian, Burdick... or somebody else had tried to poison her. They might find out that she was no longer in a coma and try again. She summoned the floor nurse, who in turn managed to track down a resident. The young doctor, seeing the urgency in her eyes, reluctantly agreed to discharge her as soon as the paperwork was finished.

After he'd left, she lay back in bed and looked through her purse for her insurance card.

She found a folded sheet of paper stuck in the back of the address book.

It was the poem that Danny Stuart had given her. Linda Davidoff's poem, her suicide note. She realized that she'd never read it, which she now did.

When I Leave

By Linda Davidoff

When I leave, I'll travel light
and rise above
the panorama of my solitude.
I'll sail to you, fast and high,
weightless as the touch of night.

When I leave, I'll become a light
that shows our love in a clear, essential way
(After all, what is a soul but love?).
After all is reconciled, and the darkness
   pitched away,
I'll travel light, transported home to you
in the buoyancy of pure and peaceful flight.

Taylor Lockwood thought of Linda, the beautiful, quiet, gypsy poet. She read the lines again very slowly.

Then she read them once more.

A moment later a huge orderly appeared in the door. "Ms. Lockwood, good news: The warden called."

He grinned; she frowned, not understanding.

Then the man delivered the rest of what would be his stock joke. "It's a full pardon. You're free to go." And he maneuvered the wheelchair into the room.

███

Taylor Lockwood had learned early who the real power centers were at Hubbard, White.

One of the most powerful was a short, round-faced woman of sixty. Mrs. Bendix had used her miraculous skills at memory and association to save the butts of almost every attorney and paralegal in the firm on more than one occasion by finding obscure file folders buried among the millions of documents residing on the gray metal shelves.

She was the doyen of the firm's massive file room.

Taylor now stood over Mrs. Bendix's frothy blue hair as the woman flipped through the three-by-five cards that were her computer. Taylor silently waited for her to finish. Mrs. Bendix—even more so than a senior partner—was a person one did not interrupt. When she was through she looked up and blinked. "I was told you were in the hospital. We contributed for the flowers."

"They were lovely, Mrs. Bendix. I recovered more quickly than expected."

"They said you were almost dead."

"Modern medicine."

Mrs. Bendix was eyeing Taylor's jeans and sweatshirt critically. "This firm has a dress code. You're outfitted for sick leave, not work."

"This is a bit irregular, Mrs. Bendix. But I have a problem and you're just about the only person who can help me."

"Probably am. No need to stroke."

"I need a case."

"Which one? You've got about nine hundred current ones to chose from."

"An old case."

"In that event, the possibilities are limitless."

"Let's narrow things down. Genneco Labs. Maybe a patent—"

"Hubbard, White does not do patent work. We never have and I'm sure we never will."

"Well, how about a contract for the development of bacterial or viral cultures or antitoxins?"

"Nope."

Taylor looked at the rows and rows of file cabinets. A thought fluttered past, then settled. She asked, "Insurance issues, the storage of products, toxins, food poisoning and so on?"

"Sorry, not a bell is rung, though in 1957 we did have a cruise line as a client. I got a discount and took a trip to Bermuda. I ate pasta that disagreed with me very badly. But I digress."

In frustration, Taylor puffed air into her cheeks.

Mrs. Bendix said tantalizingly, "Since you said toxins, food poisoning and so on I assume you meant toxins, food poisonings and so on."

Taylor knew that when people like Mrs. Bendix bait you, you swallow the worm and the hook in their entirety. She said, "Maybe I was premature when I qualified myself."

"Well," the woman said, "my mind harkens back to . . ." She closed her eyes, creasing her gunmetal eye shadow, then opened them dramatically. "...Biosecurity Systems, Inc. A contract negotiation with Genneco for the purchase and installation of Genneco's new security system in Teterboro, New Jersey. Two years ago. I understand the negotiations were a nightmare."

"Security," Taylor said. "I didn't think about that."

Mrs. Bendix said, "Apparently not."

"Can you tell me if anyone checked out the files on that deal in the past few months?"

This was beyond her brain. The woman pulled the logbook out and thumbed through it quickly then held it open for Taylor to look at. Taylor nodded. "I'd like to check it out too, if you don't mind."

"Surely."

Then a frown crossed Taylor's face. "I wonder if we could just consider one more file. This might be trickier."

"I live for challenges," Mrs. Bendix replied.

CHAPTER THIRTY-SIX

The New York State Department of Social Services worked fast.

After one anonymous phone call to the police the West Side Club became the front-page feature in the evening edition of every tabloid in the New York area.

Though gentlemen did not read such newspapers Ralph Dudley made an exception this once, since the *Times* wouldn't have the story until tomorrow morning. He now sat at his desk, lit only by a single battered brass lamp and the paltry December dusk light bleeding into his office, and stared at the same article he'd already read four times. A half-dozen people were under arrest and two underage prostitutes were being placed in foster homes in upstate New York.

Good-bye Junie, Dudley thought.

He'd made one last trip to see her—just before he'd made the call to 911, which closed up the West Side Art and Photography Club forever.

"Here," he'd said, handing her a blue-backed legal document.

She'd stared at it, uncomprehending. "Like, what is it?"

"It's a court order. The marshal seized your mother's and stepfather's bank accounts and house and they've put the money into a special trust fund for you."

"I . . . Like, I don't get it."

"The money your father left you? The court took it away from your mother and they're giving it back to you. I won my petition."

"Whoa, like radical! How much is it?"

"A hundred and ninety-two thousand."

"Awesome! Can I—?"

"You can't touch it for three years, until you're eighteen."

"Or whatever," she'd added.

"And you only get it if you go to school."

"What? That's fucking bogus."

It was also untrue. There were no strings on the money once she turned eighteen, as the trust officer would undoubtedly tell her. But she'd have a few years to think about it and might just try a class or two. Junie might just succeed at school; she was, he'd concluded, more savvy than half the lawyers at Hubbard, White & Willis.

She'd hugged him and then looked at him in that coy way that, before this, would've melted him. But he'd said he had to be going. He had an important meeting—with a pay phone. He'd looked at her for a long moment then kissed her on the cheek and left.

He wondered if Junie would say anything about him. She was, of course, in a position not only to destroy the delicate balance of his career, such as it was, but also to send him to prison for the rest of his life.

These possibilities he considered with remarkable serenity, sipping coffee from a porcelain cup. He weighed the odds and decided that she would say nothing. Although she'd been badly used by life and had the dangerous edge of those who learn survival skills before maturity, Junie was nonetheless motivated by a kind of justice. She saw essential good and essential evil, assigned her loyalty accordingly and stuck by her choice.

There were few adults with that perception. Or that courage.

Also, Dudley chose to believe that the girl loved him, at least by her wary definition of that word.

Good-bye, Junie. . . .

He now set the paper down and rocked back in his chair.

Reflecting that for once in his forty years as a lawyer he'd given up charming people and trying to win clients. Rather, he'd mastered a tiny bit of the law. In this small area of expertise he was now the best in the city: restitution of parentally converted intestate distributions (though he himself preferred to think of the subniche as "saving teenage hookers' bacon"). And he was proud of what he'd learned and done.

Still, there was one more potential problem: Taylor Lockwood knew his secret.

He picked up the phone and dialed a number he'd been calling so often over the past two days that he had it memorized.

The main operator at Manhattan General Hospital answered. He asked to speak to the floor nurse about the paralegal's condition.

They'd been reluctant to talk about details but it was clear from the tone—as well as from the gossip around the firm—that the girl was near death.

Maybe she'd died. That would take care of all the problems.

But then an orderly came on the phone. The man listened to Dudley's question and replied in a cheerful voice, "Don't you worry, sir. Your niece, Ms. Lockwood, was discharged today. She's doing fine."

An electric charge shot through him at this news. He hung up.

With Clayton dead, she was the one person who could destroy his fragile life here at the firm. She was the one risk to his budding life as a real lawyer. So much of the law deals with risk, Dudley reflected, some acceptable, some not. On which side did Taylor Lockwood fall?

He rocked back, looking out the window at the tiny sliver of New York Harbor that was visible between the two brick walls outside his office.

━━━━━

As she left the firm by the infamous back door—no longer taped open, she noticed—Taylor Lockwood was aware of someone's presence near her.

She stepped onto the sidewalk of Church Street, which at one time had been the shoreline of lower Manhattan. Now a half mile of landfill had extended the island well into the Hudson and the harbor.

Pausing, she looked behind her.

This was a quiet street, with a few bad restaurants, a girlie bar (ironically next to the rear entrance to Trinity Church) and the dingy service entrances to a number of office buildings. The street was now largely deserted.

She noticed a few businesspeople hurrying to or from one of the gyms near here and some construction workers. A number of vans were parked on the narrow street, half on the sidewalk. She had to walk around a drapery cleaning van to step into the street and hail a taxi.

Of course, there were none.

Then, in the bulbous disk of a wide-angle rearview mirror on one of the vans, she noticed a man looking her way.

She gasped.

There was nothing ambiguous about the recognition this time.

It was the man in the baseball cap, the one who'd sat next to her in the coffee shop.

The killer, the thief.

Okay. He doesn't know you saw him. You can get out of this.

Shaking her head casually, as if discouraged that there were no cabs, Taylor turned slowly back to the sidewalk.

Then instantly reversed herself and, sprinting as fast as her still-weak legs could carry her, made straight for population.

She glanced back once and saw that the man had given up any pretense—he was running after her. He reached into his coveralls and pulled out a long dark object. At first she thought it was a gun but then she realized that it was a knife or ice pick.

Still dehydrated and in severe pain from the poisoning, her muscles began to slow. Judging distances, Taylor realized that she wasn't going to make it to Broadway or one of the other heavily traveled streets before the killer reached her.

She stopped suddenly in the middle of the street and jogged down the concrete stairs to the Rector Street subway stop. This was better than the street anyway—not only would there be people on the platform but the token seller in the booth would have a hot line to the transit police. The killer wouldn't follow her here. He—

But he *was* following, grim determination—to kill her—on his face. A glance back showed that he'd picked up the speed, as if he could sense her fatigue and was moving in for the coup de grace.

"Help me!" she screamed to the startled young woman in the token booth. Three or four people scattered or ducked as Taylor vaulted the turnstile and fell hard onto the platform. One man started to help her but she raged, "Get away. No, get away!"

There were more screams behind her as the killer reached the bottom of the stairs and looked for her.

A businessman hovering nearby saw the ice pick in the hand of the killer and backed up.

Rising to her feet, she ran as fast as she could along the platform to the far exit of the subway. She heard the staticky voice of the token seller call out, "Pay your fare," as the killer jumped onto the platform and started after her.

Sprinting as best she could, she came to the end of the platform and turned to run up the stairs at the exit door.

But it was chained.

"Oh, Jesus," she cried. "No . . ."

Taylor returned to the platform and saw the killer, his face emotionless, walking slowly now, studying her carefully from thirty feet away. Anticipating her escape routes.

She jumped off the platform and dropped four feet into the muck between the rails. Turning away from the killer, she began to run through the tunnel, stumbling over the slippery ties.

He was right behind her, saying nothing, not threatening her or urging her to stop. Not negotiating—there was only one thing he needed to do—kill her.

Taylor got only about twenty feet when, exhausted, she slipped on a slick piece of tie and nearly fell. By the time she regained her balance the killer had made a leaping grab and seized her by the ankle. She went down hard against the solid piece of wood.

Catching her breath, she lashed out with her other foot and caught him in the mouth or cheek with her sole—a solid blow—and he grunted and lost his grip. "Fuck you," he muttered, spitting blood.

"No, fuck you!" she screamed. And kicked again.

He dodged away from her and swung with the pick.

Taylor rolled away and he missed. But she couldn't climb to her feet; he was coming forward too fast, swinging the steel, keeping her off balance.

Finally she managed to stand but just as she was about to start running he grabbed her overcoat and pulled her legs out from under her. She tumbled again to the ground, her head bouncing hard on a tie. She rose, exhausted, to her hands and knees.

"No," she said. "Please."

The killer was up, ready to pounce. But Taylor remained motionless, on her hands and knees, stunned. "What do you want?" she gasped, breathless, spent.

Still, no answer. But why should he respond? It was clear what he wanted. She was the tiny bird that her father had hunted, she was the victim of the Queen of Hearts—off with her head, off with her head.

The weapon drawing back, its needle-sharp point aiming at her face. She lifted her head and gazed at him, piteous. "Don't, please."

But he leaned forward and lunged with the pick, aiming toward her neck.

Which is when she dropped to her belly and scrabbled backward.

She'd been feigning, remaining on all fours like an exhausted soldier, when in fact she had—somewhere—a tiny bit of strength left.

"Ah, ah, ah, ah . . ."

Taylor squinted at him, still in the position of attack, right arm extended, clutching that terrible weapon.

"Ah, ah, ah, ah . . ." The terrible moan from his throat.

In his haste to stab Taylor he'd ignored what was just beyond her body—what she'd been trying to sucker him into hitting: the electrified third rail of the subway, which held more amperage than an electric chair.

"Ah, ah, ah, ah."

There were no sparks, no crackles but every muscle in his body was vibrating.

Then blood appeared in his eyes and his sandy hair caught fire.

"Ah, ah, ah—"

Finally the muscles spasmed once and he collapsed onto the tracks, flames dancing from his collar and cuffs and head.

Taylor heard voices and the electronic sound of walkie-talkies from the Rector Street platform. She supposed it would be the transit cops or the regular NYPD.

It didn't matter. She didn't want to see them or talk to them.

She knew now that there was only one thing to do that might save her. Taylor Lockwood turned and vanished into the darkness of the tunnel.

CHAPTER THIRTY-SEVEN

 "Do you mind my saying?...I mean, will you take it personally if I say you don't look very good?" John Silbert Hemming asked.

Taylor Lockwood said to the huge private eye, "I lost eight pounds in two days."

"Quite a diet. You should maybe write a book. I'm told you can make a lot of money doing that."

"We couldn't market it—the secret ingredient ain't so appetizing. I'm feeling better now."

They were at Miracles Pub. She was probing at a bowl of Greek chicken soup flavored with lemon. It wasn't on the menu. Dimitri's wife had made it herself. She had some trouble with the spoon—she had to keep her fingers curled; her rings tended to fall off if she didn't.

"Maybe," he joked cautiously, "you should've taken my offer to have dinner. Probably would've been better than where you ended up eating."

"You know, John, I wish I had." Then she said, "I need a favor."

Hemming, who was eating a hamburger, said, "If it's not

illegal and not dangerous and if you agree to go to the opera with me a week from Saturday at eight o'clock sharp, I'd be happy to oblige."

She considered. She said, "One out of three?"

"Which one?"

"I'd like to go to the opera."

"Oh, dear. Still, it makes me very pleased. Though nervous—considering you're balking on the other two. Now, what's the favor?" He nodded toward his plate. "This is a very good hamburger. Can I offer you some?"

She shook her head.

"Ah." He resumed eating. "Favor?" he repeated.

After a moment, she asked, "Why do people murder?"

"Temper, insanity, love and occasionally for money."

The spoon in her hand hovered over the surface of the soup, then made a soft landing on the table. She pushed the bowl away. "The favor is, I want you to get me something."

"What?"

"A gun. That kind I was telling you about—the kind without any serial numbers."

It would be near quitting time at the firm.

The end of another day at Hubbard, White & Willis.

Files being stacked away, dress shoes being replaced with Adidas and Reeboks, places in law books being marked for the night, edits being dropped in the In Box for the night word processing staff.

Four miles away Taylor Lockwood was hiding out in Mitchell Reece's loft. She was concerned that the person behind Clayton's death might figure out that she'd been responsible for the death of one hired gun and had called in a second one who was staking out her apartment right now.

She picked up the scarred gray .38 revolver that John Silbert Hemming had gotten her. She smelled it, sweet oil and wood and metal warmed by her hand. She hefted the small pistol, much heavier than she'd thought it would be.

Then she put the gun in her purse and walked unsteadily

to Mitchell Reece's kitchen, where she found a pen and one of his pads of yellow foolscap.

She wrote the note quickly—he was due home at any moment—and she didn't want him here to deter her from what she had to do.

In her scrawled handwriting Taylor promised that she'd explain everything to him later—if she wasn't killed or arrested—but she begged him to please, please stay away from the firm tonight. After all the deceit and horrors of the past two weeks she'd learned who Wendall Clayton's killer was. She'd gotten a gun and, finally, she was going to make sure that justice would be done.

CHAPTER THIRTY-EIGHT

Taylor Lockwood had never liked this room—the big conference room in the firm.

For one thing, it was always dim—a pastel room so underlit that the colors became muddy and unreal. For another, she associated it with the large meetings in which the paralegal administrator would gather her flock and give them all a rah-rah pep talk, which amounted to a plea not to quit just because the raises this year were going to be only 5 percent.

Mindless, proletariat babble.

Nonetheless, at eight o'clock in the evening, here was Taylor Lockwood, sitting in a large swivel chair at the base of the U, the chair Donald Burdick reserved for himself.

Suddenly the huge teak doors to the room opened and Mitchell Reece ran inside.

He stopped, gasping, when he saw the gun in her hand.

She looked at him with surprise. "Mitchell, what are you doing here?"

"Your note! I read the note you left. Where did you think I'd be?"

"I told you not to come. Why didn't you listen to me?"

"What're you going to do with the gun?"

She smiled absently. "It's pretty obvious, isn't it? I've got to save us."

"The U.S. attorney's coming tomorrow! Don't do this to yourself."

"The cops? The U.S. attorney?" She laughed skeptically. "And what would they do? We don't have any evidence. You and I are never going to be safe. We got run off the road, I was poisoned. I was almost stabbed to death."

"What?"

She didn't tell him about the latest assault just yet. She muttered, "It's just a matter of time until we're dead—if I don't stop things right here. Now."

"You can't just shoot somebody in cold blood."

"I'll claim self-defense. Insanity."

"The insanity defense doesn't work, Taylor. Not in cases like this."

She rubbed her eyes.

"The man who stole the note's dead."

"What?"

"The janitor or whatever he was, the one who put the poison in my food—him. He tried again. He chased me into the subway. But he got electrocuted."

"Jesus. What did the police say?"

"No." She shook her head. "I didn't go to them. It wouldn't do any good, Mitchell. They'd just hire somebody else."

"Well, who is it?" he asked. "Who's behind all this?"

She didn't answer. She glanced up, over Reece's shoulder, and said, "Turn around and find out." She hid the gun behind her back and called, "We're over here. Come on in."

Reece spun around.

A figure emerged from the dull light of the hallway into the deeper shadow of the end of the conference room. Donald Burdick, his posture perfect, like a ballroom dancer's, stepped past the doors, which swung closed with a heavy snap.

The partner called from across the room, his voice ringing dully, like a bell through fog. "Taylor, it *is* you." He nodded at Reece.

"Surprised to see I'm still alive?"

"Your call...it didn't make any sense. What's all this about Wendall's death?" He walked to within ten feet of them and stopped. He remained standing. "We thought you were sick."

"You mean, you *hoped* I was *dead*!" She slowly lifted the gun.

His mouth opened. He blinked. "Taylor, what are you doing with that?"

She started to speak. Her voice choked and then she cleared her throat. "I had a speech rehearsed, Donald. I forgot it.... But what I do know is that you hired that man to steal the note and set up Clayton's suicide. Then you had him run us off the road and try to kill me—twice."

The dapper partner gave a harsh bark of a laugh. "Are you crazy?" He looked at Mitchell for help. "What's she saying?"

Reece shook his head, gazing at Taylor with concern.

"I went through the file room logs, Donald. You checked out a file for Genneco last week. I saw your signature."

"Maybe I did. I don't remember. Genneco's my client."

"But there'd be no reason to check *this* file out. It wasn't active. As part of a contract negotiation their insurer analyzed their pathogen storage facility in New Jersey. It was basically a blueprint about how to break into the place. You checked the file out and gave the information to your hit man. He broke in, stole some botulism culture and poisoned me!"

"No, I swear I didn't."

"And when that didn't work you sent him to stab me. Well, he's *dead*, Donald. How do you like that?"

"I don't know what you're talking about." He started to turn and walk away.

"No!" Taylor cried. "Don't move." She thrust the gun toward him. The partner stumbled backward, lifting his hands helplessly.

"Taylor!" Reece shouted.

"No!" she screamed and cocked the gun. Burdick backed against the wall, his eyes huge disks of terror. Reece froze.

They stood in those positions for a long minute. Taylor stared at the gun, as if willing it to fire by itself.

"I can't," she whispered finally. "I can't do it."

The gun drooped.

Reece stepped forward slowly and took the pistol from her. He put his arm around her shoulders. "It's all right," he whispered.

"I wanted to be strong," she said. "I wanted to kill him. But I can't do it."

Burdick said to them both, "I swear I had nothing to do—"

She pulled away from Reece's arm and faced Burdick in her fury. "You may think you have the police and the mayor and everyone else in your pocket but it's not going to stop me from making sure you spend the rest of your life in jail!"

Taylor grabbed a telephone off the table.

The partner shook his head. "Taylor, whatever you think, it's not true."

She had just started dialing when a hand reached over, lifted the receiver away from her and replaced it in the cradle.

"No, Taylor...," Mitchell Reece said. He sighed and lifted the gun, the muzzle pointing at her like a single black pearl. "No," he repeated softly.

CHAPTER THIRTY-NINE

████████ She gave a faint laugh of surprise.

Much the same sound that Mitchell Reece himself had uttered when she told him a few days ago that Clayton had been murdered. Then her smile faded and with bottomless horror in her voice she said, "What are you doing?"

His face was stone, his eyes expressionless, but the answer was clear.

"You, Mitchell?" she whispered.

Donald Burdick said, "One of you tell me what's going on here."

Reece ignored him. Still holding the gun on both of them, he walked to the door, looked outside, made sure the corridor was empty and returned. He said to her angrily, "Why the hell didn't you stop when you should have, Taylor? Why? It was all planned out so carefully. You ruined it."

Burdick, horrified, said, "Mitchell, it was you? You killed Wendall Clayton?"

Taylor's eyes closed for a brief moment. She shook her head.

Reece told her, "Wendall Clayton killed the woman I loved."

Taylor frowned then said, "Linda? Linda Davidoff!"

Reece nodded slowly.

"Oh, my God . . ."

After a moment Reece said, "It was all about a man and a woman. As simple as that." His eyebrows rose. "A man who'd never had time for relationships, a woman who was beautiful and creative and brilliant. Two people who'd never been in love before. Not real love. It wasn't a good combination. An ambitious, tough lawyer. Best in law school, best at the firm . . . The woman was a poet—shy, sensitive. Don't ask me how they became close. Opposites attract, maybe. A secret romance in a Wall Street law firm. They worked together and started going out. They fell in love. She got pregnant and they were going to get married."

A moment passed and Reece seemed to be hefting the words to select among them. Finally he continued, "Wendall was working on a case one weekend, and he needed a paralegal. Linda'd cut way back on her hours— that's when she'd stopped working for me and Sean Lillick took over. But she still worked occasionally. She did a few assignments for Wendall Clayton and he got obsessed with her. One weekend in September he found out she was at her parents' summer house in Connecticut, not far from his place. He went to see her, tried to seduce her. She called me, crying. But before I could get up there or she could get away there was a struggle and she fell into the ravine. She died. Clayton left her poem to make it look like a suicide."

"This whole thing," Taylor whispered, "it was fake. You lied about everything. . . . Your mother, in the hospital? You weren't going to see her at all. You were going to Scarsdale—to take flowers to Linda's grave."

Reece nodded.

The nail of Taylor's index finger touched the marble. "Oh, Mitchell, it's so fucking clear now." She looked at Burdick. "Don't you see what he's done?" She turned to face

Reece, who leaned against the dark, dried-blood-red conference table, looking gaunt and pale. "You got one of your criminal clients from the pro bono program—what? A hit man, a killer, a mercenary soldier? You got him to break into your own file cabinet, steal the Hanover note and hide it in Wendall's office. Then you had him bug your own office so you'd look as innocent as possible. You recorded some conversations then planted the tapes with the note. You had me track him down."

She thought for a moment. "Then, at Clayton's party, I found the receipt from the security service: upstairs, where *you* sent me to search—after you planted it there.... Finally I found the note in Clayton's office." She laughed bitterly. "And after the Hanover trial your hit man killed him right away—because he couldn't very well be accused of something he hadn't done."

The lawyer made no effort to deny any of this.

She continued, "And his suicide note...It was fake, wasn't it? Who forged it? Another criminal client?"

The associate lifted his eyebrow, conceding the accuracy of her deduction.

She laughed bitterly, glancing at the partner.

Men of most renowned virtue...

Reece was gazing at her, impassive as a statue.

Eyes still on Reece, locked on his, Taylor said, "And Donald was a big help, wasn't he?" She turned to the partner. "Nothing personal, Donald, but you laid a pretty damn good smoke screen." Her hands were shaking now. The tears started. "And as for me, well, you were keeping pretty close tabs on your pawn. All you had to do was look across the pillow."

A bit of emotion blossomed in his face at this—like the first cracks in spring ice. Reece took a Kleenex from his pocket and began rubbing the trigger guard and grip and frame of the gun. He nodded. "You won't believe me if I tell you that what happened between us wasn't part of the plan."

"Bullshit! You tried to kill me!"

His eyes grew wide. "I didn't want to hurt you! You should have stopped when you were supposed to!"

Burdick said, "But Mitchell, how could you risk it? You love the law. You'd *risk* everything for this, for revenge?"

He smiled with a look as bleak as a hunting field in December. "But there *was* no risk, Donald. Don't you know me by now? I knew I'd get away with it. Every nuance was planned. Every action and reaction. Every move anticipated and guarded against. I planned this exactly the same way I plan my trials. There was no way it wouldn't work." He sighed and shook his head. "Except for you, of course, Taylor. You were the flaw. . . . Why didn't you just let it go? I killed an evil man. I did the firm—hell, I did the *world*—a favor."

"You used me!"

Donald Burdick sat heavily in a chair, his head dipping. "Oh, Mitchell, all you had to do was go to the police. Clayton would've been arrested for the girl's death."

The young lawyer gave a harsh laugh. "You think so? And what would've happened, Donald? Nothing. Any half-assed criminal lawyer could've gotten him off. There was no witness, no physical evidence. Besides, you of all people ought to know how many favors Clayton could've called in. The case wouldn't've even gotten to the grand jury."

His attention dipped for a moment to the gun. He flipped it open expertly and saw six cartridges in the cylinder. Then from his pocket he took the note that Taylor Lockwood had written to him, the note about going to confront a killer. He folded it into a tight square, stepped forward and stuffed it into her breast pocket.

She whispered, nodding at it, "I wrote my own suicide note, didn't I? I kill Donald and then myself. Oh, my God . . ."

"It's your fault," he muttered. "You should've just moved on, Taylor. You should've let Clayton stay in hell and let the rest of us get on with our business."

"My fault?" She leaned forward. "What the hell happened to you? Has it all caught up? Finally? Pushing, pushing, pushing... years and years of it. Win the case, win the goddamn case—that's all you see, all you care about! You don't know what justice is anymore. You've turned it inside out."

"Don't lecture me," he said wearily. "Don't talk to me about things you can't understand. I live with the law, I've made it a part of me."

Burdick said, "There's no way you can justify it, Mitchell. You killed a man."

Reece rubbed his eyes. After a moment, he said, "You get asked a lot why you go to law school. Did you go because you wanted to help society, to make money, to further justice? That's what people always want to know. Justice? There's so little of it in the world, so little justice in our lives. Maybe on the whole it balances out; maybe God looks down from someplace and says, 'Yeah, pretty good, I'll let it go at that.' But you know the law as well as I do, both of you. Innocent people serve time and guilty ones get off. Wendall Clayton killed Linda Davidoff and he was going to go free. I wasn't going to let that happen."

Taylor said, "The suicide note—Clayton's. 'Men of most renowned virtue...' How does it go?"

Reece said, "'Have sometimes by transgressing most truly kept the law.'"

"You meant it about you, then, not Clayton."

Reece nodded solemnly. "It's about me."

"Mitchell," Burdick whispered, "just put the gun down. We'll go to the police. If you talk to them—"

But Reece walked slowly over to Taylor. He stood two feet away. She didn't move.

"No!" Burdick shouted. "Don't worry about the police. We can forget what happened. There's no need for this to go beyond this room. There's no need...."

Reece glanced at the partner briefly but didn't speak. His whole attention was on Taylor. He touched her hair, then her cheek. He nestled the muzzle of the gun against her breast.

"I wish..." He cocked the gun. "I wish..."

Taylor wiped the thick tears. "But it's me, Mitchell. *Me*. Think about what you're going to do."

"Please, Mitchell," Burdick said. "Money, do you want money? A fresh start somewhere?"

But it was Taylor who raised her hand to silence the partner. "No. He's come too far. There's nothing more to say."

At last there were tears on Reece's face. The gun wavered and rose. For a moment it seemed to be levitating; maybe he intended to touch the chill muzzle to his own temple and pull the trigger.

But his deeper will won and he lowered the black weapon to her once more.

Alice, in this dreadful world on the other side of the looking glass, remained completely still. There was no place to go. All she could do was close her eyes, which is what she now did.

Mitchell Reece, practical as ever, held his left hand to his face to protect himself from the blast—and her spattered blood—and then he pulled the trigger.

CHAPTER FORTY

In the hushed conference room the metallic click was as loud as the gunshot would have been.

Reece's eyes flickered for a moment. He pulled the trigger three more times.

Three more clicks echoed throughout the room. His hand lowered.

"Fake," he whispered with the tone of someone observing an impossible occurrence. "It's fake?"

Taylor wiped the streaming tears from her face. "Oh, Mitchell . . ."

Burdick stepped forward and firmly lifted the gun away from him.

Taylor said, "The gun's real, Mitchell, but the bullets're just props." She shook her head. "All I had was speculation. I needed proof that you did it."

Reece leaned against the wall. "Oh, my God." He was staring at Taylor. "How?" he whispered. She'd never seen such shock in anyone's eyes—pure, uncomprehending astonishment.

"A lot of clues I finally put together today," she said. "What got me wondering was the poem, Linda's poem."

"Poem?"

"The one that Wendall left as her suicide note. I read it in the hospital and, you know, everybody *thought* it was a suicide note. But nobody really understood what it was about. It was a *love* poem. It wasn't about killing herself, it was about leaving solitude and loneliness and starting a new life with somebody she loved. Anybody who was going to kill herself wouldn't leave that as a suicide note. Danny Stuart, her roommate, said she wrote it just a few days before she died."

He was shaking his head. "Impossible. You couldn't make that kind of deduction, not from the suicide note back to me."

"No, of course not. It's just what put the idea in my head that maybe she didn't kill herself. But then I started to think about everything that'd happened since you'd asked me to help you find the note, everything I'd learned. I thought about you nudging me away from the other suspects and toward Clayton. I thought about what kind of strategist you were, about Clayton's womanizing, about how it would be easy for you to get a gun from one of your clients in the criminal pro bono program. Your trips to Linda's grave . . . I had my private-eye friend check out your mother. Yes, she was a paranoid schizophrenic. But she died four years ago. Oh, Mitchell, you looked me right in the eye and lied. I felt like crying when you told me about your mother!"

Still, he held her eye, not a flicker of remorse in his.

"Then," she continued, "I called the Boston U.S. attorney's office. Your friend Sam hasn't worked for them for four years. . . . You faked that call to him from the street in front of your loft, didn't you?" Her anger broke through. "You're a pretty fucking good actor, Mitchell!"

Then, calming, she continued. "Hard evidence? You yourself helped me there—that first day I met you, when you mentioned that the records in law firms reveal all kinds of information about where people've been and how they spend their time. I went through the time sheets going back a year and figured out exactly what happened. It's all right there: You and Linda working together, taking time off together, logging travel time to clients on the same date, joint meal vouchers. Then Linda's time drops and she takes sick leave and files insurance claims because she's pregnant. And not long after that she dies.

"Then I found the Genneco security system contract negotiation files. And, yeah, it was checked out to Donald. But if he'd used them to get access to the botulism he sure as hell wouldn't use his own name. Then I asked Mrs. Bendix to find any other files Donald had supposedly checked out recently. There was one—an insurance claim. Where a car went off the road and looked like it was going to sink in the reservoir in Westchester but ended up on a ledge of rock that kept it from sinking. In exactly the same place we drove into the reservoir that night. You needed to make it look like Clayton was desperate enough to kill us so he'd be desperate enough to kill himself. Right? Am I right?"

Reluctantly he nodded.

"Oh, sure, a lot of people had motives to kill Clayton. Thom Sebastian and Dudley and Sean Lillick...and Donald here. Even Donald's wife. And probably a dozen other people. But I decided you were wrong—when you told me that motive is the most important thing in finding a killer. No, the most important thing is finding the person who has the *will* to murder. Remember your herald, Mitchell? Preparation and will? Well, of all the people in this firm, you were the only one I believed could actually murder someone. The way you destroyed that doctor on cross-examination...you had a killer's heart. I could see that.

"But even then I wasn't absolutely sure. So I called Donald earlier tonight and we arranged this little play of our own—to find out for sure."

"You don't understand," Reece whispered desperately. "Clayton was pure evil. There was no way to bring him to justice otherwise. He—"

Taylor's hand flew up toward him, palm out. "Justice?"

she raged. "Justice?" She sighed and lowered her head, speaking into the microphone hidden under her collar.

"John, could you come in please?"

The door opened and John Silbert Hemming entered. Reece stared up at the huge man as he gripped Reece's arm tightly and stepped protectively between the lawyer and Taylor.

The man said to her softly, "You could have stopped earlier, before he tried to use that." Nodding at the gun. "We had enough on tape for a conviction."

She was looking into Reece's evasive eyes as she said in a whisper, "I had to know."

The handcuffs went on quickly, with a crisp, ratchety sound.

"You can't do this!" Reece muttered bitterly. "You have no legal authority. It's illegal detention and kidnapping. And that fucking tape is illegal. You'll be subject—"

"Shhhh," John Silbert Hemming said.

"—to civil liability and criminal charges, which I'll pursue on the federal and state levels. You don't know the kind of trouble—"

"Shhhh," the big man repeated, looking down at Reece ominously. The lawyer fell silent.

Seeing Reece standing in front of her, oddly defiant, even angry at what they'd done to him, she wondered if she was going to scream, or slap him, or even reach for his throat with her hands, which seemed to have the strength, more than enough, to strangle him to death.

Reece said, "Taylor, I can make you understand. If you'll just—"

"I don't want to hear anything more."

But she was speaking only to John Silbert Hemming, who nodded solemnly and escorted the lawyer out into the firm's lobby to await the police.

■

She spent an hour giving several lengthy statements to two humorless detectives from Police Plaza. She refused a ride home from gallant John Silbert Hemming but promised that she'd call him about their opera "date," a word that she pointedly used.

"Looking forward to it," he said, ducking his head to step into the elevator car.

Taylor walked slowly back to her cubicle. She was almost there when she heard the sound of a photocopier and noticed Sean Lillick copying sheets of music on the Xerox machine near the paralegal pen. He looked up and blurted, "Taylor! You're out of the hospital? We heard you were totally sick."

"Back from the dead," she said, glancing at the music, the copying of which he was probably charging to a client.

"You're all right?"

If you only knew . . .

"I'll live."

He nodded toward the manuscript paper. "Take a look. My latest opus. It's about Wendall Clayton. I found all of these pictures and papers and things in his office the other day and I'm writing this opera about him. I'm going to project pictures on the screen and get some Shakespearean text and—"

She leaned close and shut him up with an exasperated look. "Sean, can I give you some advice?"

He looked at the music. "Oh, these're just the rough lead sheets. I'm going to arrange them later."

"I don't mean that," she whispered ominously. "Listen up: If Donald Burdick doesn't know you were Clayton's spy yet, he will in about a day or two."

He gazed at her uneasily. "What're you talking about?"

"I'm talking about this: Pack up your stuff and get out of here. I'd recommend leaving town."

"Who the hell're you to—"

"You think Clayton was vindictive, you ain't seen nothing yet. Donald'll sue your ass for every penny of the money Clayton paid you to be his weasel."

"Fuck you. What money?"

"That you've got hidden under your stinky mattress."

He blinked in shock. He started to ask how she knew this but he gave up. "I was just—"

"And one more thing. Leave Carrie Mason alone. She's too good for you."

The kid tried to look angry but mostly he was scared. He grabbed his papers and scurried off down the corridor. Taylor returned to her cubicle. She'd just sat down and begun to check phone messages when she heard someone coming up behind her. She spun around fast, alarmed.

Thom Sebastian stood in the doorway, hands stuffed in his pockets.

"Hey," he said, "only me. Mr. Party Animal. Didn't mean to spook you."

"Thom."

"I was mega-freaked when I heard you were sick. They wouldn't let me in to see you. Did you get my flowers?"

"I might have. I was pretty out of it. I couldn't read half the cards."

"Well, I was worried. I'm glad you're okay. You lost weight."

She nodded and said nothing.

A dense, awkward moment. His voice quavered as he said, "So."

"So."

He said, "Anyway, I just wanted to let you know.... Looks like I'm leaving."

"The firm?"

He nodded. "What I was telling you about, that new firm I'm starting with Bosk? It's going to happen. Tomorrow's my last day here. I've got ten associates from Hubbard, White coming with me. And a bunch of clients too. We've already got fifteen retainer agreements. St. Agnes, McMillan, New Amsterdam, RFC, a bunch of others."

Taylor laughed. "You're kidding." These were Hubbard, White's biggest clients. They represented close to one third of the firm's revenues.

Thom said, "We're going to do the same work Hubbard, White did but charge them about half. They were ready to leave anyway. Most of the presidents and CEOs I talked to said everybody here was paying too much attention to the merger and firm politics and not enough to the legal work. They said the other associates and I were the only ones who gave a shit about them."

"That's probably true."

"The funny thing is, if I'd made partner I'd be under a noncompetition agreement so I couldn't've taken any clients with me. But since I'm just an associate the firm can't stop me."

"Congratulations, Thom."

She started to turn back to her desk. But he stepped forward nervously and touched her arm. "The thing is, Taylor." He swallowed uneasily. "The thing is, I have to say something." He looked around, his eyes dark and troubled. "I've spent a lot of time..." He swallowed. "I've spent a lot of time thinking about you and checking you out. What you found in my office, my notes about you? I shouldn't've done that, I know. But I just couldn't get you out of my head."

Taylor stood up, glanced at her arm. He removed his hand from it and stepped back. "What're you saying?" she asked.

"I'm saying I learned some things about you that're a problem for me."

She looked at him steadily. "Yes?"

"I've learned that you're the sort of person I don't think I'll ever meet again. Who I think I could spend the rest of my life with." He looked away. "I guess I'm saying that I think I love you."

She was too surprised even to laugh.

He held up a pudgy hand. "I know you think I'm goofy and crude. But I don't have to be that way. I *can't* be that way at my new firm. I'm giving up the drugs. That's what I was meeting with Magaly about the night she was killed— the night you got me out of jail. I wasn't going to score any-thing—I was going to tell her I wasn't going to buy from her anymore. I was doing that for you. Then, that night at the Blue Devil, I was going to ask if you maybe wanted to go out with me—kind of, I guess, steady." He shook his head at the old-fashioned word. "I had it all planned out, what I was going to say . . . but then Magaly got shot and you had to bail me out. The whole night went to hell and I couldn't even look you in face, let alone tell you how I felt about you."

She began to speak but he took a deep breath. "No, no, no, don't say anything yet. Please, Taylor. Just think about what I said. Will you do that? I'll have the firm, I'll have money. I can give you whatever you want. If you want to go to law school, fine. You want to play music, fine. You want to have a dozen babies, fine."

"Thom."

"Please," he begged, "don't say yes and don't say no. Just think about it." He took a deep breath and seemed on the verge of tears. "Jesus, I'm the world's greatest fucking negotiator and here I am breaking all my rules. Look, everything's in there." He handed her a large white envelope.

"What is it?" she asked.

"I did kind of a deal memo."

Now, she couldn't help but laugh. "Deal memo?"

He grinned. "For us. About how we might work things out. Don't panic, we don't get to marriage until phase four."

"Phase four."

"We'll take it nice and easy. Please, just read it and let the idea sit for a while."

"I'll read it," she said.

Then, unable to resist, he threw his arms around her and hugged her hard. He retreated before she could say anything more.

Don't get too interested in her. . . . Sebastian's comment to Bosk. It was a warning from a jealous lover, not a potential killer.

Taylor lowered her face to her hands and laughed softly. Thinking: I guess it's safe to say, *What a night.*

Her desk was a mess; Vera Burdick's ransacking hadn't left it in very good shape. When she'd called Burdick about Reece earlier in the evening she'd asked him bluntly why his wife was searching through her things.

"Vera doesn't trust anybody," Burdick had said, laughing. "Samuel Lockwood's daughter? She thought for sure you were working with Clayton, helping him push the merger through—or, after he died, sabotaging me. You should consider it a compliment."

The way a fly should feel complimented that he's a spider's first choice for dinner.

Taylor noticed a blinking red light on her phone. She lifted the receiver and pressed the play button.

"Hey, counselor."

Hello, Dad.

"Listen, hope you're feeling better. 'Cause I've made some plans for us tomorrow. I get into La Guardia in the morning. How 'bout you come pick me up? I've made lunch reservations at the Four Seasons. There's somebody from Skadden I want you to meet. A senior partner. He said they're looking for people like my little overachiever. Now, get a pen: My plane gets in at—"

Click. Taylor Lockwood hit a button.

A woman's electronic voice reported: *"Your message has been deleted."*

She hung up the receiver.

Taylor pulled on her raincoat and walked through the half-lit corridors. The Slavic cleaning women in their blue uniforms moved from office to office with their wheeled carts. Taylor could hear the whine of vacuums coming from different directions. She imagined she could smell sour gunpowder, as if Reece had in fact fired real bullets from the heavy pistol. But she realized, as she passed a conference room littered with a thousand papers, that the smell was only the residue of cigar smoke. Earlier in the evening a deal had perhaps closed here. Or maybe it'd fallen apart. Or maybe negotiations had been postponed till tomorrow or the next day. In any case the participants had abandoned the room for the time being, leaving behind only the pungent aroma of tobacco as the evidence of that success or failure or uncertainty.

The police had gone. Burdick had gone. The partner would need some rest—he'd have plenty to do in the morning. More favors would have to be called in. Taylor suspected, though, that Donald Burdick and his wife would have a sizable inventory remaining.

She continued through the firm, pressed a door latch button and stepped into the lobby. The door swung closed behind her and when the elevator arrived she stepped in wearily.

Outside, Wall Street was nearly as quiet as the halls of Hubbard, White & Willis. This neighborhood was a day-time place. It worked hard and curled up to sleep early. Most of the offices were dark, the bartenders had stopped pouring drinks, cabs and cars were few.

Occasionally someone in a somber overcoat would appear from a revolving door then vanish into a limo or cab or down a subway stairwell. Where, she wondered, were they going? To one of Sebastian's clubs, to pursue some private lust like Ralph Dudley, to plot a coup like Wendall Clayton?

Or maybe just to retreat to their apartments or houses for a few hours' sleep before the grind began again tomorrow?

What a place this was, the topsy-turvy land at the bottom of the rabbit hole....

But, Taylor considered, was this *her* land?

Alice's trips to Wonderland and the Looking-Glass world had, after all, been dreams and the girl had eventually wakened from them.

She couldn't, for the moment, say.

Taylor flagged down a cab, got in and gave the driver the address of her apartment building. As the dirty vehicle squealed away from the curb she slouched down in the seat, staring at the greasy Plexiglas divider.

Thank you for not smoking. 50-cent surcharge after 8 p.m.

The cab was a block away from her apartment when she leaned forward and told the driver she'd changed her mind.

■

Taylor Lockwood sat in the spotlight.

Dimitri twisted his curly hair and leaned over the microphone. (His habitual suspicion left when she told him,

"I'll play for free. You keep the receipts—all of them—but the tips're mine. And, Dimitri: No satin touch. Not tonight, okay?")

"Ladies and gentlemen . . ."

She whispered ominously, "Dimitri."

". . . it is my pleasure to present Miss Taylor Lockwood at the piano."

He hit the switch controlling the faux spotlight. She smiled at the crowd and touched the keys, cold and smooth as glass, enjoying their yielding resilience as she began to play.

After half an hour Taylor looked out into the cockeyed lights, brilliant starbursts beaming at her, so bright she couldn't see the patrons. Maybe the wobbly tables were completely occupied. Or maybe the place was empty. In any event, if anyone *was* in the audience they were listening in absolute silence.

She smiled, not to them but only for herself, and swayed slowly as she played a medley of Gershwin that she herself had arranged, all revolving around *Rhapsody in Blue*. Tonight she improvised frequently, playing jazzy harmonies and clever riffs, allowing the music to carry itself, the notes soaring and regrouping, then flying to risky altitudes. But Taylor Lockwood never let go completely and was careful to alight at regular intervals on the theme; she knew how much people love the melody.

About the Author

A former journalist, folksinger and attorney, Jeffery Deaver is the international number-one bestselling author of thirty-seven novels, three collections of short stories and a non-fiction law book, and a lyricist of a country-western album. His novels have appeared on bestseller lists around the world and are sold in 150 countries and translated into twenty-five languages.

His most recent novels are *Solitude Creek*, a Kathryn Dance novel; *The October List*, a thriller told in reverse; and *The Steel Kiss*, a Lincoln Rhyme novel. For his Dance novel *XO* Deaver wrote an album of country-western songs, available on iTunes and as a CD; and before that, *Carte Blanche*, a James Bond continuation novel, a number-one international bestseller.

Deaver has been nominated for seven Edgar Awards, an Anthony, a Shamus and a Gumshoe. He was shortlisted for the ITV3 Crime Thriller Award and for the Prix Polar International 2013.

His novel *A Maiden's Grave* was made into an HBO movie, and *The Bone Collector* was a feature release from Universal Pictures, starring Denzel Washington and Angelina Jolie. Lifetime aired an adaptation of his *The Devil's Teardrop*. And, yes, the rumours are true; he did appear as a corrupt reporter on his favourite soap opera, *As the World Turns*. He was born outside Chicago and has a bachelor of journalism degree from the University of Missouri and a law degree from Fordham University.

Readers can visit his website at www.jefferydeaver.com.

JEFFERY
DEAVER

THE LESSON
OF HER DEATH

When Detective Bill Corde looks at the beautiful
face of the murdered girl in the mud, he does not
know his own life is about to turn into
a terrifyingly real nightmare.

For the girl's killer is now on the trail of Corde
and his unsuspecting family: his wife, teenage son,
and imaginative but vulnerable daughter, Sarah.
Sarah, who alone knows the identity of the killer . . .

The lesson Bill Corde is about to learn – the lesson
of her death – is an education that no one
will ever forget.

Out now in paperback and ebook.

HODDER